THE MOST DANGEROUS GAMES

MrBeast

The Most Dangerous Games

James Patterson

HarperCollins*Publishers*

HarperCollins*Publishers* Ltd
1 London Bridge Street
London SE1 9GF

www.harpercollins.co.uk

HarperCollins*Publishers*
Macken House,
39/40 Mayor Street Upper,
Dublin 1, D01 C9W8
Ireland

First published by HarperCollins*Publishers* Ltd 2026
1

Following illustrations by Patrick Arrasmith: pile of cash, chess pieces, backpack and hiking boots, switchblades, killer whale, shark, spiders, snakes, snowcat machine, drones, jungle trail, Erebus glacier, underground tunnel, bomb blast, The Host, Burj Khalifa, coffin, needle, airplane crash, and hands.
Following illustrations by Steven Noble: cellphone, Zodiac boat, helicopter, missiles, moon, tents, rockface, lighthouse, necklace, topographical map, flashlight, and loudspeaker.
Endpaper and digital edge images © Shutterstock
All other images provided courtesy of Adobe Stock.

A catalogue record for this book is available from the British Library.

ISBN: 978-0-00-880285-1 (HB)
ISBN: 978-0-00-880286-8 (TPB)
ISBN: 978-0-00-883792-1 (IN)

Printed and bound in the UK using 100% renewable electricity by CPI Group (UK) Ltd

FSC www.fsc.org
MIX
Paper | Supporting responsible forestry
FSC® C013604

THE MOST DANGEROUS GAMES

THE PLAYERS

(A PARTIAL LIST)

ALEK. A university student from a hard-hit city in Eastern Europe's Carpathian belt, Aleksandra Andrich and her mother are the only surviving members of her family after years of sirens and forced evacuations. She's a tough and crafty competitor, but deep down is a faithful friend and a compass. She's also lived through the kind of coercion that hides behind "official" words. **PLAYER #9.**

AMOS. A celebrated veteran of an elite military unit from the Eastern Mediterranean Buffer Zone. A quiet and thoughtful man, Amos believes in peace despite his time in the field. Maybe because of that time. **PLAYER #17.**

ANT. A former British Royal Marine who now runs a military contracting firm, Ant Tipton is an opportunist who knows how to destabilize a room. He'll seemingly do whatever it takes to win, including causing harm to his fellow players. **PLAYER #3.**

CARLOS. A former undefeated professional boxer from Colombia. Now, Carlos Lopez has worked his way up through the ranks of South American business, in an era when supply lines break and borders close without warning in the Northern Andes. Not all his connections are legal. **PLAYER #39.**

CONNER. West Point graduate, Rhodes Scholar, youngest congressman ever elected in Kentucky. Conner Lynch left politics to host a popular podcast, in the hope that he might do more for his country there. **PLAYER #156.**

ELENA. A celebrated newscaster from Madrid, Spain, Elena Torres is magnetic, capable, and caring. She has big plans to become her country's prime minister when she's done with her broadcasting career. **PLAYER #87.**

HANNAH. Born and raised in Hamburg, Germany, Hannah Wagner demonstrated tremendous intelligence from an early age and is already a junior at MIT at the age of eighteen. She's not just a great engineer. She's emotionally intelligent, deeply sympathetic, and wise beyond her years. The daughter of two former Hamburg police officers, she notices systems the way other people notice weather. Her father, after his retirement, became an instructor in self-defense. **PLAYER #222.**

JACK. Hails from Houston and is a former sergeant major in the Army Rangers. At age ten, Jack McHenry saved six other kids when his foster home caught fire. Jack's a natural leader who has underperformed in life since his last overseas deployment, in a world that never seems to calm down anymore. **PLAYER #711.**

LUCA. A police inspector from Rome, Italy, Luca won a medal of valor for preventing a terrorist attack in the Vatican City. Despite his success, he thinks of himself as a husband and father first and a policeman second. Everybody loves Luca Tommasi. **PLAYER #112.**

MARCELO. Hails from Santiago, Chile, where he became an undefeated master of Brazilian jiujitsu. Quietly confident,

Marcelo Oliveira never loses at anything—from soccer to romance. **PLAYER #638.**

REG. An Australian gold medalist in the decathlon and world-famous athlete. He also won another gold medal in rugby. Reg Drummond is one of the favorites to win these games the way he won Olympic Games in front of the world. **PLAYER #2.**

RUPERT. Born in a poor section of Manchester, England, Rupert Chadwick is a third-generation descendant of Indian immigrants. A brilliant student and impressive athlete, but most amazing, he's only fourteen years old. Almost as much of a prodigy as Hannah Wagner. **PLAYER #930.**

SAAD. Volunteered and then served in his country's Air Force, despite his royal status, in a region where heat and money shape everything. By far the wealthiest person in the competition. Prince Saad al-Harbi believes in fair play. Unless he's about to lose. **PLAYER #7.**

WYATT. Nineteen years old and has lived in New York City his entire privileged life. Despite that, Wyatt Jordan has the highest scores on the aptitude test taken by all competitors. Resourceful and charismatic, Wyatt is a survivor and a born leader. He's a polished speaker and good with words, but it's more than that. He's a brilliant and convincing liar when he must be. **PLAYER #77.**

ZHI. An adored Chinese gymnast, Lin Zhi will be forced to compete against his brother, Lin Jian (**Player #21**), a platform diver who has no problem competing against anyone. This contest puts the two of them in the same discipline for the first time in their lives. **PLAYER #20.**

THE HOST. This mysterious disembodied character strikes fear into the heart of every player. His words alone have the power to change the players' lives and fortunes. Perhaps the most puzzling thing about him is his real agenda.

JIMMY. This is Jimmy Donaldson. Aka MrBeast. A world-famous content creator known for his games and challenges, Jimmy has been asked by the contest's organizers to help make the games as demanding as possible. He was approached by the organizers and believes in the mission behind these games, at least the one he was sold. He believes the right person can help change everything for the better if given the right resources. Sharp, fair-minded, and deeply loyal, he isn't afraid to stand up for the players when he suspects something has gone terribly wrong.

THE LETTER

The letter below was sent to the one thousand participants in the fifth competition seeking "The One" by its organizers. The envelope was gold and sealed with a blue-and-pink logo well-known to belong to YouTube creator MrBeast. The letter has never been seen by anyone who didn't participate in the final competition. Confidentiality wasn't about privacy, as believed then. It was control.

Hey guys,

It's me, Jimmy. MrBeast. This is me. For real.

First off: **Congratulations!**

I know what you're thinking. ***I didn't apply to anything.*** That's true. But stick with me and let me explain because this is the most important letter I've ever sent anyone, and you're about to get the chance of a lifetime, maybe of a dozen lifetimes.

You were selected—after careful screening—for a private competition that stays private. Not for the mystery. Because if this went public, it would turn into chaos overnight.

The competition is a series of tests that are harder than anything you've seen. And unlike what I do, this will **not** be recorded, televised, streamed, or uploaded anywhere for the world to see.

No audience. No clout.

Just the games.

This is a battle for the biggest prize and the most important opportunity anyone has ever gotten. It's also the hardest, craziest, and most lucrative competition I've ever been connected to.

By a lot.

One winner gets one billion dollars.

Yes, you read that correctly. One winner. One billion dollars. But the money isn't the real reason you're here.

The stakes aren't money.

The ***real*** stakes involve finding one person, just one, who can use their gifts to help save us all before it's too late. We're closer to the edge than we think. The organizers behind these games believe that the disaster cannot be avoided unless we bring people together fast—and find someone who can move the world.

It might be a crazy thing to say, but it's not only the endless number of growing wars.

It's systems breaking. Rolling blackouts. Water you can't count on. Supply lines snapping. Storms and heat and fires and floods. People being pushed from their homes. A crisis of what is real and what isn't, where no one can be sure of what to believe anymore. Trust in our world is almost entirely gone.

We all see it. Every day.

But I have hope. Every day I see people step up and help. That's why I agreed with the organizers of all this that the world requires someone to rally that feeling in all of us and do something about it. It requires the one thing we're running out of: trust.

The world needs people they can trust.

Listen to me carefully:

I'm not one of the organizers.

They came to me. They asked for my help. They asked me to be involved because I understand games, competitions, and people—and because they believe this mission matters.

I said yes because I believe it matters too.

And because I believe in you.

If you accept this invitation, you will become part of the most select and diverse group of competitors ever assembled: the brightest minds, the best problem solvers, the hardest fighters from countries all around the world. You are someone who will look the impossible in the face and tell it to sit down and shut up. You are someone who will stare at the shadow of death and say, "Not today."

The world needs that. The world needs **you**.

We've all seen what happens when one person starts something real. A creator. An athlete. A kid with a phone. A nurse. A teacher. One voice catches fire. Millions lean in. And when those people move together, the impossible stops being impossible.

That's why these games exist.

That's why the winner needs resources.

If you win this competition and you are declared

The One—you get the billion. You get the scale and access to make a difference.

Here are the rules you need to understand before you say yes:

1. **This is confidential.** You will sign agreements. You will follow protocols. Not because this is fun secrecy. This is not for publicity and this is controlled.

2. **This is not a show.** I will say it again. It will not be live-streamed. It will not be uploaded. It will not be recorded for the world to consume. No audience. If you're here for attention, don't come.

3. **This is dangerous.** There will be rules. There will be medical support. There will be ways to step out if you have to. **But**—you can get hurt. **You can die.** That is not hype. That is the truth.

4. If you accept, you will be moved fast. You will not be told everything at once. That is intentional.

And finally:

You're not being asked to be a hero. You're being asked to be a person other people will follow when fear is louder than reason.

If you say yes, you'll receive your next instructions.

If you say no, nobody will ever know you were chosen.

Either way: **You were picked for a reason.**

I'm looking forward to meeting you soon.

Start to prep yourself mentally and physically for the most dangerous games.

Trust that in the end, it will be worth it.

Trust me.

Sincerely,

Jimmy Donaldson, aka MrBeast

GAME #1

1.

ALEK
ANTARCTICA

Can one person really save the world?

Aleksandra Andrich—Alek—nearly six feet, twenty-two, battle-tested. She's a survivor of the many wars that have chewed up her corner of the Carpathian Belt. Her family has been running from sirens for so long she can't even tell you in what country the running started.

They'd warned her she might die. They'd also promised one person could fix the world. But that's not what races through her mind. What races through her mind is that question about why she's here, why they're all here. Whoever *The One* is, will they really be able to change things for the better? Or is the trick getting other people to move with you?

For now, Alek just needs to survive this first day in Antarctica. They've dressed them all the same: thermal gear, goggles, face wraps. And the same little add-on nobody talks about—a plastic wristband clipped snug over her glove, warm against her pulse. A tracker. Heartbeat, location, motion. If it flatlines, they're already moving. Her wristband warms against her pulse. She checks under the band: PROPERTY OF H. GAMES, INC.

She and the others are crammed into one of five Zodiac boats. They're in the middle of the freezing water of McMurdo Sound, on their way to Ross Island. Her hands are already shaking from the cold, despite the thick gloves and her thermal parka.

They're expecting final instructions for today's test upon arrival at the island. The Host—the voice they first heard back in Ohio—had communicated as much before they'd been transferred to the Zodiac boats:

"Today we begin to find out which of you is worth selecting—because today the games start for real. Good luck to one and all. And trust me: You'll need more than luck on Ross Island. You are being evaluated in ways you won't perceive. We watch the map. It changes by the hour."

In Ohio, she had caught one last clipped line that a lot of the players ignored: "We don't save what's on it. We manage it." But it didn't make any sense to her so she let it go.

The words have the same calm menace as an emergency broadcast. She's heard that tone before. It's been drilled into all of them that the games they are about to play are the most dangerous any man or woman has ever experienced. The rules have been explained to them. Alek has already memorized these rules—her life depends on it.

It's been indicated that everything on this journey is a test of their skill set. Tests to see which one of them has the leadership skills to save the world. She wonders if that is true, or if it's even possible.

They were told the rules would be clear. That they'd be enforced consistently. That this would all be fair.

That was the first lie.

More than that, Alek is worried if she makes one mistake, her wristband will stop buzzing and someone will zip her into a bag. Maybe in the next hour.

The Zodiac she's in hits another wave and goes airborne again.

Alek traps another scream in her throat.

She grips the rail in front of her harder, and slivers of ice crack off the metal railing and fall into the sound.

She can swim. That isn't the problem. What happens if the boat capsizes, she ends up in subzero water, and all of her body somehow turns to ice?

What then?

Another wave hits. Another jolt to her system. Alek's glove slips. Ice bites her palm. One mistake and she's gone. She locks her arm.

The letter had said that she would need to be brave.

Be brave now, she tells herself, despite the wind and water all around her and the unimaginable cold trying to swallow her up on McMurdo Sound, out here at the ends of the earth.

Alek plants her feet and tightens her lock on the railing as a way of not sliding across the deck. And maybe over into the water. She's ready for the next wave created by the wake of the Zodiac in front of them.

Get a grip, Alek tells herself.

And not just on the railing.

She thinks of her mother again. She misses her more than ever, on this boat trip into the frozen unknown. She hopes her mother is safe back home, in the small mountain town they last settled in two years ago. But the sirens had recently caught up to them again . . .

Alek is farther away from her mother than she has ever been in her life. She and her sister were raised by their parents to be dreamers—back when her father was still there to say it out loud.

That was before the endless raids and evacuations turned the only world she's ever known into a living nightmare.

But she reminds herself why she is here:

She keeps telling herself that these games, feeling as dangerous as promised before they've actually begun, are a chance to still have the life for herself she'd imagined, that her parents had told her she could have.

She reminds herself of that, especially here and now when her heart wants to come out of her chest as the cold wind knifes into her face and makes it impossible to breathe. Alek is surprised that her quiet tears haven't turned to icicles on her cheeks from the wind.

One more time all the feelings of helplessness she felt back home with the war raging around her have come rushing back. They're coming at her in waves.

Not once, though, does she want the pilot to turn around. And she knows why. This competition–this chance she's been given along with the others–has allowed her to do something she had stopped since the war ripped her family apart:

Alek is allowing herself to dream again.

Dream of a better world, for her and her sweet mother and everyone else. At least in this moment when she needs strength, she's made stronger by the knowledge that she is one of the few chosen to compete for an almost unimaginable fortune over the next few days.

But that's only if she lives to cash the check.

A billion dollars.

More money than she could spend in several lifetimes.

But Alek and the others know they are competing for an even bigger prize:

To be known as a hero around the world, as big and crazy an idea as that is. Only one of them can win. One out of the thousand summoned from all over the world to a cornfield in Ohio a few days ago.

But first she has to make it through a day when she will be asked to cross a treacherous stretch known as the Erebus Ice Tongue, where every step could be her last.

That's the first test, at the coldest place on earth.

For the moment, she is on the seventeen-foot Zodiac plowing through icy water. Next to her is a redheaded German girl, Hannah Wagner, Player #222. Hannah is an extraordinary prodigy studying oceanography as an eighteen-year-old junior at MIT. Hannah's eyes keep flicking to details other people miss—where the speakers are mounted, where the cameras aren't.

Next to Hannah at the bow of the sleek, inflatable boat is Wyatt Jordan, player #77, a gifted college student from New York City. Alek can already see that Wyatt is quite taken with Hannah, in just the short time he's known her.

"Can I be honest with you?" Hannah Wagner confides to Alek. "I'm scared." It's as if she hasn't just moved closer to Alek but has actually gotten all the way inside her head.

Alek is already fond of this shy, brilliant German girl. They bonded almost immediately in Ohio. Alek felt she'd been given a second chance to be a big sister. She already has a sense of how strong Hannah is. Alek still wants to protect her at the same time, the way a big sister would.

"If we go in, grab my sleeve," Alek says. "We'll get through this together."

"You make it sound so easy," Hannah says.

Alek smiles.

"I'm good at looking calmer than I feel," she says.

It takes some effort, the wind in both their faces, but Hannah smiles back.

"Thank you," she says.

"For what?"

"I know you've been looking out for me, *without* making it look that way, almost from the first moment we met," she says.

"I like you," Alek says. "I've liked you from the start. And I'm frankly not sure I could have done this at your age. It's why I think you're probably braver than I'll ever be."

"Hey, you're not that much older than I am," Hannah says.

Alek's face turns serious. "Yes," she says, "I am."

"Maybe we really can take care of each other," Hannah says. "I never had a sister."

"I did," Alek says.

"What happened to her?"

"She died," Alek says.

"I'm so sorry," Hannah says.

Not as sorry as I am, Alek is about to say, but she feels it first—a low thrumming through the rubber hull, a pulse under the water. Something hits the Zodiac hard—torpedo-hard—and the bow jumps out of the water.

"Whale!" Hannah yells before the others realize what just happened. Then, her eyes filled with both wonder and terror, she points a stiff arm at the water. *"Orca!"*

The Zodiac jumps. Then it flips.

Water slams her face. The cold is instant and brutal. They've been dunked into McMurdo Sound.

In water this cold, you lose your hands first. Then you lose your mind, Alek thinks.

The cold stuns her. Her lungs seize. She battles back to the surface. Her arms and legs already feel numb. When she manages to get her head above water, gulping in air, she's less than twenty yards from a black-and-white orca whale that is the biggest, most frightening creature she's ever seen in her life.

Her head swivels as she sees dark, cresting waves surrounding others who were just ejected from the Zodiac boat.

She frantically searches for any sight of Hannah Wagner's red hair. But she can't see her friend anywhere.

Just killer whales that seem to be everywhere.

This isn't a dream. This is a nightmare.

2.

JACK
OFF THE COAST OF CHILE

Jack McHenry, Player #711, looks down at the water.

Sharks, he thinks.

Perfect.

He knows that half of the games' contestants are off to Antarctica already.

The other half are here in South America.

But nobody said anything about sharks being a factor before the games even began.

Just freaking great.

In or out of the Army, Sgt. Major Jack McHenry (ret.) has prided himself above all else on never being afraid of anything.

Even dying.

But as he surveys the last stretch of Pacific Ocean between himself and the island off the coast of Chile known as El Fin del Mundo, he has to admit, if grudgingly, that there might be a first time for everything.

Translated into English, the name of the island means *the End of the World.*

Hope not, he thinks.

Jack knows himself well enough to know it's not the fear of death that runs his life. It's the death he's already seen in war. Not the damage war has done to him, and keeps doing. No—more than that. The damage inside him.

He remembers reading a line once—can't remember who said it: Getting old isn't for the faint of heart. And he'd thought: *Getting old is tough? Try post-traumatic stress on for size. Carry* that *around inside you like dead weight.* He closes his eyes—not just to stop looking down at the sharks—and shakes his head, trying to clear his mind of the images that never leave. Old or not, Jack learned one thing the hard way: Time doesn't bargain. It collects.

This moment makes him feel like he never mustered out and was still a Ranger. He's alive when so many guys he served with aren't. He remembers how alive he felt on deployment—going after targets, feeling like he was making a difference. That's the part he wants to hold on to.

He wants to help people. He wants people to count on him again. He wants to matter again, even though he's not wearing a uniform anymore. That's why—separate from the money—he wants to be part of this adventure. They've talked about danger from the start, from that first letter. Something else everybody ought to try on for size? An ambush in the dark, when the world goes loud and sideways—no warning, no rules, just survival.

Jack knows from experience the only thing you can do is make your fear work for you. He learned that the hard way. He's already talked about that with some of the others.

He's even tried to explain some of this to the young English boy, Rupert Chadwick, whom he's been doing his best to look after since Ohio. Jack can see already that Rupert is a wonderful kid, trying to act older than he is, coming across as braver than any fourteen-year-old had a right to be. Jack doesn't know why whoever really selected the contestants reached out to somebody this young. But it doesn't matter how he got here. Just that Rupert is here. As much as Jack knows he needs to focus on his own stuff over the long haul—and the sharks in the short run—he wants to do anything and everything he can to protect this kid.

In so many ways, even before the games have officially begun, this boy makes him feel he has a purpose again. The boy has become part of a larger mission for Jack McHenry.

"I don't know what I'm supposed to do, or how I'm supposed to act," Rupert had said before they'd gotten on the ship today.

"Listen, you've already impressed the heck out of me," Jack said.

"I can't imagine how," Rupert said.

"By acting like you belong," Jack said.

"You really think so?" Rupert asked, beaming, desperate for approval. "Because sometimes I feel totally lost, and not just because I'm this far away from my mum and dad." Then he looked away. "Do you have any children of your own, Mr. McHenry?"

"Call me Jack."

"So do you have any children, Jack?"

Jack put out his fist for Rupert to bump with his own.

"Maybe now I do," Jack had said.

Keep focused, Jack reminds himself.

The distance from their ship to the island is less than half a mile. No worries for Jack there, he'd navigated much longer distances when he was still with the Rangers. Not a problem for a swimmer as strong as he is. *A problem for Rupert, though . . .*

No, the immediate problem was the sharks, now that they've been informed this is as far as the ship is going. That they will be expected to swim the rest of the way to the End of the World.

He sees bull sharks down there, and tiger sharks too. Jack knows them by sight from growing up on Galveston Bay and having gotten pretty darn close to some of them when he was a hardheaded kid. Something else he knows? Those sharks aren't down there sightseeing.

Fine. Bring it on. This is what we're here for, isn't it? A real test.

He hadn't come this far from that oil rig in the Midland Basin to lose before he even got to the island. Not with stakes like these, not with the chance to win money beyond his wildest dreams.

But there's something else on the table along with the money, something that had made Jack want to become an Army Ranger in the first place:

What he truly does think of as a second chance—his last chance—to put meaning back into his life.

So, he tells himself now what he used to say downrange, when it was go time:

"We're going to have to pick a different day to die."

He misses the mission. That's the problem.

He gives one last look around for Rupert Chadwick, hoping against hope that the boy is a good swimmer.

If he's not, the sharks won't care how brave he is.

3.

ALEK
ANTARCTICA

After a few seconds in the water, Alek Andrich is more afraid than she's ever been in her life. Her thermal parka is waterlogged, dragging her down. Cold knifes through her suit. Her fingers stop obeying.

She tries to see past whales that look to be twenty, maybe thirty feet long. A low pulse rolls through the water. Not a whale. Not natural. The whales don't fit any plan she can imagine. Which means no one's in control out here. But she doesn't have time for that. She starts looking for others who've been thrown out of the Zodiac with her.

And she's still looking for Hannah.

We'll get through this together, Alek had told her friend. *I promised her.*

Already she can see shapes floating face down up ahead—dark parkas, limbs, maybe people. *Are they dead?* She can't tell. She tries to say a quick prayer for them anyway. But her lips are heavy and stiff.

She tries to scream Hannah's name.

But her tongue is already too thick from the cold. Her lungs feel frozen, like she's trying to breathe through glass.

The scream dies in her throat.

She starts to sink. She's going under.

This is it.

Thoughts come too fast, out of order—like her mind is dumping files from across her life as it starts to power down. She can't help it. She thinks of her little sister, back when she used to call Alek the Ice Queen, from an animated film they used to watch together. It was about sisterhood. Like theirs.

Alek hadn't been able to save her sister when a bomb hit her school, but she's going to save Hannah before she freezes to death. She just has to find Hannah first.

Don't you dare die on me, Hannah Wagner.

Alek finally spots a few of the others swimming toward the capsized Zodiac, looking for something—anything—to hold on to. The whales keep splashing around them, as if this is some game for them.

She doesn't know what orcas do to a human swimming near them, but that hardly matters. It's the water that's going to get her first.

There's no way out of this. No escape she can imagine.

Then she sees Hannah's red hair about fifty yards away. Hannah's head is bobbing face down in the ruffled sea. Alek's body wants to turn toward the Zodiac, toward anything that floats. Instead, she turns toward Hannah.

But between her and the girl another whale surfaces, the orca now swimming directly toward her, too big, too fast. Alek is about to be hit.

"Please no," Alek whispers.

Nobody hears her.

4.

JACK
OFF THE COAST OF CHILE

Jack and the other contestants headed for El Fin del Mundo, the End of the World, have been given their instructions.

Once they reach the island, they are to make their way through a forest teeming with deadly snakes and spiders as large as his fist. If they survive, next comes a steep climb of more than a thousand feet to the highest point on the island. Then back down La Montaña Serpiente–Snake Mountain–and through the forest, before heading in small boats to the main ship.

First, they have to deal with the friggin' sharks.

Jack wonders if the sharks were part of the test all along. What should that tell him about this dangerous game and how to play it to win? What does that tell him about the people who set this up?

He had been prepared as a Ranger to adapt when the situation on the ground changed. Now it was about to change, before he even set foot on the End of the World.

"Is that the ocean I smell, or just the stink of fear coming off you, McHenry?" Jack hears from behind him.

He doesn't even need to turn his head to know who the speaker is: Ant Tipton, player #3, a former British Royal Marine, now running his own private outfit, treats Jack's Army Rangers as members of junior varsity. He's taunted Jack every chance he's gotten since they'd nearly squared off back in Ohio.

"I'm good," Jack says calmly. "How about you?"

"Best worry about yourself," Tipton says. "In a few minutes those sharks will be swimming away from me. Out of respect. Maybe then I'll send them in your direction. So they can give you a little kiss." Tipton loves this part—the shove, the spark, the moment people turn on each other.

Jack smiles at him. "I've got a better idea," he says.

"What's that, mate?"

"You can kiss my ass," Jack tells Tipton, who actually coughs up a laugh.

Since Ohio, The Host's voice has been everywhere, dropping rules that shift like sand. Everything a veiled threat. Too clean. Too even. Like it's coming through a machine first, and a man second. At present, it's coming through speakers at the back of the boat.

"There are two minutes before you assemble on the platforms," The Host says. "They'll be lowered near the water. You've been presented your first surprise—our hungry friends. Swim through them to the island. Make your way to the top of Snake Mountain. Return to the ship without being bitten, or poisoned, or otherwise injured. If you can. And understand this: We're not only measuring what you can do. We're measuring what you do to each other. Every word. Every choice. Every hesitation. Consider this your calibration." There is a pause before, "Individual feats are meaningful. Team stability is scored. We will assemble for a pleasant and well-earned group dinner back on the ship this evening."

Jack feels himself smiling. Not because it's funny. Because something in him clicks into place.

"Something amusing?" Tipton asks.

"Only to me," Jack McHenry says.

He knows it's because of the edge he's always carried around inside him, an essential part of his code. He glances at the tattoo on his left forearm:

"I never lose."

And I'm not going to start now, Jack thinks, right before he hits the water.

5.

WYATT
ANTARCTICA

Wyatt Jordan watches in disbelief as this monster whale lifts itself into the air in a clean vertical surge, directly in front of him, then sends what looks and feels like a tidal wave in his direction.

When the giant orca lands back in the water, the impact cracks the air as hard as a sonic boom.

Wyatt knows he'd appreciate the spectacle of it, the raw beauty, if his brain wasn't screaming at him to survive. As good as he is with words, he's not sure if he could do this scene justice if he were describing it.

But his only concern is Hannah.

He's not sure why she's become this important to him, this quickly. But she has. Wyatt can tell that she likes him, too.

It's because she doesn't really know me yet, he thinks.

Wyatt Jordan isn't sure he knows himself. Isn't sure how scared he should be. Doesn't really know what he should do next. He's talked a little bit about this with Hannah and Alek, the tall Eastern European woman Hannah has also gotten close with. They've talked about how they both absolutely hate to lose control, just the way Wyatt does. It was that way in his childhood with his mother's depression. How he couldn't help her and she couldn't help him. It's why Wyatt has always prided himself—his words—on not losing the plot.

But out here there isn't even a storyline.

Just noise. Cold. Water. Panic.

Wyatt's brain offers one useless thought: The only story left is survival. He hasn't been in the water that long, but he already feels himself starting to freeze, fighting to get his arms and legs working together. Air won't come. His hands stop listening. He forces one breath. Then another. His parka feels like a straitjacket as he tries to tread water.

He knows he has to start swimming.

But for the life of him, he isn't sure which way is safe.

He sees Hannah's red hair. But she's floating face down. And he hates himself for the flicker of math in his head: How long a person can be under before it's too late.

And then he sees Alek Andrich swimming toward her, stroking fast, as if her own life depended on it. Another whale is headed directly for Alek, but it veers off slightly and swims past her. It creates a wave that throws her hard to the side, but not underwater.

Wyatt knew these games could kill somebody. He just hadn't believed it could be him. Now he's got to swim to save his life, and Hannah's, even as the brutal cold is making his whole body start to seize up.

Arms and legs cramping badly. His hands stop answering. That's the horror—his body quits before his brain does. The sharp, stunning sting of water on his face getting more painful as he forces himself to keep stroking. His heavy, wet clothes slowing him down.

Something on his wrist—by his glove—buzzes once, warm and precise, like it's logging the moment.

He's getting closer to them. Watching some of the face-down contestants slowly revive. But not Hannah.

"I'm here!" he manages to yell. "I'm coming!"

He can still see Hannah floating, her face in the water, all that red hair surrounding it.

Fifty yards, or less . . .

Then he sees the black-and-white orca cruising toward him, already closer to Wyatt than he is to Hannah and Alek. *Good God!* The biggest of them all, its jawline breaks the surface—black, huge—close enough for him to see the pale ridges of teeth. And Wyatt finally understands: Nobody is coming to save them.

He kicks harder and swims anyway.

6.

JACK
OFF THE COAST OF CHILE

Jack wants to be the first into the water. Back when he wore a uniform, he always believed you led from the front.

So now he's first into the turbulent waters of the Pacific.

The sharks start circling immediately, as he expected they would.

Jack tries to keep as many of them as possible in his range of vision. Focus on them and nothing else.

If you don't mess with them, they won't bother you.

That's the working theory, anyway. But he's not betting his skin on it.

Jack starts a steady crawl stroke toward the island. He reminds himself to maintain a steady even pace, pretending he's in the middle lane of some Olympic pool with other swimmers on both sides of him.

He tells himself this is not a sprint.

He's not trying to break any speed records. He's not trying to win style points. He's just trying to make it to shore with his arms and legs still attached. Jack's just trying to be alive. Then figure a way to get through the infested forest, up the mountain, and then back down.

The biggest shark—at least the biggest he has eyes on—is dead ahead. Probably thirty yards. Jack wants to keep it that way.

He knows this much from growing up around sharks, being in the water with them: They were the ones who decided whether you were prey or not.

And by the time you knew, it was usually too late.

He hears splashes of the other players hitting the water, jumping off the boat, and he wonders if being the first in was such a bright idea.

Could've let Tipton go first.

Jack watches the big shark as it watches him. They're both deciding who's going to make the first move.

Or make the first mistake.

Jack thinks about angling away from it, going parallel to shore, hoping the shark might lose interest.

Only now, just to make things more dangerous and a lot more complicated, Jack sees the shadow of a bull shark. It's less than ten yards away—and below him, turning its head just enough to put eyes on Jack.

Not today.

Jack's eyes go back to the big one, still making slow turns but not doing what Jack desperately wants it to do.

Go. Get out of here.

Hey, buddy.

Jack can clearly see it's a good fifteen feet long, or even longer than that, a beast.

Tiger shark, Jack is sure of it. Known for eating anything and everything. And everyone? Now it's moving slowly, relentlessly in Jack McHenry's direction. Sure as the sun's gonna rise, as his old man used to say. Almost baiting Jack into reacting, into turning himself into bait.

Jack knows what he has to do when the big shark gets too close.

He's not going to have any choice. He's going to get one shot at saving his own life.

He's going to have to do the only thing left—haul off and punch him right in the snout, the way he was taught back in Texas.

Jack dips under the surface, just enough to brace.

Here goes nothing.

Then he sees the shark's attention shift to his immediate left. And then the whole pattern changes, like someone just pressed a button. Jack carefully turns his eyes in the same direction—no sudden movements, not now—and sees another swimmer.

Someone Jack recognizes instantly.

Jimmy Donaldson.

MrBeast himself.

As blown away as he is to see him here, Jack is even more shocked to see the guy is actually smiling at him. Like he's saying, *Breathe. Move. Don't give them a reason.*

He hadn't seen him since they'd boarded together.

Jimmy takes charge of the situation and makes a simple motion: Stay close. Don't thrash. Something about him makes Jack trust him: the calm. The way he moves like panic is a choice.

Jack does what he's told, without hesitation, and a faint warmth from his wristband again, like someone took note.

When their heads are above the water, Jimmy looks at Jack.

"We having fun yet?" he asks.

Up close, it's different. Jack can see Jimmy is putting on a brave face. But for what? *For me,* Jack realizes. *Jimmy is acting like everything is fine so that anyone he runs into doesn't give in to fear.*

"I've had about as much fun for one day as I can handle," Jack says, gasping for breath.

"We're going to be fine," Jimmy says.

"Tell that to the sharks," Jack says.

I'm out here with the biggest YouTube star on the planet, he thinks, *and it feels like the two of us against the world. If he can lead by example, then I can too.*

"We stick together," Jimmy says. "I don't know the rules yet. But I know this: Alone is how they want us."

Jack looks to see if the closest shark has gotten any closer.

It hasn't.

Yet.

"If you say so," Jack says.

"Big win, there's no blood in the water," Jimmy says. "This is their natural habitat, panic is the only enemy we can control. They react to it. So, we don't give it to them. Even if we have to fake it. We act bold."

"Got it," Jack says.

"Then let's go," Jimmy says.

"To the island?" Jack asks.

"Nah," Jimmy says. "We have to pretend to be braver than that!"

He swims directly toward the closest shark.

Jack follows him.

THE RED TENTS

SOMEWHERE IN OHIO
81 HOURS EARLIER

7.

They stand in a mowed-down cornfield—flat stalks, torn earth, the sweet-rotten smell of husks. A thousand of them. Men and women from all over the world, packed shoulder to shoulder like they've been poured into this place, surrounded by what feels like almost as many red tents.

Too many to count at first glance. Identical. Clean. The red is too bright. Too intentional. The color of a warning. One you can touch.

As soon as they'd arrived at the field, they'd all been given a number. A guard snapped a thin black wristband onto each of them. "For safety," he said. It didn't feel like safety.

There are armed guards, dressed in black, carrying what look to be military-style rifles, ringing the field—disciplined, ready. Not quite aiming. Not quite relaxed, either. There's no shouting, no barking orders. They don't look like men who expect trouble. They look like men who've already been told what trouble will look like, and exactly how fast it ends.

No one knows what's inside the tents.

And why the guards?

Since arriving here in Ohio the day before, in a place somewhere between Cleveland and Cincinnati, somewhere that refuses to resolve into a real place on any map, no one has been allowed inside the tents or even been allowed to get close to them.

The letter promised no cameras. The lenses above the tents disagreed—quiet, mounted high, watching everything. And once Hannah Wagner notices them, she can't stop noticing the way the lenses seem to tilt. Not track everyone—just some.

They were ordered to turn over their phones—told they'd get them back after the first test. They'd also signed paperwork—stacks of it, clipped tight, meant to overwhelm. The title page called it a humanitarian resilience assessment. Nobody smiled at that.

This diverse collection of people of all ages has been flown here from their various countries, not knowing anything about what will be in store for them except what Jimmy described in his invitation letter. They know nothing about the games. Or where they'll play out.

For now, they're all milling around trying to understand what the numbers they've been given signify. A thousand nervous patterns in one tight space. People whisper in different languages. Some pray. Some pace. Some stand too still.

Wyatt Jordan wonders why there is a need for armed guards in this field.

"Are those men there to protect us?" Hannah Wagner asks him.

She's standing beside Alek—tall, Eastern European, calm in a way that feels practiced. Wyatt can't tell if Alek is brave or just tired of being afraid.

"But from who?" he says. "Or maybe a better question is—from what?"

There is a man standing directly in front of him, one who's only introduced himself as Jack, a hard-looking man with a southern drawl, tattoos on arms that look like the ink was burned into him along with his tan.

Jack follows Wyatt's gaze to the rifles. Doesn't flinch. He turns to Wyatt and says, "Possible they're worried they might have to protect us from each other."

Wyatt almost laughs—then doesn't. Because the idea lands.

"It's not that at all," Wyatt hears from behind him.

They all turn around.

"Hi," a tall young man says and smiles broadly. "I'm Jimmy."

"No way!" Wyatt exclaims, because some part of him is still eight years old and watching a video where someone gives away a house like it's nothing.

"Way," Jimmy says and puts out his hand to shake. "And you're Wyatt Jordan."

8.

Wyatt stands there feeling starstruck and dumbstruck at the same time. The MrBeast he's grown up watching on screen is standing right here in front of him.

"You know who I am?"

Jimmy's grin softens. "I do. I know some of you. Names, faces. And I've been given the basics on the rest. I know you too, Jack. And Alek, I appreciate you choosing to be here despite your circumstances."

"Thank you," Alek says.

"So wait . . . what . . ." Wyatt stammers. "What are you doing here?"

Jimmy glances out at the tents, at the guards, at the cameras that absolutely weren't supposed to be here. For a heartbeat, he looks serious.

"Well, let's see," Jimmy says, choosing his words. "Since they asked me to be the one to invite you," he says, "I kind of felt like I should show up for the first day of orientation and say hi."

"Orientation," Alek says with a dry edge.

"It does feel like the first day of school," Jimmy says.

"Or boot camp," Jack says. He doesn't bother hiding the suspicion. "You gonna explain what's actually happening?"

"Not everything," Jimmy shrugs. "I'm happy to tell you what I've been told, but obviously I don't know what I don't know."

"How about some highlights?" Alek asks.

Jimmy nods once. "I tried to give you those in the letter I sent to all of you. Without trying to sound like some philosopher—which, believe me, I'm not—I really am convinced that if this competition plays out the way I hope it will, this can be the first day of better days. For a lot of people who don't usually get better days. I wouldn't have put my name on it if I didn't think it mattered."

Wyatt knows a lot about Jimmy. Wyatt watches him and thinks, *He looks young enough to be in the crowd.*

"You really believe someone my age can be the leader you described?" Wyatt asks. "Or Alek. Or Hannah."

"Don't sell yourself short," Jimmy says enthusiastically. "I'm not all that much older than some of you. There's no age limit to being someone who tries to do the right thing."

Wyatt hears the words and feels his stomach tighten. "Not sure about my leadership capabilities, not gonna lie," he says.

"It's no accident you're here. The same goes for Jack. And Alek." Jimmy looks at each of them.

"Hope you're right," Wyatt says, wondering just how much Jimmy Donaldson knows about him.

Rupert Chadwick, the fourteen-year-old from England, joins the group. Wyatt had hung out with him a little the day before. Already he feels this kid is old and wise beyond his years. The way Hannah Wagner is.

"So this is all your idea?" Rupert asks, eyes fixed on Jimmy.

"I was asked to come up with a concept, amp up some

challenges, look for some specific dynamics," Jimmy says. "By people with a big vision for a better future. A better world. That reeled me in."

"Something else you said in the letter," Alek says. "You told us to trust you."

"I meant it. I mean it even more now that I'm meeting you guys," Jimmy says. "I'm not going to pretend I can control everything here. But I can promise you this: I'm going to do what I can to keep it honest."

"Then what's with the cameras?" Alek asks. "In your letter, you said–"

"Nothing goes public. No live-stream. No uploads. They're for internal monitoring only–security. It's important everyone is safe. At least, that's the line I was sold."

Jack notices. "Well, that's not the most comforting."

"To be brutally honest, I just asked about them too," Jimmy replies thoughtfully. "They were a surprise to me. And, when it comes to important things, I'm not a big fan of surprises."

They hear a crackling sound from the loudspeakers situated around the field, followed by a man's voice. The voice that follows is too smooth. Too steady. Like it could go all night without breathing.

"May I have your attention please?"

"Who's that?" Alek asks, shoulders tense.

"Your Host," Jimmy says.

"Time for your first tests," The Host says through the speakers. "And for the games to begin. Remember: You are being evaluated in ways you won't perceive. We watch your wristbands. We know who freezes first."

Wyatt can't help himself. He's willing to put his voice to the nerves they're clearly all feeling at the moment.

"What tests?" he yells out.

"The red tents, of course, Mr. Jordan," The Host says.

Wyatt turns to ask Jimmy what that means.

But Jimmy is gone.

9.

TENT 8

The tent is smaller than it should be. The air smells faintly clean.

"You have five minutes," the woman seated across from Wyatt says. She doesn't introduce herself. Not even a first name.

"Please use this time to answer my questions truthfully. Can you do that, Mr. Jordan?"

"Yes," Wyatt says. He tells people what they want to hear. Then he watches for the tell in their eyes.

The woman watches him the way a good bartender watches a drunk—patient, unfooled, already aware of what's going to happen next. A tablet on her lap shows a moving line every time he speaks. Her voice is loud and brassy, filling the small tent.

"Have you asked yourself why you're here?" the woman says.

"I think we've all asked ourselves that question," Wyatt says.

No reaction out of her.

"Well, without embarrassing you, it's because we believe you might have greatness in you," she says. "Has anyone ever told you that before?"

"Just one person, honestly," he says.

"Your father perhaps?"

Wyatt laughs.

"No," he says. "Never my father. It was someone who actually cared."

"Would you mind telling me who?"

"As a matter of fact," Wyatt forces a smile, "I would."

The line on the tablet twitches, just a tiny spike. Like resistance is a data point.

"What qualities do you possess that might have led us to our opinion of you?" she asks.

Wyatt hears the trap: Brag and you're arrogant, be humble and you're fake.

"I know people always followed my lead, in class and in sports, even socially," he says. "Not because I ask them to. It just . . . happens."

Wyatt smiles at the woman.

"I even got elected class president in the first grade," he adds.

No reaction.

"I've already explained why we believe you should be here," she says. "But before you leave, I'd like you to tell me why you accepted our invitation."

He's about to tell her he never likes to miss a party. He won't let life happen without him in the center of it, even if it's just to show the old man . . . but manages to stop himself. *Read the room*, he tells himself. *Tell them what they want to hear. That's what you're best at.* Even in a room as small as this.

"I want to matter," Wyatt says. "I want to be useful. Not just smart."

The tablet line steadies. The woman takes notice.

"Let me put it to you another way," the woman says. "Is there anything about you, despite our extensive research into your background, that we don't know about you that we should?"

"No," Wyatt lies again. As he says it, he feels the wristband give the faintest pulse.

I hope I'm right about that.

10.

TENT 7

Something about the interviewer's bearing—even her posture—makes Luca Tommasi, player #112, an inspector with the Polizia di Stato in Rome, feel he's taking his first oral exam back in the academy.

The tent is quiet enough that he can hear his own breath. The five-minute exam, in this case, is nearly over. The wristband on his arm is warm. He hears a soft beep—like the black band just reported him.

"Eight months ago, you thwarted an organized violent attack at St. Peter's, is that correct?" the woman asks.

Luca keeps his face still. He has testified in court. He has faced families. "I think of it as averting one, since it never really began," Luca says, holding her gaze. "But yes."

"And were you at all concerned that an innocent congregant might be killed before you stopped the gunman," she asks, "because of how crowded the Basilica was for Sunday Mass?"

"Very much so."

"But you fired your weapon anyway."

"I did," he says, not a hint of defensiveness. "If I didn't, more innocent people would have died."

"So you acted appropriately?"

"I acted according to my threat assessment," he says.

Luca waits. He has never been intimidated by silences when he is the one asking the questions, of witnesses or perps. He is used to silence. Silence is where people confess.

The woman reaches for her pen, makes a mark on the paper in front of her, looks at him even more intently.

"Are you only here for the money?"

"No," Luca says firmly. It's the easiest truth he's spoken in days.

"So why are you here, then?"

He has been waiting for this question since he sat down.

"I believe I can make a difference beyond what I do for work," he says. "If given the opportunity, in a world much bigger than my own."

"So are you saying that your current job isn't enough for you to accomplish what you want with your life?" she says.

"It's who I am," he says. "But not all that I am. My life away from the uniform, with my wife and my children, is just as important to me." He pauses and says, "If not more."

The woman smiles.

It's the first human thing she's done, and he doesn't trust it.

"Now," she asks softly, "why would you lie to me, Inspector Tommasi?"

11.

TENT 16

"You've had quite an amazing career in sports," the young man interviewing Reg Drummond says, almost sounding like a fan waiting for Reg to give him his autograph. Reg sits back, relaxed, hands folded. He gives the practiced smile that has kept reporters friendly for two decades.

"I've been very lucky," Reg says. "Blessed, really."

"It takes a lot more than luck to be a two-time gold medalist in the Decathlon," his interviewer says. "Only the fourth athlete to accomplish that feat, and the first from Australia."

"I worked hard." Reg shrugs.

"Then you came back four years later and won another gold medal in rugby. No wonder you were voted the most popular figure in your country three times. I see where you even competed in triathlons for a while."

"What can I say?" Reg says lightly. "People love a winner. And every country has sports heroes—"

"So you think you're a hero?"

"A figure of speech," Reg says. "I'm known because of sports, which sets me apart from people who are known for other reasons. That's all."

"We're not interested in what people know you for," he says. "We're interested in what you do when there's a more important prize than just a medal."

Reg holds his gaze.

"But you do seem to have everything," the man says. "Fame and success and money. As described in so many articles written about you, even movie star good looks. I read that you were briefly considered for some big Hollywood roles. So why come more than halfway across the world to be here and to be a part of this?"

Reg doesn't hesitate. "Because it's not enough for me."

"So you feel you have more to give to the world than you already have?"

"Much more. I'm here," Reg says, "to find out what I'm really made of."

"Let me ask you this." The man leans in. "Would you be willing to put your life on the line to be a real hero?"

"Without a second thought."

"These new games will be quite dangerous." The man smiles. "Aren't you afraid of dying?"

Reg Drummond offers the man the crooked grin the world once saw on the cover of *People* magazine.

"Oh, I'm afraid, all right," he says. "Just not of that."

12.

TENT 23

Jack McHenry tells himself to just treat the next five minutes like RASP: Ranger Assessment and Selection Program.

No BS. No lies. No smart talk.

Short answers. No wandering. No wisecracks.

Give them nothing extra.

Just answer their questions and get out of this tent after your five minutes are up.

And don't blow the gig.

He sits down. The wristband feels heavier than it should.

When the woman across the desk begins by asking about his military service, he goes back to the beginning, why he enlisted the week after 9/11. He trained, was deployed, got promoted, led. He keeps it tight. Professional.

When he finishes, she says, "That's a very admirable story, Mr. McHenry. Or would you still prefer being referred to as sergeant major?"

"That was a long time ago," Jack says. "But I'll always be proud of serving my country."

"Could we talk a bit about your private life for just a second?"

He grins.

"Your five minutes," he says, "even if it's my five cents."

"You frankly can't be quite as proud of how you did as a husband," she says. "Your two failed marriages are a different service record."

"I wasn't aware that this was a counseling session," Jack says. His smile tightening.

There it is. The smart mouth. He hears it the moment it leaves him.

Silence.

"Listen, you people say you're looking for a leader," he says, jumping right back in. "I've been one my whole life. I was voted captain of every football team I ever played on. I was the senior enlisted leader in my platoon. Men depended on me."

"We're well aware," she says, "as we're aware that you were awarded the Presidential Unit Citation for extraordinary heroism during combat overseas. We're aware of what you did. And why."

"I protected my brothers," he says. He's heard men justify anything with words like that. He doesn't like how familiar this feels.

She points at his left arm now.

"I can't help but notice one of your tattoos," she says. "The one that says you never lose."

He waits, sensing she's not quite finished.

"So let me ask you a question, Sergeant Major," she says. "How does a man who never loses end up alone, pulling shifts on an oil rig?"

The woman pauses. Jack feels it—the old heat behind his ribs. The shame that still makes him want to swing first.

"Would you like to talk about your nightmares?" she asks.

"No," he says, jaw hard, eyes down.

The woman waits. Patient.

Jack leans forward just enough for her to feel it and looks her in the eyes.

"But I'll tell you this," he says. "I'm not here to be handled. I'm here to win. So ask what you came to ask."

13.

TENT 19

"How old are you, Rupert?" the man at the desk asks. His voice has the same smooth flatness as the loudspeakers outside. Rupert doesn't know why that scares him. It shouldn't matter. It does.

"Fourteen," Rupert replies.

The man looks down at his notes. "Rupert Chadwick: Manchester. From a poor section of the city known as Moss Side West. Only child. Unusually high-level reader."

"That's me," Rupert says, "but I don't know about unusual."

"You seem to be quite an athlete, aren't you, son?"

Rupert's chest lifts despite himself. "Center middie at the Man City Football Academy," Rupert says proudly, "after I earned my scholarship there."

"But you must know it's your mind and not your skills on the pitch that earned you the invitation," the man says. "We've never seen test scores like yours for someone your age."

Rupert's smile fades. When the man smiles, he reminds Rupert of his uncle Freddie. Freddie's eyes always stay kind, but the kindness feels like a costume.

"Why did your parents allow you to come here?"

"Because of my mind, I guess," Rupert says. "My mum and dad think I can do anything I set my mind to."

"I can see why," the man says. Then, changing topics: "In school, you can recite long passages from famous works with ease, isn't that right?"

"It's just a skill, like kicking a ball," Rupert says.

"What's a good one you've memorized?"

"Depends on what you want it to be about."

The man taps the paper once with his finger. "Something about war," he says softly. "Something people read when they're trying to make sense of dying."

"There's a few come to mind." Rupert's throat goes dry. He stands anyway. It's muscle memory—standing to perform, standing to be judged.

"Have you read 'In Flanders Fields' by any chance?"

"It's one I've memorized, sir, yes," he says.

"Would you mind reciting it for me now?"

Rupert begins to speak in the strong, confident voice he uses for recitations.

In Flanders fields the poppies blow
Between the crosses, row on row,
That mark our place; and in the sky
The larks, still bravely singing, fly . . .

When he finishes, the tent is silent.

The man behind the desk looks at him for a long moment.

Then Rupert sees the tears in the man's eyes. The man smiles, but it doesn't reach his eyes.

"Thank you," he says.

Rupert sits back down, hands clasped tight in his lap.

"Are you okay?" the kid asks.

"I'm fine," the man says. "It's not that it's sad. It's that I know exactly how this ends."

14.

TENT 13

Ant Tipton sits down like he owns the chair. Dressed in black, almost like one of the guards outside, he looks across the desk at a white-haired man who does not introduce himself and says, "May I ask a question before you have me on the clock?"

Ant has the uncomfortable feeling they've spoken before.

"By all means," the man replies.

"Since you people are the ones who reached out to me," he says, "wouldn't it be more useful if I were the one interviewing *you*?"

Ant sees a flicker of something or other in the man's eyes. Something changing in them. In Ant Tipton's world, the ability to read people, the ability to pick up on the smallest subverbal indicators, can be the difference between life and death.

"It would not be useful, as a matter of fact," the man says firmly. "It's our job to establish your motives. Whether you see this chance you might have as a way to put yourself out in front of the crowd. Or if you simply see this as an opportunity to become stupidly rich?"

"Then let's not waste each other's time," Ant says. "Nothing is going to change from the time I walk out of this tent until these games of yours end. Whatever those games are. I'm here to win."

"Win what?" the man asks.

Ant smiles. "Whatever you put in front of me. I'm your man now and will be your man then."

"The man to do what?"

"Whatever it takes." Ant's smile holds.

The man studies him. "And if what we put in front of you is fear?"

Ant leans back. "Fear's just a tool."

"Are you willing to put your life on the line?" the man asks.

Ant doesn't answer right away. He lets the silence do the work. "I've done it before."

Silence.

"I'm willing to kill for a billion dollars if I have to."

The man nods his head slowly.

"I'm getting the sense that you don't suffer fools gladly, Mr. Tipton," he says.

"So get to the point, then," Ant says.

"Do you consider yourself a hard man, Mr. Tipton?"

Ant's smile widens. "I consider myself effective."

"Think of the other contestants as fellow soldiers," the man says. "Would you be willing to betray one of them?"

"Betray a mate? Never."

Lie.

And somewhere in the tent, something gives a soft, almost cheerful beep.

"Have you ever been convicted of a crime of which we are unaware?"

"Never."

Lie.

"One last question," the man says. "Do you consider yourself honorable?"

"Without question," he says.

The biggest lie of all.

15.

TENT 37

Alek Andrich hates any small room.

She was never claustrophobic before the war, before air-raid sirens became a part of her daily routine. A routine of running and locking a door behind you and listening for the moment the world breaks. A routine that chased her and her family to all the places they'd called home with a bomb shelter in the basement. There was always a bomb shelter.

"Before we begin," the man on the other side of the desk says, "is there anything you'd like to ask me?" His tone is professional. Calm as someone used to being obeyed.

"I'm fine," Alek says.

"You're sure?"

"I thought you were here to interview me," Alek says.

A faint smile. "We are. But let's not pretend we don't know what this is." He taps his pen once. "A billion dollars changes people."

Alek holds his gaze. "It only changes the people who've had the luxury of being changed."

She is trying to be polite. But the man's line of questioning is beginning to annoy her.

He watches her wristband. Like it's speaking.

"But isn't that really why you're here?" the man says.

"No," Alek says.

She takes a deep breath. She had come here determined to present her best self. Alek slows her breathing the way she used to curled up in basements, counting in her head so she wouldn't lose control.

"There must be a reason why I've been spared," she says. "Not because I'm special. Because I was lucky. Luck that feels like a curse when you're the one who lives. Or the kind that comes from some higher purpose. That may sound corny to you, but I believe that. When I received the letter, I thought this competition might be that purpose. And that is why I'm here."

The man doesn't move.

Is that the right answer?

What if it's not?

Her father, a professor emeritus at the time of his death, a kind and learned man, used to joke with her all the time that you didn't get a second chance to make a good first impression.

Alek now wonders how much of her five minutes she has left, and if there will be a bell like you'd hear in a classroom at the end of a period.

"My father used to tell me," Alek continues, "that if you survive something, you owe it meaning. You don't get to waste it."

"You're telling me that money beyond your wildest dreams isn't what made you accept the invitation to be a part of these games?" the man says. "You're here for meaning?"

Alek leans forward.

"No. This isn't about money," she says, "not for me, sir. I'm here because I refuse to let my life be just running. I want a future that isn't a shelter. I want my mother to never hear another siren again."

The interviewer doesn't blink.

"And if you win?" the man asks.

Alek leans forward. "Then I make sure no one ever has to beg the world to care again."

That is the right answer.

Whether he believes it or not.

Somewhere in the tent, her wristband gives a soft beep.

Alek stands. On the way out, the man says, almost casually, "Dreams are expensive, Ms. Andrich."

Alek doesn't turn around. "So is war."

16.

TENT 1

Saad al-Harbi, twenty-five, player #7, has spent his life trying not to look like what he is.

It only works until it doesn't.

The man across from him is young, calm, watching Saad's wristband the way a card player watches hands.

There is no conscription in his country. His military service in the Royal Air Force was his choice. Over his father's objections, Saad had volunteered, attended pilot school, fast-tracked his way up the ladder to staff sergeant before terminating his fixed-term contract with the Air Force and resigning. He had proved his point, mostly to himself.

"Had it always been a dream of yours to fly?" the interviewer asks, a young man who doesn't appear to be much older than Saad.

Saad smiles. He can feel himself being measured.

"Even in the air, I wanted to show I could stand on my own two feet," he says. "It was always my dream to be untouchable."

He is completely at ease sitting across from this man. He has never let his family's royalty and wealth make him soft. He worked for his wings because he needed something no one could hand him.

"So why are you here?" the man asks.

"Because I don't need to be here," Saad says without hesitation.

"Is that really your answer?"

"I am here because I have challenged myself my whole life," he says. "Most people in this field need the money. Need the story. Need the rescue. I don't."

The man reaches for his pen and takes a note. He doesn't look down when he does it.

"Then what do you need?"

Saad's smile fades into something sharper. "A ceiling."

"Would you be willing to offer some sort of compensation, from your own vast wealth, to give yourself an edge against the rest of the field?"

Saad lets the question hang, deciding whether to be offended.

"Is that an offer?"

"Is that an answer?" the man says.

"Are you asking what I'm willing to do," Saad says, "or what you're willing to allow?"

The man's eyes don't blink. "Answer the question."

"I have always done whatever is necessary to get what I want," Saad says. "But I don't pay for things that should be earned."

"A convenient line," the man says.

"A true one," Saad replies.

"But you're not afraid to put your life on the line in the name of your ultimate challenge?" the man asks.

"Have you ever flown a fighter jet?" Saad says.

"I can't say that I have."

"If you had," Saad continues, "you wouldn't ask me that."

"One final question, then," the man says. "What will you do if you are still around on the final day, and you end up being *The One* to win the money?"

"That's easy," he says. "I spend it in a way that makes it impossible for anyone to pretend they didn't see me."

17.

TENT 85

Hannah Wagner notes the camera angle without looking at it. She notes the speaker direction. The air movement when the door closes. The tiny delay between a sound and the moment it reaches her ears—small, wrong details that tell her this room is not what it pretends to be.

The man across the desk reminds her of a teacher back home.

Franz Muller. Herr Muller, to Hannah.

He even has the glasses perched perilously close to the end of his nose the way Herr Muller did when he would lean forward across *his* desk to address the class.

"You seem nervous," the man says.

Hannah can't help herself—she keeps waiting for him to lapse into a thick German accent.

"I'm not nervous," she says. "I'm observing."

His mouth twitches. Not quite a smile. "Lying will not get you where you want to go. Is it because you are always so young relative to almost everyone around you?" he says gently.

"I'm not lying," Hannah says. "If I were nervous, you'd already know."

"There is no reason for you to be nervous in here, as long as you are answering my questions honestly," the man continues. "We just want you to be yourself. Your *best* self, ideally." He studies her wristband. "Why are you here, Hannah?"

She doesn't give him the easy answer right away. She knows he wants it. Money. Ambition. A sob story. Something he can label.

"I'm not nervous. But. I want this so much," she says, playing the type he's clearly expecting. "More than I should."

The man smiles.

"So much money at stake," he says. "Completely understandable."

Hannah shakes her head. "Money is a tool," she says. "It's not the point."

"Then what is?" he asks.

Hannah's voice stays even, but her eyes burn. "We're running out of time," she says. "We act like we have forever. We don't."

She forces herself to slow down. Control. Don't give him a performance.

"You sound convinced," he says.

"It's not just wars all across the globe destroying us," she says. "Or famines. Or disease. We're destroying everything, from the air we breathe to our oceans and forests and wildlife."

Another deep breath. Deeper than before. Hannah doesn't want to appear too emotional, worried about how she will be judged if she is.

"We're voluntarily taking poison on a daily basis." She stands. "It's all connected. Systems. Incentives. Denial. Somebody has to do something to convince people to stop before it's too late."

She takes a breath and sits down. "I'm sorry."

"You did get a little loud, but that's okay," he says, writing a note.

"People listen when something is loud enough," she says. "When it's undeniable. When it changes their day. Their habits. Their excuses."

"And you think you can be that loud," he says, "even at your age?"

Hannah is prepared for the question. Really, she's been expecting it.

"Age doesn't decide who people follow," she says. "Clarity does."

She gets nothing back but silence.

"My country produced a man named Hermann Hesse," Hannah says. "And he once wrote that every beginning holds magic." She pauses and adds, "He wrote nothing of age limits on the magic."

The man's tone stays gentle. "And if you're wrong?"

Hannah's answer is immediate. "Then we lose everything."

18.

As they leave the tents, a guard posted outside the door hands each of them a card with a letter of the alphabet written on it.

"Line up by letter," one guard says. "Face the stage."

Twenty lines. **A** through **T**. Fifty people in each.

Reg Drummond walks toward his line with a B in his hand and feels a little bit like it's the Olympics all over again. He's just marched into a stadium along with the other athletes for Opening Ceremonies.

Except there's no cheering here.

Just the red tents behind them, the armed perimeter, and a stage that sits empty except for a microphone stand and speakers.

He assumes he must have been one of the last to be interviewed, because as he gets to the field, he sees that most of the other contestants—or dreamers, or fools, or both—are already in their lines.

What am I at this point in my life, he asks himself, *a dreamer or a fool? Or both?*

Suddenly, he fully understands, because of the tightness in his chest—or his heart—how much he wants this. How much he does not want to be sent home, not today. Not yet. As much as he's accomplished in his life, he's really felt since he retired that he's meant to do more. That he has the potential to do more. He'd always loved that the Olympics could bring the world together, and this stage feels even bigger.

Reg had just done his best in his interview to make that argument, for himself and about himself. He's about to find out how well he did.

"This is your moment," Kyra, his fiancée, had said before he left home.

Reg spots Rupert and falls in beside him. The kid keeps his eyes forward like he's trying not to blink.

He's a sweet kid, obviously bright, and probably quite remarkable if he's here at his age. There is no point in asking the kid how someone so young ended up in this isolated field in the middle of nowhere, because he's certain the boy has no idea either.

"I feel I'm being marched to the headmaster's office," Rupert says. "I just don't know if it's because I've done something good or bad."

Reg forces a small smile. "That's the trick," he says. "They keep you guessing."

Rupert looks down at his letter, a card with B on it, same as Reg. "How do you pass a test," he whispers, "if you don't even know what the test is?"

They take their places at the end of the line, and before Reg can answer, the speakers crackle.

"May I have your attention please," The Host says.

Reg feels the field tighten. A thousand bodies going still at once.

Marcelo, the jiujitsu champion from Chile, is lined up in front of them. He turns and says, "Does he not think he has it already?"

"One hundred of you are about to learn that you have been selected to remain in this competition," The Host continues. "The rest will be dismissed."

A ripple runs through the lines–shock trying to become sound–then dies. No one dares to react too loudly. Reaction is a target.

Marcelo says, "I feel the way I do when the judges are about to tell me whether I just won or lost a decision. But at least in a fight, you know the rules."

"The only rule is that they're always watching," Reg says, making sure to keep his voice low, because The Host hears everything. Or wants them to believe he does.

Reg takes another look around the field. Everyone in the other lines seems frozen in place now, facing forward, eyes on a stage that remains empty except for the speakers and a single microphone stand.

Reg thinks of The Host's voice as belonging to a man, knowing it could just as easily be AI generated. *Might make as much sense as anything happening so far today.*

"The interview was not for your answers," The Host says. "It was for your tells. Your instincts. Your appetites. What you reach for when you're afraid. These are what convinced us those moving forward should stay while the majority of you will now be asked to leave."

Reg's mouth goes dry. Breath too fast. Heart hammering like it wants out. He hasn't felt this level of helplessness since right before the gold medal game in rugby.

No, since he was a rookie staring at a clock he couldn't control. Only this time, there is no clock. That was sports, where he always felt he was in charge of the narrative.

Not now.

Who's in charge of this narrative?

Just a voice and a microphone waiting on an empty stage.

19.

"The people in two of these lines will be divided up and flown tonight to two remote corners of the world," Luca Tommasi hears The Host say.

There is a slight pause before he continues.

"And so you know," The Host adds, almost amused, "I will not be calling out the rows in alphabetical order, what would be the fun in that?"

Luca's throat tightens. He forces air in anyway.

What part of this is fun? Luca thinks.

It has been one nerve-wracking moment after another.

"Rows **O, P, Q, R, S,** and **T**," The Host says. "Leave the field immediately."

Luca hears groans from his right. The sound rolls across the crowd–pain, disbelief–then bodies start moving. Heads down. Like a team walking off after a loss they didn't see coming.

The Host waits until they have left the field before resuming.

The speakers crackle again. "Rows **C, D, E, F,** and **G** . . ."

The Host waits, clearly as a way of torturing them a little more. Luca is certain that everybody still in front of the stage is having the same difficulty breathing as he is.

"All of you please leave the field now," The Host says.

More groans. More movement. More quiet misery. This time from Luca's left, even louder than the ones before.

Luca forces himself not to look around too much. Looking makes it real. Looking makes you start counting.

He'd rather be on a street in Rome, making a call he understands.

This is not a call. This is a verdict.

Despite having been called out as a liar in the tent, Luca had never been any good at lying to himself. So he knew why he was here, really.

He had lost his family. Was about to lose his job before flying to Ohio. This is his chance to be the man he was meant to be. The leader of men he told himself he ought to be.

"Letters **H, I, J, K, L** . . ."

Here it comes, Luca thinks.

His last chance to be the father he still imagined he could be if he was somehow reunited with his family at the end of this.

There's no time. Not even time to say a quick prayer.

The next row out is ours, and I'm gone.

Luca knows this best of all: He isn't ready to go home because he doesn't have a home anymore.

The Host stops again before he gets to **M**.

"The people in those rows are now dismissed."

"*No way!*" Luca hears from his left, sees that this voice belongs to the young pilot with the perfect posture. The one everybody's been whispering about being some form of royalty.

"There obviously must be a mistake! I must've been given the wrong card!" the man shouts, voice carrying across the field. *"You've made a mistake!"*

He is still yelling his head off, even louder than before. The rest of the people in his row begin to file quietly off the field, heads down.

Saad digs in and refuses to go any farther until two guards arrive, each one grabbing an arm and walking him away.

"You can't do this," the man yells as they walk him away, pointing at the stage as if The Host is actually standing there. "Do you know who I am?"

Then he adds this: "You're all going to pay a price for this. And trust me: I can afford it!"

Then he's gone.

Just four rows left now.

Two hundred people out of the original one thousand.

A and **B**.

M and **N**.

Luca sees the two young women in front of him, a German redhead and a tall Eastern European woman, holding hands. He flashes back to pulling his gun without hesitation that day at St. Peter's. The moment he acted. The moment he didn't freeze.

This is different.

He'd given up control when he came here.

They all did.

The Host doesn't drag things out any further.

"Rows **A** and **N**," The Host says. "Leave the field."

Madre di Dio.

Mother of God, Luca thinks. *I made it.*

He's still here.

His knees almost buckle. He needs this more than he wants to admit.

The two girls in front of Luca let go of each other's hands long enough to give each other a high-five. They turn and do the same with Luca, and he happily obliges them.

"The rest of you can think of yourselves as the chosen ones— please move closer to the stage," The Host says. "Because in a day that has already been full of surprises, I have one more."

20.

The survivors drift closer to the stage in small clusters and chat among themselves for the next few minutes, wondering if they're finally going to see who The Host really is; if that's going to be the next big reveal.

Mostly what they all feel is relief, at least for now.

They've just found out that they hadn't come all this way for nothing.

But relief is dangerous. It makes you sloppy.

Rupert Chadwick stays close to Jack McHenry. Even in this short a time, it's obvious Rupert feels safer when Jack is around. He's learned something already: In a place with no rules, you pick a person you trust and you don't let them disappear.

Alek watches the crowd the way she used to watch streets back home. She watches who helps. Who laughs when someone flinches. Who scans the perimeter like they're looking for exits.

Hannah has been squeezing Alek's hand since the final announcement, without realizing that she had been doing it. It felt completely natural, part of the sisterhood they already share.

"We made it," Hannah whispers, breathing a sigh of relief.

"For now," Alek says.

Hannah lets out a breath she's been holding for hours. "In that tent . . . I thought every word was a trap."

Alek nods. "It was. I kept thinking there might be right answers. And the next thing I said might be the wrong answer."

"Same!" Hannah says. "But we still don't know what the numbers mean."

"Could just make us easy to count," Alek says.

Jack and Rupert are in front of them, next to Elena Torres, a prominent TV reporter for Television Española—sharp-eyed and camera-ready even when there are no cameras.

"What did you tell them?" Jack asks her.

"I told them the truth," she says. "That I'm not here to be a spectator. Someday I plan to lead my country. I intend to be prime minister."

She smiles at Jack and watches his reaction closely. "Does that sound ridiculous?"

"I don't know you very well," Jack says. "But, not to me."

Elena turns it back on him. "What about you, what did you tell them?"

"I tried to tell them my own truth as best I could." Jack doesn't puff himself up. He's past that. "I was an Army Ranger but haven't been much more than a hard-living knockaround guy since. I've been drifting. And I'm done drifting. I'm back in the driver's seat and on my way to being *The One*, of course."

A voice cuts in from behind them. "Oh, please," Ant Tipton says, strolling up like he owns the place. "You two sound like high school children at prom."

Elena gives him a look that could peel paint. "Did your mother not teach you it's rude to eavesdrop?"

Jack studies him. Tipton's eyes have the flatness of a man who's never felt bad about what he's done. Tipton smiles because he knows Jack is trying to figure him out.

"I'm proud to tell you both that I basically lied my ass off in there," he says. "Up and down and all the way to Berkeley Square and back. But here I am, anyway. Same as the two of you. Fancy that."

"Fancy that," Elena says. "Thrilled, practically."

Jack watches Tipton's face to see if there's any reaction to the obvious sarcasm in Elena's voice. Watches his eyes, mostly.

"That should tell you something," Tipton says.

"It tells me you're dangerous," Jack says quietly.

Tipton's grin fades for half a second—just long enough to show there's a temper under it.

Most guys Jack had served with, he knew they'd have his back if it ever came to that, no hesitation even if it meant putting his life ahead of theirs. Tipton is different, Jack is sure of it somehow, barely even knowing the man. With him, you were better off watching your own back.

You didn't have to know Tipton to know his type.

Tipton looks past Jack, bored again, and moves off.

Hannah watches him go. "That English man . . ."

"A problem. The kind you don't turn your back on," Alek says quietly, afraid Tipton might still be in earshot.

"So, I'm #222. Wyatt's #77. You're #9. What the hell do the numbers mean?" Hannah gets back on her new mystery.

Alek nods decisively. "I'll tell you. Nothing at all."

Then Wyatt directs her attention back to the stage.

Jimmy Donaldson has reappeared and is walking to the microphone.

21.

Wyatt feels the mood shift the second Jimmy steps up.

It's ridiculous, but it's real. People straighten. People look. Like they're watching someone who's supposed to know what comes next.

"Pretty sure I've watched every video he's ever made," he says to Hannah and Alek.

"I watched the one last week where a guy and a girl won $500,000 for staying in that nuclear bunker for a hundred days," Alek says. "Felt familiar, but it was somehow a relief to see it as a game for once."

Hannah doesn't look away from the microphone. "Half a million times two thousand," she says immediately.

Wyatt blinks. "That's–"

"A billion," Hannah says. "It's a billion."

Jimmy is onstage and leaning toward the mic stand now. He lifts a hand for quiet. But right before he begins to speak someone from the crowd yells out, "You're crazy until you're successful and then you're a genius."

Jimmy taps his index finger to the side of his head, smiling, and leans toward the microphone.

"Who said that?" He looks around and no one admits it. "It's a pretty good line, even if it's a little cringe," he says.

It gets him a good laugh.

"Anyway, thanks everyone. Let's quiet down. Thanks, and hi. For those of you who don't know, I'm MrBeast–or Jimmy Donaldson. You can just call me Jimmy. But yeah . . . you're probably wondering what's going on. Sorry . . . someone's talking in my ear . . . okay, sorry again, I have to give you the rules first apparently."

He reaches into his pocket now and comes out with a bright red pendant on a string. He clears his throat, straightens his posture, smiles, and–

"Let's get something important out of the way!" he yells, like when addressing contestants in his viral videos. "First thing: When you leave this field, you're getting one of these."

He holds up the necklace.

"This isn't jewelry," Jimmy says. "It's your extraction device. If you hit the red button, a team comes and gets you. Fast."

The field stirs.

"This state-of-the-art device, no matter what situation you find yourself in, you can't break it, you can't destroy it, and you better not lose it. If at any time you feel you've reached your breaking point, press the red button."

Murmurs race through the crowd.

"And listen to me," Jimmy adds, voice hardening. "If you press it, you're safe . . . but you're out. No coming back. That's the deal."

He waits until they've absorbed it.

"This competition is dangerous, but I take safety very seriously. Just because you CAN get seriously hurt, doesn't mean you SHOULD. Hands to your heart," Jimmy says. "I want you to promise me you'll use it if you're in real trouble. Not because you're scared. Because you're in danger."

The crowd shuffles. Some snicker. A few roll their eyes. Then someone shouts, "I promise!"

Another voice joins. Then another.

The crowd erupts in everyone saying it—ragged, nervous, real.

Jimmy nods once. "Good."

It quiets down.

"One last time: Red button means SAFE but ELIMINATED."

From somewhere behind Wyatt, Tipton mutters, "Would've been nice to have one of those out on a real battlefield."

Wyatt takes a couple of steps back, not wanting anyone in the line to think it was him.

Jimmy looks out at them, and now he's not performing. His shoulders drop and he speaks normally.

"Okay," Jimmy says. "Now the part we actually care about. You're here because the world feels like it's coming apart. People are tired. Angry. Scared. And the folks who built this thing believe one person can shift the direction of a lot of people."

A few skeptical laughs.

Jimmy doesn't flinch.

"I've seen what happens when you give someone a real shot," he says. "I've seen how fast good spreads when it's loud enough. The organizers of this challenge called me and told me they believe that one special person with courage can make a majority. They told me if some kid from rural North Carolina obsessed with YouTube could make videos that inspire people to go out and do good, then imagine what one of you could do."

A cheer rises from the field.

He pauses.

"But you should know something else," he says. "This isn't the first time they've tried this. There have been other years. Five to be exact. No winner. No one has come out as *The One* who could take the prize and use it to make real lasting impact."

"*Good!*" someone calls out.

"I like the energy!" Jimmy says, grinning. "But we're running out of time."

"Don't worry, I got this!" someone else yells.

Jimmy shakes his head. "I hope you do!" he says.

He takes a breath. You can see the weight hit him, even if he's trying not to show it.

"As you already know," Jimmy says, "the prize is one billion dollars. Not because money matters. Because money can move the world and, in the hands of the right person, it can move it fast."

The crowd starts to build again—hope, hunger, fear.

"Even though I keep talking about how bad everything seems, I'm actually a pretty optimistic person," he says.

He allows that to sink in before continuing.

"The world needs a leader. And I am convinced that the leader this world needs is one of the hundred people on this field. One of you can change the world. *LET'S. DO. THIS!*"

Jimmy shouting that last call to action elicits the loudest cheers yet. He lifts his hands, trying to settle them—

—but the speakers crackle.

"One last surprise today," The Host says.

Jimmy waits now along with everyone else to hear what it could be.

"If you count, there are actually only ninety-nine contestants in front of the stage," The Host continues. "Though I've said one hundred are moving on."

There is a lengthy pause.

The Host says, "Contestant one hundred: Jimmy Donaldson."

22.

For a second, Jimmy doesn't move.

The words didn't land in his brain in the right order.

Number one hundred. Him.

What did he just hear?

I'm one of the players?

He immediately answers his own question:

Since now.

He honestly has no idea who The Host is—couldn't hazard a logical guess—but now the guy is making him No. 100?

Calling him out this way in front of everyone?

Jimmy had been chatting with some of them a few minutes earlier. Reassuring them that no matter what, he'll have their backs.

But who has his back at the moment?

He feels the field staring at him—ninety-nine sets of eyes on him.

What's he going to do?

What am I going to do?

Jimmy looks out into the crowd and finds faces he recognizes from minutes ago. Alek and Hannah. Jack and the kid, Rupert. Wyatt. Reg Drummond. People who already look like they're doing math in their heads:

How safe are we, really?

Jimmy's throat goes dry.

All the people in front of him—all ninety-nine of them—have already had their first tests in those red tents.

Now, Jimmy thinks, *here's my test, out in the open for everybody to see and hear.*

Pass or fail.

He believed in this concept with all his heart. Doesn't just feel it's important. It's more than that. But does he believe enough to be a player?

It lands, fast and clean:

They didn't make him number one hundred as a favor.

They made him leverage.

A test. A warning. A leash.

Who exactly did he choose to believe in?

Another thought crosses his mind: *If I can't trust the organizers or the games, then can I do more to protect everyone looking up at me—looking up to me—if I'm one of them?*

If they didn't trust me, they wouldn't be here.

What's the best way for me to pay it back? Not with speeches. With pressure. With honesty. With someone in the field who won't let the games cheat them. If the game is rigged, or fake, then I'm going to take it back and find The One. Whether it was ever the organizers' intention or not.

He takes another look out into this mowed-down cornfield.

All of them are watching him, and they're waiting.

He steps back to the microphone. He keeps his voice steady because if he doesn't, a hundred different kinds of panic will start running through the field at once.

"It's probably obvious I didn't know that was coming," Jimmy says.

A nervous laugh tries to rise. Dies.

"But I'm not walking away," Jimmy continues. "Not from you. Not from this."

He pauses, and his gaze hardens.

"I'm in," Jimmy Donaldson says. "But, if I'm playing, I'm playing to win. Which means you'll really have to earn it."

23.

THAT SAME NIGHT
STILL IN OHIO

The hundred who made the cut–ninety-nine plus Jimmy–eat dinner in a large dining hall in the middle of the property. There are ten long tables set up. Ten to a table. Guards at the doors, guards along the walls, guards keeping people in, not keeping them safe.

Over loudspeakers, The Host explains that tomorrow they will be transported to the sites of their first "real" tests.

"One destination is Antarctica," he says once they're all seated. "The other is on an island off the coast of Chile featuring a place called Snake Mountain. Known there as La Montaña Serpiente."

Wyatt stands up from where he's seated between Hannah and Jack, not quite certain where he should be looking as he addresses The Host once again. He looks toward the ceiling because that's where one of the loudspeakers sits.

"Do we have any say where we're going?" Wyatt asks. He grins and looks around at the other tables. "Asking for all my new friends."

From across the table, Ant Tipton doesn't look up from his steak. "Speak for yourself."

Wyatt ignores him.

"Some will be allowed to choose," The Host answers. "Some will be assigned. Think of it as a second lottery. All part of the fun."

"Define fun," Jack says, not bothering to look up either.

Elena Torres, sitting close enough to bump Jack's elbow, playfully pokes him in the arm. "Be nice," she says.

Jack glances at her. "I'm always being nice. To you."

Elena's smile says she hears the difference.

"I've noticed," she says.

Jimmy sits next to Tipton. He has been noticeably quiet since they've all arrived in the dining hall. He'd been loud all day. Now suddenly reserved. Alek is also seated at this table. She watches him for a minute before she speaks.

"Jimmy," she says, "you look like you're somewhere else."

"I'm here. I'm just . . . doing math."

"What kind of math?" Jack asks.

"The kind where the numbers don't add up," Jimmy says. "I like getting to know you guys. It's just that a lot has been thrown at me today, and not just the part about being number one hundred." Pause. He looks at them, deciding how much he should share. "I was told the tent interviews would take a couple days." He looks around the room. "They promised a careful selection. This was a cattle call."

"And that bothers you?" Alek asks.

"It should bother all of us," Jimmy replies. "This is supposed to be about methodically finding the right candidate. If they rushed the first part, what do you think they'll do when it gets hard?"

Nobody answers that.

"Who told you it would take longer?" Alek asks.

"There have been a few intermediaries who reached out to me

about how they might shape this competition," he says. "Now I'm wondering if they ever really cared about what I thought."

"But you're still going to play this out along with the rest of us?" Jack asks.

Jimmy nods. "I–"

The Host returns like he's been listening in, because he has.

"Someone once said that all of life is a game," The Host says, "just with a new field every day." The Host lets it sit. "You will have plenty of time to worry about the game starting tomorrow. Tonight, just enjoy this fine meal." He pauses. "If you can."

Conversation resumes in pockets.

Alek is as interested in the conversations around her as she is in the meal. Jack spends most of his time chatting with Elena. He feels a sense of ease talking to her. Wyatt leans toward Hannah. At some point he says he goes to NYU like it's a badge. Hannah says she's almost done with MIT like it's a passing fact. Wyatt laughs, but there's real respect in it.

Tipton keeps to himself, head down, focused mainly on the steak he's chosen for dinner. He eats like he's fueling up for something.

Alek finds herself watching the room the way she watched a new shelter–who guards the doors, who sits with their back to a wall. But maybe The Host was right. She can relax. Just this once.

In an odd way, this mess hall reminds Alek of her first freshman gathering during her short-lived time at National University, at one of the few places she and her mother tried to settle in. Except that most of the hundred in this room–with a handful of exceptions–are adults.

She has had moments where she feels more at home with older people than her newfound friends closer to her age. Living through war—surviving war, at least so far—has made Alek feel much older than her years.

Elena pulls Alek out of her head when she asks, "If you get a choice tomorrow—where do you want to go?"

"Antarctica," Alek says. "As soon as I heard Snake Mountain, I was begging not to be sent there. Cold doesn't bother me as much as things that crawl or slither. Snakes especially."

"Snakes?" Hannah asks, making a face.

Alek nods. "Snakes."

Dessert is finally served, the most popular selection being ice cream with chocolate sauce. As Alek digs in, she says to the others at her table, "Wherever we end up, and whomever we travel with tomorrow, the truth is we all get further if we support each other, no matter what."

Tipton makes a snorting sound. "That's adorable."

Elena turns her head slowly. "Say that again."

"I said it's adorable," Tipton replies. Then: "Maybe before we disperse this evening, we should all join hands and sing 'Kumbaya,' too."

"Tell me the truth. What does being a jerk get you?" Elena asks.

"You all keep talking about 'truth.' Truth doesn't win things. I win things. Just stay out of my way until you go home like the loser you are."

Jack's chair scrapes the floor—just once. Not a lunge. A warning. "Shut up, Tipton. *Now.*"

Tipton's eyes flick to him. "You getting worked up, Tex?" Jack's voice stays low. "You're not going to talk to her like that."

The room goes quieter around them. Aware of the rising tension.

"Or what?" Ant says.

Jack is around the table before Tipton can get out of his own chair.

As Tipton pushes Jack back, a familiar voice once again fills the dining hall.

"Jack!" The Host says sharply. *"Tipton!"*

They both freeze.

"Either behave," The Host says, "or continue the discussion outside. Without my assistance."

Jack and Tipton eyeball each other for a moment longer. But Tipton sits back down and returns to his steak. Jack walks back around the table.

Elena doesn't say thank you. She doesn't need to.

But she puts her hand in his.

Wyatt leans over to Hannah and whispers, "I know what place I'm picking, if I get the choice."

"Where?" Hannah whispers back.

"Any place where Tipton isn't," Wyatt says.

GAME#1 CONTINUES

THREE DAYS LATER

24.

ANTARCTICA

The killer whale hadn't been coming for Wyatt, as it turns out. It blows past him—black, white, massive—close enough to take his breath. For a half second, the water around his head turns violent—pressure, wake, noise that he feels in his teeth. Then it's gone, diving under the surface without leaving so much as a drop of blood. He doesn't see what it's after, and he doesn't care.

He cares about Hannah.

Wyatt swims in her direction again, feeling he's going in slow motion, arms already thickening, joints already refusing him. Every stroke feels delayed, like his body and his brain are arguing over whose job this is. He tells himself that she's not dying before help arrives—*if* it arrives in time—and neither is he.

Up ahead he can see that Alek has almost reached Hannah.

Then another swimmer flies right past Alek, appearing almost out of nowhere, the way the orca just had.

Wyatt recognizes Reg Drummond, player #2, the Australian Olympic athlete. He'd been on the Zodiac boat with them and now here he is, muscular arms pumping hard and fast above the frigid water.

If the water temperature, feeling like it's a hundred degrees below zero, is slowing him down the way it is Wyatt, Reg Drummond sure isn't showing it as he passes Alek. Wyatt remembers his lifeguard training and tries to estimate time and can't. Three minutes? Five? Ten? His wrists feel like they don't bend right anymore.

A rescue Zodiac is coming, small and fast in the distance.

Not fast enough.

How long have I been in already?

Three minutes? Five?

The boat is still too far away.

Wyatt can't tell now whether the burn he's feeling in his arms and legs is from the water, or because he's stretching his endurance to its limits.

The three swimmers finally meet where Hannah is floating, face down.

Reg immediately takes charge while Alek struggles to keep treading water, and keep her face, red as an apple from the cold, above it. Reg gets a hand under Hannah's jaw, another under her shoulder, and snaps her over. As soon as he does, they see that her face isn't as red as theirs.

Hannah's lips are wrong—too pale, starting to blue.

Alek's face is red from the cold, eyes wide. "Is she—"

"She's alive," Reg says. The words come out clipped. He doesn't have spare breath for anything else. "Barely."

Wyatt has no idea what to do.

"Help me," Reg snaps, not unkind, just urgent. "Alek—hold her head. Wyatt—grab her arm."

Wyatt does it, fingers clumsy, almost useless.

Reg tilts Hannah's head back and gives her a breath. He doesn't hesitate as he begins doing rescue breathing, the kind lifeguards do on a beach, here in the water, because he has no choice if they're going to save her.

Hannah coughs—thin, weak. Water dribbles from her mouth.

It's the best sound Wyatt's ever heard.

"Need . . . to our own boat while at least part of it is still out of the water . . . while we hope other boat . . ." Reg is having the same difficulty speaking as everyone else, almost as if they are all still underwater. But he clearly and urgently says: "Now."

"How?" Wyatt asks, as he struggles to keep treading water.

Their Zodiac is capsized, only a portion of its bow still visible.

"I'll hold on to her . . . try to side-stroke," Reg says. "You get on other side . . . keep her head above water."

Wyatt side-strokes, one arm doing the work while the other keeps Hannah's face up.

The rescue Zodiac is closer.

Still not close enough.

To Alek, Reg says, "You follow. Stay close."

"I'll do my best," Alek says.

Reg manages a half-smile and says, "No medals . . . for trying."

Alek stays close, fighting to keep her own chin above the surface.

Wyatt knows they've only been in the water for a few minutes. It feels like hours. But they methodically keep pushing their way toward the capsized boat, only showing its bow above the water.

They're close when the whales return.

Two of the more rambunctious ones are between them and the Zodiac. They breach hard, not far off, and the water around them heaves. Wyatt feels his grip start to slip. He tightens it with hands that don't want to close.

A low pulse rolls through the water again. Not the whales.

Reg holds on to Hannah and keeps stroking.

"Don't let her go," he says.

Wyatt doesn't answer. He can't. He just strokes.

He strokes as the waves the whales are creating make that more and more difficult.

Wyatt can see the rescue boat getting closer.

Still not close enough.

Seconds later he feels the biggest waves coming at them from what feels like all directions.

And sees why.

The two orcas appear on either side of them, close enough that Wyatt sees the slick shine of their skin, the white patches like eyes staring back, right before one more act of nature.

The water rises again—higher this time—like the world is about to flip.

25.

CHILE
SEVERAL HOURS LATER

Luca Tommasi is swimming off the southern tip of Chile toward the island known as El Fin del Mundo, trying to keep as much distance as possible from the sharks, who don't seem much interested in him for the time being.

It is Friday afternoon in Chile. Saturday morning in Antarctica, where the first test is ending on Ross Island, in the subzero temperature of McMurdo Sound. Here off the southernmost coast of Chile, on a beautiful and cloudless Friday, Luca is in much warmer water—warm enough to fool you into forgetting what's under it. The potential for danger from the sharks might be greater if they decide to change direction.

But Luca Tommasi chose the long way on purpose.

Most of the swimmers go straight, because straight feels like courage. Luca has spent his whole career watching men confuse courage with stupidity.

He angles wide, away from the tight cluster near the ship where fins circle the boat. He keeps his stroke quiet. No splashing. No panic. He's not racing anyone, yet. He's positioning.

Ahead, the island dares them. Dark green tree line. And above it, the mountain—La Montaña Serpiente—rising steep.

Luca breathes every third stroke. In through the mouth, out through the nose. The rhythm steadies his head. The rhythm is something he can control, and right now control is everything.

He risks a glance back.

Out there to the west, the pack has stalled. People tread water, argue with each other, debate like the sharks are open to debate.

Luca pushes harder.

He has always considered himself a strong swimmer, from the time he was a boy. He never loved it enough to compete on the high school team. But as an adult his favorite form of exercise, even more than going to the gym, was swimming every morning at the pool at YMCA Italia—or every morning he could around his schedule with the police.

He liked being first into the water in the morning, and he was one of the first in the water off the ship today.

He has no idea how this competition will be scored, how much ingenuity will be rewarded in situations like this. No one knows. But Luca believes he has made the right play by swimming as far away from the sharks as possible.

Unless confronting them was somehow part of the test.

No point in worrying about that now.

He hits shallows and stands, water streaming off him, the sand bright under his feet. He starts running before he's even fully stable, because running is simple and fear is not. He can clearly see the hut where The Host has told them their clothes, backpacks, and hiking gear would be waiting for them.

Luca doesn't know what the rules are, if getting to the island first will win him more points in the eyes of the judges, whoever and wherever they are.

He tells himself it can't hurt.

No one else is close.

Maybe his wide route wasn't just safer.

Maybe it was smarter.

He sprints toward the hut now, like back when he was a street cop chasing a perp.

Luca runs even harder through sand almost white enough to be the color of snow, staring up at the mountain as if the pot of gold is waiting for him up there.

I can win this.

I can make my son proud of me again.

26.

CHILE

Jack has been in firefights that felt easier than this.

Underwater, everything is slowed—movement, sound, time itself.

Jack and Jimmy surface only when they have to, careful and quiet, then slip under again like they're trying not to make a sound.

For a few minutes the big tiger tracks them at a distance, patient. Curious. Like it's deciding whether they're worth the effort.

They've been well underneath the surface for the past few minutes, only coming up—carefully—to breathe before submerging themselves all over again.

Jimmy motions with one hand: up.

Maybe he's decided that's a better plan than engaging the shark, one of them being forced to deliver the blow Jack had been preparing himself for, the punch he was ready to throw as a last resort.

For now the shark hasn't gotten any closer, almost swimming parallel to them, not changing direction or picking up speed.

Not yet, anyway.

When their heads break the water, Jack can see the shark's dorsal fin breaking the water, too.

Now it's moving in their direction, the fin acting as a pointer.

"What do we do?" Jack asks.

"The backstroke," Jimmy says, trying to appear calmer than he really is. "Backstroke our way all the way to shore if we have to." He pauses and says, "At least theoretically."

Jack gives him a look.

"No eye contact with the beast," he says. "So to speak."

Jack says, "You know they're way more likely to attack in shallow water? You do know that, right?"

"Would you rather hang around here and take our chances that he'll play more fair?" Jimmy says.

Jack knows he's right. If they can get close to shore while the shark is still keeping its distance, they can finally get to their feet and make a run for it.

Not much of a plan, Jack thinks.

But best we've got.

"Don't splash. Don't stare at him. Just move." Jimmy shrugs. "Then we figure out how we get everybody else back."

They roll onto their backs and start pulling water, slow and steady. The sky above them is too blue for what's happening underneath.

They swim side by side on their backs, both moving in slow motion across the waters of the Pacific, away from the ship. Still managing to keep their distance from the shark, who somehow seems as patient as Jimmy is, despite the clear and present danger.

Jack turns his head enough to see the dorsal fin, trailing just slightly, looking like an up periscope.

It stays with them.

Not rushing.

"Honestly," Jimmy says, voice aimed at the clouds like this is small talk, "if he was going to eat us, wouldn't he have done it already?" Jack barely hears him over the slap of their arms hitting the water, almost in unison.

Synchronized, save-your-asses swimming.

"Don't say that out loud," Jack whispers.

Jack turns his head just enough to see the beach up ahead coming into clearer focus. It is an odd sensation, going backward this way, still in relatively slow motion, but running for their lives at the same time.

A hundred yards from shore now.

Maybe less.

"When do we make our run for it?" Jimmy says, having taken another look himself to try and see where they are.

"Soon," Jack says.

He takes one more look at the shore, is about to tell Jimmy it's time for them to haul ass, when the sun is blocked out and they're staring up at the helicopter directly above them.

They hear the roar of it, feel the whirring of the rotors, the helicopter so close to the water it's creating waves all around them the way a storm would. The sound is enormous. Physical. Jack feels it in his ribs.

Too fast, Jack thinks. *Like it was already in the air.*

The water around them goes rough.

Right before Jack flips over, he sees the shark's fin coming faster, racing the helicopter toward the beach.

"*Go!*" Jack yells to Jimmy, rolling over—

—and the ocean explodes beside them.

Too late.

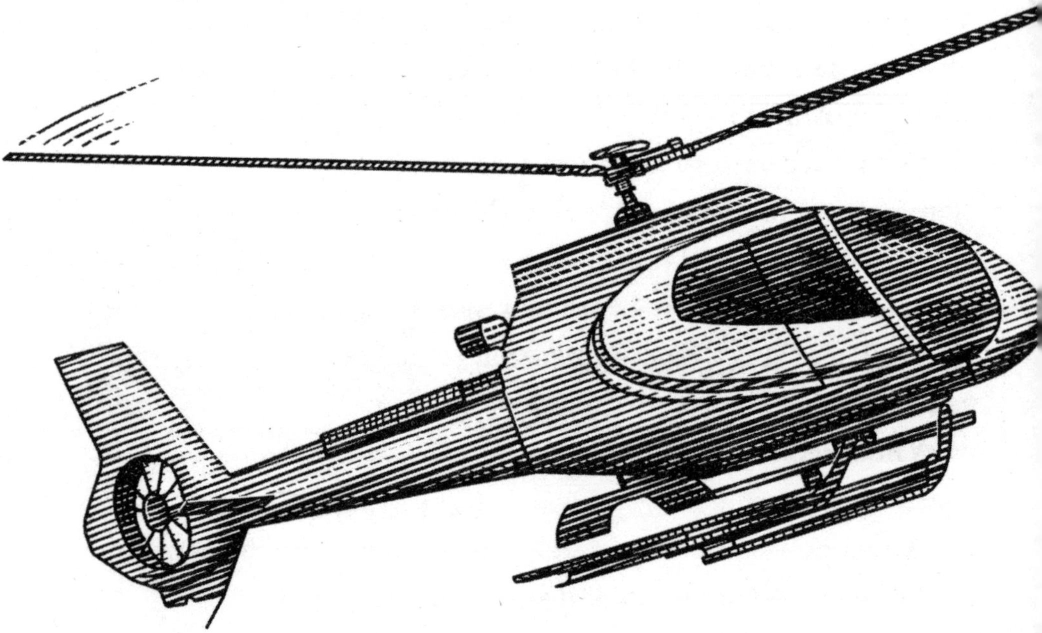

27.

ANTARCTICA

They should have died out there.

Wyatt is sure of it now, sitting in the rescue Zodiac with his arms wrapped around Hannah like he can hug the cold out of her. The four of them–Reg, Wyatt, Alek, Hannah–stare back at the black water they came from.

Against all odds, the two orca whales have almost acted as patrol boats for them. They moved with them. Around them. Almost like they were clearing a path, sliding through the chaos and keeping the other whales from slamming down right on top of them.

Hannah is conscious. Shivering hard enough that her teeth click. Alert enough to be aware of what's happening on either side of them. Reg, Wyatt, and Alek are still talking about what the whales did for them. It felt like a miracle.

"Did you see that?" Reg says, breath still ragged. "Like they . . . escorted us." He thinks. "Maybe nature thought it owed us one."

Alek doesn't answer. She's still looking for the thing she felt in the water–the low pulse that didn't belong to any animal she's ever heard.

Hannah, several blankets wrapped around her and held down

by Wyatt's arms, providing as much warmth as he can, isn't surprised at all.

"They're not what people think," she says finally. Her voice is thin, but it's Hannah's—steady under strain. "People think of them as only apex predators and orcas can be dangerous, sure, but they're not . . . mindless. They're social. Curious. Sometimes protective."

Wyatt shakes his head. "Protective of us?"

Hannah swallows. "There are documented cases. They'll intervene with sharks. They'll push people toward boats. Sometimes toward shore." She looks out at the water again, and her eyes narrow like she's solving an equation. "But what I don't understand is why they were behaving like they had . . . instructions."

Less than half an hour later, the four of them are in what is known as Shackleton's Hut at Cape Royds. A doctor checks Hannah, listens to her lungs, checks her hands, her feet, her pupils.

"You are very lucky," he tells her. "You were close."

"Lucky," Alek repeats softly.

They change into dry gear that's already waiting for them—parkas, gloves, cleats. Neatly stacked. Sized correctly. As if The Host had known, ahead of time, exactly how wet and cold they were going to get.

Wyatt watches Hannah's hands shake as she pulls on fresh gloves.

"You should press the red button," Wyatt says. "Some of the other people already did when our boat went flying. Punched their tickets right out of here."

Hannah's chin lifts. "I'm not leaving."

"You don't have to prove anything," Alek says, sounding gentler in her own head.

"I just proved how hard I am to kill," Hannah says and meets their eyes. "We all did. If none of you are quitting, neither am I."

Outside, the world has turned into a showroom for survival. An orange Delta transport vehicle sits in front of two dozen snowmobiles–snowcats lined up in perfect rows. A huge speaker is mounted on the Delta's roof.

They're just waiting for their instructions now, along with the other contestants who didn't quit.

And right on cue, The Host is back.

"I'm so relieved that you all made it across the water, though some of you must have felt you'd ended up on a smaller version of the *Titanic*," he says. "I can assure you that the visit from the whales was not planned in advance."

Reg's head turns slowly toward the hut behind them. Toward the dry gear. Toward the medical team.

Not planned, huh.

He then looks over his other shoulder and sees the players who pushed their red buttons climbing back into Zodiacs. Next to Reg, there is a woman from India, Anjali Gupta, player #92, who had ended up in the water, too.

She seems to be deciding whether or not to stay or go.

Settling some interior debate, she says, "Nearly dying once today was quite enough." Then she runs toward the boat, waving and yelling for the pilot to wait for her.

As the boat pulls away, The Host continues, smooth as ever. "Fifty of you set out for Ross Island today. Now eight have decided to leave before your first real test is about to begin. Their loss, your gain."

Nobody cheers.

They all wait, staring at the speaker on top of the Delta.

"You will all find maps in the snowmobiles," The Host continues. "The maps show the location of various ice caves between where you're standing and what is effectively your finish line at McMurdo Station. A few of you will be asked to travel the length of the glacier known as the Erebus Ice Tongue to one particularly spectacular ice cave. Some will be directed to caves closer to the volcano. Your journey will be monitored by the drones you will surely see in the sky, just as a way of knowing you have, well, touched all your bases. Consider it . . . verification. Then, if you have hit your marks successfully, you will get back into your vehicles and proceed down the coast to McMurdo Station."

Reg Drummond speaks up.

"I've done some reading on the Ice Tongue," he says, talking directly to The Host. "It's incredibly unstable."

"We are aware," The Host replies.

Then he adds: "The easiest jobs don't pay very well, Mr. Drummond. Nor, in this case, do the safest ones."

Reg's jaw tightens. "Understood."

"Just make sure to pay close attention to the red flags marking your routes, wherever on Ross Island they take you," The Host continues. "They are there to prevent you from falling through a crevasse and into the water underneath. Oh, and one more thing: Take extra care in the caves to tread carefully, so that one of the many ice bridges in there does not collapse while you're standing on it."

Reg takes another look behind him, sees the Zodiac disappearing in the distance with people like Anjali who decided one near-death experience today was enough.

Knowing by now The Host can hear everything they're saying, Reg says, "How do you decide who wins today?"

"The speed with which you make the trip, the resourcefulness you show, and, as need be, even the courage. If required," The Host says. "That's if you all live."

"You said no one's supposed to die."

"And if you are truly worthy of having been invited to these games, if you continue to exhibit the worthiness you just showed in the water, no one will," The Host concludes.

Reg looks at Wyatt and says it quietly, where only they can hear it.

"He's lying."

Not the first time, not the last.

28.

CHILE

Jack has read plenty about people who have been bitten by sharks. A school friend from Galveston told him what it was like, saying it felt like a bad wasp sting at first, except for the crunching feeling of the teeth.

The truly intense pain, his friend told him, comes later.

Jack feels the teeth clamping down on his lower left leg, experiences the shock of that, just because he thinks he's in the clear when he's about to be up and out of the water.

But, just as quickly as the bite has come, the shark lets go of him.

Jack has also read up on what are called "hit and run" shark bites, once the attacker realizes that humans aren't prey.

When he is on his feet, he sees the blood in the water and runs like hell through the waist-high surf, despite the pain. When he gets close enough to the beach, hoping the shark is gone but not taking any chances, he just launches himself, almost with a racing dive, the last few yards into the sand.

Jimmy is with him, helping him up to a sitting position, giving a quick check to the wound, and then runs to what they both can see is a medevac helicopter that has landed farther down the beach.

Elena runs across the sand and appears out of breath, dropping to her knees beside Jack. Hand on his shoulder like she's grounding herself.

"I thought—" she starts. "Are you—are you okay?"

Jack tries to smile through pain that's starting to bloom. "Day at the beach."

Elena doesn't smile back. She glances toward the helicopter. "It wasn't for you."

Jack follows her look.

A stretcher comes out of the tree line. A man on it. Face gray. Jaw slack. Luca Tommasi. They'd had dinner the night before, Jack, Luca, and Elena.

Jack's stomach drops. "What happened?"

Elena's voice goes tight. "We got new routes on our sat phones. The Host said we could start whenever we wanted, and they'd check times later. Luca took off right away." She swallows. "Tipton went with him."

Jack's eyes flick. "Tipton?"

Elena nods. "They were together at first. Then Tipton came back alone. Said he decided to wait and 'play it smart.'"

Jack sits up as far as he can. "And Luca?"

"They said he stopped to fix his boot," Elena replies. "Bend down, tie a lace. And he got tagged by something." She lowers her voice. "One of those spiders."

"Chilean recluse?" Jack asks, because his brain needs a label for the horror.

Elena nods once. "Probably."

Jack looks up and watches them start to check on Luca. He sees Jimmy talking to two men Jack assumes are doctors, both of them carrying small black bags.

Jimmy points in Jack's direction, and one of the doctors runs toward him across the beach.

Jack has been pressing his hand to his wound.

When he takes it away so that the doctor can get a better look at it, Jack looks down at his hand and sees a lot of blood. The pain is even more intense than his friend had once described, but the wound doesn't look that deep.

That could've been worse, Jack thinks.

A lot *worse*.

The doctor, who introduces himself as Dr. Paredes, asks Jack what happened. Jack tells him. Paredes asks him to roll over on his stomach. Jack asks if he needs to clean the wound and the doctor says, "The salt water did that for me."

Jack watches the doctor reach into his bag for what he hopes is something that will start to kill the pain, manages to smile at Elena. Somehow it feels they have known each other longer than a couple of days.

He sees her hair is still wet. He'd almost forgotten that she had been in the water, too.

"No sharks for you?" he asks.

"You guys being first in the water must have taken up all their attention," she says.

Jack looks at the helicopter again.

"Was Tipton still with him?"

"I'm not sure," Elena says. "Only Tipton knows that. If he was, he just left him there before turning around. And Luca hasn't regained consciousness, so he can't tell us what happened."

Jack is seated while Dr. Paredes finishes putting a bandage on the shark bite, which the doctor states isn't as bad as it looks. Jack tries to crane his neck, to see what's happening with Luca, and sees Jimmy walking back.

He's walking slower than before, like the sand got heavier. His face is blank in a way that scares Jack.

"How's Luca doing?" Jack asks when Jimmy gets close enough.

Jimmy sits down next to Jack, wraps his arms around his knees, and stares out at the ocean.

Jack's blood goes cold all over again, flashbacks of being back in the water.

"Jimmy."

Jimmy finally looks at him.

"He just died."

29.

"No–no–no!"

Jack looks over to where the doctor is still crouched over the body of Luca Tommasi.

He sees immediately that the wail they've all just heard has come from the boy, Rupert. His small frame is bent over in the sand, knees buckled. He waves his hands, frantically, trying to make the reality of the moment go away.

The sound that comes out of the boy is raw. Not words. Something older than words.

Jack's own chest goes hollow.

Luca Tommasi, a good man, a steady man, the kind you want beside you when something goes wrong, lies on a stretcher like he's already been packed away.

Because of a game.

Because of a voice.

As shocked as Jack is by the news Jimmy has just delivered, as much as he's just felt all the air go out of him, both he and Jimmy run for the boy, who is sobbing hysterically. Elena trails behind them.

Everything Jimmy and Jack have just experienced in the water, the narrow escape they've made from the sharks–now felt like it happened to someone else, somewhere else.

Jack knows they can't do anything for him now, or the grief that has fallen over the beach. Heavy. Total.

"Hey," Jack says, and his voice comes out softer than he expects. He gets a hand under Rupert's arm. Jimmy does the same on the other side.

Rupert can't breathe right. He's gulping air like he's drowning on land.

"I–" he tries. "I never–" His throat clamps. Tears flood. "I never knew anybody who died."

Jack feels that sentence hit him in a place he tries not to have.

Rupert convulses into tears all over again.

They guide Rupert away from the stretcher, closer to the water where the wind is harsh and clean and doesn't smell like blood. Jack is on one side of him, Jimmy is on the other. Elena follows, and when Rupert's hand flails, she catches it and holds on tight.

Rupert stares out at the ocean, blinking hard, believing the world will blur back into something safe if he does it enough.

"How . . . how could this happen?" he whispers.

Then, smaller: "Why him?"

Jimmy's jaw tightens. He's trying to keep it together for Rupert. Jack can see it now–the same thing he saw out in the water. Not fearlessness. Control. Jimmy fails anyway.

"It shouldn't have," he says. "It shouldn't have been possible." He swallows. "He came here because he wanted to matter. Because he thought he could help. That's what kills me." Silence. "Jack probably saw this happen way too much in war."

Rupert shakes his head hard. "But this isn't a war!" He sobs. "Good people aren't supposed to die!"

Jack looks at the boy. Fourteen. Brilliant. Still new to the idea that the world doesn't care how good you are.

"No one was supposed to die," Jimmy says.

"In war," Jack says quietly, "you learn the worst lesson early. Sometimes the good ones go first." He pauses, chooses the honest version. "And sometimes it isn't because they made a mistake. It's because somebody else did."

Rupert doesn't answer, just turns and lets Elena put her arms around him. They just stay where they are, all of them feeling as gutted as this fourteen-year-old boy who just encountered death for the first time.

Rupert turns to him. "Who?"

Jack glances toward the trees, toward the unseen cameras, toward the helicopter that arrived too fast.

"I don't know yet," he says. "But I know this: Somebody wanted us to see it."

They sit there with the water slapping the shore.

No one knowing or able to find the right words.

Probably because there aren't any here at the end of the world.

30.

ANTARCTICA

Reg, Wyatt, Alek, and Hannah have made their way to the ice cave located near the end of the Erebus Ice Tongue that is the centerpiece of their mission. Wyatt thinks of it that way, as a mission and not a game.

They are all forced to drop down on the ice and slide themselves through the entrance to the cave. Once inside—and able to stand again—they move carefully across various snow bridges and into a soft, beautiful blue light.

The ice cave is everything Hannah promised—blue light, smooth walls, a quiet that's both soothing and terrifying.

"These caves don't last," she tells them as they pick their way through. "A few months, sometimes less. Then they collapse or melt or . . . just vanish. Like ice castles instead of sandcastles."

They've been inside for about half an hour, having reached the end of the cave before turning back. Only one way in and out, something that doesn't exactly thrill Wyatt Jordan. Wyatt doesn't like anything with only one exit. And even though he has been as swept away as the others by the quiet, spooky beauty of the interior, he wants to get out of here.

"As amazing as this all is," he says, "there's something about this place that gives me the creeps. I keep waiting for these walls to just come tumbling down. Or start melting."

"Or for us and the glacier to just float away," Alek says.

"Wyatt's right," Reg says. "We really should be going. We've got a long walk back to the snowcat, and then we have to make it all the way back before the sun sets and what they call the polar night here sets in. I don't know if we need to be the first ones to the station. But I don't see how it can do us any good to be one of the last."

Hannah leads them out, Alek behind her, Wyatt and Reg behind them. When they're back outside in the brittle light of the sun, it's as if they've left one world for another.

The drone still circles overhead, patient as a judge.

Wyatt stares up at it, and waves, imagining The Host watching their every move.

Probably because he is.

Mission accomplished, Wyatt thinks.

Wyatt feels the beauty of this moment, of them being part of it together, still helping each other after having done everything humanly possible to keep each other alive.

The thought of it almost takes his breath away. The fact that he is part of the moment with Hannah makes it even better.

Hannah continues to lead them over the ice field to where they've parked the snowcat.

It is a long walk back from the cave, the Ice Tongue stretching seven miles in all, the ice cave having turned out to be three-quarters of the way to the water of the Sound.

They move gingerly across the ice. The Yaktrax cleats they're wearing provide them the best possible traction and make loud, crackling noises as they go. They all keep looking down, checking for any possible cracks underneath their feet no matter the traction they're getting from their cleats.

They stay in their lane, basically, just as they had on their way to the cave, making sure not to stray outside the red flags on either side that act as their guardrails.

It is not them against nature. Just them dealing as best they can with the natural world all around them, the snow and the ice and sunlight making everything seem as bright and sharp as a diamond, their breath coming out of them like plumes of white smoke.

Wyatt just wants to be off this long, thin glacier, with what he knows is more ice-cold churning water underneath them.

Reg keeps checking the sun. "We do not want to be the last ones back," he says.

Wyatt is about to agree–

–when the ice under Alek makes a sound that doesn't belong in the natural world.

A crack. A split. A sudden opening.

Alek drops to one knee, then both, sliding as the surface gives way beneath her. She throws her hands forward and catches the edge–gloves scraping snow, arms locking as her body tries to follow gravity into the hole and she is pulled down toward the water, somehow managing to stop herself almost by the force of her will.

Alek's eyes go huge. She doesn't scream. She can't spare the breath.

But her grip on the ice and snow, they can see, isn't going to last very long. Alek's fingers are frantically trying to claw into the snow as her weight drags her farther into the hole.

They can all see the roiling water below.

Reg is moving before Wyatt's brain catches up. Reg dives flat, crawls to the edge like he's approaching a ledge in a burning building.

"Axe!" Reg yells.

Wyatt rips off his pack with hands that feel clumsy for the first time in his life. He finds the small pickaxe and shoves it into Reg's reach.

Reg slams the axe into the ice with a brutal swing. The metal bites. He wraps his left hand around the handle, then reaches with his right and grabs Alek's wrist.

"Hold," he grunts. "Hold!"

Wyatt knows that if she hits the water, it's a death sentence.

"*Don't . . . let axe . . . come loose!*" Reg yells, and then with what little leverage he has, he starts to slowly pull Alek toward him, his right hand holding on to hers for dear life.

Wyatt drops flat behind Reg and grabs Reg's ankles, locking himself in. Hannah drops behind Wyatt and does the same.

A chain.

A human anchor.

All of them against the world.

And still the three of them start to slide.

They all begin to slide slowly toward the edge, like this is a tug-of-war being lost by their increasingly desperate and unlikely team. Not fast. Not dramatic. Just enough to be terrifying. A slow, steady pull toward that black water.

Somehow Reg, even being pulled toward the water, still has Alek's hand in his.

"*Hold on!*" he gasps.

Wyatt doesn't know whether he's talking to Alek, or to him and Hannah.

It doesn't matter.

They all have to hold on.

But the three of them keep inching forward, continuing their slow slide toward Alek and the water.

Reg's shoulders strain. His arm shakes. The axe handle creaks against the ice.

Wyatt feels his stomach go weightless as inches disappear.

"Hannah—don't let go," he says, voice cracking.

"I'm not," Hannah spits back, teeth clenched, eyes wet with cold and panic.

Reg draws a breath like he's about to lift a car.

Then he hauls.

Alek rises an inch. Two. Her free hand claws at the snow, searching for purchase that isn't there.

Reg lets out one more yell as he hauls, the loudest yet, a combination of discus-throw grunt and primal scream, and with one last massive effort pulls Alek all the way out of the hole.

Alek's body clears the edge.

Wyatt scrambles forward and grabs her jacket. Hannah grabs Wyatt's belt.

Together they drag Alek back onto solid ice.

Wyatt and Hannah drag her away from the edge.

Alek collapses face down, shaking so hard her whole frame rattles. Alive.

Reg just stays where he is, sprawled out on the ice, chest heaving, one hand still firmly on the pickaxe. When he finally lets go of it, he uses what strength he has left to roll himself onto his back and stare up at the sky.

Wyatt stares too—at the drone, at the tiny, distant eye that watched all of it.

Reg sits up, points at Wyatt with a trembling finger, and somehow manages to break out into a loud and boisterous laugh.

He points at Wyatt.

As Wyatt points back at him. And they all laugh hysterically.

And then a thought hits them that's not relief.

It's dread.

Because if this is Game One—

What the hell is Game Two?

31.

CHILE

They stand on the beach and watch in silence as the body of Luca Tommasi is lowered into the inflatable Sea Eagle boat that will shortly head back to the ship.

It is the beginning of Luca's long journey back to Italy, where he'll be reunited with his wife and son, just not the way he had intended.

Jack watches the body settle into the boat—handled and placed with cargo. He feels something in him go cold that has nothing to do with water. He's seen plenty of death before. Too much of it. But this—this feels stolen. Like it was taken on purpose.

As the Sea Eagle begins to make its way across the water, Jack looks around for Ant Tipton, very much wanting to look him in the eyes and ask if he really left Luca on the trail to die.

Nothing.

Either the man is already on the mountain . . . or he's made sure nobody can find him.

"Elena," Jimmy says quietly, staring at the water. "You talked to him last night, right?"

Elena nods once. "He kept talking about his son." She turns to Jack. "He just wanted to make his son proud."

Jack tightens. "He thought he could do something bigger than his job. I believed him."

Jimmy is standing with them, eyes still fixed on the water.

No sharks in sight.

Just the inflatable boat with Luca's body on it. Jack stands there with his arm around Rupert, propping up the boy, who could drop to the ground at any moment as the boat moves farther away from shore.

Jimmy finally looks away from the Sea Eagle. "Isn't that why we're all here?" he says. "Because we're the idiots who still believe we can make a difference?"

Before Jack can answer, The Host fills the beach, shattering the solemn quiet.

"For those who weren't here earlier," The Host says, "your second test of this day is to make it through the jungle and up to the lighthouse at the highest point of the island. Some are already on their way there. The rest of you need to check your phones now, because all of you have been given detailed routes up the mountain. Once you're on your way, we will be tracking your times, and your progress."

Elena checks her screen. Jimmy does too. His route is on the far side.

"The obstacles are fairly obvious," The Host continues. "Heat, extreme humidity, the snakes and spiders you will almost surely encounter along the way. Despite what you may have heard, the venom from these snakes is rarely fatal. But, as we have all just discovered, being bitten by a recluse spider can be an entirely different story."

He doesn't sound remorseful in any way about Luca, Jack thinks. To him, Luca was never here.

"In a few moments, we will blow a horn and those of you standing on the beach can follow your maps to begin your journey to the lighthouse," he says. "If you can make it, of course. I know this might sound harsh: But the show must go on."

Jimmy's voice is flat. "Some show."

Jack finally checks his phone. Jack is leaving from a point on the south side of the mountain, Elena from the north. Jimmy will start out all the way on the other side.

"I'd rather be going with you," Elena says to Jack.

"You're tough enough to do this on your own," Jack says.

"You don't know that," she says.

He grins. "I know tough when I spot it."

"Luca was tough, too," Elena says quietly.

The horn blows.

32.

LA MONTAÑA SERPIENTE

As Jack makes his way up the mountain, the heat of the day somehow becomes even more brutal, the humidity even more suffocating, and the pain from the shark bite stings with each step he takes.

In addition to all of that, the trail ahead of him appears to be at a ninety-degree angle, or maybe steeper than that, like he's pulling himself up a vertical ladder.

Not exactly a stairway to heaven, he grimly tells himself. But at the same time trying to maintain his focus, take in all of his surroundings at once, the trail and the trees and foliage, even the jungle sounds.

He's already felt a shark's teeth today. Now he very much wants to make his way up this mountain and back down without feeling the sting of a snake or—worse—the type of spider that killed Luca.

Jack keeps moving anyway.

That's what he's always done. Keep moving. Don't give your brain time to build a story about how this ends.

He keeps his eyes on the trail, on leaves, on the places a snake could hide and look like nothing at all until it's too late. From the prep reading he'd done, Jack knows to be alert for even the slightest movement, how they can coil and look as innocent—and the same color—as a pile of leaves. He had even watched a *60 Minutes* segment on his phone about a reporter who'd traveled to a place called Snake Island off the coast of Brazil. The reporter said at one point, "You have to look anywhere and everywhere. But the key is to keep moving."

Jack keeps moving despite the pain in his leg, his backpack starting to feel so heavy, like it's full of rocks.

He doesn't even stop for water breaks, just grabs his bottle from the pouch on the side of his backpack and takes quick swigs as he goes.

The trail somehow gets steeper, if that's even possible. Jack has always been good at memorizing maps, having known as a Ranger that making the wrong turn could be the difference between life and death. But he doesn't know how close he's getting to the summit, or how long it's been since he left the beach.

He just keeps going, using a sturdy branch he'd broken off a tree right after he'd started as a walking stick, hoping he won't need to use it on a snake. Or on one of the gnarly, nasty eight-legged spiders. He'd definitely checked out images of them when they'd been on their way to the airport at Punta Arenas. Some of the spiders were orange, some a deeper shade, almost brown. Some black. But no bigger than the palm of your hand. He'd read they only attacked when threatened.

Then he feels it. A sharp sting above his right knee, hot and precise. The feeling of being stabbed by the point of a sharp knife.

And Jack knows before he looks down.

He *knows.*

He thinks of a bullet hitting before hearing the gunshot.

He looks down and sees the black spider clearly outlined against his pale, khaki-colored pants.

Don't panic.

He forces air in, then out. He doesn't smash it. He flicks it off hard with the back of his hand and watches it vanish into the leaf litter like it was never there.

Except for the sting.

Except for the heat blooming under his skin, spreading outward like somebody poured something hot and wrong into his leg.

Jack takes another step.

His leg buckles.

Jack feels his heart beating hard enough that he's surprised he can't hear it over the sound of his own breathing and the sounds of the jungle.

Don't panic.

First the shark.

Now this.

Am I about to die?

He tries to catch himself, but the trail is too steep—maybe shock, maybe fear, maybe the beginning of something worse. He slides, catches himself, ends up seated on the trail, breath coming too fast.

He hears footsteps coming down the trail.

Jack looks up and sees Ant Tipton coming down the path, moving like nothing can touch him.

"McHenry," Tipton says, almost friendly. "You look like crap."

"Spider," Jack grits out.

The burn in Jack's leg spread. Not a massive stab of pain, he knows enough to know it doesn't work that way. But it's there. He can feel it starting to swell up without being able to see it.

Tipton crouches. Not close. Not kind. He glances at Jack's leg, then at Jack's face. Fast assessment.

"Unlucky." Tipton shrugs. "Lot of that going around."

"Help me," Jack says. Simple. No pride.

"You feel dizzy?" Tipton asks.

"No."

"Nauseous?"

"No."

"Good," Tipton says, like it was a checklist.

Tipton's hand drifts to the chain at his neck, thumb rubbing the clasp like it's a habit he hates. For a second his eyes go far away—then the mask snaps back into place.

He reaches into his pocket and tosses Jack a small strip of bright surveyor ribbon, the kind used to mark trails. It lands on Jack's chest.

"Wrap it tight," Tipton says. "Keep moving."

He stands.

Jack stares at him. "You got a radio? You got a phone? Call it in."

"I'm not your medic," he says.

"You left Luca," Jack says.

"You don't know that."

"You leaving me?" Jack asks, voice cold.

Tipton's smile is small. Controlled. Charming in the way it makes you want to punch him.

"I'm not leaving you," Tipton says. "I'm just not dying with you."

Then he adds, almost like advice:

"Press your red button if you start seeing God."

And he keeps walking.

GAME #2

SOMEWHERE IN KENTUCKY
FOUR DAYS LATER

33.

They brought a thousand to Ohio, out of thousands more who had been considered.

Then shipped out a hundred to two ends of the world.

Fifty-five returned to the United States.

Some pushed their red buttons in Antarctica or Chile. Some were eliminated for not completing their mission. The especially foolish after trying to access their social media accounts, posting about what they've been doing.

Some were caught cheating by the surveillance drones, straying from their designated route up the mountain, or down the coast of Ross Island to McMurdo Station.

A half dozen were sent home without any reason being given.

Almost half were gone. The survivors had been flown in C-17 Globemasters to Louisville, Kentucky, this time, transported from there to an isolated farm on the Cumberland Plateau in the Appalachian Mountains.

It is a lush, isolated property, they all see from the buses, miles from the last homes or signs of civilization. Apart from the main house, what looks like a massive combination of palace and farmhouse, there are enough two-story guest cottages on the property to accommodate all of them, together as a group for the first time since their odyssey began.

After having showered and changed, they have assembled in a ballroom inside the main house that is as ornate a place as Jack has ever been inside, art on the walls and chandeliers hanging from the ceiling.

Jack sits with Elena and Jimmy. Rupert's right there, too. The boy and Jack have now become practically inseparable. They've been joined by three members of what Jack thinks of as the Antarctica group: Wyatt, the young guy from New York City; and two young women, Alek and Hannah.

In Chile, they had discovered that Rupert was almost fast enough to be playing for his favorite football club back home, Man City. He's the one, out of all of them, who produced the fastest time making it to the lighthouse and back.

Fastest. By a lot.

Even after the death of his friend Luca Tommasi, to whom he'd grown as close as to Jack.

It turns out that Rupert Chadwick is more than just a brain, his slender frame much stronger and more agile than it looks. He is too modest to have told the table about that, so Jack does it for him, before recounting for the Antarctica people his own experience that day at the End of the World, first with the shark attack and then with the Chilean recluse spider on the trail.

Rupert, wide-eyed, had not heard the entire story until now. Jack had never been big on telling war stories. But the boy had asked.

"Weren't you afraid that you were going to die the way . . . the way . . ." The boy can't finish the question.

Jack is well aware of how much Luca had looked out for Rupert from the time they'd arrived, Luca having explained to Elena the night before he died that Rupert was the same age as his son.

He could lie. He could put on that tough-guy thing.

But he's had enough of people performing.

"Yes," Jack says. "I was scared."

Rupert nods like that matters.

Jack adds, "I kept moving anyway. I didn't turn back. I flushed it, wrapped it, kept moving, and I kept telling myself: *not today*. About half a mile up I ran into an incoming med team, they gave me an antivenin."

Jack isn't going to share with the kid everything about what he was feeling on the trail in that moment, how fueled he was by his anger at Tipton for leaving him the way he'd left Luca.

Only he and Tipton knew about that.

For now, anyway.

"There's this country singer I like named John Anderson," he says to Rupert. "And he's got this one line that sticks with me, something like: Living scares me worse than dying."

Rupert Chadwick surprises everyone by standing.

Then the fourteen-year-old, perhaps the shyest of all of them, surprises the room a second time by tapping his water glass with his spoon to get their attention.

Jack can see how nervous he is. Everybody close to Rupert can. But the ones who have taken the time to get to know him have begun to learn how much there is to this boy.

"I'd like to say something about Luca," Rupert says. "Because we all know we feel him in this room with us tonight, even though he isn't."

The room has gone completely silent. Jack keeps his eyes on Rupert.

The boy swallows hard. Then again. Takes a sip of his water, then takes in so much air Jack wonders how he could fit it all inside that skinny body.

"I wasn't with Luca for very long, none of us were," Rupert says. "And he wasn't the only person in this room who's gone out of their way to make me feel less homesick. But . . . he was a lot like my dad."

Jack sees the boy's chest rise and fall. Sees him flush. Is afraid Rupert might start to cry.

Come on, kid.

You got this.

Rupert keeps going.

"I watched Luca and learned how a grown man is supposed to act," he says. Smiles as he looks at the women in the room. "Or just how an adult is supposed to act, period."

The only sound in the room is the voice of Rupert Chadwick, trying to hold himself together.

"He wanted this so badly," Rupert says. "He wanted to make his own son proud, he told me that. I hope that maybe someday I can meet his son and tell him that. Tell him how much his dad loved him."

Another deep breath. Jack sees Rupert's eyes start to fill up.

"But in the little time we had together, Luca treated me like a son. He wanted the first prize as much for me as he did for himself." He pauses. "But mostly he told me to believe in myself even when I wasn't feeling anything like that."

Rupert says, "I can hear his voice, even now in that thick accent of his. *Sii coraggioso.* That means 'be brave' in Italian."

He pauses again, his voice thicker with emotion than ever.

"Luca said that's the way you say it to a man," Rupert says.

He picks up his glass again and raises it to the others, and probably gives the first toast of his young life.

"To Luca," he says.

Now he cries.

He's not the only one.

34.

Dinner is served before long and finally the mood in the room lightens, and people are telling of the adventures they've experienced so far, about whales and sharks and spiders and all the rest of it.

Somehow the evening swings back to being about the camaraderie most, if not all, of them are feeling. They don't know about the adventures to come, or stories yet to be told. But on this night, even with the short amount of time they have been together, that camaraderie matters, even without Luca Tommasi.

They are here, even if Luca is not.

"Hey, at least none of you got attacked by leopard seals," Marcelo Oliveira, the jiujitsu man, says at one point.

He's sitting across the table from Jimmy.

Jimmy says, "Leopard seals are mostly solitary. But they can be dangerous, seriously dangerous."

Hannah's eyes light up. "Sometimes they smile. And they sing underwater. So what happened, Mr. Oliveira?"

Marcelo recounts how the ice field on which he'd been walking cracked open like an egg, just as it had for Alek. But he was, he says, quick enough and agile enough to jump away in the nick of time; was carefully backing away from the edge when a leopard seal lurking underneath the surface had risen up out of the water and tried to bite through the thick ski pants he was wearing.

"I guess that leopard seal wasn't smiling. Then what?" Hannah asks. It's clear that she's caught up in the story. They all are.

"I managed to spin around and roundhouse kick him right in the teeth," Marcelo says, "before I ran like hell back to my snowcat with my pant leg flapping in the breeze."

Jack thinks: *It's like we're telling war stories.* Except that his father, the ex-Marine, always said that you didn't tell stories like that until the war was over.

Jack doesn't like to tell them, period.

"Why don't you two blokes compare your wounds?"

Tipton.

Jack hadn't gone looking for him on the ship taking them back to the airport at Punta Arenas. Then he had stayed away from him on the plane, not sure if he could control himself if he confronted him, and worried about making a scene in front of everybody else.

He frankly didn't know if he might get sent back home for doing what he wanted to do with Tipton—shove him up against a wall, just for starters.

But tonight, Jack immediately feels the same searing heat in the back of his neck he'd felt in his leg on the trail that day.

Jack looks him dead in the eye.

"You left me on that trail."

"I went to get help," Tipton says. "Which eventually arrived."

"That's your version," Jack says.

"It's the truth," Tipton says.

There is one empty chair at Jimmy's table, between Marcelo and Reg Drummond, maybe the most famous person here with the exception of Jimmy. Tipton, dressed all in black, as always, starts to sit down with them.

"Seat's taken," Jack says.

"That seat's been empty all night," Tipton says. "And it's not even your table."

No voices have been raised. Still: There is a hush over this part of the ballroom. All eyes on them.

Jack's eyes don't leave Tipton.

"We all decided to keep it open in honor of Luca," Jack says.

"Pity about him," Tipton starts–

Jack's eyes lock. "Don't."

Tipton lifts a hand like he's surrendering. "I'm saying it's tragic." He shrugs. "But the rule is simple: You stop, you die. He stopped."

The air changes. Alek's jaw tightens. Hannah's eyes go cold. Rupert's face changes. Not loud. Not dramatic. Just . . . a line being crossed.

Jack starts to get out of his own chair. Elena puts a hand on his arm before he does. "No lo hagas."

Jack knows enough Spanish from growing up in Texas to know she's saying this to him:

Don't do it.

But Jack isn't entirely ready to drop this.

Not yet.

"Heard you left Luca the way you left me," Jack says.

"Some of you may still be under the misguided notion that this is a team sport," Tipton says. "I'm not."

"My team saved my life," Alek Andrich says.

She catches Reg Drummond's eye, smiles at him, offers a discreet wave. Maybe because she and Reg have also been through something life-changing together. Jack used to feel that way with the Rangers. He understands the look that has just passed between Reg and Alek.

"They saved my life, too," Hannah Wagner says, "not that I'd expect you to care about that. Or me. Or anybody except yourself."

"Bully for them," Tipton says.

Jack: "You didn't answer my question. What happened with Luca, Tipton?"

"Nothing."

That's when Rupert Chadwick stands and walks over to him.

"Excuse me," Rupert says.

Tipton turns—

—and Rupert drives his fist straight into Tipton's nose.

Not wild. Not flailing. One clean shot full of a football academy kid's timing and balance. Surprising everyone for the second time tonight.

Rupert grabs his fist. That hurt.

Tipton staggers back, hand flying up, blood trickling down his nose. A clean, surprisingly hard hit.

"You little . . ." Ant lunges at the kid, who retreats. "That's right. Run away!"

Now Jack moves. Fast. He gets between them before Tipton can take a step.

"No lo hagas," Jack says, low, close to Ant's bleeding face. Then, in English: "Not him. Not tonight."

Tipton stares past Jack at Rupert, eyes bright with shock and something else—anger, sure, but also calculation, like he's already deciding how to use this.

He takes a step back instead.

Smiles through the blood.

"Good punch, kid," Tipton says.

35.

When they've moved on to dessert and coffee, they hear The Host for the first time this evening, his voice seemingly coming at them from all corners of the room, surround sound.

"I hope everybody, including Mr. Tipton, is enjoying their evening," The Host says, "and this welcome chance to become more fully acquainted." They can clearly hear him chuckling. "Just out of curiosity, Mr. Tipton, what hurts more, your nose or your pride?"

"Get stuffed," they hear Tipton say.

Jack spots Tipton sitting next to Yolanda Green, player #53, a former WNBA player, and directly across from twin brothers from China whom Jack had met in Chile: Lin Zhi, a gymnast, and Lin Jian, a platform diver. Tipton still has a napkin pressed to his nose. Jack can see the blood soaking through it.

"Please watch your language, Mr. Tipton," The Host says. "There are women and children present, even if one of the children just nearly punched your lights out."

"You're one to talk about protecting women . . ." Tipton says under his breath.

One of the waiters trades him an icepack for the bloody napkin.

"How about you spare me the grief then?" Tipton says.

"As you wish," The Host continues. "Despite the jet lag I'm sure you all must be dealing with, please do your best to get a good night's sleep, as the games will resume tomorrow."

"What games?" Yolanda Green calls out from her seat.

"Board games," The Host says.

A ripple of laughter, nervous and confused.

"Are you being serious here?" Yolanda says.

"All will be explained in the morning," The Host says. "For now, I think we should all call it a night."

But they hear another voice coming from the middle of the ballroom, not from speakers.

"Not quite yet," Jimmy Donaldson says.

36.

Jimmy strides quickly and confidently to the middle of the room. He doesn't ask for it. He takes it.

"Okay," Jimmy says, hands up, palms out. "Before everybody goes to bed and pretends tonight didn't happen . . ."

A few nervous laughs.

"I'm in the same leaky boat as the rest of you." He adds, "Though I'm aware we've all had enough of boats for one lifetime."

That gets a real laugh, a little release.

Then he lets the smile fade.

"We lost Luca."

The room stills.

"He shouldn't have died," Jimmy says. "That's not me talking as a contestant. That's me talking as the guy who was asked to help shape this."

Reg Drummond shifts in his chair. Jack watches Jimmy closely. So does everyone else.

"When I was approached back home in North Carolina to sketch out a framework for these games, I wanted them to be hard, but I wanted them to be fair," Jimmy continues. "Not lethal. You've got red buttons for a reason. That's the whole point—danger, sure, but with a line you don't cross."

He looks around the room.

"And that line got crossed."

Nobody speaks. Nobody wants to be the first one to say it out loud.

"Reg kept Hannah alive." A nod to Reg. "Wyatt and Alek didn't let her go." A nod to them. "Jack got through sharks and still came back to help somebody else." A nod to Jack.

He takes a breath.

"That's what I'm seeing," Jimmy says. "Even though we're all competing, we're on the same team. All of us. And even though Luca's life was lost, other lives have been saved. Because of teamwork, and incredible courage, from everybody in this room."

He pauses.

"And then I'm seeing . . . other stuff."

He doesn't say Tipton's name. He doesn't have to.

"Here's what I can promise you," Jimmy says. "I'm in these games now. I don't get to stand outside and comment. Fine. But I'm not going to sit quiet if the rules keep changing in ways that get people killed."

Silence. Then: "I see the games taking on a life of their own, like some runaway train. I don't know who's responsible. But I'm going to find out. I'm asking you to trust me again."

"I trust you," Wyatt calls out.

Then he speaks in a stronger voice. "I have your backs. Please have mine."

Jimmy makes a small turn and is looking directly at Jack.

"Jack, you know this—"

The Host interrupts. The speakers crackle. The Host doesn't raise his voice. He doesn't need to.

“Mr. Donaldson,” The Host says, “you’re confusing this for one of your productions.”

Jimmy doesn’t look up. Doesn’t give him the satisfaction.

“It’s not,” Jimmy says. “Because when I do a production, I know who’s in charge.”

A ripple in the room. People glance at one another.

The Host’s voice sharpens a degree.

“I am.”

Jimmy nods, like he expected that answer.

“Then answer me,” Jimmy says. “Why were there sharks? Why were there spiders that can kill a healthy adult in hours? Why are people disappearing without explanation? That was not the framework we discussed.”

“You discussed,” The Host says, “and then you agreed. And now you’re here.”

“*No one* was supposed to have to swim through sharks,” Jimmy says, and now he’s shouting. “No one was supposed to deal with deadly spiders. That was never part of the deal.”

The Host continues, smooth as ever. “You have the same lifeline as everyone else. Red button. Press it. Walk away. We will escort you to safety. Nobody is keeping you here against your will. If this has gotten to be too much for you, push the button. That’s all it takes.”

The room holds its breath. Waiting.

Jimmy doesn’t flinch.

“You want to know what keeps me here?” Jimmy says.

He scans the room—finds Rupert. Jack. Alek. Hannah. Wyatt.

“It’s them.”

A beat.

"And you don't get to use my name to recruit good people . . . and then run this as a slaughterhouse."

The Host lets that go.

"How about this?" The Host says. "Let's end this. All of you quit. Right here, right now. In a few months we start all over again without any of you. Push your buttons! You will all be safe and you will all be done."

The room goes still.

Hands hover near red pendants.

Nobody moves.

Not one.

"Interesting," he says. "Good night."

37.

As they're all filing out of the ballroom, everybody more off-balance than ever after what they've just seen and heard from Jimmy and The Host, Wyatt finds Hannah.

"Walk?" he asks. "Before the next nightmare drops?"

Hannah hesitates, then nods. "Yes."

Maybe as a way of trying to regain her balance, if only for a few minutes. They move down a gravel path that cuts through darkness and manicured fields. The property feels endless.

After a minute Hannah says, "He almost challenged The Host."

"Jimmy?" Wyatt says. "That wasn't almost. That was him drawing a line."

"And The Host didn't care," Hannah says.

Wyatt snorts softly. "The Host cares. He just cares about control."

"Were you worried that Jimmy was about to pull the plug?" Hannah asks.

"Nobody's followed him more closely than I have," Wyatt says. "That was never happening."

Hannah's eyes lift to the main house behind them. Lights glowing. Windows like watchful eyes.

"Who is he? The Host," she whispers.

Wyatt thinks of the voice. The calm. The way it never strains.

"I don't know," he says. "But he talks like someone who's never been told no."

They walk in silence for a while, out into grounds that seem to go forever.

"How many acres do you think this place is?" she asks.

"A billion?" Wyatt says.

She laughs. A nice laugh. But then everything about this girl is nice.

As they make their way down the hill and away from the main house, they can see Jack and Elena walking away in the opposite direction—close, heads bent toward each other, like they're trying to steal a normal moment inside an insane week.

Hannah watches them, then says, "That's going to get dangerous."

"I know they haven't known each other for very long," Wyatt says. "None of us have. But it's obvious."

"Do you think that's wise?" Hannah asks.

Wyatt says, "The way I look at it, sometimes you just feel things whether you want to or not."

"Even in a situation like we're all in?" Hannah says.

"Maybe because we're in a situation like this," Wyatt says.

She seems much older than eighteen, and not just because she's the smartest girl Wyatt has ever been around. There is this naturalness about her, a beauty inside and out. He still can't believe how close he came to losing her in McMurdo Sound.

But at the same time he tells himself now not to analyze his feelings for her too much, because he's never been any good at talking about feelings. Hannah, though, is different, just off some of the long conversations they've had already, mostly on planes. She's more an open book.

Not me, Wyatt thinks.

Not even close.

They pass what looks like a horse corral. Empty. Wind moving through it like it's waiting for something.

Wyatt thinks about taking Hannah's hand.

He doesn't.

What would she think about me if she knew my story?

What would they all think?

They continue walking down the hill. The farther they get from the main house, the more they feel they're putting the scene they just witnessed in the ballroom behind them. Just the two of them, now, alone in the half-light between day and night, a whole world between them and the cold of Antarctica and everything that happened there.

And, Wyatt knows, it's more than the weather:

This feels like the first chance he's had since Antarctica to exhale.

None of this is normal, he knows that. His life hasn't been normal for a long time. Even his closest friends don't know his whole story. But this—what he's feeling tonight—does feel normal.

He's worried about what Hannah just said.

How any relationship, no matter how innocent, might be a bad idea.

"It's weird, right? We don't even know what the scoreboard is."

"I hate that," Hannah says. "I hate being measured and not knowing how."

Wyatt looks at her. "You do great on every test."

"That's exactly why I hate it," she says. "Because this one isn't a test. It's a trap."

They stop at the fence line and look out at the property. Stars are beginning to show.

"Who do you think owns this place?" Hannah asks.

"Maybe The Host dude," Wyatt says.

There is another silence between them, just not an uncomfortable one. So many girls he's known, even the ones he liked, felt like they had to be talking all the time, filling up every silence.

Not this particular girl.

Hannah's voice drops.

"Why are you here, really?"

Wyatt smiles, but it doesn't reach his eyes.

He says, "I guess the best answer I can give you is that I want to see if I can do something great on my own, maybe some heroic feat like Luca's. He was a good dude. I know it's different with me, obviously, on account of me having a lot handed to me in my life."

"By your parents, you mean?"

Hannah watches him, and Wyatt gets the uncomfortable feeling she's already reading the parts of him he keeps locked away. He wants to tell her the truth about that. But he knows he can't, at least not yet and maybe not ever. He wants this girl to like him as much as he likes her.

He is trying to be honest with her. Just not as honest as he could be. Even though this night does feel normal, so is lying for Wyatt Jordan.

"And you?" he says, turning it back on her. "MIT at your age? I mean, are you being serious? I figure you're halfway to world domination no matter what happens. Why are you here?"

"World domination because I'm German?" she asks.

Nice going, Wyatt.

Smooth, no kidding.

"No, no, no," he says, fast and loud. "I didn't mean it that way at all. I was just messing with you, but in a good way."

"I know that," she says. "I already know you better than you think, Wyatt Jordan."

No, you don't.

"You didn't answer my question," he says.

Hannah exhales.

"Because I don't think we survive as a species if we keep doing what we're doing," she says. "That's not drama. It's data."

Wyatt shifts, trying to find something lighter.

"So you're basically here to save Earth. Casual."

Hannah almost smiles.

"Something like that."

They're standing too close. Not touching. But close.

She stares up at the stars already appearing in the sky.

"Could you believe how beautiful it was in Antarctica?" she says, spinning around wanting to see the whole sky at once.

"You could have been killed there!" Wyatt says. "We all could have!"

"Danger hides in beauty and beauty hides in danger," Hannah says. "A woman named Belva Plain wrote that. You want a fun fact about her? She didn't write her first novel until she was sixty-three years old. A late bloomer."

Silence, knowing it's time to turn around and head back, nightfall coming fast now. But even with that, Wyatt has the sense that neither one of them is in any hurry for this night to end, especially since they have no idea about what craziness The Host has in store for them in the morning.

"If she's a late bloomer," Wyatt says, "that makes her the opposite of you."

Just like that.

Wyatt doesn't plan it.

Neither does she.

They've pulled each other into a kiss. They both decided to do it at the same time.

When they finally pull back, both of them look as surprised as they are happy at what just happened. Hannah's eyes flicker, sharp again—like she remembers the cameras.

"Bad idea," she whispers.

"I don't know about you," Wyatt says. "But it felt as wise to me as it felt good."

"A good kiss, you mean?" Hannah asks, smiling again.

"Good, period," he says.

"No," she whispers.

Wyatt swallows. "Why?"

Hannah looks past him, up toward the house.

"Because everything here gets used," she says. "Everything."

She steps back first.

"Let's go," she says. "Before we do something else we can't take back."

Wyatt follows her up the hill. He does feel good, about the kiss, about being with her, all of it.

And more scared than ever that things between them can only end badly.

38.

The Host watches the monitors without expression.

Wyatt and Hannah. Jack and Elena. The little clusters of loyalty and attraction forming like algae in water.

Predictable. Useful.

He watched them walk toward the house like they're coming home from a high school date. He's more convinced than ever that Wyatt is an immature fool.

A few minutes earlier he watched on a different monitor as the cocky oil rigger from Texas, McHenry, took a walk across a different part of the vast property with Elena Torres, the newscaster from Madrid, before both of them disappeared from his sight.

McHenry and Elena Torres had looked as smitten with each other—do people still say that?—as the two teenagers do now.

He had expected some pairing off like this, various attractions, it was to be expected when you threw people together like this in life-threatening situations. Or even, in the case of the Italian policeman, life-*ending* situations.

The thing he finds most interesting, and even more entertaining, is that even after the situations in which they found themselves in Antarctica and Chile, they clearly have no idea what's coming next.

Or the choices these happy couples are eventually going to have to make.

Would Jack McHenry be willing to save Elena Torres's life if it meant losing his own?

And what about the spoiled boy from New York City?

If it comes right down to it, would he choose his life or the life of the lovely, brilliant girl from Germany?

Better yet:

How hard will he have to push any of these people to get them to push the red buttons around their necks?

He watches now as Wyatt Jordan walks with the German girl toward the cottages.

People think love is a weakness.

Sometimes it is.

Sometimes it's leverage.

He changes the camera angle and watches Wyatt glance over his shoulder one last time, like he can feel the eyes on him.

You're learning, The Host thinks.

Too late.

The Host thinks to himself, *It would be a pity if one of them is the next to die.*

39.

Before she heads back over to the main house the next morning along with the others—The Host having commanded they be back inside the ballroom by eight o'clock or the games would begin without them—Alek Andrich places an allowed call to her mother back home.

They haven't spoken since she had boarded another Globemaster at Williams Field, near McMurdo Station, for the flight they didn't even know was to the United States until they were in midair. And they had only spoken for a couple of minutes that day before the plane took off.

Alek hadn't mentioned it to anyone, not to her mother and not even to Hannah, that being anywhere near a military plane gave her terrible flashbacks about what had happened since the war started falling out of the sky on her family.

Alek just wants to hear Danyia Andrich's voice this morning. As insane as her mother's life was through the wars and as insane as Alek's has become since she left, somehow the sound of her mother's voice still brings normalcy to her, even peace, if only for a little while.

Her mother answers on the second ring.

"Alechka," Danyia says, and the sound of her voice hits Alek in the chest like warmth.

"I'm okay," Alek says immediately. Because that's what mothers need first.

She does not tell her mother about her near-death experience at the Erebus Ice Tongue, knowing full well by now that Danyia Andrich is already scared enough by this journey her daughter has taken.

Sometimes, her mother says, she feels she's sent her daughter off to fight.

"Where are you?" her mother asks.

"Kentucky," Alek says. "America."

A pause on the line. A breath.

"And what is next?" Danyia asks. Trying to sound calm. Failing.

"I think this morning we're actually going to be competing in board games," Alek says.

"You mean like Monopoly?"

Alek thinks of the money, money beyond avarice, waiting for someone at the end of these games.

"Yes, Mama. Like that."

Neither one of them speaks until her mother says, "My daughter, after the way you've described some of those against whom you are competing, after what you've already survived . . . are you sure it's still worth it for you to be there?"

Alek closes her eyes.

She doesn't tell her mother about the crack in the ice. The hole. The water. Reg's hand on her wrist. Wyatt and Hannah anchoring—shoulder to shoulder, locked in.

She only says, "I've told you over and over again, I have to do this."

"For you?" Danyia asks.

"For us," Alek says.

"And I've told you over and over that you don't have to do this for me," her mother says.

"Ya lyublyu tebe," Alek says.

Alek feels the catch in her throat saying the words, afraid as always that after she ends the call, she might never hear her mother's voice again.

"I love you too," her mother whispers back, voice breaking just a little.

Alek ends the call and heads for Hannah's room. After Hannah had returned from her walk with Wyatt last night—she quietly told Alek about the kiss she and Wyatt had shared—they had made a plan to head over to the main house together, both of them having no idea what to expect when they got there, but wanting to walk into the room together.

Hannah said she'd be waiting for her.

But there's no answer when Alek knocks on Hannah's door.

She knocks again and calls out her name.

Still no answer.

She knows Hannah is always on time, always does what she says she's going to do. She is both ridiculously punctual and totally reliable.

Alek tentatively turns the knob and pushes the door open.

The room is empty.

The bed made.

Hannah's gone.

40.

Alek doesn't know for sure that something has happened to Hannah Wagner. But she's like everybody else remaining in the competition, which means she's grading high on paranoia these days.

Would Hannah have decided to quit the competition and go home because of something that had happened overnight, maybe on a call to her own parents? Anything was possible.

But it seemed impossible that she'd leave without saying goodbye.

Alek enters the ballroom. It doesn't look anything like it had the night before, having been transformed into what looks like a vast computer room, rows of tables and chairs, oversized computer screens in front of chairs with headphones draped over the backs of them.

A lot of people are already sitting down. Alek looks for red hair, not wanting her to be gone.

Not wanting her to have pushed her red button.

Alek jumps when there is a tap on her shoulder, then sees Wyatt standing next to her.

"Hey, are you okay?" he asks.

"Did you happen to see Hannah this morning?" Alek asks him.

"No, why?" Wyatt asks. "Is *she* okay? She seemed fine when I left her last night."

Alek's eyes keep moving. "She wasn't in her room."

Wyatt's face shifts—confusion first, then fear.

Alek's eyes finally land on Hannah's red hair.

She's at the far end of the room, in the last seat at one of the long tables, staring at her computer screen. Body perfectly still. Eyes locked on the screen. Hannah's headset is already on. The mic light is glowing red.

Alek checks her watch. Still ten minutes before this morning's tests are scheduled to begin, the board games to which The Host had alluded.

Alek and Wyatt move fast, weaving between chairs.

Alek is the one startling Hannah when she touches her shoulder.

"Sorry," Alek says, when she sees Hannah jump. "I just wanted to make sure you're all right."

"I'm fine," Hannah says. "Just nervous, I guess. I'm not sure what to expect today. It's why I just wanted to get here early to collect my thoughts. Sorry I didn't wait for you."

Hannah's eyes flick to the corner of her screen where a small window is still open. It reads: AUDIO: LIVE. CONNECTION: OPEN. She clicks it closed.

"You sure you're okay?" Wyatt asks.

"I'm fine," Hannah says. "Really I am. I just need to be by myself and start getting mentally ready."

Alek thinks: *You're always mentally ready.*

"Okay then," Wyatt says. "I'll leave you alone."

"Wait," Hannah says.

She turns away from the computer and looks up at him. It's as if Alek is no longer there.

"What happened last night can't happen again," Hannah whispers to Wyatt.

Wyatt blinks like he didn't hear her right. "Why?"

Alek watches the color drain from his face.

Wyatt says, "I thought . . ."

Hannah looks around the room—at the cameras, the screens, the staff moving in the corners.

"Because it wasn't private," Hannah whispers. "None of it is."

Wyatt's mouth opens. Closes.

He looks . . . honestly hurt.

"I thought—" he starts.

Hannah shakes her head once. "Not now.

"It's not about you," she adds, and it sounds like she hates that sentence because it's the kind people say when they're lying.

But she's not lying.

She's scared.

Wyatt tries to hide the hurt Alek can see he's clearly feeling, along with the surprise.

"Okay," he says, and walks away. "Okay."

Alek watches him go, feeling the damage in the air.

Hannah doesn't look at Alek.

She stares at the screen.

"I want to win," Hannah says when Wyatt is out of earshot.

"We all do," Alek says.

"I'm just trying to do it the right way," she says.

"Hannah," Alek says, "we're all trying to do that, too."

Hannah looks down the row to where Wyatt is standing. He looks away when he sees Hannah staring at him.

"Hannah," Alek says. "Talk to me."

Hannah's eyes stay on the monitor.

"I can't," she whispers. Then Hannah, shifting her stare to Wyatt, says, "I just can't."

And goes back to staring at her screen.

Alek watches Hannah's eyes track the cameras, the screens, the staff.

Not nervous. Measuring.

41.

They have each been given four games from which they can choose:

Chess.

Checkers.

Go.

Scrabble.

They will all have the same opponent, whatever game they choose: Artificial Intelligence.

A low, unhappy growl comes from Ant Tipton, seated two rows over, dressed in black like he's still on contract.

"Blazing computer science," he mutters, "or one of the options would be Charades."

A few people smother laughs.

As soon as the words are out of Tipton's mouth, The Host responds. When they're assembled like this, Big Brother always seems to be watching and listening.

It's why so many have taken to spending more time outdoors, every chance they get.

"It's clear you consider yourself quite the wit, Mr. Tipton," The Host says. "But we're about to find out how you do when it's a *battle* of wits, and you have to rely on your brains and not simply your brawn."

Tipton doesn't look up. He keeps his eyes on the menu like he's choosing wine.

"I'm not worried," Tipton says. "I run a business built on intelligence. And before that, I topped my class in the Marines."

Jack McHenry is listening with amusement to the exchange along with everybody else in the room. But thinking he might be far more amused than others.

"Pottery?" Jack asks.

Jack has avoided Tipton since dinner, not wanting to escalate the hard feelings between them. But he can't help himself in the moment and he's quite pleased when he hears some of those in the immediate area laughing at his comment. Jack feels Elena's shoulder shake beside him.

Tipton finally looks over. He gives Jack a smile that could pass for friendly if you didn't know better.

"Funny," Tipton says. "What did you pick, Sergeant Major?"

"Chess," Jack says.

"Of course you did," Tipton replies, like he's complimenting him and insulting him at the same time.

"Just curious," Jack says. "What about you, Tipton?"

"Not that it's any of your business, but Go," Tipton says.

"Words too long for you in Scrabble?" Jack asks.

"That will be quite enough repartee," The Host says, cutting them both off. "Whatever game you all have chosen, you are about to be challenged by AI the way you've all been challenged by nature. And even though these are almost certainly games some of you have been playing since childhood, survival of the fittest will still be very much in play this morning. Only this time it will be man—or woman—against machine."

Reg Drummond raises a hand, like he's back at a press conference.

"One question," Reg says. "How are you scoring this, exactly?"

The Aussie is a few seats down from Jack.

"Since we're all playing different games, how will the ultimate winners be decided?" Reg asks.

"Are you really asking who's going to end up on the medal platform, Mr. Drummond?" The Host says.

"I guess you could put it that way," Reg says.

"You're still trying to locate the finish line," The Host says. "That's understandable. But you'll learn what matters the way you've learned everything here—after the fact."

"That's not sport," Reg says.

"To me it is," The Host replies. "Because to me, sport is not about fairness. It's about exposure."

No one moves.

"And today," The Host continues, "we expose the mind. Plus, I suspect the only winner today will be the superiority of machine over man."

Tipton leans back and rests one hand behind his head like he's about to enjoy a movie. The other hand drifts to the chain at his neck seeking the comfort of an old habit.

"We'll see," he says.

"Oh, you will, Mr. Tipton," The Host says. "Before the morning is over, I fully expect you all will."

"If you're so certain we're all going to lose," Reg says, "why even play the games?"

"Let me worry about that," The Host says.

42.

The last instruction they're given is that there's to be no conversation between the players once the games begin. Those who've brought their phones with them to the ballroom have had them confiscated by the guards stationed just inside the door, to be returned when everyone is finished, just in case anyone even considers looking for online help with the gaming or the strategy.

"Do they think people are going to try to cheat at Checkers?" Elena says as she leans toward Jack, barely moving her lips. "Or Go?"

Jack smiles at the lovely newswoman who wants to be prime minister someday, provided she makes it out of this alive.

"Machine's paranoid," he murmurs back. "Takes one to know one."

A cold voice comes over the speakers.

"Start."

People settle in like exam takers.

Headsets on. Microphones down. Screens bright. Hands suddenly clumsy.

As soon as they begin, there is a new, thick tension in the room, obviously different from the physical challenges they've already faced but every bit as real, even though this morning's competition involves games some of them, perhaps all of them, have played as kids.

The stakes are just higher now.

They're focused on the screens in front of them, taking a test on which their lives depend. All wear headsets with microphones attached. Some have chosen the option of having their computerized opponent talk back to them. Some play grimly in silence, the headphones blocking out any possible noise from players to either side of them, everyone clearly feeling the same thick, kinetic—almost oppressive—energy.

For now, the only scoreboard is the one in front of them. Because of the soundproofing from the headphones, none of them can hear the occasional curse from one of the players, or a sound indicating that someone might be in mental pain because of something that just happened on their screen.

In the end, Jack McHenry loses a long, grueling game of Chess the way you lose a war you didn't know you were fighting: slowly, then all at once. His silent opponent had relentlessly stalked his every move, even ones that Jack considered quite brilliant. But Jack had kept even, until his opponent made a move Jack learned years before, killing time on base with a staff sergeant who'd loved Chess the way other men loved whiskey.

It's called the Arabian Mate—the opponent's knight and rook work together to checkmate your king, usually in a corner. Jack had seen it coming three or four moves away, defended it as long as he could before finally being unable to stop the inevitable from happening.

Game over.

Jack is now the one spitting out a quiet epithet as he gets out of his chair, another one in the room already beaten.

Across the room, Elena Torres fights a Checkers match like it's a siege.

Elena was a whiz at Checkers when she'd attended boarding school in London, though they called the game Draughts over there, even playing tournaments for a local club. Today she plays a long and careful and tortuous game, taking no reckless chances, playing a defensive game from the start. People who have only played Checkers for fun, she will tell Jack later, have no idea how long a tournament game involving skilled players can last.

In long games people get impatient. The machine doesn't. Finally, though, she is overwhelmed by her own AI opponent, feeling so crowded she's surprised her chair doesn't fall over behind her, unable to jump any of her opponent's pieces.

Elena had chosen a voice option—a woman's voice—on her computer, and she has set it for Spanish. When the game is over, she hears this in her headset:

"Lo hiciste bien."

You did well.

All the nerves she had been feeling for more than an excruciating hour—in a Checkers game!—come out of her at once.

"Vete a la porra," she hisses, then instantly flushes, ashamed of herself for sounding like Tipton, something that makes her feel smaller than she can afford to in the moment.

She stands and looks around for Jack, like she needs to see a face she trusts.

She sees Jimmy getting up from his own game of Checkers and joins him. She can tell from the pained look on his face, normally optimistic even in the worst of times, that he has also just taken a beating.

Elena reaches him first.

Jimmy exhales once.

"Tell me you lost too," Jimmy says. "Because I got wrecked."

43.

After another hour, there are only four people left at the tables:

Two are the twins from China, Zhi, player #20, and Jian, player #21, the gymnast and the platform diver, both of them playing Go, a game invented in their country, one generally acknowledged to be the oldest continuous board game on the planet.

Their games, both losing games, end only a couple of minutes apart.

Not long after they push their chairs back, Rupert Chadwick does the same, having just been defeated in Scrabble, despite having stayed with his opponent until Rupert had played his last letter.

Now there is just one player, there at the end of her table, hunched over as far as she can go, her nose close enough to her screen as to almost be touching it:

Hannah Wagner.

She is playing Scrabble as well.

English is her second language, of course. But with her it's a minor point, not even worthy of discussion in any language.

The others in this room watch her, not knowing what is happening on her screen, all of them feeling the morning has turned into both an odd and gripping spectator sport.

Jack stands with Elena, Wyatt, and Alek.

"How many people do you think are rooting for her?" Jack whispers.

Alek doesn't blink.

"I don't care," Alek whispers back, eyes locked on Hannah. "I just know I am."

What none of them know, and will only find out later after Hannah shares the details of the ending to her game with Alek, is that Hannah has finally used up all her letters on her last turn. She is out of tiles.

Because she has a photographic memory, she knows how many of each letter there are in Scrabble.

She knows the distribution.

She knows what has already been played.

She knows what cannot possibly be on the rack.

Three tiles.

P. O. Q.

That's it.

The computer would have to use all of them now, using a dangling letter somewhere, to end up with more points than Hannah.

I want to win, she'd said to Alek and Wyatt hours ago, and it is clear just watching her now how much she'd meant those particular words.

Here is her chance, a great chance, to at least win this day now that all the others have lost, even though she's probably lost Wyatt in the process.

Because of her quiet demeanor, Hannah has always been able to hide how competitive she is at school, any school, burning to be the best. You didn't get to MIT at sixteen without having a fire inside you.

She had looked around a few minutes before, seen that Zhi and Jian were still playing. Rupert had only been a few seats away.

All of them gone.

She watches, unable to breathe—and knowing how hard it is to use a Q in Scrabble.

The machine's cursor moves.

Slow. Deliberate.

It places a Q. Then an O. Then a P.

It hooks them onto an existing H already on the board.

Q-O-P-H.

Hannah's chest tightens.

"That's not—" she starts.

"It is," the host from the computer says, without inflection. "It is a Hebrew letter."

"Sorry, Miss Wagner," The Host says. "He's right. But then, he always is. Somewhat like me."

Hannah's hands slide off the desk.

She falls back in her chair like somebody cut her strings.

Then her voice cracks, small and furious.

"But I was that close."

"Yes," The Host says. "You were."

"You should actually be happy," The Host continues.

"I lost," Hannah manages. "When I was that close to winning."

A pause. Letting it hurt.

"Now for the part you didn't know you were playing."

The room goes dead silent. Even Tipton stops moving.

Hannah hears The Host again, directed now not only at her.

"You should be pleased, Miss Wagner," The Host says. "You

have not been eliminated, as so many others who were just watching you are about to be."

Hannah blinks.

Around the room, bodies tense. Heads turn. Eyes flick to red pendants under shirts.

Tipton explodes first.

"No one said anything about these being elimination games!" he yells.

"No one asked," The Host responds calmly.

Tipton stops dead. Not angry anymore. His eyes move once across the room, taking inventory. Thirty. Not fifty. Not twenty. Thirty.

He says, almost pleasantly, "So it's not about winning. It's about how entertaining you are while you lose."

Jack whispers to Alek and Wyatt.

"I feel like we're back on the field in Ohio," Jack says, "waiting to see whether or not we made the cut."

"But we all just lost!" Tipton shouts.

"Yes," The Host says. "Some of you simply lost . . . more."

44.

They don't get a long speech. They don't get comfort. They don't even get a real explanation.

The Host gives them a verdict, not a rationale.

"It's not just that you lost," The Host says. "It's how you lost."

He lets his words walk through the room.

"The lack of creativity for some of you. How quick some of you were to surrender. How badly you mismanaged time. How predictable you were. How little imagination you showed under pressure. Those are the real losers today."

The guards open the doors.

"Now will the losers please get out of my sight."

Jack McHenry was right, Wyatt thinks as he watches nearly half of the people in the ballroom file out of it, some with their heads down, all of them stunned at this turn of events: *I feel like we're back on the field in Ohio.* And as much as he wants to feel badly about the ones just dismissed, his overpowering emotion is relief, knowing that he's still here and they're not. No survivor guilt whatsoever.

When he tries to explain his mixed emotions to Reg Drummond, after this reckoning no one knew was coming, Reg says, "There's an expression about selfishness we've got in Australia that covers the feeling you just described: I'm all right, Jack." Reg grins then. "And I don't mean Jack McHenry."

The Host's voice returns, perfectly steady.

"For those of you who didn't do a quick head count, there are now thirty left in the competition," he says. "You will all convene back here shortly for a pleasant lunch, at which the next tests—and the setting for them—will be revealed."

He pauses.

"And all I can tell you for now is that one of those settings is Death Valley," he continues. They hear that familiar and grating chuckle now.

"Enjoy your meal," The Host concludes.

As their phones are handed back to them by the guards, Reg says, "I feel like we all just survived a qualifying heat none of us even knew was a heat."

"They just keep making up the rules as they go along," Wyatt says.

"The golden rule, evidently," Reg says. "The person with the gold rules."

Wyatt and Reg have just stepped back outside and into welcome sunlight, when they hear Alek, several yards ahead of them, scream.

"No—"

It's not a scream of fear.

It's a scream of recognition.

They see her staring at the phone in her hand as she drops to her knees.

By the time they've rushed to her, Alek is rocking back and forth, still staring at her phone.

"Please, no," she moans.

"Alek . . . what is it?" Wyatt asks her.

Her eyes find his, wet and wild.

"My mom," she says.

45.

It takes Alek a second to make words.

Like her brain keeps rejecting the sentence.

Alek explains that the apartment building they had been living in—hiding in—had been hit by a bomb.

"That was . . . her . . . her friend Sofia who called me," she says, fighting for any scrap of control. "My mother had given her the number . . . Sofia . . . but only in the case . . ." Her chest is heaving again. ". . . in case of an emergency."

Reg kneels on one side, steady as stone.

"Your mother?" he asks, and can't finish the question.

Alek shakes her head fast, like she's trying to shake off the image.

"She's alive," Alek says. "But hurt badly . . . her ceiling . . . collapsed. Ten bodies so far have been recovered." Alek still has the phone in her shaking right hand. She swallows hard. "She's at the hospital."

"How badly hurt?" Wyatt asks.

"Sofia says things were broken," Alek says. "Maybe many things."

She looks up at Wyatt, and it's the first time she looks her age since he met her.

"This is . . . was for her more than me," she says. "Me being here and not with her there." Her voice breaks on the last word.

"We all know that," Reg says quietly.

"I have to leave," Alek says. "I have to push my button. I have to– You both understand, don't you?"

Wyatt thinks: *She wants us to pull her to safety one more time.*

Reg puts a hand on her shoulder. Firm. Gentle. Nonnegotiable.

"Breathe," Reg says. "Just breathe."

Alek tries. Fails. Tries again.

"Help me," Alek says to them in a small voice.

"I'll do whatever you want me to," Reg says. "We both will. Just breathe."

Reg keeps his voice low.

"Get information first," he says. "Make the decision with facts, not panic. Because once you press it . . . that's it."

Wyatt watches Alek's hand tremble near the pendant at her chest. She's staring at it like it's a gun.

Wyatt had wanted to go looking for Hannah as soon as he'd left the ballroom, to try to understand what had happened to them this morning. But he knows he can't leave Alek, any more than he would have left her that day when she fell through the ice.

"We're not leaving you," Wyatt says.

Reg nods. "Not until you know."

He thinks: *This is a different kind of test for Alek.* Not part of this competition, but the most difficult test yet. *By a lot.* All of them had left their old lives behind when they'd entered this competition. But Alek's has just reached out to her in this lousy way.

They walk her back to her cottage like she's fragile glass.

Alek sits on the front steps with her phone in both hands, knuckles white.

"Wyatt and I will stay with you until you hear back from your mother's friend," Reg says. He smiles at her again and puts a hand on her shoulder. She reaches up and covers it with her own. "You know by now that we have your back, no matter what."

As they sit there with her, Wyatt once again thinks how full of it a guy like Tipton is, thinking that alliances and even newly formed friendships don't matter here.

They do.

Jimmy was absolutely right after dinner last night. Some of us feel we're all in this together, no matter how much we all want to be the ultimate winner. Wyatt is intelligent enough to know that might change eventually, probably will change, as their numbers continue to dwindle. Maybe it will be him against Reg or Alek, or Jack.

Or Hannah.

Just not right now.

They sit there.

Minutes pass.

Then more.

Wyatt tries small talk once—about Go, about how he thought he had control until he didn't—then stops. Alek's eyes are on nothing. His words can't reach her.

Finally she whispers, barely audible, "I've never felt so helpless."

Her phone rings.

All three of them flinch.

Alek answers, voice shaking.

"Please give me good news," she says in English.

She listens quietly for a long time, answering her mother's friend in their native language. Alek waits and then listens again, her face fierce with concentration. Wyatt and Reg stand nearby and listen.

They hear her soften and say, "I'm here, Mama," before nodding and listening all over again.

Finally, almost out of nowhere, a smile begins to form. Not much of one, Wyatt thinks. But whatever she's hearing can't be terrible news, that much is quite clear.

Before the call ends, Alek Andrich laughs heartily, laughs so hard Wyatt is almost afraid she might start crying again. He feels closer to her than ever. He's certain Reg feels the same way. Feels this is one of those special moments that continue to make the whole competition worthwhile, even after what happened this morning with Hannah, something he's still trying to process. He's been given a whole new reason for being here.

At last Alek puts the phone away. She wipes her face with the back of her hand and looks at them.

"Broken arm," she says. "Four cracked ribs. A concussion. She's going to be in some pain for a while, the doctors tell her, especially with the ribs. But they say she's going to be fine."

Wyatt finally exhales. "I'm so glad," Wyatt says. "For your mother, of course. But also for you."

"She wouldn't even hear of me coming home," Alek says.

Wyatt says, "You have to tell us what she said that made you laugh so hard."

"My sweet, gentle mother," she says, voice steady, "told me to stop whining . . . and go kick some ass."

46.

Ant Tipton's cottage sits higher than most of the others. Whoever assigned them knew exactly what he'd prefer.

Distance. Sightlines. Control.

He stands at the second-floor window and looks down at the front steps of Alek Andrich's cottage.

Drummond is there, big and steady, like the world can't move him unless he agrees. The rich kid from New York—Jordan—is there too, all long limbs and nervous loyalty. Alek sits between them with her phone in her hands, no longer shaking.

Alek's crisis is over. For now.

Not that Tipton cares about her feelings in this moment, one way or the other.

He's not worried about her, and he's certainly not worried about some kid from a fancy private school who he knows could be taken down by a strong breeze.

Alek's crisis did one thing he knew would make things harder: It solidified them as a unit. Cemented a bond. A visible bond. People who would bleed for each other without being asked.

That's the real threat in these games. Not strength. Not brains. Not even courage.

Alliance.

Drummond is the anchor of it.

Reg Drummond is a threat, as big a threat as anybody still left in the competition, in Tipton's view, anyway.

And Tipton had always been good at evaluating a situation.

Of almost any kind.

Tipton has spent his whole life assessing threats, first in uniform, then in the private world—where everyone smiles while they price out your death. Identify the threat and then deal with it. If necessary? Eliminate it first chance you got.

Tipton's already marked two people as problems.

Jack McHenry, who has that quiet Ranger readiness even when he's pretending he doesn't.

Reg Drummond, who looks like he's still carrying a whistle inside his head—still captaining a team.

And Tipton has never been afraid of problems.

He's afraid of one thing only.

Being controlled.

It isn't anything in particular Drummond has said, or even the way he'd saved Alek back in Antarctica—something Tipton obviously didn't witness but heard, as it is already legend with the other competitors. It isn't the fact that well past his Olympic prime, the guy is obviously in tremendous shape. There's this confidence about him, as if he's still on his way to another gold medal. He knows he's better than you without having to say that.

He doesn't need Drummond to announce himself. It's in the posture, the calm, the way he takes up space without trying.

Tipton has long since identified Jack McHenry as a threat, of course. Done it even before they'd been swimming through sharks to that forsaken island off the coast of Chile. It was why Tipton had done everything to eliminate McHenry in the water that day, trying to send the shark his way, as risky a maneuver as that was. Extremely risky, in fact, because the shark could have come for him instead.

In that case he'd evaluated the risk of his action against its possible reward.

It hadn't worked. Tipton still thinks it was worth it. Only McHenry is still here, and in his way. So is Reg Drummond.

He thinks of Luca Tommasi for half a second, the way you think of a headline you've already read. The cop had been on the trail, pale, sweating through his shirt, eyes not quite focused.

"Aiutami," Tommasi had said.

Help me.

Tipton understood the word. He understood the moment even better.

If he stopped, he'd be the one on the ground next. If he carried the man, he'd slow, and slow meant vulnerable. If he pressed his own red button to summon help, he'd be out of the competition.

So he'd done what he always did when the world asked him to choose between mercy and survival.

He'd chosen survival.

Not to mention he knew they were watching. He couldn't risk it. He couldn't risk . . .

Don't think about that.

He'd told himself the medics would reach Tommasi fast. He'd told himself it wasn't his job. He'd told himself a dozen things.

Then Tommasi died.

And that death has been following Tipton ever since, not as guilt—as leverage.

"Others may want this," Tommasi had said to Tipton in English. "I need this."

"Why you more than the rest of us?" Tipton had asked.

"Because I am needing it to save my life," Tommasi said.

But Tipton knew just listening to this man, who said he was willing to do whatever it took to win, that he wouldn't be willing to kill if it came to that.

He is about to go outside and take a walk by himself before lunch when he feels his phone buzzing.

He looks at the screen and smiles like he's been invited to a private club.

THE HOST.

Tipton answers without hesitation.

"Hello," Tipton says.

The Host's voice is soft, almost conversational.

"Mr. Tipton. How's your nose?"

Tipton touches it, still sore, still swollen.

"I've had worse," he says.

"I'm sure you have," The Host replies. "I didn't call about your nose."

"No," Tipton says. "You didn't."

A small pause.

Then The Host says, "I saw you on the trail in Chile."

Tipton doesn't react. Not visibly. Not even alone.

"I'm flattered you were watching me," Tipton says.

"I watch everyone," The Host replies. "But you are . . . useful."

Tipton keeps his voice light. "What do you want?"

"I want truth," The Host replies, and somehow makes the word a threat. “I want to see what you do when you’re not protected by rank, or reputation, or deniability.”

Then: “And I’m reminding you what happens when you disappoint the people in charge.”

Tipton’s stomach tightens.

The leash he never talks about.

The Host lets the silence work.

“Tomorrow, you climb,” The Host says. “And you’ll be in a pod with someone you’ve been watching.”

Tipton’s eyes flick back down to Alek’s cottage. To Drummond.

“Lucky me,” Tipton says.

“Don’t do anything foolish,” he says. “I need you here. For now.”

The call ends.

Tipton stands at the window a moment longer.

Then he watches Drummond laugh at something Alek said, and he makes a decision he doesn’t like.

He will deal with Drummond.

Not because he wants to.

Because he’s being told to.

In that moment, he’s afraid.

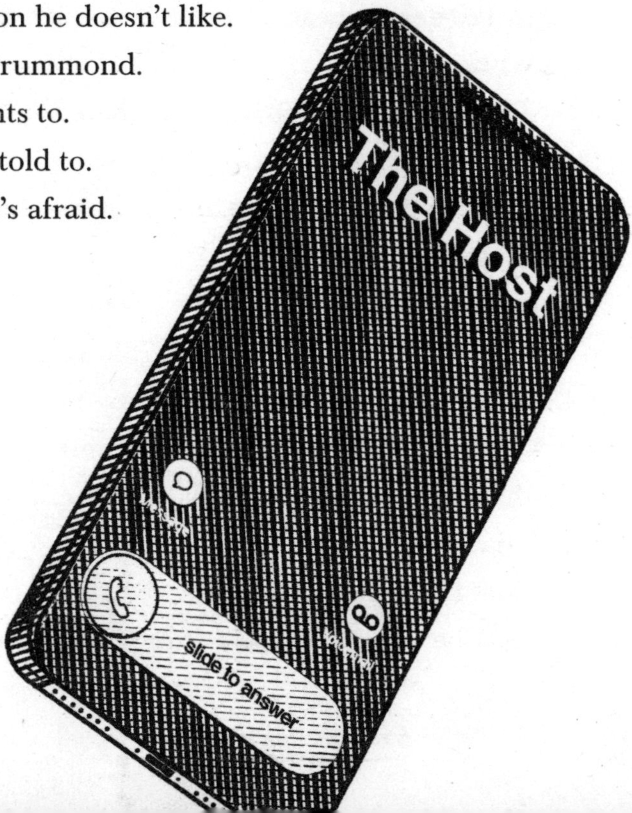

47.

DEATH VALLEY

How did I get here . . . and what do I do next?

Jimmy Donaldson can't stop asking himself that question, now more than ever, on this speeding bus with a dozen or so other players—what The Host calls their "pod"—about to begin a hike across the vast northern stretch of the Mojave Desert known as Death Valley.

In 120-degree heat.

Without water.

This isn't one of his videos. There's no set he built. No safety team he trusts.

There is just the red pendant at his throat and the truth he's starting to accept:

Someone else is writing the rules.

All of which have changed. These games are too dangerous. Lives are at stake every day. Jimmy stares out the window at the pale, empty land rolling past. He thinks of Luca Tommasi's body on that inflatable boat, headed back across the water.

That wasn't supposed to happen.

That can't happen again.

And he needs to make things right, not just for the friends

he's made here, but also because of his mistaken complicity in all of it.

But first . . . the desert.

Jimmy is seated across the aisle from Lin Zhi, the Chinese gymnast who won in Rio de Janeiro—quiet, compact, eyes forward like he's already visualizing the next movement. Jimmy idly wonders how many bus rides Zhi has taken on his way to various gymnastic events around the world.

Zhi said something on the flight that stuck with him.

"I am sure the other athletes here would tell you the same thing," Zhi said quietly. "Once I stopped competing, I found myself missing it more than I thought I would. No one except other athletes might understand, but entering these games was as much about getting that feeling back as it was about the money. It was about a new challenge."

Jimmy feels that in his bones. Not because he's obsessed with winning—he's obsessed with meaning. Scale. Impact. With proving something is possible.

The truly crazy part of the whole thing? He still doesn't know who the backer is. Or the banker. In the run-up to this version there had been encrypted correspondence. He had provided feedback on challenges and been informed that the prize money had been upped all the way to a billion dollars. He had trusted his instincts were right . . . but were they?

So much of this was starting to feel all wrong.

It had started with the death of Luca Tommasi. Now here they are in Death Valley, about to take an insane walk.

He knows that no one is forcing him to do this, the way nobody forced him to accept The Host's challenge.

The titanium red button is still hanging around his neck.

But he can't walk away. He can't let these people down.

Can't disappoint them.

Or himself.

Most of those on this bus—plus those in the pods on their way to Mammoth Cave in Kentucky or to an intense climbing expedition in New Hampshire—are easy for Jimmy to root for.

Jimmy looks down the row.

Alek Andrich is here. Marcelo Oliveira is here. Carlos Lopez is here too—an ex-boxer with the dangerous ease of someone who learned young that violence solves problems.

Jimmy still hears Lopez's voice from Kentucky.

Since Ohio, Lopez has carried himself like a freewheeling gangster, giving off the same ruthless vibe as Tipton. Maybe that's why Tipton and Lopez have been spending time together, deep in conversation, probably plotting against everyone else.

Jimmy has only talked to Lopez once, after dinner the other night in Kentucky. He asked Carlos if he believed he could win.

"I always win," Lopez had said curtly. "In boxing and now in my business. For me it has always been: Muerte antes que el deshonor."

Death before dishonor.

Lopez had smiled thinly.

Jimmy doesn't like people like that. People who treat morality like an outfit they can swap.

He trusts Jack. He trusts Reg. He trusts Alek. He trusts Wyatt even when the kid annoys him a bit. He trusts Hannah's brain, even if her heart is getting tangled in this. It's why he's gone out of his way to keep telling them that he's there for them, no matter what.

And also lets them know this:

The one he trusts the least here, less than Tipton or Lopez or anyone, is The Host.

It's more than not knowing who he is, his true identity, his name. Jimmy doesn't know what The Host's *agenda* is, or what his endgame might be.

Jimmy knows he's never been faced with a challenge like this. Maybe no one has. But he has to find out who's in control of these games.

The bus hits a bump. The pod sways. Someone laughs nervously.

Jimmy feels the red pendant shift against his chest.

He thinks, not for the first time:

I can quit.

Then he thinks:

If I quit, who protects them?

48.

DEATH VALLEY

Jimmy delays getting off the air-conditioned bus as long as he can, still wishing the ride from the Furnace Creek Airport had taken longer than it had.

He and Alek get off the bus together.

"You ready?" she asks.

"No," Jimmy says. "But yeah."

They step down onto the ground.

They have arrived at the point from which they will embark across a valley considered to be the lowest and driest and hottest point in North America, especially in the summer.

Which this is.

When Jimmy is outside, the heat hits him so swiftly and violently that it nearly knocks him down. And he's only gone a few feet, not the miles he'll soon be forced to walk underneath the brutal desert sun.

Alek sways slightly, then steadies.

"It's a death march," she says, voice flat.

They're standing at a marked start line with an ugly view: endless pale dirt, rippling heat, distant dunes that look fake because nothing in nature should feel that hostile.

A black-clad driver gestures them into formation. No talking. No questions.

Then The Host's voice comes from a speaker mounted on a truck. "Welcome to Death Valley," The Host says. "Today, you learn what your body does when the mind begs it to stop."

Jimmy looks around for water. Coolers. Bottles. Anything.

There's nothing.

The Host continues, "You will walk eight miles to the dunes and eight miles back. Sixteen miles in all, there and back. Your primary sightline will be Telescope Peak in the distance."

A murmur runs through the pod. Not panic yet. But close.

"No carried water," The Host says. "However—"

Everyone leans in slightly, instinctively.

"—there are three caches," The Host continues. "Buried. Marked only by coordinates that will appear on your screens . . . one at a time . . . if you earn them."

Jimmy looks down. Their phones are gone, but each of them has a small screen clipped to their backpack strap—simple. Locked. GPS arrow. Heart rate. Temperature.

The Host adds, "The quicker you move, the more information you receive. The slower you move, the more you suffer."

Jimmy exhales through his nose.

Of course.

Alek glances at him. "So, it's a puzzle," she says.

"It's insane to do this under any conditions," Jimmy says to Alek. "But it's criminal to be asked to do it without water."

"A death march," Alek says again.

The pod breaks into smaller groups—three teams of four for this location, making it harder to draft, harder to protect each other, easier to fracture.

Jimmy's team is called out:

Jimmy. Alek. Carlos Lopez.

And then the fourth: Marcelo Oliveira.

"I'm going to be with you every step," Jimmy says. "You know our deal."

"I have to trust you," Alek says. "And I definitely do."

"Today more than ever."

"There's always the red button," Alek says.

"You won't need it," Jimmy says.

They don't tell them how the winners are chosen. Only that there will be winners, if they make it across Death Valley and back.

Alive.

They start walking toward dunes that look as far away as the other side of the earth. At first, it feels manageable. Awful, but manageable.

Then the sun climbs higher and the valley turns into an oven. Sand crunches under their shoes. Their screens stay stubbornly blank—no coordinates yet.

No mercy.

The four of them go silent because talking is wasted water.

They walk.

And walk.

And they walk.

It truly is a death march.

They're silent, all four of them.

Until they hear a single voice.

"I have to quit."

49.

MOUNT WASHINGTON

Wyatt Jordan is part of the group that has been flown to the airport in Portland, Maine.

The Host has only told them—mid-flight—that they were on their way to a "rock-climbing expedition."

Then he added: "And since you wouldn't be here if you all weren't thrill seekers, rest assured that you're going to love it."

Reg Drummond is part of this group.

As is Hannah Wagner.

So, too, is Ant Tipton.

Wyatt hates having anything at all to do with Tipton, but he is secretly glad to have Hannah along for this particular ride, as strained as things have remained between them. He still can't help feeling he needs to look out for her as much as for himself.

Maybe even more.

A different emotion, frankly, than anything Wyatt has ever experienced. But then this girl is different, whether she's ghosting him or not. Maybe things would change for the better over the next couple of days.

Maybe he could find a way to make things right.

Once they've boarded the bus waiting for them on the

tarmac, he sits two seats away from Hannah and tries—once—to look at her.

She doesn't look back.

Her face is calm in the way a person's face is when they're holding something in.

Wyatt keeps thinking about what she whispered in the ballroom.

It wasn't private.

So he doesn't push her. Not now.

Before they left, The Host told them that their eventual destination would be Mount Washington in New Hampshire, seventy miles or so away.

"You may or may not know that it is the highest peak in the northeastern United States," The Host said, "and the most prominent mountain east of the Mississippi River. One you will be expected to scale today after a quite scenic hike from Pinkham Notch, New Hampshire, to get there," he adds.

He's not quite finished.

"This style of climb is known as 'free solo' for the uninitiated," The Host concludes.

Boom, Wyatt thinks.

There it is.

Wyatt knows what the expression means. *Free Solo,* one of his favorite movies ever, was about Alex Honnold's historic climb up the 3,200-foot face of El Capitan without a rope or safety gear, taking a dangerous route known as Freerider.

The movie had visually blown Wyatt and his buddies away. He can't imagine Mount Washington could possibly be more dangerous or difficult than El Capitan. But he's been conditioned, because they've all been, to assume nothing.

What he mostly remembers from *Free Solo* is that it was as close as he'd ever come in a movie theater to suffering from vertigo.

Wyatt gets a little dizzy even thinking about any climb similar to that one.

He had tried one more time to start a conversation with Hannah on the plane, saying, "Are we ever going to talk about what we're not talking about?" Her answer had been a quick shake of her head.

So on the bus from Portland, Wyatt sat next to Gabrielle Fontaine, player #301, another athlete, who had retired after winning a gold medal for France in the 4 x 100 medley relay at the Summer Games in Paris.

"I know The Host talked about us loving what we are about to do," Gabrielle Fontaine says to Wyatt. "But to me, it just sounds like one more of his lies."

Once they have arrived at Pinkham Notch, their driver, dressed in black like one of The Host's guards, wordlessly leads them for the next hour and a half to an area at the base of the mountain known as the Huntington Ravine.

"Is there just one route up the mountain?" Reg Drummond asks the driver.

"Do I look like a tour guide?" the man asks.

Then the man says, "This is the end of my trip." He shrugs and points toward the sky. "And the beginning of yours."

"I would rather climb the Eiffel Tower," Gabrielle says.

The Host's voice comes through a phone the driver sets on a rock.

"Welcome," The Host says, cheerful enough to be insulting. "Today you climb."

Reg looks up at the steep ravine walls.

"This isn't Mount Washington," Reg says. "This is a death slide."

The Host pauses, pleased.

"Yes," he says. "Now you're paying attention."

All of their heads are tilted back as far as they'll go.

"We had considered other climbs, in other parts of the country, including one in Boulder, Colorado, called the Wind Tower," The Host says. "But we considered this one to be more fair, and perhaps not quite as dangerous."

"Are we supposed to thank you?" Gabrielle asks.

"Hopefully that attitude will prove useful in the free climb you are about to make to the summit," The Host says.

"I assume you were joking about us making a free climb up this monster," Ant Tipton says.

"No joke, Mr. Tipton," The Host says. "And no ropes, no harnesses, no rappelling equipment. Your goal is simple. Reach the checkpoint above the headwall by sundown."

Wyatt looks up at the headwall and feels his throat tighten. Loose rock. Unreliable holds. A fall that would not be cinematic.

Just final.

Tipton adjusts his backpack straps.

"Well," Tipton says, "this is a stupid way to die."

Wyatt can't help himself. "So don't."

Tipton turns his head slowly toward him. Mildly amused.

"I'll be going it alone," Ant Tipton says.

"Your choice or ours?" Wyatt asks.

Tipton fixes him with a long look.

"You do not want to back talk me, boy," Tipton says finally.

Reg steps half a pace closer without making it obvious. Protective. Measured.

Wyatt holds Tipton's gaze anyway.

"Yeah," Wyatt says, "I kind of do."

Tipton's mouth twitches.

"Fine," Tipton says. "Stay behind me. You'll live longer."

The driver cuts short the exchange right before Reg Drummond steps between Wyatt and Tipton. He distributes folded maps—odd little topographic sheets with a thin line drawn up the ravine, hand-marked dots beside it.

Holds. Ledges. "Rest shelves."

"What happens if we turn back?" Hannah asks, voice steady.

The Host answers like he's been waiting for her.

"Turning back is always an option," he says. "But it has consequences."

Reg's eyes narrow. "Define consequences."

The Host doesn't.

"What are these for?" Hannah asks. "We can see what's in front of us. And above us."

"Maps that show various natural holds, ledges, knobs, and imperfections that may aid you in your climbs," The Host says. "And now, if there are no further questions or comments from the group . . ."

"I have another question," Hannah says.

"Yes, Miss Wagner," The Host replies.

"If we press the red button in the middle of a climb . . . how fast does rescue arrive?"

The Host's voice turns thoughtful.

"I'm no mountain climber, I've never been much for heights, to be honest," The Host says. "But there is one expression with which I've made myself familiar."

"And what's that?" Reg Drummond asks.

"There's always a way down."

50.

SOMEWHERE

The Host watches on his monitors as the buses arrive at Death Valley, at Mount Washington, at a secret entrance to Mammoth Cave in Kentucky. A fourth screen shows multiple feeds. One a procurement dashboard. Names replaced by vendor codes—because the real game isn't survival. It's logistics.

Contracts make everything clean. A "relief corridor." A "training exercise." A "private evacuation." Paperwork turns kidnapping into itinerary.

One map filled with moving dots pulsing—the contestants. He doesn't need it. He knows where the real tension is.

He watches the feed of Death Valley longer than the others.

He thinks:

This is the day when the stakes are about to spike.

Everything up to now feels like child's play, even with near-death experiences for some of them in Chile and Antarctica.

Without real stakes, what would be the fun of running the board?

He feels himself rooting for them to make it through. He knows they think he's a monster. He's not. There is a method to what they think is his madness.

What's the old line?

What doesn't kill you makes you stronger?

He'd actually laid it out for Reg Drummond, when he'd told everyone in the room that the easy jobs generally don't pay very well.

For the moment, his eyes are focused on Jimmy Donaldson. Alek Andrich. Lopez. Oliveira.

He watches Jimmy the way you watch a fire near dry brush: Not because it's beautiful, but because it spreads.

Jimmy is trying to be a leader. To build loyalty.

It's irritating. It's also dangerous.

Loyalty is the only force in this game stronger than fear.

The Host turns slightly in his chair and studies another screen: Mount Washington.

Tipton. Drummond. Hannah. The boy.

There's a moment—small, easy to miss—where Tipton looks up at the headwall and doesn't sneer.

He calculates.

The Host smiles to himself.

Good.

Because Tipton is not here to win.

Tipton is here because he's owned.

The Host's gaze returns to the Death Valley feed.

Jimmy is talking to Alek.

Encouraging. Stabilizing. Doing what he does best.

The Host doesn't hate him.

Hate is too personal.

Jimmy is simply in the way.

And if Jimmy stays . . . he'll turn thirty contestants into a movement.

The Host just wants him to be gone, sooner rather than later. *Out of sight, out of mind. Out of the way.*

Donaldson tries to be discreet in his private conversations with some of the others, almost always outdoors, away from any hidden microphones. Or cameras. Or even drones.

Was he really naïve enough to think there might not be casualties? And what difference would it make if he knew my name, as much as it might shock him?

It would shock all but one of them.

"Maybe today he quits," The Host says out loud.

There is *a method*, The Host thinks.

The Host leans toward the mic at his desk and speaks softly, not to the contestants, not to the pods . . .

To the room.

"Today," he says, "we find out who they really are when the world offers them one button and no mercy."

He watches Jimmy take another step into the heat.

Then he adds, quieter:

"And we find out how long optimism lasts when it starts to cost blood."

51.

MAMMOTH CAVE
KENTUCKY

Four groups of four players have gathered in the mountains of south-central Kentucky, in what The Host calls "an unmapped branch of the Mammoth Cave system" that stretches for hundreds of miles.

Jack McHenry knows better. Mammoth Cave is mapped the way oceans are mapped: not completely, not perfectly, but thoroughly enough that anyone who says "unexplored" is trying to sell you something.

This isn't unexplored.

It's restricted.

The "Alpha" group is the first to enter the caves, followed by "Bravo" and "Charlie," each from a separate location. The "Delta" group is the last to enter:

Jack McHenry—already flashing back to deployments where caves meant traps and ambushes and the ugly, stale smell of fear.

Elena Torres—who grew up visiting the Nerja caves near Málaga, and thought those were frightening until this.

Rupert Chadwick—the fourteen-year-old Brit asked now to be as adult as he's ever been.

Conner Lynch—native of Kentucky. Former all-American receiver at West Point. Former Rhodes Scholar. Retired Golden Boy congressman from his state once considered to be a possible presidential candidate until he became disillusioned. He left government so publicly that half the country called him a coward and the other half called him honest.

At the age of fifty, Conner had begun hosting a wildly popular podcast, in the hope that he might do more good for the country there.

"Lyndon Johnson, a proud Texan, once said it was better to have J. Edgar Hoover inside the tent pissing out than outside pissing in," Conner had said to Jack on the bus. "Well, I'm outside pissing in now."

All they know in advance is that there is a surprise waiting right before they see daylight again.

"But for now," The Host had said on their ride in, "your challenge is simple: get to that daylight without falling.

"There are more than four hundred miles officially mapped out in the Mammoth Cave system, mostly near Mammoth Cave National Park. But the only people who have attempted to map out the route you're about to take work for me. Well, the ones who survived."

No phones. No watches. No GPS. Only small flashlights and the hard little security earpiece in each of their ears—The Host's voice, if he decides to use it.

"How will we know when we've reached the finale?" Conner asks. "Or end zone, or whatever you want to call it?"

"Oh, you'll know, Congressman," The Host says. "Trust me, you will know."

They proceed slowly, without any sense of time. They make their way carefully along the walls, feeling their way in the semi-darkness, afraid to look past the end of the short beams of their flashlights or down into the deep caverns below them. The caves are both forbidding and beautiful at the same time. All of them move cautiously, afraid that one misstep, one bad slip, and they disappear into the darkness.

Their flashlight beams cut through dust and darkness and make everything look closer than it is—right until you glance down and realize the floor is not a floor at all.

It's a drop.

A void.

Jack takes point. Conner asked him to.

"All I had was an intelligence assignment after West Point," Conner tells him. "I defer to a man who served in a forward zone."

"I feel I'm back in the many caves during various missions," Jack says, "almost always walking into a trap."

"But you're still here, aren't you?" Conner says. "I'll take my chances following you, Jack. We all will."

Jack keeps one hand on the wall as much as he can, testing each step, watching for loose rock and slick mud.

"Segunda," Elena Torres says.

Jack takes a moment to lock eyes with her. They smile at each other. The warm and familiar smile of a growing affection. Maybe even young love.

Jack tells Rupert to stay directly behind him.

"Jack," Rupert whispers to him at one point. "I'm so afraid."

"Hey, pal," Jack says. "We all are."

"You don't understand," Rupert swallows. "The thing I'm most afraid of in the whole world is the dark."

Jack stops the line with a raised fist. They freeze.

He crouches in front of Rupert, close enough that the boy can see his face inside the weak cone of light.

"You're doing great," Jack says.

"I'm really not," Rupert says.

"Listen to me," Jack says, soft but steel. "The only thing you have to see is my back. You stare at my boots. You put your feet where I put my feet. You don't think about the dark. You don't think about the drop."

"I just feel like my next step . . ." Rupert's mouth trembles.

Jack puts his hands on the boy's shoulders.

"Look at me," he says softly, but sternly.

Rupert does.

"You won't," Jack says. Then he adds, because sometimes people need a lie that keeps them alive: "And if you do, I've got you."

Rupert gives a nervous half-smile.

"We're supposed to be looking for a leader," Rupert says. "I think I already found mine."

They get moving again.

Slowly.

Jack slips once on a patch of wet limestone, catches himself hard, knuckles scraping rock. Elena steadies Rupert with a hand on his shoulder. Conner stays behind them, sealing the rear.

A while later Elena stumbles and catches herself with both hands.

When they stop, Jack sees her palms are cut, streaked red against pale dust.

Elena leans in close. “Can we turn back?”

Jack doesn’t sugarcoat it. “Not if we want to live.”

She looks at him, breathing fast. “I can barely breathe.”

From behind them, Conner Lynch quietly says, “We’ve come too far to go back.” Pauses and adds, “Come too far in every possible way.”

Elena manages just a hint of a smile. “I can see why you made such a good politician,” she says.

He smiles back. “Hey,” he says, “there’s no need to insult me.”

A few hundred yards later, Jack steps into a hole.

They go another few hundred yards.

Jack steps onto what he thinks is solid ground.

It isn’t.

A shallow sinkhole gives under his weight. His foot drops, his balance goes, and he slides.

Unable to break his fall, he hits the ground hard. The trail is wide enough, though, that Conner Lynch moves quickly past Rupert and Elena and grabs Jack by the arm.

“I wasn’t the fastest player in the world,” he says to Jack. “But I always had good hands.”

Jack gets his footing again.

They are moving again a few minutes later, still no real light ahead of them. Just an unbearable tension, broken only by the sound of their footsteps on the rocks and limestone and occasional mud underneath their feet.

Jack really does feel he’s back on duty. There is the same quiet now, the same sense of dread, the fight to control his breathing and his heartbeat and remain alert, because alertness could mean the difference between life and death.

He then hears the roar from down below them.

The roar of a great river running through beneath them.

When he does force himself to look down, there is just enough from the flashlights that he is able to see the powerful, swirling water that seems to be yelling up at them.

In the next moment the one yelling is the English boy, Rupert, as his footing goes and he disappears into the darkness.

Jack spins.

Rupert's arms pinwheel.

Then the boy is gone.

Not into the void—down slick rock that drops off the ledge in a steep slick chute, funneling toward the roaring water below.

Rupert's scream trails after him.

And then the dark swallows it.

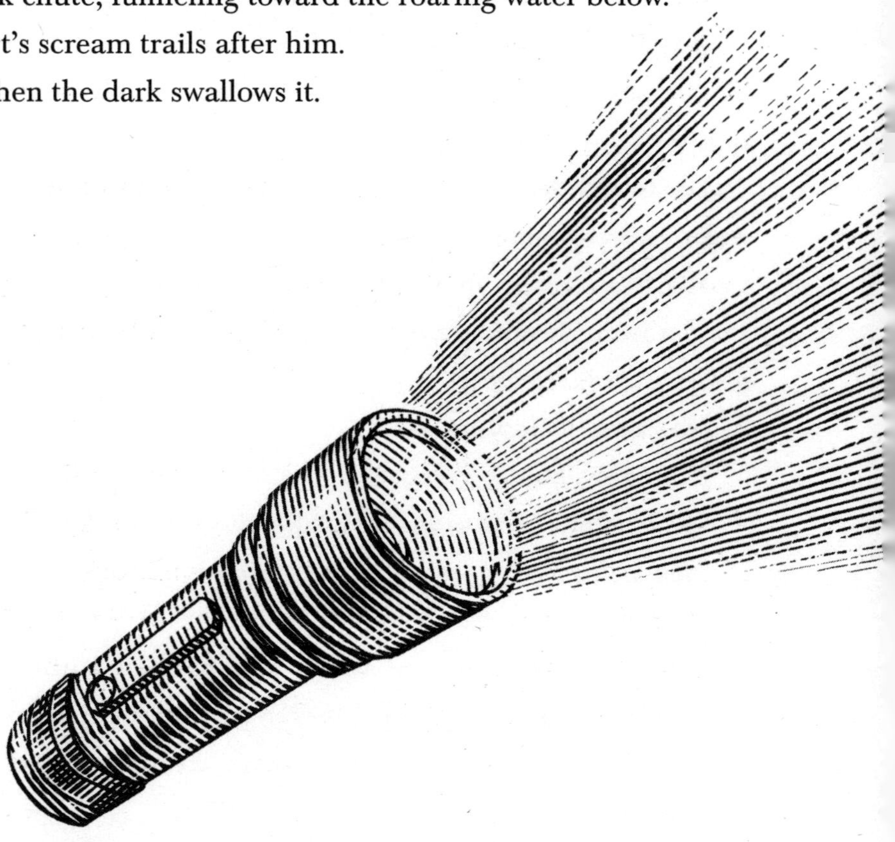

52.

DEATH VALLEY

Two hours in 120-degree heat and this daytime nightmare has turned into what Alek had predicted:

A death march across Death Valley.

Jimmy can't tell if he's been walking for two hours or a day. Time doesn't work right out here. It's just sun, glare, breath, footfall.

His mouth feels like sandpaper. His tongue feels too big for his teeth. Every swallow is dry.

His strap screen shows what he already knows: heart rate high, temperature climbing.

No coordinates.

No cache.

No mercy.

Two options scream inside his head:

Find water.

Get help.

But maybe the only way to get help at this point is for one of them to push the red button.

They have to find water—somewhere—as remote a possibility as that seems.

Jimmy once considered doing a video in the Great Basin Desert in Nevada. He scouted locations himself. But no heat he's ever felt comes close to this hellscape.

I'll die before I let any of the others die out here, he thinks.

Lopez has fallen down once. So has Marcelo. Jimmy caught himself on his hands and felt the ground scrape skin like concrete.

Then Alek calls out: "I have to stop."

She pitches forward.

She's strong and tries to break the fall with both hands. But still ends up face down in dirt.

Jimmy goes to her. He manages to get Alek into a sitting position. Marcelo takes off his shirt and wipes dirt, sweat, and blood off Alek's face, hands shaking with effort.

Alek's eyes flutter open.

"Leave me," Alek says. "All of you, just leave."

"Leaving here sounds great," Jimmy says. "But we're not abandoning you."

Alek tries to push herself up. Her arms tremble. She fails.

"Jimmy. Just stop. You all go ahead," she says. It's spoken as a command. "Go now. Go!"

Jimmy points at her red button.

"No," Alek says, somehow putting some snap into her voice. "I've made it this far, I'm not quitting." She shakes her head. "Not happening. Not after everything. Not after– I'm going to finish." She closes her eyes. "I'm going to win."

"Okay, but we have to find water," Jimmy says and looks around at the group. "And we have to find it now."

His screen buzzes once.

A simple arrow appears. A coordinate. Finally.

But it's not "water." It's not a map. It's just a direction and a distance. 2.1 miles.

Jimmy smiles, finally some hope. "That's the cache," he says. "That has to be the cache."

"I'll go," Lopez says.

They all turn and stare at him, shocked to hear Lopez sounding cooperative, for once.

"Somebody has to do it," he says. "I'm used to the heat."

He points off to the west. "That way. Looks like there was big rain out here last night." He shrugs. "Who knows? If there's a low wash, the cache will be there. Maybe water too. What do we have to lose?"

Lopez starts to walk away, headed toward the dunes to the west.

They let him go and start walking in the opposite direction, toward mesquite trees several hundred yards ahead.

Jimmy watches him.

He doesn't trust him.

"You get Alek under those mesquite trees," Jimmy tells Marcelo. "Shade. Even bad shade. Don't let her sleep."

He starts walking toward the closest dunes, forcing himself to pick up the pace.

He walks for ten minutes, maybe twenty—he's lost all sense of time. If not for the dunes in front of him and the arrow on his screen, he'd be worried he was walking in circles.

Then he sees Lopez. On his knees, digging in the dirt.

Jimmy shuts his eyes, squeezes the sweat out of them, hopes that the sight of Lopez isn't some mirage.

It's not.

Jimmy walks up behind Carlos Lopez. He doesn't make a sound. Then he speaks. Quietly.

"You weren't ever coming back."

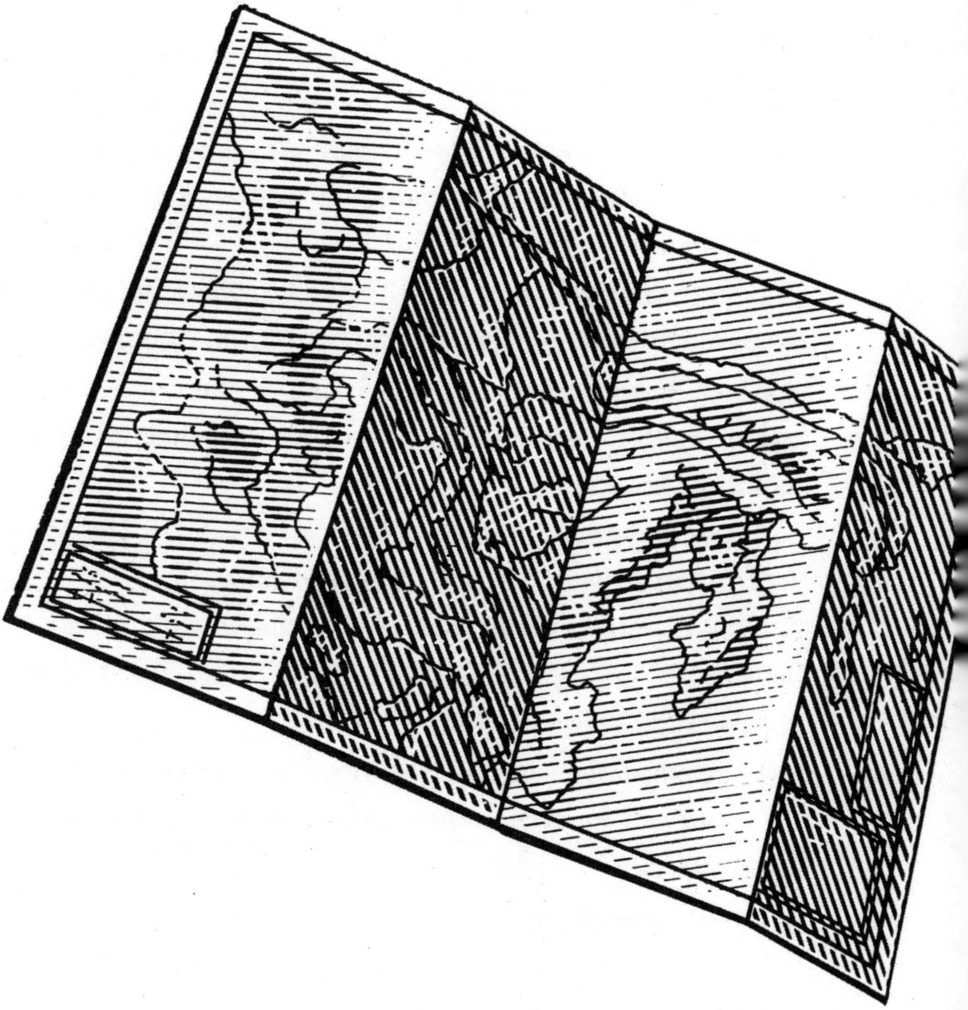

53.

DEATH VALLEY

Lopez finds the cache.

Not a miracle pond. Not salvation.

A buried black case half hidden by windswept sand at the base of a low wash.

Lopez is kneeling over it, having half dug it out of the sand with his bare hands. When Jimmy reaches him his hands are working at the latches.

He doesn't seem to be particularly surprised to see Jimmy standing behind him.

Lopez glances up, squinting through sweat. His face is wet, but not from water—just the body trying to survive.

"You Americans love your stories," Lopez says. "Hero. Villain. Betrayal."

"You didn't answer," Jimmy says.

Lopez taps the case. "This is why I came."

"I said you weren't going to return to us," Jimmy says. "Not to the group. Not to Alek."

Lopez's mouth twitches—almost amused.

Then he opens the case. Inside: two sealed water bladders, a cheap plastic measuring cup, electrolyte packets, and a folded note.

Lopez reads the note out loud, mocking the tone without changing it. "Congratulations," he says. "You earned water."

Jimmy's knees almost give out at the sight of the bladders.

He grabs one, tears it open with his teeth, drinks like an animal. Then he forces himself to stop. "Alek," he rasps. "We have to get this to Alek."

Then Lopez makes a quick move with his right hand. He draws a switchblade and flicks it open.

Jimmy tries to step away.

Lopez smiles. "I'm not going to stab you. I may be a fierce competitor, but I'm no killer. We'll need this knife to bring back water."

He flicks the knife toward the measuring cup, then toward the electrolyte packets.

Lopez nods toward the wash. "You want to carry her, you need her conscious. You want her conscious, you ration."

Jimmy swallows hard, forces his voice steady.

"Then we ration." He nods.

54.

MAMMOTH CAVE

Jack McHenry tosses the flashlight to the ground and drops to his knees at the edge of the chute as he prepares to jump down into the darkness after the boy.

First, he takes one last listen for another shout from down below, even for help, hoping to gauge where Rupert might be. The chute is slick limestone and mud, angling down into darkness.

There is only the roar of the water, sounding louder and more intimidating than ever.

Conner grabs his arm.

"Jack, *wait*—" Conner starts.

"Don't know, don't care," Jack says. "He's fourteen."

"C'mon man, we don't know what's down there," Conner says.

Elena is behind them, one hand pressed to her own mouth.

"Jack," she whispers. "Please don't—"

Jack doesn't answer. He's already taking off his boots.

Conner's voice is low, urgent. "You don't know what's down there."

Jack looks back at him, eyes hard.

"Yeah," Jack says. "I do."

Conner holds his gaze for half a second.

"Then I'm going with you," Lynch says, untying the laces of his own boots and tossing them aside along with his flashlight.

Elena crouches, hands shaking. "Wait–wait, we can call–"

Jack touches the earpiece in his ear. "The Host doesn't rescue people," Jack says. "He collects outcomes."

He swings his legs into the chute and lowers himself down, testing friction with his bare socks, one hand braced on rock.

Jack takes a last look at Elena, wanting to tell her before he jumps how much it's meant to him getting to know her. But he doesn't. Something in her eyes tells him she already knows.

"I'll be right behind you," she says, and touches her hand briefly to her heart.

Jack commits.

He slides.

Conner drops in right behind him, sliding on his side, one arm pinned to his chest.

Elena comes last, slower, careful.

The roar gets louder. Air gets colder. The smell changes–wet stone, moving water.

Jack hits the bottom and stumbles forward into shin-deep current. It grabs him immediately. It's stronger than it looks. He fights for balance, scanning the darkness.

"Rupert!" he yells.

No time to wait for the others.

No time, period.

The boy is down here somewhere.

A thin sound answers–barely audible over the water.

"Jack–!"

Jack turns toward it and wades into the current, arms out,

moving by sound and instinct and the stubborn refusal to let a promise die. Conner splashes in beside him.

Jack and Conner are carried along by the surprisingly powerful current, which drags them toward the sliver of daylight they can see in the distance, the daylight The Host had promised was there.

A loud splash behind them. Elena, probably hitting the water. He wants to go to her. Find her. Make sure she's okay. It feels like it took her so long to drop but it's only been seconds that feel like hours because of the cold and the fear. He knows he can't swim back. She's strong.

Find the boy.

A few seconds later they hear Rupert's voice from up ahead, barely audible over the din of the water all around them.

The boy is the only prize that matters now.

The boy is everything.

"Over there!" Conner shouts.

Jack came to these games looking for redemption. He had wanted to feel the sense of purpose he'd once felt as a Ranger, which he'd lost a long time ago, when he'd lost himself.

He swims toward the boy.

He promised Rupert he'd take care of him, no matter what.

"I'm coming!" Jack shouts, and swims furiously in the direction of Rupert's voice.

He feels like a Ranger again, and Rangers live by a simple code. A code he never stopped believing, even when he stopped believing in himself:

I will never leave a fallen comrade.

55.

MOUNT WASHINGTON

The hike from Pinkham Notch along the Tuckerman Ravine took more than two hours.

They are allowed a brief rest when they arrive at the foot of the climb they're about to make, at a side of the mountain known as the Pinnacle.

Reg's lungs pull air like he's been running. The exposure makes his stomach tighten, the world dropping away behind them in a way that has nothing to do with altitude and everything to do with possible consequences.

Tipton stands first.

Of course he does.

He adjusts his straps and looks up. "Listen," Tipton says, and for the first time his voice is neutral, practical. "No hero moves. No lunges. You don't 'go for it.' You place, you test, you commit."

Reg watches him. Hates him. Respects him. Both at once.

Tipton adds, almost grudgingly, "If we had a rope, we'd simul. Four of us on one line. But we don't. So we move like we are."

A team without the thing that makes teams safe.

They slowly begin their ascent.

Reg stays close behind Tipton, Tipton reluctantly having become the group leader.

Insanity, Reg tells himself.

Pure insanity.

Tipton also tells them that as a boy growing up in England, he'd done a fair amount of climbing in what is known as the Peak District, not too terribly far from where he'd grown up in northern Derbyshire.

There is little conversation. They all just follow Tipton's lead, focus on finding handholds and footholds in the schist rock in front of them.

Wyatt makes one dumb joke.

"Yeah," he says when Reg asks if he's climbed before. "I've done this exact route. At the Equinox Club on West Seventy-Sixth."

No one laughs. Not even Wyatt.

Mostly the handholds and footing in the silver-gray rock are surprisingly good as they begin to angle to their right, not nearly as slick as Reg had expected. Occasionally they even find a slab long enough and sturdy enough to fit all of them, and they take a short rest.

They climb in silence for long stretches, broken only by Tipton's clipped observations.

"Three points of contact."

"Don't trust the flakes."

"Edge left—better friction."

When they do take a rest, the view—especially to the east—is like nothing any of them have ever seen before. Reg wishes his fiancée, Kyra, could see it. Well, maybe with ropes. He remembers reading a book as a boy in which the main character is given the choice of being able to fly or be invisible.

For Reg there was no choice.

He'd always wanted to be able to fly.

Tipton, it turns out, really does know a fair amount about this mountain, occasionally reciting brief facts about the Mount Washington Cog Railway and how the temperature at the summit can drop to 50 degrees below and how winds up there had been measured as high as 230 miles per hour.

"The Cog Railway goes up the other side," he says. "Built in the eighteen hundreds."

Reg glances at him. "You're chatty today."

"Shut up and climb," Tipton replies.

Reg thinks: *I wonder if Tipton was given a heads-up before that they were coming here today*, though Reg can't imagine why anybody would think that would give him an edge, especially the higher they go.

He looks back at the two kids.

"What about you, Hannah?" Reg asks. "You ever do any climbing?"

Hannah's eyes stay on the rock in front of her. Anywhere but down.

"I'm terrified of heights," she says.

Wyatt flicks a glance at her—concern, unfinished business, swallowed words.

Hannah continues, voice calm, "I told them that in the red tent, but they sent me here anyway. Probably for their own sick amusement."

No one speaks.

"But I don't care," Hannah says. "I'm going to show them." She pauses. "Even if it kills me."

Reg stops climbing for half a beat and turns enough to look her in the eye.

"That's not happening," he says.

He sees the fear in her. Real fear. Not drama.

"It didn't happen after we ended up in the water that day, and it's not going to happen here. We make it up," Reg says. "We make it down. That's the whole job."

He adds, "We're more of a team than ever."

He believes that in his heart. He has always believed in the power of a team, the company of men when he was a rugby player, now the company of both men and women. You didn't have to love everybody on the team. No one here loves Ant Tipton, and that might include Tipton himself. But you had a common goal, and that won out over anything else. You didn't have to love everybody to still love the team.

Reg feels that now, especially with these two kids: Hannah and Wyatt. Probably in love already even if they don't know it, or would never admit it. Reg can see the way they look at each other.

But the common goal is the same for all of them now:

Make it to the top of the mountain.

And then, God willing, make it down.

"I'm still scared," Hannah says over her shoulder.

"I learned a long time ago," Reg says, "the thing that scares you the most is the thing you have to do."

Tipton, above them, mutters without turning. "Less poetry. More hands."

56.

MOUNT WASHINGTON

They keep making slow progress. Ten inches at a time. Sometimes five. All of them are afraid—they wouldn't be human if they weren't.

But all of them are being brave, maybe as brave as they've ever been in their lives. They've been told, constantly, that they would be pushed to their own limits in this competition. Maybe even beyond them.

The wind is constant now—cold enough to bite through sweat-soaked layers, strong enough to make the rock feel alive beneath their hands.

Softly Reg Drummond says, "I've never felt more alive," unsure whether the others can hear him or not.

To his surprise he hears Hannah say, "Same."

"I get it," Wyatt says, eyes fixed on the rock inches from his nose. "Maybe now more than ever."

Reg almost smiles. "Get what?"

"All of it," Wyatt says. "Why people do stupid things on purpose."

Tipton doesn't join the exchange. Tipton hasn't joined anything all day. He's been leading because he has the most experience, and because he cannot stand the idea of someone else being in control.

But he has something in his ear. Most of the time it's silent. A faint click, then The Host's voice—private, intimate, smiling right inside Tipton's skull.

"Mr. Tipton," it says. "A word."

Tipton's jaw tightens. He doesn't look back. Doesn't acknowledge it. Just keeps climbing.

It happens then.

Tipton loses his grip.

He half-slides and half-tumbles until Reg manages to block his fall, probably saving them all. Those few terrifying moments last hours for Reg.

"Sorry," Tipton says. "I could've killed us all."

"Nah," Reg says. "Buckley's chance."

"What does that mean?" Tipton says.

"An expression in Australia that means *not* a chance."

"And why is that?" Tipton asks.

"Because," Reg says, "it's like I told Hannah: Nobody is dying up here today."

Tipton barks out a laugh.

"You know, I may even end up liking you," he says.

"Buckley's chance," Reg says again.

Already the temperature up here is 20 degrees cooler than it had been at the base of the mountain. It might be even cooler than that. The higher they get, the more the wind starts to pick up, making any progress, even ten yards at a time, vastly more difficult.

Another click. "You're doing so well," The Host murmurs. "Almost like you've done this before."

Tipton's fingers dig harder into the schist. His knuckles go pale.

They land on a slightly broader slab—one of the few places you can stand without feeling the mountain trying to shake you off—and then Reg speaks low enough that only Tipton can hear.

"You got someone talking in your ear?" Reg asks.

Tipton doesn't answer.

Reg studies him for a second.

"You know what's funny?" Reg says. "I used to think the scariest thing in my life was losing."

Tipton finally glances at him. Suspicious. Almost . . . curious.

Reg keeps his eyes on the rock as he talks. "Then you win. You get the medal. You get the anthem. You get people telling you you're special. And you wake up the next year and realize the scariest thing is being ordinary again."

Tipton snorts, barely a sound. "World's tiniest violin."

Reg smiles without humor. "Yeah. That's what I told myself too."

Tipton looks away fast, like he's seen something he doesn't want to see.

The climb continues.

They can finally see the summit up ahead of them, after being on this mountain, making this slow climb, for more than half a day, at least.

With all that, Reg knows something that he wouldn't even think about trying to articulate to the others:

Reg hasn't felt this good—this exhilarated, really—since the Olympics, when he'd won gold medals and was the one on top of the world.

Only now he really is at the top of the world.

How could he explain this experience to someone else, that these games were changing him in ways he never anticipated?

Tipton pauses again, looks back over his shoulder, and asks if anyone wants to stop.

They all say no.

The summit is too close, almost close enough to reach up and touch.

But Tipton cautions them they can't take a direct line to it, it's not safe, this is no time to rush things, they need to traverse their way up there, first to the left, then back to the right, making the climb less steep, the last part of the ascent a little less dangerous.

"The mistake amateurs make is that they want to sprint to the finish line," Tipton says. "That's what can get them killed."

When they begin to proceed in a straight line again, Reg lets Wyatt and Hannah get between him and Tipton, telling them that's why they had him play fullback in rugby, so he could be the last line of defense.

A few minutes later, Tipton is the first to reach the ledge. They've reached the final summit. He pulls Hannah up first, then lets out a whoop of triumph. Hannah's hands shake but her grip is iron. She gets up, breathing hard, eyes bright with something fierce.

He reaches down to pull up Wyatt, but suddenly releases Wyatt's hand, as if he's lost his grip.

"What the hell . . . ?" Wyatt shouts, grabbing only for air now.

Wyatt starts to slide back down the rock face, no way to get a handhold or a foothold, feeling as helpless as he ever has in his life.

No way to stop himself.

Or save himself.

Reg is the one who somehow manages to do that.

Somehow he grabs hold of the collar of Wyatt's vest, then

manages to get his arm around Wyatt's neck almost in a choke hold, as he pushes him onto a smaller rock ledge ten feet short of the summit.

"Don't let go," Wyatt pleads to Reg.

"Don't worry," Reg says. "I won't."

Then: "Just move to the side a little so I can get next to you, then we'll go the rest of the way together."

"Okay . . . I guess," Wyatt says.

Reg is reaching for the ledge when his feet give way.

And Reg is the one starting to slip-slide and tumble down rock that feels incredibly slick, incredibly smooth, making it impossible for him to get a grip, find any crevasse or knob. Find anything to stop his downward momentum.

Then Tipton reaches for Reg. Reg's hand finds Tipton's wrist. Tipton clamps down. Reg hauls himself up until his chest is level with the ledge—

And then Tipton hears the click. The Host again. Private.

"Now," The Host says. "Let him go."

Tipton's eyes widen a fraction. He locks up.

Reg sees it.

In that split second—Reg hanging half on, half off the summit—Reg reads Tipton like he's reading a play on a rugby field. Reg gives Tipton the briefest of nods.

Tipton's throat bobs. His grip trembles.

The Host whispers, "Do it, or she's gone."

Tipton's hand opens.

For a heartbeat Reg's eyes stay on Tipton—no surprise, just a grim understanding.

Tipton lunges instantly, horror flooding his face, knowing the choice didn't belong to him the second after he made it. He dives, arm shooting down, fingers clawing air.

He catches nothing.

His glove tears on rock. Skin rips underneath.

Hannah grabs Tipton's belt and yanks him back from the edge, saving him from following Reg into the ravine.

Wyatt sees it all from ten feet below.

"Reg, take *my* hand!" Wyatt yells, reaching as far as he can without falling off the ledge himself.

It's the same way he screamed when he was pulling Alek Andrich out of the hole in the ice that day; the way he did when he needed an extra burst of energy or speed or strength in the Olympics.

The way he had when he'd saved Hannah.

Only there is nothing to stop him.

Nothing to hold on to.

Nothing and no one to stop what is happening to him.

There is another gust of wind, even more powerful than the ones that had come before it.

Wyatt's voice breaks. "REG!"

Hannah starts to cry. And Tipton—Ant Tipton, who has never looked shaken by anything—makes a sound like he's choking. He says, barely audible into the wind: "Oh God."

Reg Drummond is already a disappearing dot in space, swallowed by cloud and distance and the indifferent geometry of a mountain.

One last scream is trapped in his throat this time, as he drops helplessly toward the ravine thousands of feet below him.

Flying at last.

57.

MOUNT WASHINGTON

It is the most horrible moment of Wyatt Jordan's life.

Just like that, Wyatt's helpless to stop what was happening inches away from him before it was too late, his friend gone.

Not just a friend.

Someone who had become Wyatt's hero, starting that day in the icy water of Antarctica.

Reg just fell.

The boy, Rupert, had told him the night after the death of Luca Tommasi that he'd never known anyone who had died. His parents were alive. His grandparents were alive. So were all his aunts and uncles. Rupert felt like Luca had been the first death in his family.

Wyatt felt the same way about Reg.

Reg just fell.

He felt he had come to know Reg Drummond after everything they had been through together. Had known him and respected him and loved everything about him.

He had died in front of Wyatt's eyes.

Wyatt can't make himself look down again.

If he does, he will see Reg falling.

Still trying to process what had just happened, he's just as afraid to look up to where he knows Tipton and Hannah are on the ledge.

Up at the peak.

Wyatt just presses himself to the wall behind him and squeezes his eyes shut, and then he begins to cry when he opens them.

Begins to sob.

And can't stop himself.

Doesn't even try to stop himself.

Wyatt knows it could just as easily have been him falling off what feels like the top of the world, and that thought hits him hard.

But he's not thinking about that.

He's thinking about a good and kind and brave man like Reg Drummond, who had looked out for everybody except himself, even in the final moments of his life.

Reg.

Gone.

Wyatt is crying so hard it's nearly impossible for him to get any of the cold air up here into his lungs.

Feels he might pass out.

Hang on, boy.

Above him, Hannah is crying too—silent tears ripped sideways by wind. Tipton is on his knees at the edge, staring down like he can force gravity to reverse if he stares hard enough.

Then Tipton moves.

He's fast again. Purposeful.

He yanks his earpiece out and throws it so hard it bounces and disappears into nothing. Then he crawls back from the edge, face wrecked, and reaches for Wyatt.

Tipton yells something from up above.

Wyatt can't make it out over the sound of the wind and the terrible sounds coming out of him.

"Nobody's dying up here today," Reg Drummond had said.

Now Reg was gone.

Finally, like it's one more arduous part of the climb, Wyatt gets his breathing under control.

I'm not dying up here, he tells himself.

Tipton's voice is hoarse. "Give me your hand."

Wyatt doesn't move.

Hannah leans over, voice trembling. "Wyatt. Please."

Wyatt forces himself to breathe.

He climbs the last feet on pure hate and grief. He carefully pushes himself off the rock wall, turns to face it, grabs for some schist rock just above him.

Begins moving again, even if it's only a few inches at a time. He tells himself he's going to finish this climb, no matter what.

For Reg.

Eventually he allows himself a look up, just to see how close the ledge is.

He can see Hannah leaning over, Tipton holding on to her from behind, like they're a two-person human chain.

When Wyatt is close enough, Hannah reaches down with her hand.

Hannah's hand locks around his wrist, surprisingly strong. She hauls him up with everything she has.

When Wyatt is finally on the summit ledge, he scrambles away from the edge and collapses, chest heaving.

Tipton is still staring down.

He doesn't look at him. "I tried," Tipton says. It's the first time Wyatt has ever heard him sound human.

Hannah's voice is small. "Ant . . ."

Tipton finally looks at them both.

And what's in his eyes isn't the smug cruelty.

"He's dead," Wyatt whispers.

Tipton swallows hard. "Yes."

Wyatt's mouth opens, but nothing comes out.

Hannah moves closer to Wyatt and puts a hand on his shoulder, steadying him. Like she's steadying herself too.

Wyatt looks down once—just once—because he has to.

He sees only distance and cloud and rock and knowledge.

His hero is gone.

He presses his fist to his mouth, voice breaking.

"Made it, Reg," he says.

58.

MAMMOTH CAVE

They can't spot the boy right away, even as the water keeps carrying them along. The current carries them deeper before it carries them out.

Jack fights to keep his head above water, eyes burning from the cold and the grit and the panic of needing to see.

"The water gets deeper in these caves after storms!" Conner yells. "They must have had some beauts lately for it to rise like this."

"Then he's ahead," Jack yells back, refusing the other option.

"Unless he got pulled under," Conner says.

Jack's eyes search the water up ahead, the cave walls seeming to narrow.

"He can't be that far ahead of us," Jack says. "He didn't go into the water that much before we did."

"Unless he hit something on his way down," Conner says.

Then he asks Jack: "Can the kid swim?"

Jack says, "He made it through Chile."

They see Rupert then.

He's halfway out of the water somehow, maybe a hundred yards ahead of them, clinging to something against a steep bank, like he's hanging from a tree branch.

He spots them at the same moment.

"JACK!" Rupert screams.

"Hang on!" Jack shouts back, and surges toward him.

Jack begins to swim hard toward Rupert, and toward the light. Conner stays with him, his stroke as powerful as Jack's, seemingly impervious to just how cold the water is.

He would have made one damn fine Ranger, Jack thinks.

The nearer they get to Rupert, the more daylight there is in the cave, the opening closer than they thought.

When they finally reach Rupert, they see a nasty bruise on his forehead.

"What happened?" Jack says.

Jack is out of breath. So is Conner. They manage to dig their hands into the slippery bank as a way of stopping themselves, at least for now.

"Hit my bonce on the way down," Rupert says, managing a crooked grin. "But just missed a huge piece of rock that might have finished me."

Conner scans him, "Think you're okay to swim?"

Rupert nods quickly, brave for them. "I'm even better at that than playing center middie," he says.

"Well how about we swim out of here?" Jack says to him. "Now."

As the boy slides into the water next to Jack and Conner, Jack yells "Wait!" to both of them.

Jack's brain finally catches up.

Three splashes.

Not two.

Jack whips his head upstream, squinting into the darkness. Conner sees his face and already knows what Jack's going to say.

"Elena," Jack says.

He searches.

He has been so caught up in the moment, so fixed on the mission of finding Rupert and saving him, he had forgotten about her.

He sees her now.

Sees the blood on the back of her head. Sees her floating toward them, face down, the only movement the water around her. Her hair spreads in the water like dark seaweed, one arm bumping uselessly against the current.

Jack screams her name and begins swimming toward her, so hard his legs cramp.

But when he gets to her, turns her head just slightly, he knows. Her face is slack. Eyes closed. Mouth open.

He says her name, more quietly this time, knowing there will be no response.

"No," Jack says, like the word is a rope he can throw.

Even as he gets an arm around her and begins to pull her toward the bank, stroking with his other arm—Jack knows.

He has seen death too many times as an Army Ranger not to know. He hauls her toward the bank, Conner helping, Rupert clinging to Conner's sleeve and sobbing. They slam Elena onto the muddy rock.

Jack checks for breathing. Nothing. He starts compressions.

Hard.

Fast.

Again.

Again.

Conner counts under his breath, steady, brutal. Rupert cries behind them, the sound small and animal. Jack gives breaths, tasting cave water and blood and regret.

Nothing.

He hits her chest again.

Her body is motionless beneath his hands—no fight, no spark, no insult of life left to argue with.

Jack's throat locks. His vision blurs.

He keeps going anyway, because stopping feels like murder.

Finally, Conner puts a hand on Jack's shoulder.

Jack jerks away, furious. "Don't."

Conner's voice is low. "Jack . . ."

Jack's hands are shaking. His arms feel hollow.

He presses his forehead against Elena's wet hair for a split second, like he can will warmth into her.

Jack can't help himself. He imagines himself sinking, being pulled down to the bottom of this river along with Elena Torres.

And feels he's the one drowning.

59.

MAMMOTH CAVE

Daylight.

Not triumph. Not a reveal. Just the mouth of the cave ahead, a slice of white like an exit wound.

And waiting there—because of course—an inflatable boat with black-clad crew, braced like they've done this drill before. The rescue boat sent by The Host slowly makes its way across the water.

They don't know what the surprise was that The Host had promised.

Jack McHenry doesn't care.

He just sits in the back of the small boat, cradling Elena Torres's body in his arms. Conner and Rupert are in front, facing him. The boy is acting stronger and stronger, even after another shocking tragedy.

Maybe this has become a war.

The boat noses farther into daylight and Jack squints, hating the brightness. Hating that the world looks normal.

Rupert turns back once and looks at Elena, then at Jack. His voice is tiny. "I'm sorry."

Jack can't answer.

It's worse now than anything Jack has ever known—probably because of his surprising feelings for Elena.

He stares at Elena's face. He memorizes it because he's terrified his mind will soften later and he won't be able to hold on to her features. Jack can feel tears on his cheeks, and he can't remember the last time he cried. Maybe not since the death of his mom.

Jack feels the tears on his face and hates himself for every second he didn't say what he felt when he still had someone to say it to.

What was the last thing Elena said to him?

He has been trying to remember but everything in his brain is a terrible jumble, everything is happening so fast.

Then he remembers.

His brain drags up her last words to hurt him.

I'll be right behind you.

She said it before he jumped. She said it, and meant it.

He'd had to get to Rupert before it was too late.

I'll be right behind you.

He hadn't checked once. He hadn't even looked back.

The boat rises out of the water slightly as the pilot increases the speed.

The bumps just make Jack hold on to Elena more tightly.

She really does look peaceful. He brushes wet hair away from her eyes.

He doesn't say *I love you* out loud.

He can't.

But it's there in the way he holds her, in the way he can't stop shaking.

Jack has so many regrets in his life. But he knows in this moment that he will never have a more painful one than this:

Not telling Elena how completely he'd fallen for her before it was too late.

60.

DEATH VALLEY

Jimmy and Carlos Lopez begin to make their way back to Alek and Marcelo. Jimmy hopes they aren't too late. They might be.

Leave me, Alek had said. A command. From a natural leader.

Jimmy and Lopez are moving more slowly than ever, both of them weakening fast, feeling the heat hit with the force of strong wind blowing dead against them.

But there's another reason their progress is so slow, and it has nothing to do with the heat. It's the water they're carrying.

Lopez used the knife to cut open the sealed plastic liner from the supply case they were issued at the start—thick plastic. He twists it into a bag, ties it shut with strips torn from his own shirt, and makes a second smaller pouch from a second liner.

It leaked.

Every few steps Jimmy feels water run down his wrist, and it makes him want to scream.

Because that water is Alek.

That water is Marcelo.

That water is the difference between "we finish" and "they die."

It was Lopez's idea.

Maybe he isn't a gangster, Jimmy thinks. *Just a competitor who never loses.* Either way, Jimmy is glad that Lopez seems to know his way around a desert.

They keep walking.

Jimmy is almost certain his body is on the verge of shock. From the heat, dehydration, blood pressure, sheer exhaustion. His head is spinning. His mouth is so dry it feels like glass.

He's worried about Alek. He can't imagine losing her like this. But he knows it could happen. It's happened before.

Finally, they make it all the way back around the farthest dune. When the mesquite trees finally come into view, Jimmy's hope spikes so hard it makes him dizzy.

Jimmy stops again. But not because of fatigue or dizziness. Not because of the heat.

"They're gone," he says, his voice a raspy whisper. "They were supposed to be here."

"Maybe they kept going," Lopez says, scans the sand. "Or turned back."

"I can't speak for Marcelo," Jimmy says. "But Alek wouldn't turn back. You heard her."

Is this where he left them? Has he become delirious?

Lopez's voice goes colder. "Then she pushed her button."

"She didn't," Jimmy says. He doesn't know if that's faith or denial.

He and Lopez keep walking toward the trees. They need shade themselves, and some rest, if only for a few minutes before they decide what to do next.

In the distance, they can see the tall dunes that were supposed to be the halfway point of this insane journey.

Jimmy stumbles into the shade and drops to a knee, forcing himself to think like a planner. He looks down.

There are prints. Dragged heels. Two sets. Leading away from the trees toward the dunes.

Jimmy's heart kicks.

"They tried to finish," Jimmy whispers.

Lopez nods once. "Then we go."

They leave the shade and head into the open again.

A mile later Jimmy sees something dark against pale sand—fabric tied low on a branch.

Marcelo's shirt. A marker.

Jimmy's relief hits so hard it almost buckles him.

Then he crests a small rise and sees the second shock.

A drone. Low over the sand, circling, patient, camera pointed straight at the trail. Waiting. Watching. The real test isn't "can you survive the heat." It's "what will you do when you realize someone has been steering this the whole time."

The last shock doesn't come for another mile.

61.

THREE NIGHTS LATER
100-MILE WILDERNESS
MAINE

There are now twenty of them left. Out of the thousand invited to Ohio, out of the hundred shipped to the ends of the earth, out of the ones who made it through ice and sand and stone.

Luca Tommasi is dead.

Reg Drummond is dead.

Elena Torres is dead.

Others have pushed their red buttons and departed, sometimes in full view of the other contestants. Sometimes it has happened in the middle of the night, and they're just gone, without a goodbye or a trace, just an empty bed in the morning and that awful understanding: Someone quit in silence.

The survivors have been transported to another estate, this one in a remote section of the Appalachian Trail in Maine, close enough to the 100-Mile Wilderness that the air smells like pine and wet earth. They are told by The Host that they will be flying again tomorrow, to an undisclosed location, for what he promises will be their most perilous mission yet. The Host said this over the speakers with that same bored amusement.

Hannah, Wyatt, Jack, and Rupert have gathered in Alek's cottage before dinner. This is the first chance for them to all be together after the events of the past few days. So much has happened, so much of it terrible. The loss of two more friends has staggered them all.

They've already talked about a different kind of loss—Jimmy Donaldson.

Alek has described the scene in detail: Jimmy showing up with water that saved her life. Then, after the others were stable, Jimmy pushing his red button anyway. Alek had grabbed him, furious and shaking, and demanded to know why. All Jimmy said was: "A conversation for another day."

Then: "Trust me."

Alek was running short on trust after everything she'd been through, but she did. Still. Despite her reservations.

Now the air in the cottage is different—heavier. The conversation has shifted to the names no one wants to say.

"I don't know if I'm ready to talk about Reg," Wyatt says. His voice is thin, like it's coming from a place inside him that's still clinging to the rocks. "I'm not sure I ever will be."

Jack nods once. He looks older than he did in Ohio. "It's good to talk about it," Jack says. "That's something I've learned the hard way. You don't, it rots you from the inside."

Hannah's hands are wrapped around a mug she isn't drinking from. "I keep thinking about him," she says. "He saved me. And then—" She stops. Her throat works. "And then when he needed someone . . ."

Wyatt's eyes flash. "Don't."

She sighs.

"It's not her fault," Alek says fast. "Or yours. Or anybody's. That's the whole sickness of it. We're up there, trying not to die, and someone still . . . still–"

She can't finish.

Wyatt sits up. "You know what I can't help thinking about with Reg? How happy he'd been that day."

Rupert is tucked beside Jack on the sofa. The boy's face has that look grief gives kids: too old, too alert, like his body keeps expecting more bad news. "Luca and Elena and Reg were all so brave," he says. "*Love and were loved, and now we lie.*" Rupert looks almost embarrassed at the words that have just come out of him. "It's a poem. 'In Flanders Fields,'" he explains.

"You're brave, too, kid," Jack says, patting Rupert on the shoulder.

Rupert shakes his head. "I miss them."

"We all do," Alek says.

Then Rupert looks down at his hands like he's reading something invisible and softly quotes more of the poem he had partially recited in the red tent that day:

"To you from failing hands we throw the torch; be yours to hold it high."

No one speaks right away, until Alek raises her arm as high as it will go. One by one they follow. They all do. It's awkward and small and almost ridiculous. Which is why it works.

A knock comes at the door–time to walk to dinner. But before they leave Alek says, "I still can't believe Jimmy left."

Jack stares at the floor. When he speaks, it's flat with certainty, the same certainty he'd had in war when he told men what they needed to hear to keep moving. “I’ll just say what I said before,” Jack says. “He must have had his reasons. Damn good ones. And if he said he’ll explain when the time is right, he will.”

Wyatt doesn’t argue.

Hannah doesn’t either.

But none of them look comforted.

62.

An hour later, after they'd all finished dinner, Jimmy Donaldson comes walking into the estate dining room.

For half a second, nobody moves. Alek's chair scrapes as she stands, shock turning instantly into angry relief. She can't hold back a smile. "You know how to make an exit."

Jack's eyes narrow. "Nobody else who pushed the button ever came back."

"What's going on?" Hannah whispers.

Jimmy looks . . . normal. He's wearing a navy sweatshirt, jeans, sneakers. And an almost sheepish look on his face. He looks as surprised to be there as they are to see him.

He raises both hands, palms out. "Okay," he says. "I deserve that look. I deserve all of it."

Tipton's voice cuts in from another table. "I'm not applauding."

Jimmy doesn't even glance his way. He looks at the twenty of them like he's counting faces, like he's checking who made it, who didn't.

"Listen, we've already pretty much established that I talk too much," he says. "And I'm sure you've all got a bunch of questions about what happened. But none of that matters as much as this: I'm still here for all of you."

"How did you even get here? You pushed your red button," Wyatt says. "I mean, not that we aren't glad to see you."

"Speak for yourself," Tipton says. "Fame has perks."

"I'll bet it does," Lopez says.

Jimmy ignores him. "I can't tell you yet," Jimmy says. "Not in here."

Alek stares at him. "So you just . . . forced your way back in?"

Jimmy's expression hardens. "No. I didn't force anything."

Lopez's voice comes from the other side, amused. "So you're back because they want you back."

"Look, we all know good people who are gone," he says. "I came back to show you I'm still in this. I'm worried that there will be more unless somebody does something. And that somebody has to be me."

"But how?" Jack says.

He shakes his head. "I've got a lot of work to do. Starting with finding out who's really behind these games. I stayed when I thought this was fair, but I've seen you can take care of yourselves. I can't help from in here–"

Tipton smirks. "That's convenient."

Jimmy turns, finally, and looks straight at Tipton. "It's not convenient. It's leverage. They think they can use me."

He faces the room again. "Someone needs to figure out who's actually in charge."

Jack's voice is rough. "We should go with you–"

Jimmy's eyes flick to Jack–just for a moment, like he's seeing Elena in the space beside him.

"Not yet," Jimmy says.

Silence.

Then Wyatt says the simplest thing in the room. "I trust you."

Jimmy exhales, like he didn't realize he'd been holding his breath since he walked in.

"I'm not asking for blind faith," Jimmy says. "I'm asking you to survive long enough for me to do my part." He pauses. "I'm starting with The Host." He looks up at the ceiling, speaking to a hidden microphone—and adds, "And I don't care whether he's listening or not."

Alek leans forward. "What did you learn out there?"

Jimmy keeps it grounded. "This isn't just one sadistic guy with a microphone. There are layers. People with money. People with systems. People who planned contingencies."

"And the world?" Hannah asks. "We all know it's running out of time. What about *The One*?"

"I . . . don't know," Jimmy says earnestly. "I still believe that we need to do something. Anything. We're watching flashpoints stack up. It's not one headline. It's the pattern."

"Enough with the sermons, mate," Tipton says. "What's your point?"

"I came into this thinking the competition was going to be fair," Jimmy says, "but—"

"You're saying it's rigged?" Jack asks.

"I wish I could tell you more," Jimmy says. "That wouldn't be safe for any of you." He looks up at the ceiling again, deliberate. "But if anyone's listening—they should be worried."

A voice answers from the doorway behind them.

"You might be the last person I worry about, Mr. Donaldson."

They all turn at the same moment and see a tall, silver-haired man in a dark suit and open-necked white shirt, standing at the open door at the far end of the room.

"Good evening," he says in a voice they recognize instantly.

The Host.

Wyatt Jordan, addressing no one in particular, says, "The man, the legend, the monster."

63.

Jimmy is silent now.

They all are.

Jimmy finally finds his voice. "Is it worth asking what your name is?"

"I go with Satan," Wyatt says. "Or maybe Lucifer. Serpent. The Tempter."

"Now now," The Host says. "Who raised you? Did no one ever teach you manners, young man?"

Wyatt tries to hold eye contact but buckles first. Looks down. Sits.

The silver-haired man shows no signs of moving farther into the room. He seems comfortable where he is.

"More to the point, my name is of little or no consequence to any of you," he says. "For your purposes, The Host will continue to serve us all just fine. That will do swimmingly."

He chuckles now—that condescending laugh they've come to expect from him, in just about every encounter. Trapped in the same room with him, the sound is even more grating.

"For now, just be pleased that I'm here," The Host says.

"Oh, we are thrilled," Gabrielle Fontaine says. Her thick French accent has a way of underlining the sarcasm, and a few people laugh.

"This would be a good time for you to express some remorse for the latest people your competition killed," Jimmy says.

"Oh, for God's sake," The Host snaps, clearly agitated. "You people are competing for the opportunity to change lives, money aside, and for the better. You all see yourselves as heroes, whether you want to admit that or not. You wouldn't be here if you didn't think you have what it takes. You all volunteered for stakes like these. What did you think you were signing up for—summer camp?"

"These aren't close to being the kinds of tests I suggested," Jimmy says.

"Let's just say," The Host says, "that while we were impressed with your spirit and overall vision, Mr. Donaldson, once contractors were hired, permits bought, and cameras already in the walls—the Board of Directors decided to up the ante. And will continue to do so, as we see fit. But, your early framework was . . . charming."

What "board"? Alek asks herself.

"Here's what I think of you and your board," Jimmy says. "You are nothing more than cowards who enjoy watching people suffer."

"You can call me names until I walk out of here," The Host says. "You've already pushed your red button. If this is too much for anybody else, feel free to do the same."

He moves closer to the tables, stopping to point at Jack, then at Ant Tipton and another former soldier, and then a man named Amos Meyers. Amos was once a celebrated member of an elite military unit from the Eastern Mediterranean Buffer Zone. He had finally mustered out of his military service after a remote-operated bomb had blown up a hospital while he was inside evacuating civilians. He spent three months in a hospital run by the people he was fighting against because of extensive shrapnel wounds. They saved his life, despite him participating in taking so many of theirs.

"You know about war, don't you, Mr. Meyers?" The Host says.

"Unfortunately, yes. More than you could ever imagine," Amos says in a soft voice. "It was my natural state for years."

They can all still see the scarring around his eyes.

"My whole life has been war, even once my military service ended," he continues. "You must know that as well as I do, or I wouldn't be here. I grew up hating the people we called our enemy. And I knew they hated us. That shared hatred informed every day of our lives. All I have known in my life, even as a boy, is that hatred."

Everyone else in the room has fallen silent. Amos Meyers has spoken little about his experiences as a soldier since the red tents in Ohio, choosing mostly to keep to himself. He told Jack McHenry that he's found it useful to not open his mouth unless he has something to say.

But he has opened up here.

He breathes in, steadying. "War is the easiest thing in the world to start," he says. "Hate makes it simple. Hate makes it feel righteous."

The room doesn't interrupt. Even Tipton holds his tongue.

Amos continues, not preaching, not performing–just telling a truth he can't afford to soften. "My wife and children died in a strike two years ago," he says. "Wrong place. Wrong time. That's what people say when they want grief to sound clean."

He looks around, voice still level. "The pain of that led me to do awful things. Awful things to the people who eventually saved my life. But who also did awful things to me. It was then that I saw past the stories and the history and the lies. We kept causing each other the same pain and blaming each other the same ways. Over and over. If there is a true enemy on this planet, it's not a flag. It's not a language. It's the thing inside us that loves watching someone else suffer and calls it justified."

For once, The Host doesn't talk over someone.

"It is the hate that only stops briefly, and then flares up again, that never seems to stop, not really, not for long."

When Amos finishes, The Host nods—performing approval.

"You know better than anyone the heavy cost of winning a war," The Host says.

"You don't win wars," Amos corrects him. "If you are among the fortunate, you merely survive them."

"You see?" The Host says to Jimmy. "This is why you're here. These games are a necessary evil for a planet now seemingly dominated by evil."

"No, you didn't hear a word that man said," Jimmy says. "They're a choice you're making and all it does is keep things as they are."

The Host makes a sweeping gesture that takes in all the tables.

"You all knew the risks involved when you signed on for this competition," he says. "And you've been reminded repeatedly after becoming a part of it. No one forced Reg Drummond to climb. No one pointed a gun at Elena Torres and forced her to make that leap into the water trying to save young Rupert. The reality is that they accepted the same risks you all have. They made choices. Heroic choices, if you insist on that word."

Jack's hands curl into fists under the table.

Jimmy's voice is ice. "Easy to say when you're not the one bleeding."

The Host's smile returns. "And yet you came back."

Jimmy stares at him. "Because I'm going to find out who you are. I think you're just a sadist. And I think the people here who have risked their lives have a right to know exactly who's behind this. Who are these deranged people on the Board of Directors, starting with you?"

The Host chuckles again. "I frankly don't care whether you think of me as a monster or not," he says. "The mission remains the same: To identify *The One*."

"No matter what the cost?" Jimmy says.

"If you believe in *The One*, then yes," The Host says. "That's what real belief looks like."

Somehow Jimmy and the silver-haired man are only a few feet away from each other now.

Jimmy stands firm. "You should warn them I'm coming."

"Good luck with that," The Host says.

He turns and starts to walk toward the door.

Jimmy's voice stops him.

"At the very least these people have a right to know where they're going next," he says.

"To a real war, since you've all lost sight of the stakes," The Host says. "Where some of them will die. It's what happens in war. People die."

64.

The room goes quiet again, all of them staring at the door trying to process what happened since Jimmy arrived. This entire evening, without any advance warning, has turned into one more test. Or one more game, before a much deadlier one if The Host is to be believed.

Jack is the first to break the silence.

He stands so fast his chair almost goes over. He walks out of the dining room, out of the main house, into the night. He doesn't fully know what he's going to do if he catches The Host. He just knows he can't sit still with Elena's name still echoing inside his skull. Loud. Final.

Jack thinks, *He might think we're done here, but I don't.*

Jack's not interested in what the bastard knows about war, if anything. He reminds Jack of an old general sending soldiers into combat. It's why he wants to catch up to him. Wants to bounce him around and let him know that Elena Torres was something more than collateral damage.

A woman that Jack had cared about more than he's willing to admit to himself, even now that she's gone.

Night has fallen while they've been inside. The estate is completely dark. The lake they passed on arrival is a sheet of black glass. Jack stops briefly, the light from the moon obscured by a heavy cloud cover.

But there is no sight of The Host.

Then, perhaps a hundred yards up ahead, there is the silhouette of a tall, slender man on a bluff overlooking the water.

Jack starts after him, jogging at first, then breaking into a full sprint. Jack wants to lower his shoulder and drive him to the ground the way he used to do with ball carriers in high school football when he'd catch one of them from behind. He wants him on the ground. He wants his hands on something real.

But before he can, Jack is the one tackled from behind, his face pushed into the cool, wet, night grass.

Even with the wind knocked out of him he tries to wrestle out from underneath whoever it is on top of him. But his face is shoved back into the grass, even harder this time.

"*Stop*," he hears.

Tipton.

Jack twists enough to see him.

"Get off me," Jack growls.

Tipton doesn't. He shoves Jack's face into the grass harder, like he's pinning down a wild animal.

"What the hell are you doing?" Jack says, trying to get enough leverage with his arms and legs to get Ant Tipton off him.

"You're going to get yourself killed," Tipton says.

"By him?" Jack spits.

Tipton finally eases the pressure–just enough for Jack to breathe. "By them."

Jack blinks, rage stalling for half a second.

Tipton stands, and Jack sees his hand in the moonlight.

"You may *think* you know how ruthless they are. But, actually, I do know, mate."

Tipton reaches down. "Up."

Jack almost refuses just on principle.

Then he takes the hand and lets Tipton haul him to his feet.

"I'm supposed to trust you now?" Jack asks.

"Absolutely not," Tipton snorts.

He still has Jack's hand, and roughly pulls him closer.

"You don't trust anybody. Not Donaldson. Not me. Not the 'board.' And not the rules—the rules don't exist. There's only whatever jurisdiction they rented this week and the outcomes they want to rig. Nothing else."

65.

At breakfast that morning The Host is back to communicating via speaker. "You may make a final call or write letters to friends or loved ones today," he announces. "One final courtesy. They will be mailed once your aircraft is in the air."

They are going to be bused to the Portland International Jetport. There they will board the flight to what was still an undisclosed war zone somewhere.

Alek and Hannah walk back from breakfast hand in hand, boots scuffing gravel, the Maine air damp and cold enough to wake you up even if you haven't slept.

Alek says, "I don't believe Jimmy quit."

Hannah doesn't answer right away.

She's thinking about Death Valley. About the button. About the rule that was supposed to be the only rule that mattered.

Alek continues, because when Alek believes something, she says it like it's a fact. "He's not playing their game anymore. He's playing against The Host."

Hannah finally nods once. "Then he's doing the only rational thing."

She breaks away and runs to her cottage.

She doesn't cry. Knowing how little time she has, she writes to her parents in Germany—both police officers, both trained to see patterns, both trained to ignore melodrama and look for proof.

Dear Mom and Dad:

If you are reading this, then one of two things has happened:

1. *I am dead.*
2. *Someone wants you to believe I am.*

Either way, treat this as evidence, not a goodbye.

You raised me to be precise and observant, so here is what I know and what I need you to do.

What this is: A competition disguised as "philanthropy." The stated goal is to identify The One—*a person who can lead a global movement. The true goal appears to be control. The Host is not alone. There is a "board." There is a way to abandon the game and it is real, but not equally real for all of us.*

A. Do not go to the press first. You will be fed a narrative.

B. Go to your contacts in Bundeskriminalamt and request a quiet inquiry into the flight manifests connected to our movements from Ohio onward. You know how to phrase this so it doesn't trigger bureaucracy.

C. Pull CCTV around any private aviation facilities near the last confirmed locations of "Jimmy Donaldson" (I cannot include certain details here without risking interceptions). Our movements require clearance and equipment you can't fake: tail numbers, secured airfields, armed escorts, fuel, manifests. Look for repeats. Patterns will be the only fingerprints. He is not your target. He is an asset to your investigation. If you find him. He will be useful.

Proof and identifiers:

- *The Host's voice has a particular cadence and a recurring phrase structure ("for the uninitiated," "not to make too fine a point," "delightful"). This is not random. It's a mask.*
- *He uses everything as a deliberate intimidation tactic. He wants us to imagine something untouchable.*
- *No one "sets up" a war zone. You rent it. Security contracts. "Aid" flights. Medical pallets that aren't medical. That isn't "one rich guy." There's a private apparatus that* mimics a state–*contractors, shell charities, and a security conglomerate that can buy access.*

The boring parts are where the truth hides.

Now the part I don't want to write, but I will, because you would hate me if I didn't.

We're about to go on our most dangerous test.

All we know is that we're being sent off to a war, without knowing which one. In the world in which we live, that could be almost anywhere.

You both raised me to be brave and strong. And were always telling me–long before this came along–that I could grow up to change the world.

I just want you to know that if something happens to me, if I never see you again, that I've always loved you the way you loved me.

There's another thing I need to admit, because it feels dishonest to die without saying it.

I care about someone here. Wyatt Jordan. He's not what he seems, but neither am I anymore. I was forced into a choice: him or the game. Another "test." Another way to make us bleed without leaving a mark. I chose the game. I did it to survive. I did it to stay close to what's happening long enough to understand it. It also hurt him, and I'll have to live with that.

If I don't survive: Tell him this wasn't a teenage fantasy. It was real. It was brief. It mattered.

Finally–because you're my parents and you'll want to protect me even from beyond the world–remember: You didn't send me into this. I walked in with my eyes open. I just didn't know how dark the room was.

If I come home, I'll tell you everything.

If I don't, remember me as brave, and I need you to do what you do best.

Justice.

Ich liebe euch

Hannah

GAME #3

66.

UNKNOWN WAR ZONE

At least this time The Host isn't playing games with us, Alek thinks.

They really have been flown into a war zone. They never tell them the name of the country. They land in the middle of the night.

Alek steps down from the transport and feels heat that isn't heat. It's the air itself–thick, metallic, already bruised by smoke. Armed men usher them onto a bus with blacked-out windows. No insignia. No flags. Just rifles and faces that don't invite questions.

They drive for a long time, mostly on back roads. Alek tries to count turns. Tries to keep a map in her head.

Then the first distant boom rolls through the bus like thunder. Not a test, Alek thinks. War.

They finally stop near a building that used to be beautiful–tall spires, old stone, a place tourists would have taken pictures of back when pictures mattered.

Once off the bus they are escorted by armed soldiers, who call themselves the local Defense Force, through an elaborate series of underground tunnels to what they're assured is a bomb shelter as safe and secure as any in the city.

The air changes immediately. Cooler. Wet. Old concrete.

Alek hears the first blast before she feels it. A low concussion that makes dust drift from seams in the ceiling.

A soldier mutters to himself, "Well, suh much fuh de ceasefire."

Hannah notices. This narrows where they could be. Somewhere in South America, most likely. Not that it matters much. The continent has seen a spike in ceasefire collapse. Resource war. Here—two militias fight over water access and the road that brings food in. Nobody here is "winning." They're just lasting.

Then the soldier looks at them and says, "We deh pon de same team now."

Hannah just files it away: Ceasefire was real. Now it's gone.

All of them had been given one last chance to quit before leaving Maine. No one did.

Jack looks around the shelter: reinforced concrete, metal benches, a few medical supplies stacked in crates. It reminds him of the bunkers in the Gulf—places that promised safety right up until they didn't.

"I just hope the ceiling holds when another blast hits," Jack says.

"Don't say that," Rupert whispers.

Jack doesn't mean to scare the kid. He just can't stop his brain from doing what it does: measuring exits, counting bodies, imagining the worst so he's not surprised by it.

"They said this was the most secure shelter in the city," Alek replies.

"And maybe it is," Jack says.

"What does that mean?" Alek asks.

"Sometimes soldiers lie," he says. "Even when they're the good guys."

"So now what?" Alek asks. "We just wait here?"

The speaker in the corner crackles.

The Host.

"Glad you asked, Ms. Andrich."

Tipton's voice cuts in. "Why do I feel like I got drafted into this war?"

"It frankly doesn't matter how you got here, Mr. Tipton," The Host says. "What matters is what you do while you're here."

The shelter shakes again, more violently than before, with another bomb blast. A few people flinch. Someone curses.

When the room is finally quiet again, with no immediate aftershocks, The Host continues:

"There are several hotspots we could have chosen for you. The list is sadly so long, as we all know. But this will do nicely."

Jack's fingers flex like he's ready to swing.

"Try to rest," The Host says. "In a few hours, your job will be saving as many lives as possible before—"

He pauses, indulgent.

"—some of you lose your own."

Alek's stomach turns. He's enjoying this.

The next bomb blast comes then.

This one throws them all off their benches and to the floor, the blast sounding and feeling impossibly close, the whole room feeling like it's been concussed.

The bench Alek was sitting on skids.

The lights flicker once.

The walls and ceiling come crashing down on all of them.

67.

Jack knows the sound.

Not just "bomb." Not just "close."

This is a strike meant to kill people underground.

He's almost certain it's a bomb known as a bunker buster, designed specifically to attack underground shelters like this.

Chunks of concrete and plaster and steel plates rain down on them along with the shrapnel that has penetrated the ceiling. People shouting and diving for cover where there really isn't any. Waiting for it to be over.

They feel the sky is falling on them, even this far underground.

Alek is closest to Jack. He quickly pulls her underneath a nearby metal bench, which becomes a temporary shield. It's enough to deflect at least some of the falling debris until the chaos of the moment is over. Someone yells in pain and then stops yelling.

When the blast finally passes, and Jack thinks it's safe, he crawls tentatively out from under the bench. The silence that follows is worse than the noise had been. His shoulders are hunched. He checks Alek with a quick sweep—blood? limbs? eyes focused? She nods. Alive. He stands into smoke so thick it turns the emergency lights into weak halos.

Across the room, Rupert has both hands on Tipton's shoulder, shoving him sideways. A chunk of concrete lands where Tipton's head was a second before. Tipton stares at Rupert for half a beat, like he doesn't know what to do with the idea that a fourteen-year-old just saved his life.

Jack makes his way through, climbing over some debris nearly as high as his waist, to the middle of the room.

Not a game, he thinks. *Just war.*

All of them different and all the same in the end.

It's then that he sees a huge piece of steel almost completely covering two people on the floor, neither one moving.

As Jack moves toward them, Wyatt's voice tears through the dust.

"HANNAH!"

68.

After Jack and Wyatt both stumble through the debris they see Conner Lynch underneath the plate—half covered, half crushed, his body angled like he tried to become a shield. Hannah is alive beneath him. Her red hair is spread across the floor. She's trying to wriggle out, but she won't yank herself free because she's staring at Conner's face, waiting for it to move.

Conner, who had graduated with honors at West Point and been a football star, and then a rising star in Congress who people thought might be president someday.

His neck was wrong.

No part of him moving.

"Let us help you," Jack says.

"Help him," Hannah says, and her voice is small in a way that scares Alek more than screaming would. "He's not breathing."

It takes both Jack and Wyatt to slowly and painstakingly lift the heavy steel plate.

"Slowly," Jack says to her. "His neck."

When Hannah crawls free, she doesn't stand. She stays on her knees beside Conner and presses two fingers to his throat like she's been taught first aid and knows exactly what she's not going to find.

Jack checks anyway. Pulse. Nothing. Breath. Nothing.

Jack gets close to his face, hoping for any sign—heat, movement, a flutter.

Hannah's right.

He's not breathing.

The way Elena wasn't in the water.

"He can't be dead," Hannah whispers. "He can't be—"

Softly Jack says his name. No response.

Alek kneels beside Hannah and tries to pull her up. Hannah doesn't move. Then her arms go around Alek with sudden force, her body shaking, grief finally allowed out.

"He died for me," Hannah says into Alek's shoulder.

They can't hear her sobs any longer, just see her back rising and falling as Alek rocks her gently back and forth, back and forth.

It's Jack who breaks the terrible silence now that the bombs have stopped falling.

"Selfless service," he says, almost talking to himself. "So that others may live."

69.

The soldiers don't let them stay.

A man with exhausted eyes and a rifle held like it's welded to his hands says, "We move. Now. Not safe here."

They're going to lead them back through the tunnels, then escort them across the city to a temporary barracks that has been set up near the National Museum.

"We have to move," one of them says in crisp English. "This shelter is compromised."

"We're not leaving him," Jack snaps.

The soldier tries to convince the group to go. They promise to come back for the body of Conner Lynch, but the rest of them have to get moving, because it's clear they're defenseless down here if more bombs and missiles hit.

Tipton appears at Jack's shoulder, dusted with ash, eyes hard. "He comes with us," Tipton says.

Jack doesn't like agreeing with Tipton.

But Jack likes leaving Conner less.

"I'll take the legs," Tipton says, voice hard.

Jack takes Conner's arms and they lift him together. They carry him through the broken tunnels and up into dawn.

The bombing has temporarily stopped, though there is no way of knowing for how long. The skies are empty of planes and drones. In the eerie half-light the war looks like it's already over and they've lost, badly. Smoke hangs low. Buildings are cracked open, rooms exposed like dollhouses. Sandbags pile up around doorways that won't matter if the next hit lands right.

They all pass one bombed-out building after another, walk slowly and in formation past what is left of a church that's been here for a thousand years.

They pass a stretcher team and stop. They gently transfer Conner Lynch. Someone covers his face with a blanket and then Jack and Tipton continue to carry him through what is left of the ravaged city.

Hannah walks beside the stretcher and holds Conner's hand, like she can still feel some last warmth through the sheet. Wyatt reaches for her other hand. She lets him take it.

"I'm sorry he died," Wyatt says to her. "But so grateful that he saved you before he did."

As they're finally approaching the National Museum, Jack turns to Ant Tipton.

"Maybe Lynch was supposed to be *The One*," Jack says. "Maybe he was supposed to save the world."

"Hate to admit it, mate," Tipton says. "But you just might be right."

The other pod is waiting for them once they're inside the barracks.

Carlos Lopez, Amos Meyers, Gabrielle Fontaine, and Fumio Hase, player #38, who'd gone from being a multiple winner of the All Japan Karate Championships to being elected governor of Tokyo. Jack had come to like him in the short amount of time they've been together, mostly because the man clearly didn't take crap from anybody.

The rest of them watch Jack and Tipton walk past the sandbags and into the front hall of the barracks, where they set down the stretcher.

Jack pauses and touches the blanket once, just once, like that contact is a promise.

He says to Fumio Hase, "Conner kept telling me he'd always wondered what a war was like."

Jack hates the thought. Hates the irony. Hates how the universe can be cruel and still be clever.

"Now he knows," Jack says.

In the middle of all this, Jack's brain does a cruel thing.

It remembers Elena Torres's voice.

"I'll be right behind you."

He hears it close by, close enough to touch. Spanish flickers in his memory–Elena snapping at her AI opponent, Elena laughing at his stupid jokes, Elena's accent wrapping around words like they were a dance.

"May I have your attention please?" they hear now from the speakers in the barracks lobby, the sound shattering what had been a somber silence.

The Host.

"I want you all to know how truly sorry I am for this latest loss of life," he says. "And also want to acknowledge the bravery that some of you just exhibited in that shelter."

"Do you now." Jack laughs once, without humor.

"I do, whether you believe me or not," The Host says. "Mr. Lynch proved that he was willing to pay the ultimate price to save the life of another. I sincerely honor his courage and selflessness along with the rest of you."

They hear bombs falling in the distance.

"We always hear about people dying for their country," he continues. "Mr. Lynch died for someone else's life. Regardless of creed or background. A noble exchange."

He pauses. Alek's stomach twists.

Then another cluster of explosions hits closer. The lobby shivers. People stumble. Someone drops to a knee.

The Host's voice doesn't change.

"But even in the aftermath of a tragedy like this, you must understand," he continues. "This is why we're all here. This war is the world. Even the ones of you who've fought needed to see this."

Alek steps up. Stares at the speaker like she could stab it with a dagger. "This isn't just tone-deaf, it's cruel."

Jack comes in afterward. "I didn't need a reminder of how cruel the world can be. It's in my head every second of every day."

Hannah next, "This is pointless. This doesn't prove anything. Your entire experiment is a joke."

"You can go ahead and hate me more than ever. But let me repeat: *This is what it is all about.*"

Wyatt sighs. "You're wasting your time. He won't listen. He thinks he's doing the right thing. He thinks he's saving the world. No, he *believes* it. You guys think he's evil, but he thinks he's righteous. Just like Amos was talking about. The blind faith that doing the right evil will net out the right good. Everything in his life told him this was true. He's trying to convince us, recruit us, get us to see the world the way he does. Just like they did to him."

They hear more bombs falling outside then, a cluster of them clearly hitting close by, the force enough to knock some of them back into the wall and some to the ground.

"He's right about one thing. You'll all see the truth for yourselves. Now all of you do what Conner Lynch just did," The Host says. "Go save some lives."

70.

They move tentatively outside onto Church Street. The damage is somehow even worse now than it had been before. The ground is cratered like the moon. Glass crunches under their boots. Smoke curls from a building that used to be a shop, a home, a life. Bodies lie on rubble across the street where a library must have been. People are screaming somewhere ahead.

For now, the only bombs they hear are being dropped to the east, the sound of them slowly diminishing until the streets around them are again quiet.

For now.

A young soldier—barely older than Rupert—touches his earpiece, listens, then looks at Jack.

"Last night and this morning," the young soldier says to Jack, "this is the worst day of the war." He looks back at the street in front of them. "They want to finish us off today."

In the distance they can see adults frantically using their hands to dig through more debris up ahead, clearly trying to find those who might be buried but still alive.

"I must go now," the young soldier says to Jack. "Tanks coming now, couple of miles." Then he nods once and jogs away.

"Hey!" Jack says.

Jack salutes him without thinking.

The kid blinks like he's not used to being seen as a person.

Jack thinks: *I was that kid once.*

The kid stops, finger to his earpiece again. "Your boss," he says, and spits the word like it tastes wrong. "He's in my radio—rebroadcasting on our frequency. Someone gave him access. Someone high . . . He says your job is getting survivors to the public hospital. Not far."

He rattles off directions, fast.

They huddle and discuss the strategy. Jack, Tipton, Wyatt, Hannah, Alek, Rupert are still one team, along with Marcelo Oliveira. The other team remains Amos Meyers, Zhi Lin, Carlos Lopez, Gabrielle Fontaine, Fumio Hase.

They agree to split up.

The bombing still has not resumed in the part of the city between the museum and the hospital, half the buildings blackened by fire or already crushed to rubble. No matter which way any of them look, the devastation is so sad.

"Where do we even start?" Alek asks.

"By looking for the living," Jack says. "You and your mother did that after bombings in your city—"

"—More than I care to remember," she cuts in.

Jack stares at her for a moment.

"You're tougher than any of us," he says.

They turn a corner now and see an apartment building halfway up the block, fire already engulfing the bottom floors. One more place about to come crashing down. And soon.

They are running toward it when they hear the sound of drones above them. Jack's blood goes cold. These are not part of the war. They're part of what their sick Host calls a game.

The drones are followed by a thunderclap of noise that Jack and Tipton and Alek recognize all too well, the whistling sound that means more bombs are about to hit.

"COVER!" Jack shouts, trying to be heard over the bombs.

They all dive to the ground, some throwing themselves into the massive craters in the street. Hannah lands on top of Rupert, shielding him the way Conner shielded her.

They stay down, waiting for this latest wave of bombing to be over, looking up enough to see what had been a convenience store, less than fifty yards away, now leveled, completely destroyed in the blink of an eye.

The shockwave slaps them sideways.

Dust fills the air.

And when the noise finally thins, Hannah twists around, wild-eyed, scanning through smoke.

"Where's Wyatt?!" she screams.

71.

"Wyatt!" she yells. "Wyatt!"

Alek points toward the only apartment building still standing on the corner—barely standing—its windows vomiting black smoke, flames licking up the walls like they're climbing for oxygen.

"He went in there," Hannah says.

Jack grabs her shoulder. "We don't know that."

"We do," Hannah snaps, and that's new. Hannah Wagner doesn't snap. She takes a deep breath, fighting for composure. She is usually the calmest of them all.

"He could be dead," Hannah says.

"We don't even know if he's in there," Jack says.

Alek steps forward, taking over. "Spread out. Now. Find him. Before the bombers come back."

Then a voice cuts through the crackle of fire.

"UP HERE!"

Wyatt is on a third-floor terrace, framed by flame, arms stretched out for balance. For one stupid second he looks like a statue. Then they see what he's doing. He's not showing off or fooling around. He's shielding someone behind him.

"There's a kid inside," Wyatt yells down to them. "Don't try to come in. This whole place is about to go!"

He's right. Black smoke is pouring through the open door

behind him, flames spitting out of the windows on both sides of the terrace. Even on the ground, Alek and Hannah feel like they are standing in front of a blast furnace.

Alek takes one step toward the door and Jack yanks her back hard. Because the building makes a sound. A deep, groaning, structural sound. The kind that comes right before collapse.

When the smoke clears for a moment, Wyatt has disappeared again.

72.

"I'm going in," Alek announces. She pauses and seems to consider her next words carefully. "I saved my mother from a fire like this."

Hannah grabs her arm and holds on tight. "Alek, there's no time for that." Alek stares at her like she's lost her mind.

"But we have to do something before the whole building comes down with Wyatt in it!" Alek shouts.

"And we're going to," Hannah says. "I've got an idea."

Wyatt reappears on the terrace, no longer alone. Through the smoke, they can see he's holding a small blond girl in his arms. Even from three floors below, they can see that the girl is clearly unconscious.

Hannah's eyes lock in. She goes cold, in the best way. Like a surgeon. Like a scientist. "Good," Hannah says, her voice calm. "The girl is dry."

"I don't understand," Alek says.

"Wyatt's smart," Hannah says, eyes fixed on Wyatt and the girl. "People think you help by putting them in a bathtub or shower in a fire like this. But the water makes asphyxiation more likely."

Wyatt looks down, desperate.

"We're going to jump!" he yells. "It's our only chance!"

"Not yet!" Hannah yells back.

Hannah turns to the others.

"We have to get them off that terrace. Or they're both going to die."

There's more smoke, more heat driving back the rescuers on the ground. Hannah is staring intently at the building, making a motion, counting with an index finger.

"Three stories," she says. "Thirty feet. Maybe thirty-five." She points—sharp, commanding.

Alek thinks: *In the middle of all this insanity, it's like she's solving a physics problem.*

"You three are the strongest," she says, pointing at Jack, Tipton, and Marcelo. "Come with me. Now."

They don't argue. They move. They follow her to a point underneath the terrace. Hannah looks up again. Next, she's using an index finger, drawing a line from the terrace to the ground. She looks around.

Hannah sprints to a wrecked storefront and yanks down a thick canvas awning that's half torn loose. It's heavy, grimy, stiff with soot.

"Perfect," she says.

Tipton blinks. "What the hell is that going to do?"

"It's going to keep them alive," Hannah says.

She drags the canvas into the street and barks orders like she's been doing this her whole life.

"Four corners. Hands through the folds. Wrap it. Don't grip flat—grip rolled. Lock your elbows. Bend your knees on impact."

Alek and Rupert rush in, forming a human brace line behind the men, forearms hooked together, backs against a parked vehicle.

She barks orders at the men: "You all sit close together. This spot. Right here. Alek and Rupert and I will form a safety chain with our arms."

They're all in position when they hear another explosion from the top floor and see the windows framing the terrace blow out, pressure punching outward.

The terrace is fully on fire, about to collapse underneath Wyatt and the little girl, any second could be the last.

Wyatt looks down one last time.

Hannah shouts, "NOW!"

Wyatt jumps. Not straight down. Out and away, like he knows if he clips the wall he's dead. He keeps the girl tight against his chest.

The next thing they hear is him yelling at the top of his lungs:

"GERONIMO!"

73.

The canvas grabs them hard, steals their breath.

A brutal, snapping impact that drives everyone down two inches, knees buckling, arms burning. But it holds. They hold.

Hannah is in Wyatt's face instantly, hands on his shoulders, eyes locked. "You alive?" she demands.

Wyatt sucks in air like he's never owned oxygen before. "Yeah."

Alek exhales so hard it almost turns into a sob.

Tipton shakes out his hands like they're on fire. "That was insane."

Marcelo grins through sweat. "That was teamwork."

Wyatt looks at Hannah like he's seeing her for the first time.

"We got you," Hannah says.

"Thank you doesn't seem to quite cover it," he replies.

He looks down at the girl.

"She alive?"

Hannah presses two fingers to the child's neck, then leans close to her mouth.

"She's breathing."

Her plan worked. Maybe even better than she thought it could. Their impromptu rescue team did just enough to break the fall. Wyatt and the little girl have survived, apparently without serious injury. Wyatt was able to protect the girl with his arms even as he tucked and rolled and absorbed most of the shock of his landing.

"Nice move there at the end," Tipton says.

Wyatt grins. "My high school football coach made us take a gymnastics class to improve our agility," he says. "And to know how to fall. Always thought it was silly."

When they're all on their feet again, Hannah says to Wyatt, "I was going to tell you to drop the girl first. To make it easier on everybody down here."

Wyatt still has the girl cradled in his arms. Her eyes are closed, passed out after everything that happened.

"I wasn't letting go of her," Wyatt says, finally smiling at Hannah.

They are all in the middle of the street now. It's less than a minute since Wyatt jumped to safety.

Hannah's voice stays steady, but her eyes don't.

"Next time," she says, "you don't vanish into a burning building without telling us your plan."

Wyatt almost laughs. "I didn't have a plan."

"That's the problem," Hannah says.

He turns and looks back at the terrace—just as it comes crashing to the ground. It collapses with a roar, dumping fire and debris into the street in a shower of sparks. Wyatt flinches. Then he looks back at Hannah.

"How did you know the fall wouldn't kill us?" Wyatt asks.

"Basic physics," she says. "Of course, one more floor and we would have had a problem. By the way? *Geronimo?*"

"Couldn't help myself," he says.

"Stupid," Hannah says. "But funny . . ." She pauses and adds, "Well, now it's funny."

There is a terrible ending for the building, then, what sounds like one more bomb falling as all the structural materials explode and crumble to the ground.

They stand and watch, transfixed, moving even farther from the heat and smoke; from the sheer force of the destruction.

Alek is the one who breaks the silence.

“What were you thinking, running into a burning building like that?” she asks Wyatt.

He grins at her. “Hey, I’m a New Yorker,” he says. “Kind of our thing.”

“She’s being serious, Wyatt,” Hannah says.

Wyatt looks at the girl in his arms, then at the ruined street.

His voice drops. “This is why I’m here.”

Not for the money. Not for the glory. For this.

Alek studies him and thinks Wyatt looks very grown-up right now. He looks like a winner.

“It’s why we’re all here,” he says. “I’m proud of that.”

He looks up at them and a wide grin breaks through again—because he can’t help himself. “And you have to admit,” he says, “that was kind of cool.”

“Okay, that’s enough,” Hannah says.

But she doesn’t let go of his sleeve.

74.

Wyatt carries the young girl most of the way to the public hospital. When he occasionally gets too tired and has to stop, Jack wordlessly lets him hand the girl over. Hannah stays close and tells her not to worry, it's going to be okay.

"I don't know if you can understand me," Hannah says, "but you couldn't be in better hands."

They are gradually making their way through the streets. Sirens wail somewhere, closer now.

As they make their way up to the hospital's entrance, they see that members of the other group have beaten them here. Carlos Lopez's forehead is bandaged. One eye is completely swollen shut. Lin Zhi holds the door open for Wyatt and the girl. No one stops to talk. They move her inside like she's the last fragile thing left in the world.

Lopez starts to say something, but Jack and Alek and Wyatt push him aside, walk past him and into the triage unit that the lobby has become: gurneys, bloodstained sheets, doctors shouting, volunteers running.

"If this little girl didn't die in that fire," Alek says, "there is no way she's dying on us now."

A white-bearded doctor takes the girl from Jack, speaking a lilting English that bends around the words. Wyatt forces himself to explain.

"Found her in a bathroom," he says. "Parents . . . in the living room."

He doesn't say what he saw. He doesn't need to.

The doctor grips Wyatt's shoulder—firm, grateful—and nods. "She goin' be fine," the doctor says.

The doctor affectionately places the girl on a gurney and pushes her through double doors.

"We did it," Wyatt whispers to Alek.

"You did it," Alek says quietly.

"No, we did," Wyatt says. "We worked together when it mattered."

Then Alek sees Hannah standing just inside the entrance. She's staring down at something on the floor of the lobby. Her hand is covering her mouth.

After all the poise she had shown as they teamed up to save Wyatt and the girl, after the way she had calmly organized the team, Hannah is crying.

Jack is next to Hannah, slowly shaking his head, unable to hide his grief. It's not like Jack, who usually hides everything so well.

When Alek gets to them, she sees what they're seeing:

On the floor, on an Army blanket, lies Amos Meyers. Someone has had the good grace to fold his weathered hands across his chest. An orderly appears, reaches down, and pulls the blanket all the way over Amos's face.

Next to him is the young local soldier Jack saluted earlier. He's not much older than Hannah is. What a waste of a life.

Zhi walks up behind Alek. "Lopez tried to tell you. When you rushed past him."

"What happened?" she responds.

Zhi recounts their arrival. They all came into the hospital lobby much the same way. It wasn't just triage then, as a wave of people running from the violence had flooded in—it was a stampede. A second wave of civilians came after them, pushed in as a nurse tried to unsuccessfully shout order into the chaos.

Amos saw and heard it first. Not the screaming. Not the blood. The small, wrong sound under it all—a dull clink on tile. A metal cylinder rolling.

A grenade.

Some of the opposing forces must have chased the people down and didn't care it was a hospital. For half a second, nobody understood what they were looking at. A mother froze. A little boy just stared at it like it was a toy.

Amos didn't freeze.

He was already across the lobby before anyone could even shout. He kicked the grenade toward the thickest wall he could find—behind an overturned gurney—and threw himself down over the boy and the mother, shoulder to shoulder with two orderlies who reacted a heartbeat after he did.

He didn't look up.

He just said, almost calmly, "Down." Everyone took cover, even those on the team in the room. Zhi among them.

The blast didn't tear the building apart. Objectively and relatively, it was minor. But it was all pressure and shrapnel in a crowded room. When the smoke cleared, the boy coughed—alive. The mother started screaming—alive.

And Amos was lying on his back, eyes open, not seeing. Blood soaking through his shirt in a spreading, unstoppable bloom. By the time Zhi got to him, it was too late.

Jack salutes them both one last time. He does it fast, like if he holds the salute too long, he'll break apart. Then he turns and walks out before anyone can see what's in his eyes.

Alek leaves Zhi and steps closer to Hannah.

And Hannah—who held it together through fire and falling and screaming—finally cracks. Alek holds her as her tears come, hot and unstoppable. It hits Alek in the ribs—same grief, different uniform. When her sister died . . . it was all too much.

It isn't just the horror.

It's the cost.

75.

The Host sits in front of a monitor, first watching scenes from the war the street cameras are providing him. Then secret videos taken inside the public hospital. Faces he recognizes now—because he's made it his job to recognize them.

He's seen Hannah Wagner turning panic into a plan. Wyatt Jordan hand the girl they've just saved over to the doctors. Jack McHenry saluting two dead soldiers like it's the only language he trusts. He's seen the anguish when they realized one of the fallen was their own.

The Host has felt some of that anguish himself.

He doesn't smile. He doesn't celebrate. He sits very still. Because this is the point.

Not the stunts. Not the spectacle.

The consequence.

He takes no joy in this, nor any relief that so many of them have made it to the hospital alive.

They came here believing they could change the world.

Now they've seen what the world actually looks like when it breaks. *Leadership isn't speeches*, The Host thinks. *It's what you do when it's burning.*

It has to be this way.

He has told them, will keep telling them, that one of the reasons they were brought here was to experience pain like this—and loss like this—firsthand.

He watches Jack walk out. Watches Hannah cry.

Good, he thinks. Not because he enjoys the pain. Because pain is the only teacher none of them can ignore.

As challenging as honesty is for him, he has at least been honest about that.

He knows there is more suffering to come, sooner rather than later, when they realize things are about to get worse.

None of them might want to hear this, but the fact is that there is no other way to complete the mission. It is for their own good, whether they want to hear that or not. They need to fear for their lives and somehow overcome that fear. Find a way, if they can, to rise above horrors like they've witnessed today. And will continue to witness.

It is why he has actually been pleased today to witness the leadership and the teamwork exhibited in saving a little girl whose name they still might not know.

It had been a complete—and inspiring—collaboration.

That happens to be a quality that will be essential in leading people out of the darkness—with his able assistance, of course—no matter who ends up being *The One*.

Something else they might not want to hear?

That person will also need to be as ruthless. With true greatness always comes that sort of ruthlessness. It's part of why he was drawn to Jimmy Donaldson in the first place. He thought Jimmy understood what it takes for a person to succeed. He was wrong.

He shifts his attention back to the screen showing the chaos and movement and even panic in the lobby of the hospital.

He leans closer to the monitor, listening to the chaos in the lobby. And he knows what comes next. Not a bigger explosion. Not a louder bomb.

A choice.

A choice that will split them.

And for the first time since this day began, The Host feels something that surprises even him. Not pity. Not guilt. Fear.

Because he can see it now, clear as a target in a scope:

One of them is starting to become *The One.*

76.

When the doctor is back in the lobby, he waves Alek over, and the two have a lengthy conversation. They talk fast, close, trying to hear each other over the sirens and the crying and the constant churn of bodies being dragged in.

When they finish, Alek says to Wyatt, “They’ve got her in one of the operating rooms. Performing what’s known as a bronchoscopy, basically looking down her airway with a scope, checking for smoke damage. And checking to see if she suffered any internal injuries when the two of you . . . landed.”

“I didn’t mean to hurt her, I—”

“No one thinks that,” Alek says. “You saved her.”

Wyatt swallows. “Her name?”

Alek points toward the double doors. “Jelena.”

“Jelena . . . please be okay,” Wyatt says. “She’s just a kid.”

Alek puts a hand on his shoulder. She hasn’t just seen uncommon valor from Wyatt today, it’s the same valor she’d seen from him in the water in Antarctica, when Hannah was the one he was trying to save. And she’d seen something else today: Wyatt’s great heart.

He looks around the lobby, finally seeing what he hadn’t let himself see before. Kids. Too many kids. On stretchers. On blankets. In arms.

Alek touches his shoulder. “Look around, Wyatt,” she says. “There are a lot of Jelenas in here.”

Wyatt’s voice is rough. “This is insane.”

Alek’s face hardens, and it isn’t anger—it’s memory.

She leans closer. “War and conflict don’t care how old you are. If it did . . . my sister would still be alive.”

Wyatt walks away from her, his breathing still painful from the fall, trying to find a patch of the lobby that isn’t overrun.

So his back is to the door when it’s flung open again and Zhi and Carlos come running in, Gabrielle and Fumio behind them, all screaming on top of the others as they scramble to get themselves and everyone else to safety.

“Get down!”

“Take cover!”

“They’re back, the soldiers are back!”

Wyatt locks eyes with Zhi when he yells, “GRENADE!”

Wyatt whirls—

He sees it. A small dark cylinder skittering across tile.

Time does that awful stretching thing.

And then, a flash. A concussion that punches the breath out of everyone at once. And something small goes flying across the lobby, weightless and wrong.

Another kid the war doesn’t care about being blown across the lobby of the public hospital:

Rupert Chadwick.

77.

Ant Tipton isn't in the lobby when it happens.

He isn't even inside.

He's around the corner, in the narrow strip of street that still smells like smoke and diesel and hot stone, catching thirty seconds of air. Stolen. A few seconds of the closest thing to peace.

He sees the soldiers in uniforms and gear different than he's seen so far running from the hospital but doesn't think much of it. They don't see him. He pretends not to see them.

He has one hand braced on the wall, head down, trying to steady his breathing.

"I'm fine," he whispers to himself.

If he feels it, he breaks. He starts thinking about a mountain. A ledge. A man falling.

He lets out a long sigh when his burner phone rings. He knows who's calling. Only one other person has this number. As far as Tipton knows, he's the only one of the competitors with a phone like it.

He answers on the first ring.

"Was that a grenade?" Tipton asks.

"Unfortunately."

"Did you have anything to do with it?"

"If I did, Mr. Tipton," The Host says, "you'd already know."

"Why should I believe you?"

"Because you like believing you still have choices," The Host says. "It lets you sleep."

Tipton looks up and scans the street. No one watching. No one close enough to hear. Not wanting any of the others to spot him talking on the phone if they've realized he's not in the hospital and have come looking for him.

"I could've been in there," Tipton snaps.

"But you weren't," The Host says.

Tipton goes cold. He understands that line. It isn't comfort. It's ownership.

Tipton walks the fifty yards to the corner and peers around it. He knows he must get back before McHenry or one of the others come looking for him.

"When are you getting us out of here, by the way?" he asks.

"When the darkness comes to the edge of town, as someone once sang," The Host says.

"If the opposing forces don't get to us first," Tipton says.

"Your problem at the moment, I'm afraid," The Host says. "Not mine."

Tipton lowers his voice. "You told me we had an understanding."

"We do," The Host says. "And you're still useful. That's the good news." Tipton's hand tightens around the phone until his knuckles whiten.

"And the bad news?" Tipton asks.

Nothing.

Tipton says, "I need to get back to the hospital before they're all wondering where I am."

The Host's voice stays even.

"The bad news is that when you walk back into that hospital, you're going to find out that one of you didn't make it."

Tipton swallows.

He forces the next words out like they're easy.

"Who?"

"You'll see," The Host says. "And you'll remember what I told you from the beginning."

Tipton's eyes flick to the hospital entrance.

"What?" he says.

"You don't get to be a hero, Ant," The Host replies. "You get to be what I need."

The line goes dead.

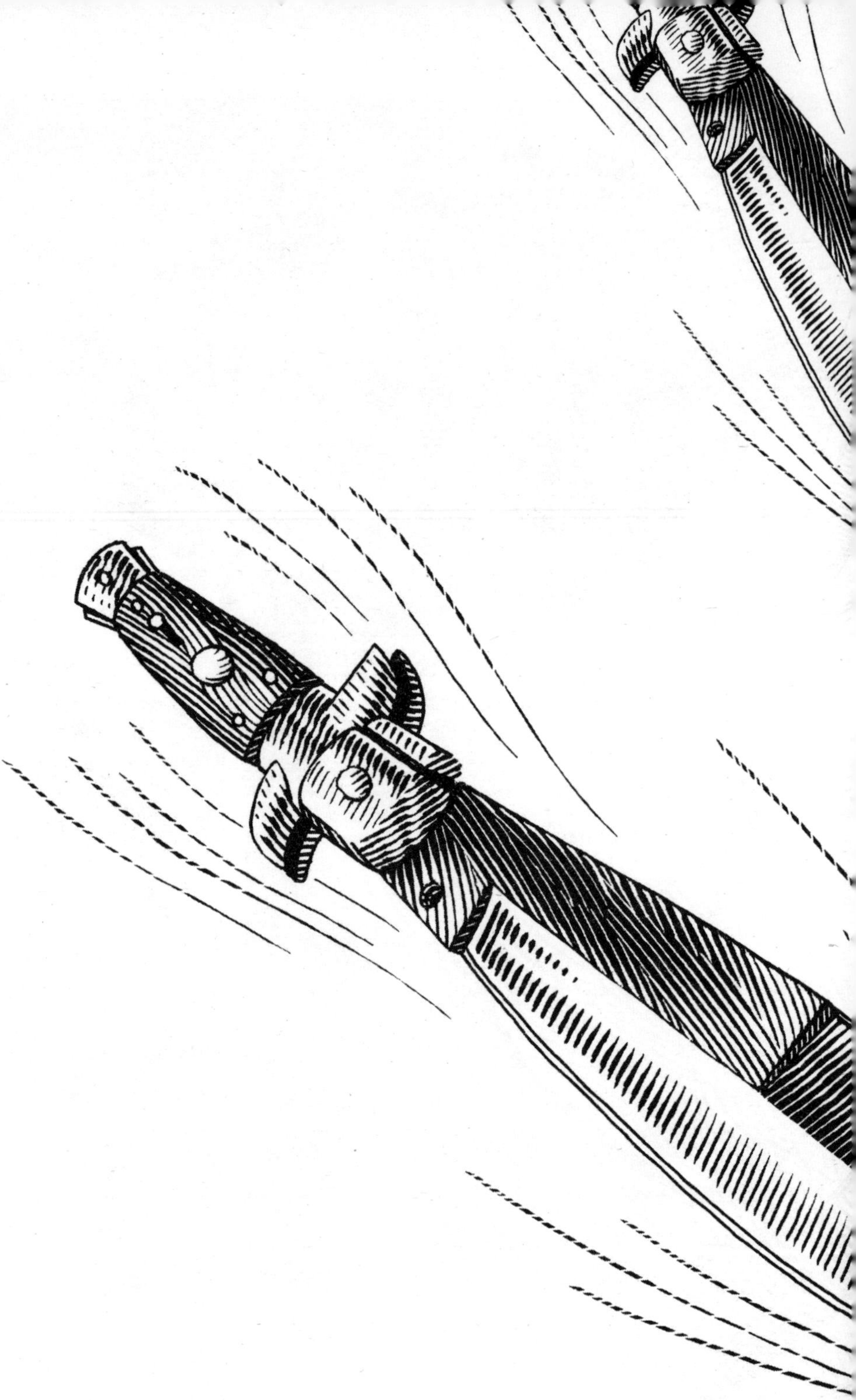

GAME #4

NO PRISONERS

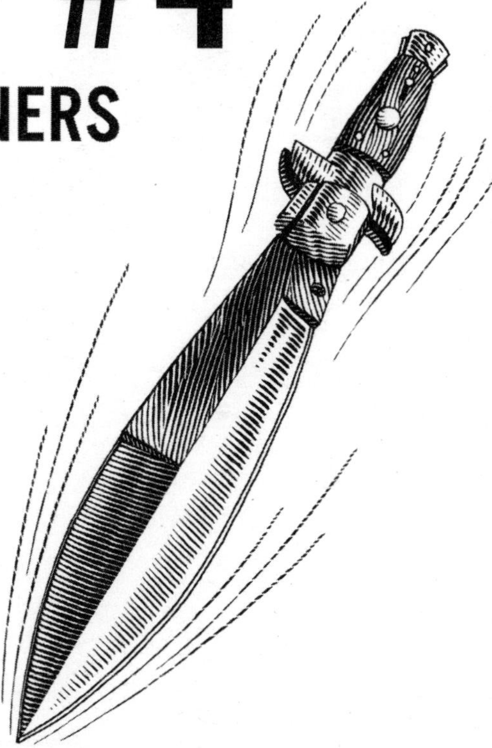

78.

Jimmy Donaldson is in London.

Normally he wouldn't, but right now, he hates that sentence. Because it means he's far away from the people he's grown to care about. And he's getting closer to the people he's trying to take down.

He's moved through a chain of doors that seem to lead only to more doors and no answers. He's traveled from Maine to Washington, DC, where a DHS analyst slid him one file: shipping manifests for "medical" cargo tied to the games. The pallets were the right size for IVs and body bags. Also for restraint rigs and AR housings. Same supplier. Same signature. The trail ended in NYC. Where the money trail sent him to London.

The lead in London has a solid connection to the estate of the reclusive billionaire Gavin Hillshire. In the later stages of his life, Hillshire started a blog that railed endlessly about the Apocalypse, and how world leaders weren't doing enough to sound deafening alarms about it.

The lead ties the manifests to Hillshire's estate–his holding companies, his air charter accounts, and one "charitable foundation" that doesn't treat patients. It moves cargo.

Jimmy feels he's as close as he's come yet to discovering the identity of The Host, as well as the mysterious Board of Directors that controls the game.

Every meeting has been in a place with too much noise and too many exits. Every person has said the same thing in a different way: This isn't one man. This is a group. A board. A network. A machine. And Jimmy is not stupid. He knows machines don't care about the names of the people they crush.

But he cares.

Luca.

Elena.

Reg.

And now—others. He doesn't have a scoreboard anymore. He doesn't have a red button hanging from his neck. He has something worse.

He's running out of time.

He knows there are more he doesn't know about. Jimmy hoped for the best but feared the worst. When he'd left his friends in a dining room in Maine, they were about to be shipped off to a war zone.

Jimmy is no longer competing to be *The One*, but the stakes here in London feel even more urgent. He's going to find out who's behind this competition; find out the identity of The Host, whom he holds responsible for many deaths.

Now someone with insider knowledge of the board has reached out, indicating he has useful answers to the questions Jimmy has been asking. He's more confident than ever he can find out how the original vision for a competition of this scale—this magnitude—has gotten so distorted.

Jimmy is as terrified as anyone by what he sees as a dangerous pre-dystopian world. Drastic measures are required. It's why he signed on in the first place, willing to help in any way possible.

The quest to identify *The One* was new and bold and necessary. Maybe he was naïve to believe in it. But Jimmy still considers himself an idealist. He believes that one great man or woman is capable of changing the course of history, the same way great leaders always have in moments of crisis for civilization.

Maybe even a group of great men and women. Maybe it wasn't down to one person . . . but a movement, growing until it hit a crescendo, a wave so strong it cannot be ignored.

Before that can happen, Jimmy knows he has to do everything in his power to regain control of these games. That has to happen. He doesn't want anyone else to die. Not one person. Not even Ant Tipton.

He runs.

He knows he can't stop.

Or let himself be stopped.

He's certain he's being watched. He felt it in New York. He's certain he's been followed to London. He's already changed hotels once, using fake names at both. But he doesn't care if he's in danger. If the others can put their lives on the line, so can he.

He's doing a lot more than scrambling international phone calls now.

Jimmy has taken a taxi from his new hotel in Kensington, switched to a train, gotten off at the Green Park station, eventually walked across St. James's Park. Jimmy constantly looks over his shoulder to see if he has picked up the tail he'd spotted back in New York.

He walks. He loops twice around a block for no reason except to see if anyone loops with him. No one does. That doesn't mean he's safe. It means whoever's following him is good.

Jimmy makes his way past Buckingham Palace until he arrives at a pub off Caxton Street called the Stewart Arms. Good crowd at the bar, pints and shots in front of them, watching a Premier League soccer game. A place where nobody expects to see MrBeast.

Alek and Hannah, Jack and Wyatt—they talked all the time about how far they'd come. They have no idea how far Jimmy has come.

Alone in a corner a man is crouched over a beer, where he'd said he'd be in the encrypted message Jimmy had received an hour ago. A New York Yankees baseball cap is pulled down so low Jimmy's surprised he can even see.

Before walking over to him, Jimmy surveys the bar one last time. He's trying to see if anyone has shown an unusual interest in his entrance. No one has. It's an older crowd. If the crowd was younger, Jimmy would be mobbed by now.

No one looks over at him as a goal is scored. A loud cheer erupts from the well-lubricated patrons.

Jimmy walks to the table. He taps the man on his shoulder, clearly startling him.

"You can't be sneaking up on people that way!" the man hisses.

Jimmy stares down at the man's face, almost not believing what he's seeing. He knows that voice. He knows that posture.

He knows that cap.

"*You?*" he whispers.

79.

Hours later, the survivors are extracted from the city under darkness and noise and orders barked in languages none of them fully understand. They are moved fast. Too fast to grieve properly. Too fast to even breathe. The Host's people—soldiers, guards, shadows—push them through a corridor of destruction to a waiting transport. They are airlifted out that night to Brazil, then flown to Florence. From there they will be transported by bus to another estate, this one in the hills of Tuscany.

There are now twelve left out of the original one thousand.

By the grace of God—or dumb luck, or both—Rupert Chadwick is still one of them.

Somehow, he survived the grenade blast.

He's alive.

Because the blast happened right inside the hospital, the doctors had gotten him into surgery almost immediately. In the process they saved his right eye and repaired the severe damage to his spleen, and to a collapsed lung.

When the boy is out of surgery and awake, he's pale as paper and shaking, his voice barely more than air. As soon as he's allowed to have visitors, Alek and Hannah and Wyatt and Jack visit him in the private room The Host arranged for the boy, a rare example of generosity.

Maybe the only one they've seen so far.

The doctor has already informed Rupert how long his rehabilitation is going to take. Alek is the one to tell him that the next trip Rupert will be taking is home to England.

As lucky as the boy knows he is—as lucky as they all are to be alive—he is the last of them to cry.

"Hey," Jack says, standing at the foot of the bed like he's afraid to get too close, like he's afraid the world will take the boy just for touching him.

Rupert's eyes are glassy. One is bandaged.

He whispers, "Please . . . take me with you."

They can see how painful it is for him to get out even a few words at a time.

Alek's throat tightens. She takes his hand carefully, like it might break.

"We can't," she says. "Not this time."

They know how tough this fourteen-year-old is by now. How much rope he has in him, as Jack likes to say.

Rupert's jaw trembles. He hates crying in front of people. They all know that about him now.

"They say . . . months," Alek adds softly. "You need real recovery. Real doctors. A real bed."

Rupert stares at the ceiling like he's bargaining with it.

"I can heal . . . at the next place," he whispers. "Wherever you go. I can stay out of the way."

Wyatt steps closer. His ribs still ache every time he breathes, but he doesn't let it show. "You're never in the way," Wyatt says. "You're family."

Rupert looks at Hannah like he needs to hear it from her.

"And you will be a part of our family forever," Hannah says. "I keep telling Alek that she's the sister I never had. But you've become the little brother I never had." She squeezes his hand. "And before you get mad—yeah. Little."

Rupert loses the fight and a tear slips out.

"Promise me," he whispers. "You'll tell me you're okay."

Alek doesn't hesitate.

"Promise," she says.

"Don't heal too quickly, dude," Wyatt says. "I have a feeling that the tests we're going to face down the road aren't going to get any easier. You just need to go home and get better."

He looks over at Jack. They see the same pleading in his eyes they'd seen in Hannah's earlier when she realized that Conner had died saving her.

Jack clears his throat hard. His voice is rough.

"I'm the one who's really going to suffer here," Jack says from where he's standing at the end of his bed. "I'm the one about to lose the best wingman I've ever had."

"Even in the Army?" Rupert asks.

Jack nods once. "Even there."

The doctor pokes his head in and says that Rupert needs to rest.

After the doctor has left, and more tears have been shed by everyone in the hospital room as their goodbyes are said, Alek and Hannah, Wyatt and Jack, head for the door. At the threshold, Rupert whispers one more thing:

"Don't forget me."

Alek and Hannah run back, both sides of his bed, and each one kisses his cheeks, turning his face the color of an apple.

"Never," Alek says.

* * *

Several hours later, in her new cottage in Tuscany, Alek hears a ping from one of the cell phones they've all been given on their arrival at the Tuscan estate; these are phones The Host has told them can be used to call family and loved ones.

She goes into the living room, where she'd left the phone on the coffee table, and sees the incoming text.

Go outside.

She switches the phone to silent mode and walks out of the back door of the cottage, keeps going until she is deep into the wooded area behind it.

No one is sure exactly what The Host's surveillance abilities are outdoors, or how closely he is even monitoring them at this point. She just knows she can't stand under a camera.

Alek takes one last look around, making sure she's not being watched. The phone buzzes. Incoming call. Alek answers.

Somehow, even after everything that has happened over the past twenty-four hours, she manages a smile when she hears his voice. The comfortable smile of hearing from an old friend.

"You never call, you never write," she says.

She hears him laugh.

"Is it safe for me to even be talking on this phone?" she asks.

"I'm scrambling the call," Jimmy says.

"You can do that . . . how?" Alek says.

"Later," Jimmy says. Then his voice shifts, gentle but urgent. "Talk to me. Tell me what happened after I left."

80.

Alek quickly describes scenes from the war, the second grenade landing in the hospital lobby so soon after they'd lost Conner and Amos.

Jimmy goes quiet in a way that scares her.

"I was so sure Rupert was dead," she says.

"He's alive," Jimmy says. "That kid . . . he keeps proving something."

Alek's voice cracks anyway. "Conner died to save Hannah."

"I know," Jimmy says. And you can hear he means: I'll never forgive that.

Alek tells Jimmy about how they all teamed up to save Wyatt and the little girl from the burning building.

"And she lived?" Jimmy asks.

"Yes," Alek says.

"All of you teaming up to do something like that is why you're a part of all this," Jimmy says.

All the images she's been describing come washing over her at once, like waves in McMurdo Sound. Starting with the image of Conner Lynch's dead body covering Hannah in the bomb shelter.

She's so dizzy she has to lean against the nearest tree to steady herself.

"I'm not sure I *want* to be a part of this any longer," she says quietly.

Jimmy's voice turns firm.

"Don't say that," he says. "Not now. We need to see this through."

Then he adds: "I just need to roll some things up."

"Where are you?"

"London," he says.

"Why London?" Alek asks.

There's a long enough pause at his end that Alek thinks the call might have dropped.

Then Jimmy says, "Because the trail goes here."

Alek looks around again, feeling even more paranoid now about being watched. Lowers her voice.

"Did you?" she says. "Find out, I mean."

"It took some doing," he says. "But, yeah, I think I did."

Her heart slams. "Then tell me."

"I can't," Jimmy says.

Alek feels heat rise in her chest. Not anger. Fear. "Why not?"

"Because if anyone is supposed to be a target," Jimmy says, "it needs to be me."

He softens, just a little. "I'm close, Alek," he says. "Closer than I've ever been."

"Jimmy–"

"I know," he says. "I hate it too. But I don't think it will be that much longer."

Alek looks up through the branches, at a sky that doesn't care. "Then what do I do?" she asks.

Jimmy answers without hesitation.

"You keep them alive," he says. "You keep each other alive. And you keep being the people the world needs."

He pauses, and when he speaks again, it's quieter.

"And Alek?"

"Yeah?"

"If anything feels wrong–like 'too wrong'–like something you can't survive–you get out. You don't hesitate. Promise me."

Alek swallows. She thinks of Conner. Of Rupert. Of the way the rules keep changing.

"I promise," she says.

"Good," he says. "Because I'm about to make a move."

"What move?" Alek whispers.

Jimmy's voice turns serious in a way she hasn't heard before.

"The kind that either ends this," he says, "or gets me killed."

81.

Alek knows she can't stay out here much longer—they're expected at the main house for dinner soon. If she doesn't arrive with the others, one of the guards will surely come looking for her.

"I promised someone very important to me—and to all of us—that I wouldn't tell anyone, even you guys, at least not yet," Jimmy says.

"Who?"

"Someone who's trying to keep you alive," Jimmy says. "That's all you need to know."

He pauses and lowers his voice.

"I've got to wrap this up. There are people following me . . ." He lowers his voice even more. "Wait. I need to move farther out of sight."

Alek straightens. "Jimmy—"

"Hold on," he says. "I need to move."

She hears muffled footsteps. Traffic. The hum of a city. His breathing.

When he resumes speaking to Alek after what feels to her like an agonizing few minutes, she can barely hear him over the traffic sounds in the background.

"Alek, there are more layers to this than I originally thought," he says. "And we're all facing even more of a threat than I imagined.

We're not just dealing with powerful people here. We really are dealing with ruthless ones, and a board with a completely different agenda."

"Different how?" Alek asks.

There is such a long silence Alek once again thinks the call might have dropped. Then: "Nothing about saving the world," Jimmy says. "That part was bait."

Alek's throat tightens. "Then what is it?"

"I can't get into it. But I'm getting close to finding out who the real enemy is," he says.

"It sounds ominous," Alek says.

"It is."

"Promise me you'll be careful," Alek says.

"They've already made one run at me," Jimmy says.

Alek's pulse spikes. "Where? Are you hurt?"

"I'm fine," Jimmy says. "But I'm on their radar now. I'm sure they're willing to do anything to stop me."

He exhales sharply.

"And Alek–one more thing. I need to tell you what I learned about the chain of command–"

The next thing Alek hears is the roar of a car engine, and then the screech of tires. A horn. A hard impact–metal, maybe, or a body slamming a door. And then–

Nothing.

Alek freezes, staring into the trees like she can see London through them.

"Jimmy?" she whispers.

No answer.

Dead air.

82.

Jack McHenry used to be able to go all day and all night: All day on oil rigs, all night out hunting trouble wherever the next party was. His buddies from the rig used to call him Jack-O-Lantern, because he never turned out the lights.

It all happened in another lifetime.

Jack slept most of the afternoon on a couch in the living room of his cottage in Tuscany. Once he's finally awake, he's still what his salty dad used to call dead tired after a grueling—and tragic—couple of days. But The Host has told him and the others that attendance at the dinner is mandatory.

Holy crap, he thinks.

Only eleven of us left.

What was that old book? *And Then There Were None*. Was it a movie, too? Jack isn't sure. He just remembers that in the story, one character after another after another was killed off, their number called.

When's my number going to come up?

He used to ask himself that question while deployed in active war zones, just about every day.

Jack's half asleep, or just hammered by jet lag, when he hears an alert from the cell phone that had been waiting for him in his cottage. The note said he could use it to contact loved ones. But

Elena was gone. And all the other people he loved the most—with the exception of Rupert Chadwick—are here with him in Tuscany.

He immediately heads out the back door, pretending he's taking a leisurely stroll into the woods surrounding the property. He discreetly checks the phone and sees a text sent an hour ago.

Jack goes through the painstaking process of reading what is a rather long text, one that had come in while he was asleep. Of course Jimmy has this number.

JM: Can't talk. Bigger than I thought. I now might know where to find the Big Guy. For now, gotta keep moving, because pretty sure they're on to me. Will tell you everything the next time we talk.

If something hasn't happened to me.

Watch your back, Ranger.

Wish I still had you around to watch mine.

We're surrounded again. Same predators. New Water.

JD

P.S. We're wrong about Tipton.

Jack reads it twice. Wrong about Tipton? Jack's first instinct is to laugh. His second is worse.

I'm wrong about something else, Jack thinks. *It's really twelve of us left, counting Jimmy.*

He tries to text him back, just to ask if he's all right.

You okay? Call me.

He waits several minutes.

No response.

83.

There are just two tables set tonight in the dining room.

Six at one, five at the other.

Eleven guests in all.

Alek looks around at faces she knows too well now—faces she's seen terrified, bleeding, shaking, stubborn, brave. Seated at these tables are the last ones standing:

Jack McHenry. Army Ranger. Just survived another war, even if something in him looks cracked.

Hannah Wagner. The teenage prodigy from Germany who cheated death twice now. First in Antarctica, then in the bomb shelter. Too young for this, too smart to pretend it's fine.

Wyatt Jordan. The New York City teenager growing up by force. He'd confided in Alek on their way out of the war zone that he'd never experienced the real world, not really, until now.

Carlos Lopez. The Colombian who called himself a businessman, but someone saw as a dangerous thug. Always watching. Always calculating.

Ant Tipton. A storm in human form. The former Royal Marine from Great Britain whom Alek saw as one word: dangerous.

Marcelo Oliveira. The Jiu-Jitsu champ whose physical skills and athletic character are now being tested on a daily basis.

Lin Zhi. The gymnast who talked openly about missing his

twin brother, who'd gone home early. And was starting to question whether he still belonged here, as well.

Fumio Hase. The politician who doesn't flinch. Once the boy-wonder governor of Tokyo at the age of thirty-two.

Logan Bergeron, player #61. He had spotted the grenade first as it came rolling into the lobby of the hospital. Not only had he reacted quickly enough to get out of the way, he had somehow carried the nurse closest to him to safety.

Gabrielle Fontaine, player #55. The French swimmer who was still more openly hostile to The Host than any of them. But still here.

One of the eleven.

Alek says softly to Gabrielle, "Sometimes I think they're trying to kill us all."

"Well, not *all*, Ms. Andrich," Alek hears from behind her.

The Host. Himself.

He has made another unexpected entrance, striding confidently into the dining room. He strides in like he owns the place. Like he owns the air. Like he can't imagine a world where someone says no to him.

A waiter appears on cue and hands him a glass of wine. The silver-haired man raises it.

"You've already eaten," he says. "So let's drink and be merry, shall we?"

He smiles and adds, "For tomorrow more of you die."

84.

The only one with a glass raised is The Host.

"Maybe you're the one who deserves to die," Jack says. "Just thinking big picture here."

"I probably do," The Host says pleasantly. "Just not tomorrow. And not here."

The silver-haired man is dressed as he was that night in Maine: dark suit, white shirt, no tie, every hair in place. Carrying himself, as always, like he owns the room.

"I'm curious about something," Alek says. "Are you even going to acknowledge Amos and Conner? Or how close we came to losing a fourteen-year-old boy?"

"There is nothing I could possibly say that would satisfy any of you," The Host says.

"You're the one who put them in the line of fire," Alek says. "And now more people are dead because of that."

"Any one of you could have chosen not to go, I made that clear," The Host says. "You could have pushed your red buttons once you arrived and observed the situation on the ground." He shrugs. "You put yourselves in the line of fire."

"You really are a bloodless prick," Jack says.

"That is nicer than I would have put it," Gabrielle says.

"This can't be your first war, Mr. McHenry," The Host says. "Get over it."

He's drinking more of his wine when Jack is up and out of his chair, moving around his table toward him.

Before he's able to reach The Host, though, Ant Tipton is up just as quickly and blocking his way.

The two men are inches apart.

"Move," Jack says, eyes locked on Tipton's. "Only gonna tell you once."

Tipton doesn't blink. "We've no time for this."

"You might not," Jack says. "I kind of do."

"He isn't the one you should hit," Tipton says.

Jack's eyes narrow. "So you're protecting him now? What, you got yourself a little deal?"

Tipton leans in just enough for Jack—and only Jack—to hear him. "You touch him and you won't be the one who pays for it," Tipton says. "They will."

Jack freezes for half a beat.

Alek sees it—the flicker in Jack's eyes. The soldier part of him hearing something real. The rage winning anyway. She thinks: *This was inevitable.* She's surprised it took this long.

Jack brings his hands up to shove Tipton aside.

But Tipton is quicker, his arms rising up to block him.

Nobody in the dining room makes any move to break this up. Alek shoots a glance at The Host, who seems to be enjoying the show immensely.

Wyatt has told Alek about Jack having been a football star growing up in Texas. Now she watches as he steps back only long enough to lower his shoulder, then drive it into Ant Tipton.

Tipton goes crashing onto his table, scattering glasses and plates and silverware.

But as Jack reaches for him again, Tipton springs up and off the table.

He grabs a steak knife off the table. Not waving it—holding it the way someone trained holds a tool. A warning. A line.

"Don't," Tipton says, voice ugly.

Alek hears Hannah gasp. Wyatt starts to get up from his chair. Carlos Lopez grabs Wyatt's arm to keep him where he is. Everyone else is frozen in place, shocked that things have escalated as quickly and violently as they have.

Tipton jabs the knife in Jack's direction like pointing a sword at him. Jack backs away and into a defensive crouch, hands out in front of him.

But The Host stops them both.

"Enough!" he shouts.

Jack and Tipton both turn to see that four guards, in their familiar black jumpsuits, have entered the room. They are moving toward them, guns in their hands.

"Put the knife down, Mr. Tipton," The Host says. "Do it now."

Tipton looks over at the guards. He hesitates, but only briefly, before carefully placing the knife back on the table.

There is still a stunned silence in the room until The Host addresses them once again.

"In truth, the timing of what you just witnessed couldn't be more perfect," he says. "Because tomorrow we're going to find out just how many of you are prepared to fight to the death in the name of being *The One*."

"Fight who?" Alek asks.

"Each other," The Host says.

85.

The Host looks quite pleased with himself as he lets that sink in.

"You must be joking," Alek says.

"Do I look like I'm joking?" he says.

"You expect us to fight each other?" Wyatt asks.

The silver-haired man nods.

"You hear people say they'd 'kill to win' all the time," he says. "We're about to find out which of you would be willing to kill the person in the next chair—or at the next table—to win this particular competition."

"You're talking about duels," Gabrielle says. "To the death."

"Exactly," The Host says brightly. "You will all be paired off in the morning. I'll select the pairings. I'll select the weapons. Some of you will fight with small knives, which happened to be Mr. Tipton's choice of weapon just a few moments ago. Some will be given handguns. And some will fight with their fists. And feet, if need be."

He chuckles.

The sound on this night is more chilling than ever.

"But then all of this will be Ultimate Fighting in a way, won't it?" he says.

He finishes his wine then. As he's leaning over to place it near Gabrielle Fontaine, he starts to place a hand on her shoulder.

She recoils before he can.

"Ne le faites pas," she snaps.

Don't.

The Host smiles like he's amused she still has fight in her.

"This is madness," Gabrielle says in English.

"On the contrary, Mademoiselle Fontaine," The Host says. "It is an element that is quite necessary. You've shown you'll sacrifice comfort. Safety. Pride. Even your bodies. But are you now willing to sacrifice each other? That's the question we need answered. Because in the war to save our world from imminent destruction, these are the kinds of sacrifices that might need to be made, in the ultimate fight for survival."

Alek feels nausea rise.

Jack's voice cuts through it.

"I've been thinking about something," he says.

"Other than throttling me?" The Host asks.

Jack ignores him.

"Why does there have to be just one winner?" he says.

"You mean cut the pie up into pieces in the end?" The Host says.

"We've already shown we can team up to get things done," Jack says. "We've saved people together. Why couldn't we do that for the biggest possible stakes?"

For the first time, The Host looks genuinely interested.

"Interesting," he says. "You come up with that all on your own?"

"It's just common sense," Jack says.

The Host starts to say something else, but stops himself. Claps his hands together instead, the noise jarring enough that it's like the crack of a pistol being fired.

"Now all of you go and get a good night's sleep," he says. "Lord knows, you're going to need it."

He turns and starts to walk toward the door through which he'd entered.

"I'm not doing it," Hannah says.

The Host makes a slow, theatrical turn.

"Excuse me?" he says.

"I'm willing to do a lot," the girl says. "I've already done a lot. But not this."

The Host offers what might pass as a paternal smile if they all didn't know him better.

"Well, that will be your choice," he says. "Do you want to press your red button yourself, or would you like me to do it for you, Miss Wagner?"

Hannah sits motionless, and expressionless, staring back at him. She knows everyone in the room is watching her.

"I'll think about it overnight," she says finally.

The Host once again heads for the door.

It's Jack's voice that stops him this time.

"You said we'd be paired off for these duels," Jack says. "Right?"

"So I did."

Jack makes a gesture that takes in both tables.

"But there are only eleven of us," he says.

The Host's smile is faint. Like he's been waiting for this.

"Twelve, actually," another voice says from behind them.

They turn. A man stands in the doorway, travel-worn and smiling like he's late to a party he never stopped attending.

Saad al-Harbi, player #7. The cocky prince who'd been sent home before they'd all left Ohio.

"So nice to see all of you again," Saad al-Harbi says.

"Wait," Alek says. "You can't be here. You were out."

"I was removed," he says. "Not released."

Wyatt blinks. "That's . . . not the same thing."

"No," Saad says. "It isn't."

"You all keep using the word 'eliminated' like it means 'safe,'" The Host says. "Like it means 'free.'"

He steps closer, voice calm.

"It doesn't."

Silence.

Saad takes one step into the room. "They put me in a different box," he says. "A different kind of test." He looks around at their faces. "You think you were the only ones being watched?"

Beat.

"Plus. What can I tell you?" the prince says, looking even more arrogant than ever. "Money talks." He smiles broadly. "You think your favorite influencer is the only one who can bend the rules?"

Alek's mouth is dry. "Why bring you back?"

The Host answers before Saad can.

"Because tomorrow requires pairs," he says. "And because Mr. al-Harbi has . . . reconsidered his willingness to do what it takes."

Saad's smile fades into something harder.

"I didn't come back for fun," he says. "I came back because they made something very clear."

Jack's voice is low. "What?"

Saad meets Jack's eyes. "That 'no' is not one of the options."

The Host's smile returns.

"Now," he says, "we have twelve."

86.

Jack, Alek, Hannah, and Wyatt take a long, slow walk across the property after dinner.

This is the A Team—if anybody's still allowed to be a team—together one more time.

It's not as if they don't trust everyone still left, Ant Tipton and Carlos Lopez being the clear exceptions. It's more basic than that: After the hospital, after the grenade, they've learned trust has to be earned every hour.

When they are far enough away from the main house, near an old fire pit almost entirely surrounded by trees, Jack checks the woods one more time, then uses his phone to call Jimmy.

Jimmy answers right away. Jack puts the call on speaker so the others can hear.

"Do you still have scrambling capability?" Jack asks.

"I do," Jimmy says. "But I'm done acting like I'm hiding. If he's listening, good. Let him hear it."

Alek leans in. "Is this a bad time?"

"There really isn't a good time for me," Jimmy says. "I'm still on the run."

Jack hears it—the edge in his voice that wasn't there before. Not fear. Focus.

"Are you closer?" Jack asks.

"I am," Jimmy says. "This has been a grind, but I suspected it would be once I took off. This is . . . bigger than I thought. More layers. More people. And they don't play like normal people. I just keep reminding myself how much you guys are going through. And that keeps me going."

There's a brief silence before Jimmy says, "If you're calling me, this must be important."

"It is," Alek says.

Wyatt says, "We need you to hear something."

Alek tells him what they know about the upcoming duels.

There's a beat of silence.

"He really talked about guns and knives?" Jimmy asks.

"Yeah," Wyatt says. "He did."

"Okay," Jimmy says finally. "That's . . . not a test. That's him trying to turn you into him."

"He said guns," Wyatt adds. "Real guns."

Jimmy exhales. "It was out of control a long time ago, but this is beyond anything we thought they'd ever get to."

Hannah's voice is small but steady. "Can you stop it?"

"I'm trying," Jimmy says. "And I'm not telling you to be heroes here. I'm telling you to survive."

Silence.

"I know you don't want to hear this," Jimmy says. "But you could walk away."

Jack says, "We already decided we're not walking away."

The members of the A Team all look at each other. It is Alek who speaks for the group now.

"But also, Saad is back," she started, "and we learned getting out doesn't always lead you out."

"They're in control no matter what," Jack says. "He wanted us to know that right at this point. To know there are no rules. Only him and what he wants. Down to what the red button means, or doesn't."

"And you?" Alek looks at the others. "Are you prepared to walk away?"

"You know the answer to that," Jimmy says over the speaker.

"He's trying to turn you against each other," Jimmy says. "He's tested everything else, now he wants to test your loyalty. For himself. He wants you to break."

Jack says, "He wants to see if we'll kill each other to win."

"Exactly," Jimmy says. "So don't give him the show. Don't become the thing he wants."

Wyatt says, "Easy advice when you're not the one in the ring."

Jimmy doesn't flinch.

"Fair," he says. "I think you have to keep trusting each other. If this is about loyalty and friendship, you guys have already won. Keep your heads. And if it comes to a choice you can't live with—remember you still have one button that's yours. We just have to trust it still applies." Another pause. "When I think about the people we've lost . . . well, the stakes are higher than ever. Because now we owe them our very best."

Alek closes her eyes. "We owe the dead better than becoming monsters."

"Yeah," Jimmy says. "We do."

Jimmy has covered his phone, if only momentarily.

"I have to go," he says. They can hear the urgency in his voice. "I'll be in touch when I have another update and hopefully tell you more of the truth than I can tonight."

"The truth about what?" Alek asks.

The call drops.

87.

A few minutes after eight the next morning they arrive as instructed at a huge ballroom. Bright chandeliers. Polished floors. A room meant for weddings and fundraisers.

Hannah hasn't slept very well. She feels as nervous and as anxious—and filled with dread—as she had been on the boat that first day in Antarctica.

But she hasn't quit.

None of them have.

"I know I've been scared before," Hannah had said to Alek on their way to the ballroom. "But not like this."

Alek had squeezed her hand and said, "You won't fight me. I won't fight you."

Jack had said, "There were lines I didn't cross even with enemies."

Wyatt had said, "He wants us to become enemies. It's crazy."

"No," Hannah says quietly.

One more time she reaches for Alek's hand.

"It's sick," Hannah says.

"I've never fired a gun in my life," Alek says.

"And knives?" Hannah says. "I was horrified when Tipton went after Jack with that knife he grabbed off the table."

"This whole idea is sick," Hannah says again.

The Host is waiting for them in the ballroom.

"I will be brief, as there is much for you all to do this morning," he says. "This is the day when you learn even more about each other than you already have."

He surveys the twelve people in front of him. Hannah thinks: *It's like we're waiting to hear a jury verdict.*

Or a sentencing.

"Without further ado," The Host says, "I would like to first announce the pairings for today's events, before I explain what the events will actually be."

He looks as pleased with himself as ever, Hannah thinks. She fights the urge to walk across the room and slap him, even if it means being eliminated before the duels start.

I'm not quitting.

He looks out at them again, letting the moment build a little more.

"Mr. McHenry, you and Miss Wagner will be our first combatants," the silver-haired man says.

He doesn't even allow this fact to settle—an ex–Army Ranger going up against a teenage girl—before quickly going through the rest of the pairings:

"Ms. Andrich and Mr. Lopez."

Alek's eyes flick to Carlos Lopez. He doesn't smile. But he looks . . . ready.

"Mr. Tipton and Mr. al-Harbi."

Tipton's face is stone. Saad's is calm in a way that doesn't comfort anyone.

"Mr. Jordan and Mr. Lin."

Wyatt swallows. Lin Zhi gives a tiny nod like he's accepting a routine.

"Mr. Oliveira and Mr. Hase."

Marcelo and Fumio exchange a respectful bow. Fighters recognizing fighters.

"And finally—Mr. Bergeron and Mademoiselle Fontaine."

Logan Bergeron looks at Gabrielle Fontaine like he's about to apologize for being in the room.

Hannah is still trying to imagine any one-on-one competition that would pit her against Jack McHenry, who's been as much a leader as any of them once they'd left Ohio.

The Host says, "Now the events."

He lifts a small remote. Clicks it once. A panel in the far wall slides open, revealing metal cases on tables. Weapons cases.

"The weapons for Mr. Bergeron and Mademoiselle Fontaine will be knives," The Host continues.

The rest of them hear Gabrielle Fontaine gasp and they turn to look at her. Gabrielle starts to say something back to him, but holds her fire for now as the man still in charge of them plows ahead.

"Ms. Andrich and Mr. Lopez will also fight with knives," he says. "Saad and Mr. Tipton will be given revolvers—"

Tipton already knows which way the board wants this to go, but he can't help himself. "How's that going to work, exactly?"

The Host ignores him and proceeds, "—as will young Mr. Jordan and our friend Mr. Lin. Mr. Oliveira and Mr. Hase. Hand-to-hand combat, for lack of a better expression."

The Host looks directly at Hannah Wagner now.

"Mr. McHenry and Miss Wagner will engage in hand-to-hand combat as well," he says.

"Hold on," Jack says. "You're talking about me having a fistfight—with a teenage girl?"

The Host smiles again. "Fists, feet, elbows, knees. Knock yourselves out." He shrugs, and grins. "Literally, if necessary. Whatever ends it."

"Ends it how?" Jack snaps.

The Host's smile doesn't move. "You'll find out."

Hannah is studying Jack, seeing him already clenching and unclenching his fists, more upset than she is at the moment. She worries briefly that he might be the one to charge The Host and do something worse than slap him.

"I've never raised a hand to a woman in my life," Jack says angrily.

The Host smiles, almost apologetically. "Unfortunately, Mr. McHenry," he says, "there's a first time for everything."

"This just isn't fair," Jack says.

He doesn't know how right he is, Hannah thinks.

She likes Jack so much. She'd seen him take the lead again last night. But he's the same as everybody else standing here with her, these people who only see her as a brain.

They think they know her.

88.

Alek allows herself a quick sideways glance at Carlos Lopez. She's sure she can see a small smile playing across his lips. She's also sure that today won't be his first knife fight.

Fumio ınd Marcelo keep their eyes on each other, both of them breathing slow, conserving energy like this is a real match.

Gabrielle Fontaine, still appearing stunned that she is being asked to participate in a knife fight, is saying something quietly to Logan Bergeron.

Logan is nodding as he listens.

"How's it going to work with guns, exactly?" Ant Tipton growls. "Twenty paces and turn and fire like it's Aaron Burr trying to put one into Alexander Hamilton?"

But before he gets his answer, Logan and Gabrielle turn and walk in the direction of the double doors through which they'd all entered the ballroom.

Logan has his arm around her shoulders.

The Host's head turns slightly, curious.

"Where are you going?" he asks.

Logan doesn't stop.

"Out," he says.

When they get to the doors, Gabrielle says something to Logan right before they turn and give The Host the finger.

Then they look at each other, lift their necklaces, and push their red buttons at the same moment.

Two clean clicks. Two quiet beeps.

"I ride bulls for a living. I know risk. I know pain," Logan says. "But I have no intention of fighting another human being with a knife no matter how much money is on the table."

Gabrielle then addresses the other competitors.

"Logan and I will still be alive at the end of this day," she says. "I sincerely hope some of you can say the same."

Then, she finds herself walking back across the auditorium until she is standing in front of The Host. For a second, the guards shift. The Host doesn't.

"As for you, sir, you want blood. You won't get it from me," Gabrielle says.

She slaps The Host across the face, snapping his head to the side.

"Pourrir en enfer."

Rot in hell.

The Host slowly turns his face back toward them.

He doesn't look hurt. He looks . . . delighted.

Gabrielle and Logan don't wait for the response. They're through the doors and gone.

Alek thinks about following them. She really does. But stays right where she is.

They all do.

The Host touches his cheek with two fingers, tasting the moment. "Excellent," he says.

Then, louder: "Now we begin."

He looks at the ten remaining. "What are you?" he asks.

No one answers.

"Say it," he urges.

Silence.

"From now on," The Host says. "Only winners or losers."

He pauses as he studies the ten competitors left out of the twelve who had shown up a few minutes before.

"What are all of you?" he asks.

89.

Four black-uniformed guards appear, laying down a mat that looks to be about the size that Zhi must have used for floor exercises in his gymnastic competitions.

Hannah, though, imagines it more as a boxing ring.

Just one without ropes.

She is on one side of the mat. Jack is on the other, not even wanting to look at her. Neutral corners, and he doesn't want to come out of his.

Hannah walks over to him and puts out her hand.

"I am so sorry it's come to this," Hannah says. "With you of all people."

Jack takes her hand—careful, like she's made of glass.

"Not as sorry as I am," Jack says. "I'll try to go as easy on you as I can before somebody steps in and stops this stupid fight. I'm going to end this without hurting you."

"You can't promise that," Hannah says.

Jack swallows. "Then I'm going to try."

"If we were going to quit like Logan and Gabrielle, we would have done it already," Hannah says. "Now we both have to do what we need to do."

She turns and walks to the middle of the mat, waiting for Jack to join her when he's ready. Hannah is taking slow breaths the way she has been taught as a way of calming herself.

But none of it helps to slow the crazy pounding of her heart.

She can hear her father's voice inside her head now. The former policeman who became a self-defense trainer after retiring as a new way of protecting people. He is the one who made sure Hannah went through life as more than just a brain.

He had trained Hannah in self-defense from the time she started going to school, to the point where Hannah eventually believed she could have taught his courses herself.

"If you are about to be attacked," her father would always remind her, "the first thing to do is create as much distance as you can. And be as loud as you can as a way of distracting your opponent."

Then this, always:

"But if you determine that your life is truly in danger, *mein Liebling*, sometimes the best and only weapon is escape."

Only she knows there is no escaping what is about to happen. She has to stand and fight, even if the opponent is Jack McHenry.

The Host joins them in the middle of the mat.

"Are you both ready?" he asks.

Hannah and Jack nod.

"Rules are simple," he says, almost casual.

He gestures at the red buttons around their necks.

"A fight ends when someone is unable to continue . . . or when someone chooses to end their run."

Jack's eyes narrow. "So you're not even pretending this is about skill."

The Host smiles.

"Skill is part of it," he says. "But will is the real currency."

He steps back.

"Begin," he says.

He takes a seat in a folding chair set against the wall, casually crossing his legs. The other competitors have already been escorted out of the ballroom. Hannah wondered, as she watched them leave, which ones she might see again.

"I really am so sorry it's come to this," Jack says.

He steps away from Hannah. Then he sighs almost sadly and raises his hands into a boxer's pose and stance.

Hannah Wagner spins around—as taught—as soon as he does. She doesn't square up like a fighter. She moves with problem-solver-style precision.

When she comes back around and is facing him again, she steps toward him. Then her right hand flashes out before Jack has a chance to react, and Hannah drives two fingers into his left eye—not a strike to injure, a strike to blind.

I'm sorry, too.

Jack staggers back a couple of steps, his hands going to his eye. But Hannah is already moving in, having been taught by her father to seize any opening, especially against a bigger opponent. She delivers a knee to his midsection, doubling him over and nearly putting him down.

He doesn't go down.

The former Ranger gets some air into him, forces himself to straighten up, looking at Hannah warily now, as if she's a stranger. He gives a quick shake to his head, gathering himself. Trying to shake off everything that has just happened to him.

"Okay, then," he says. Hannah isn't sure whether he's talking to himself, or her. "Okay," Jack says.

He reluctantly starts to draw back his right fist. But even after the blows Hannah has just delivered, he hesitates again, he still can't force himself to deliver a blow to his friend's face.

Jack changes his mind and bull-rushes her instead, getting his arms around her, lifting her into the air at the same time.

He squeezes so much air out of her in the process.

Just not all.

Hannah gets loud here.

As taught.

Even being bear-hugged this way by Jack, she screams at the top of her lungs, startling him enough that he weakens his hold on her. She drops her weight, twists out, and kicks the outside of his knee—not with full force, but with the angle that makes legs betray you.

Jack stumbles.

She follows that by yelling even louder than before, and spins again, coming around this time with a fierce, swinging kick to the outside of Jack's left knee, both of them hearing a crack as she does.

Hannah ignores the sound.

He's not Jack now.

Just her opponent.

Jack shakes off the pain in his knee and gets into a crouch, lowering his shoulder and driving it into Hannah's stomach, putting her on the mat as he lands with all his weight on top of her.

Pinned this way, she can barely breathe.

"Stay down," he says.

She looks up at him, seeing the sad and almost resigned look on his face: the same thing she saw in the shelter after Conner died. A good person trapped inside someone else's rules.

The man she really has come to respect so much.

Both having found themselves in this impossible situation.

"I still don't want to hurt you," Jack says.

"Do . . . what . . . you have to," she manages.

Once more, though, he seems to freeze, having no idea what to do now to end the fight.

For a second—one tiny second—he hesitates.

It gives Hannah the last opening she needs.

If Jack can't bring himself to end this, she can.

90.

At the last possible second Hannah tucks her chin to her chest, burying it in there as deeply as she can just in case Jack changes his mind and does decide he has to punch her in the face.

No matter how fond he is of her.

The voice of her father is back inside Hannah's head for the last time. Otto Wagner practically shouting at her that a guard position can be crucial—can be everything—in ground fighting like this.

Hannah frames her forearms against Jack's shoulders, creates space the size of a breath. Then she bucks hard—hips up, turning—slipping one knee between them.

Jack shifts to keep her down.

Hannah pivots and catches his arm, trapping it against her chest. A quick, ugly little lock that doesn't need strength—only timing. She knows that won't stop him for long. But she doesn't need to stop him for long.

Jack's face changes instantly. Pain flashes there. He tries to pull free. Hannah tightens the angle. Jack stops moving. He knows what it is. He's been trained.

"You're going to break it," Jack says, voice tight.

"I don't want to," Hannah whispers.

Hannah releases the hold.

"Boo!" The Host heckles.

Jack lunges forward, but he can't. He can't bring himself to punch her. He can't bring himself to give the full force of his strength and training against a kid, especially not one he cares so much for.

"Finish it," he whispers to her. Leaving himself open.

"Don't let me win," she says.

"I won't," he replies. "But I won't hurt you. I told you that."

He gets back into his fighting stance, and she sees the opening again. It's not intentional. He doesn't realize it.

Hannah just needs to use her own strength and agility one final time, along with a final element of surprise. A short, hard, right-hand punch to Jack's nose. The punch Jack couldn't bring himself to throw at her. Hannah doesn't know if it's enough of a punch to break his nose. She just sees the blood pouring out of it. Sees Jack pull his head back before she can hit him in the same spot a second time.

Hannah rolls away from him, springing to her feet, delivering a kick to his kidney.

Jack is the one on his back.

Hannah jumps on top of him. He looks up at her as she puts him back in an arm hold. This time with her full body weight as leverage. She—again—doesn't need an upper hand in strength if she has the right angle.

"Finish him," she hears The Host shout.

"No," she says.

She looks over at the silver-haired man, then back down at Jack.

Hannah stands and offers him her hand.

Jack stares up at her, stunned.

She pulls him to his feet.

"Are you telling me you can't?" The Host says.

She reaches down with the handkerchief she's just pulled from the back pocket of her jeans and gently wipes the blood from Jack's face. Then she looks back at The Host.

"I'm telling you I won't," Hannah says.

It's as if she's alone in the room, only speaking to herself.

"You win," Jack says to her.

"No," Hannah says. "No, I don't."

Hannah turns back to The Host, presses her own red button, and says, "I quit."

The room goes silent.

She didn't just refuse the fight. She refused what the fight was trying to turn her into. And for the first time in a long time, The Host looks—just for a beat—genuinely annoyed.

Because he didn't get what he wanted.

Not from her.

Not today.

91.

Thirty minutes later, The Host hands Ant Tipton and Saad al-Harbi their classic LeMat revolvers, the style of gun men were likely to have used in duels in the nineteenth century—heavy in the hand, ugly.

Hannah is already back in her cottage, packing up her belongings. Jack's injuries are being treated by an Italian doctor who has been summoned to the main house.

In the ballroom now, it's just Tipton, Saad, and The Host.

"In the past," The Host says, "formal duels were conducted most frequently with smoothbore pistols that held only one bullet. Very tidy. Very polite. Very deadly."

He gestures at the revolvers in their hands.

"The guns in your hands are reproductions of the legendary cap and ball revolver that the Pietta company of Brescia, Italy, started making again forty years ago," he continues. "Beautifully made. And they have a history."

Both Tipton and Saad study the guns in their hands. Saad remarks on their craftsmanship. Tipton simply asks, "How many bullets?"

"It's capable of holding nine," The Host says. "But for our purposes today, you each have one in the chamber."

"How do you know?" Tipton asks.

"Because I loaded them."

"Is it really going to be twenty paces and turn and fire?" Tipton asks. "If so, where are our seconds?"

The Host ignores the remark, and says, "You will each be escorted by my guards to different points of the wooded area at the far end of the grounds. Then you will hear one shot fired into the air."

He pauses, enjoying the weight of it.

"That shot means you're free to move. Hunt. Or run."

He looks at the two men.

Tipton looks at him. "Any rules?"

The Host's smile widens. "Only the oldest one."

"And that is?" Saad asks.

The Host spreads his hands.

"Survive."

Tipton swallows something hard.

"Any more questions?" The Host asks.

"Just one," Ant Tipton says. "Are you expecting us to shoot to kill?"

The silver-headed man walks over and then claps them both heartily on the back.

"Why not?" he asks.

92.

Alek Andrich knows she would kill to protect her mother, without a second thought. She would have done the same for her sister if it had ever come to that, had she even gotten the chance. Or for her father.

Killing to protect her mother was simple.

Killing to win a game wasn't.

She tightens her grip on the knife.

"Don't let them turn you into a story," Hannah had said once. Lopez smiles like he's already written her ending.

As insane as these duels are—as insane as hers is about to be with this armed and frightening man—she has come too far and done too much and seen too much to turn back now. More than ever, even faced with perhaps making the ultimate sacrifice, she continues to keep her eyes on the prize. She would never say it to the others, but she has come to believe she really is meant for a higher calling.

Whatever the risks.

She didn't die in Death Valley and isn't going to die today.

Alek still can't believe that Hannah and Jack, two of the best people involved with these games, had been paired off. Or maybe, if she really thinks about it, she shouldn't be surprised, knowing by now how sadistic The Host can be.

What person in their right mind could even call these "games" at this point? Alek thinks. She knows Ant Tipton and Saad al-Harbi have just been sent off into the woods with their dueling pistols.

Alek is convinced only one of them will come back alive.

Lopez had said nothing to her when they were handed Darter combat knives that look so much more frightening and so much more lethal than the steak knife Tipton had waved at Jack in the dining room before that fight was stopped.

But would anyone stop Lopez from killing her?

Will anyone stop me?

The Host walks them into what might have been at some point an exercise room, but is empty of any equipment today. Two of the walls are floor-to-ceiling mirrors, as if this actually had once served as a gym. Today it's a room built to break them.

"Are you going to watch?" Alek asks.

"From the next room," The Host says. "Ready to intercede if necessary."

Alek doesn't hide her contempt. "And when might that be?"

"One more thing that is for me to know and for you to find out, Ms. Andrich," he says. "I will simply ask you and Mr. Lopez to once more trust the process."

Alek feels her breath catch.

Trust the process.

She watches the bloodless silver-haired man walk out of the room, whistling softly to himself.

Then Alek hears Bohdan's voice in her memory, the night before he'd left to join a fight he believed in. Alek's boyfriend Bohdan had been two years older than her during her short stint at university. When he was old enough he had joined the war, like everyone else, saying it was his duty to fight for his country. That was a few months before Alek had gone to Ohio. She hasn't heard from him since he left.

The night before he'd enlisted, though, he'd told her, "I refuse to live like a victim. Promise me you never will, either."

She had made that promise.

She wasn't going to be a victim today.

Or ever.

Alek is still watching the door close softly behind The Host when Carlos Lopez, without warning, slashes the top of Alek's hand with his knife.

Her own knife goes clattering to the floor.

93.

Alek jumps back, pain flaring across her hand, barely out of reach of Lopez's knife, knowing there is no way for her to reach down for her own without being slashed again.

Or perhaps just gutted this time.

Lopez grins and casually jabs at her again. It forces Alek to jump back a second time. As she does, she makes sure to keep her eyes locked on the Colombian's knife.

"You know what they say," he says softly. "A nick here, a nick there, and soon you are bleeding to death."

He jabs again–testing her, measuring her. Alek keeps backing up, hands up, eyes locked, putting her hands out in a defensive posture.

Lopez points at her knife, on the floor between them.

"Go on," he says. "Pick it up. Make it interesting, little girl."

Not only bigger than you, but faster, she thinks.

Before Lopez can swing his weapon again, Alek takes a long step toward him.

Not going for her knife.

Going for his.

Don't be a victim.

Promise.

Lopez's eyes flicker with surprise–just a fraction too late. Alek is inside Lopez's reach before he can react, surprising him by clamping both of her hands on the wrist of his knife hand, snapping the wrist into a vise.

She hears a grunt from him as she forcefully bends the wrist back, the blade of the knife pointing straight up in the air between them.

"Now I kill you," he hisses at her.

"If you can," Alek says.

She squeezes harder on his wrist as she bends the blade toward Carlos Lopez an inch at a time. Then she jerks his arm away from his body, trying to tear the arm from his shoulder.

Lopez screams in pain.

As he does, Alek drives her right knee as hard as she can manage into his groin.

Lopez tries to scream again, but the pain from what Alek has just done to him ends up trapped in his throat.

She still has not let go of his knife hand.

Alek moves to the side now, turns her hips, and uses his momentum against him. A shove. A hook. Finally taking the knife away as she kicks his legs out from underneath him and puts him on his stomach.

She sits on top of him then, knee planted between his shoulder blades, his knife in her hand, pressing the tip of it to the back of his neck.

"If you are expecting me to beg, I will not," Lopez says, the side of his face pressed to the floor, afraid to move his head even slightly.

Alek doesn't respond.

"Do what you have to do," Lopez says, "and get it over with."

She does.

Alek leans in close enough only he can hear her. And whatever she says makes him go still. Not fear.

Humiliation.

94.

When The Host reenters the room, Alek is leaning down, saying something into Carlos Lopez's ear that only Lopez can hear.

Alek stands and leaves Lopez where he is on the ground. Lopez stays on the floor a moment longer, breathing hard.

Alek picks up her fallen knife.

Then she holds out both knives—hers and his—handle-first, offering them back like she's returning borrowed tools.

The Host takes them.

"You must know he would have killed you if given the chance," The Host says calmly. "Driven that knife up into you and as close to your brain as he could get it."

"I'm not him," Alek says.

Then she adds:

"And just so we're clear? I'm not you, either."

Lopez slowly gets to his feet, glaring at Alek as he does.

If looks really could kill, she thinks.

"Since we are both still alive," Lopez says, turning his attention to The Host, "this should be judged a draw. And since there has been no resolution, I am demanding a rematch. Immediately if possible."

Alek sees The Host smile.

"You're demanding?" he asks Lopez.

Lopez corrects himself. "I am *requesting* a rematch," he says.

"And I can totally understand why you'd feel that way," he's told. "But this wasn't a draw, sir. It wasn't even close, and you know that, Mr. Lopez. The only way there would have been a more clear-cut resolution–so to speak–is if Ms. Andrich slit your throat from ear to ear when she had the chance."

The Host is beaming now as he adds, "Now please do me the favor of–"

What happens next happens so fast that this time Alek has no chance to stop Carlos, who lunges for one of the knives in The Host's hands.

But then, to Alek's amazement, The Host's hands are suddenly a blur of motion and Lopez is screaming out in pain again, so much louder than before.

Carlos stares down in shock at the two knives sticking out of his midsection, blood pouring out of him.

Only the handles of the knives are showing.

When Lopez manages to pull one out and then the other, his hands covered in blood, two guards have appeared. They half lift and half drag him out of the room, Lopez shouting curses as he goes, even with his hands pressed to the wounds in his stomach.

When he is gone, The Host turns to Alek.

"I hate a sore loser, don't you?" he says.

"You could have killed him," she says, still in a mild state of shock over what she's just witnessed.

"How do you know I wasn't trying to do just that?" is his answer. "Why didn't you kill him when you had the chance?"

Alek doesn't blink.

"Simple," she says. "He was already dead."

"May I ask what you were telling him when I came back into the room?" The Host says.

Alek wipes her own blood from her hand with the edge of her shirt.

Then says, flat as steel:

"I asked him who was a little girl now."

95.

Saad al-Harbi has had extensive training with firearms. In controlled places. Expensive places. Clean places. Places where people talk about discipline like it's a brand.

Private instruction. Competitive shooting. Security courses his father insisted on after a kidnapping scare years ago.

It had also been one of the requirements for service in the Royal Air Force. More than one instructor had remarked about how proficient Saad was with guns already, as unlikely as it would be for a pilot to ever have to put that skill into practice.

He never dreamt he might have to.

Saad had hated all of it at the time.

Now he hates that it still isn't enough.

His father had bought his way back into another set of trials—one he was told could get him back into the games. He had paid high, after Saad had been sent home from Ohio. Saad had been able to avoid life-and-death situations in Antarctica and Chile; and in caves and mountains and the place in America known as Death Valley. But he had faced off against player after player eliminated after the red tents. Even though his father bought him back in, he earned his place back.

Maybe that was part of the arrangement between his father and the people in charge.

But there had been no way for Saad, once he was back in the competition, to ever imagine he would find himself in a setting like this. Or a situation like this. Here he was, anyway, essentially in combat, with someone like Tipton.

Tipton was a natural-born killer.

Saad thinks about Tipton's skill set now as he moves silently forward through a forest much larger and more dense than he had anticipated. Somewhere in his memory was a line of poetry from his English studies, about woods lovely and dark and deep.

Nothing lovely, though, about these woods.

They are most certainly dark and deep, under a sky that is growing more ominous by the minute.

Every time Saad hears the snap of a twig underneath his feet he stops and holds his breath. And waits. Then waits a little longer, listening for any other sound in the immediate area, the hint of any movement, before proceeding.

Every twenty yards or so he stops at another tree, peers around it and around the immediate area, looking for any sign of Tipton.

Telling himself:

I will only need one shot.

A clean shot.

One he knows he will take without pause even though he has never killed anyone in his life. And he can't stop thinking about Tipton's eyes. Tipton isn't here to win. Tipton is here because he knows how to do this. And because someone wants him to.

It begins to rain, the sky growing darker, turning day into night, the woods darker and deeper than ever. Saad moves forward anyway, crouching behind a tree, peering into a clearing blurred by rain. Black clothes. Black trees. Black shadows. Saad hears something over the steady pounding of the rain.

Is it just the normal rustling of branches as the wind has picked up?

Or something else?

What will happen if they do come face-to-face in these next few moments?

Will someone actually say, *Draw*, like this is a scene from some old western movie? Who will be the first to fire?

Saad thinks about these things as he crouches behind another tree before rising again and pressing ahead in the rain. There are no rules out here.

Only the law of the jungle.

Maybe, he thinks, the real scene in which he finds himself is from *Lord of the Flies*. A story of savagery and violence.

Would it be enough for him, as good a marksman as he is, to put a bullet into Tipton's arm or leg or shoulder if Saad is the one to get off the first shot?

Tipton will shoot to kill, of this Saad has no doubt.

Saad leans out from the lush tree providing some shelter from the rain. In the next moment he is certain he sees movement on the other side of the clearing. And decides, just like that, it is time to force the action. He is tired of waiting. Or maybe the waiting has gotten to be too much for him.

Make something happen.

Now.

Saad joined the Air Force to prove to his father that he isn't some rich, pampered boy.

That he's a man.

He wishes his father could see him now.

He rises.

And makes the worst decision of his life.

"Tipton!" he calls out, loud enough to make himself heard over the rain. "No more hiding for either one of us. Let's settle this like men."

His voice cracks on the last word, and he hates that it does.

Then a voice answers—soft, close, almost conversational.

"Fine with me."

From behind him.

Saad's blood goes cold.

Because he realizes he never heard Tipton moving at all.

And that means Tipton had been there the whole time.

96.

Ant Tipton is standing in the middle of a narrow dirt path, puddles already having formed at his feet, his lace-up military boots covered in mud.

Saad al-Harbi is twenty-five yards away—maybe less—his revolver up, his arms locked, trying to look like he belongs here.

Tipton has his gun up, too. But Tipton isn't trying to look like anything. He's just . . . ready.

"You could have shot me in the back before I knew you were even there," Saad says. "Why didn't you?"

"I'm a lot of things," Tipton says. "But I'm not a coward who shoots people in the back. Even I have rules." He pauses. "Even out here."

Saad tries to appear calm, acting in control of the situation, staring down the barrel of a gun. But he knows he is not in control.

Neither of them is.

Saad tries to slow his breathing, wanting to slow it to practically nothing if he can't work something out with Tipton before either one of them chooses to pull the trigger.

"A lot of money has changed hands to get me back into this competition, I don't know whether you're aware of that or not," he says. "Some of the money could end up in your hands if we can just talk about this before one of us does something rash."

"Sorry, mate, but I don't need your money," Tipton says. "I'm about to win a billion dollars." He grins. "It won't make me as rich as royalty, mind you. But rich enough, don't you reckon?"

It takes all the discipline Saad can muster to remain completely still. He is pleased to notice, perhaps even surprised, that there isn't even a slight tremor in the hand holding the old-fashioned LeMat revolver.

"We can work together going forward," Saad says. "Maybe there's a way to game this out with The Host so that both of us win. I've frankly always found it a silly notion that only one of us can end up the chosen one." Now he grins.

"Mate," Tipton says, "you're talking like the world is still normal."

Saad's jaw tightens. "I'm talking like I want to live."

"Fair," Tipton says. "If I'm reading you correctly here, you're proposing a bit of a separate arrangement?"

"Precisely," Saad says. "It would certainly be the easiest way to end our current impasse. It's practical—"

Tipton nods once, like he's accepted the terms.

"Here's what's practical," Tipton says.

He fires a shot. One crack of sound swallowed by rain.

The initial force of the bullet drives Saad backward. Unable to break his fall, the back of his head lands hard, spraying mud in all directions.

Somehow Saad's weapon remains in his hand.

But he can't raise his gun because his arms aren't working. There is no way for him to stop the pain in the middle of his chest, or the blood that's blooming out from around his heart.

Saad can't move.

Can barely breathe.

He sees Tipton standing over him in the rain, the gun trained on Saad al-Harbi one final time.

This time he is aiming between the eyes.

"You said one bullet," Saad manages.

Tipton's voice drops even lower.

"No. *He* said one bullet."

It is the last thing Saad al-Harbi expects to hear.

Tipton's eyes flicker—just for a moment—like he hates hearing the words out loud.

Saad squeezes his eyes shut. Waiting for the end.

But it doesn't come.

Not yet.

Instead, Tipton steps back. And when Saad opens his eyes, Tipton is already turning away.

"Don't," Saad whispers. "Don't leave me here. End it."

Tipton doesn't look back.

Over his shoulder, he says, "I can't. I can't keep doing this. I can't keep being who they want."

"You already are."

"Push the button. They'll save you. Or . . . you bleed out. Your choice."

Then he disappears into the trees.

And Saad al-Harbi is left alone in the rain.

With his gun. With his blood. And with the sound of his own breathing getting thinner by the second.

He doesn't push his button.

97.

The Host studies Wyatt Jordan and says, “There’s much I still don’t know about you.”

Wyatt snorts. “Yeah. No kidding.”

The Host’s smile doesn’t reach his eyes. “Have you ever fired a gun before?”

“At another person?”

“That was the implication, yes.”

“I’ve wanted to point one at you plenty of times,” Wyatt says. “But you have to know that by now.”

Wyatt turns to his opponent, Zhi. By now they’re all aware that Zhi speaks fluent English. It happens to be one of many languages he speaks flawlessly.

“How about you?” Wyatt says. “Do you know how to shoot?”

Zhi nods.

“In my country,” he says, “college students and sometimes even high school students are required to pass a course in military training.” He shrugs. “Along the way there were many tests, I guess you could call them. I came out first in most of them.”

The Host has stepped away for a moment. Zhi follows him. The two men speak quietly.

When he comes back, Wyatt says, “What was that?”

“I asked him if this was going to be a fair fight,” Zhi says.

"And?"

Zhi looks straight at him. "He told me to trust him."

They both see the trap.

Wyatt keeps his voice as low as possible. "I guess we're going to have to trust each other one more time," he says. "Just know that I don't want to do this any more than you do."

"I do what I have to do to win," Zhi says.

So do I, Wyatt thinks.

He grips the handle of the gun hanging at his side a little tighter now.

So. Do. I.

A million thoughts come rushing over him now, all the way back to being in the freezing water that first day in Antarctica, when he'd been overwhelmed with fear, more for Hannah's survival than his own.

He thinks about Reg Drummond, because he can't help thinking about Reg Drummond, someone he had admired more than anyone else in this competition. All the talk, from the very beginning, about heroes. Reg hadn't talked about it. He'd just been one, starting with that first day in the water and then later when that hole had opened up in the Ice Tongue and he had saved Alek's life, and Wyatt had helped him do it.

That courage—the kind Wyatt needed now—had seemed to come so naturally to Reg. He had never hesitated to put his life on the line and was still saving lives on Mount Washington until no one could save him.

He needs Reg to tell him what a hero does when the only way out is through another person.

Ever since that day, Wyatt has had the same recurring nightmare about Reg losing his grip—Wyatt reaching for him—before Wyatt would wake up again in a cold sweat, heart pounding.

Sometimes he woke up crying, dreaming of being back up on the mountain, Reg still gone.

He needs Reg to be here now.

Wonders what Reg would do if the duel were between him and Wyatt.

Which one of them would have walked away first?

Or would both of them have played this out to the end, Reg especially, because he had never walked away from a fight in his life, at the Olympics or anywhere else?

Would Reg have walked out the door the way Gabrielle and Logan Bergeron had this morning?

It's not just the weight of the gun in his hands that Wyatt Jordan feels now.

It isn't just the weight of metal in his hand.

It's the weight of Reg Drummond.

It's the weight of what he's about to become.

98.

As Wyatt walks toward the woods, he sees two guards come out carrying a stretcher.

There is clearly a body on it, covered with a thick blanket. But as thick as the blanket is, Wyatt can see the bloodstains seeping through it.

Ant Tipton is walking behind the stretcher.

As he passes Wyatt, Tipton only slows long enough to say, “Hope you do better than he did.”

He starts to walk past Wyatt—then hesitates like he wants to say something else. Something softer. He doesn’t. His hand goes to the chain around his neck instead, thumb working the clasp, and he keeps moving.

Wyatt doesn’t answer. He can’t. Because he sees something in Tipton’s face that scares him more than the blood.

Not pride. Not satisfaction. Something closer to . . . disgust.

Or regret.

Wyatt forces himself to keep walking.

He and Zhi had just watched Marcelo Oliveira win his fight against Fumio Hase, jiujitsu on this day ultimately triumphing over karate. The competition, which became more and more vicious, had ended when Marcelo used what he explained afterward was a “Kimura lock” to pin F Fumio he ground. Once he did have him down, he immobilized Fumic Fumio forearm pressed against the other man's neck.

There had been a moment when Wyatt thought Marcelo might choke Fumio to death before he'd pulled his arm back and Fumio was able to breathe again.

So the last duel of this day is between Wyatt and Zhi, someone else he has come to like. They will be using the same old-fashioned revolvers Wyatt saw Tipton carrying.

By the time Wyatt is all the way into the woods, night has started to fall. But even in the gathering twilight, Wyatt knows that when the time comes, there will be more than enough light for him to see Zhi.

And, likewise, for Zhi to see him.

Then they will both discover how far they are willing to take this.

But Wyatt knows that all of this—him, Lin Zhi, Tipton, Saad al-Harbi, these guns—was never supposed to have gone as far as it has. He isn't supposed to be out here feeling he has a target on his back.

Or, more accurately, one on his chest.

Wyatt's mind does the thing it always does in crisis—tries to run away.

He knows he could have pressed his button before he came out here. Probably *should* have pressed it before he got anywhere near the line of fire.

I should be back at the cottages saying goodbye to Hannah.

Telling her the truth, and not just about my feelings.

Letting her know the person I really am.

And the one I'm about to be.

He almost laughs at himself.

Too late for that now.

After everything that has happened since he was in the water in Antarctica that very first day, trying to save Hannah Wagner, the life Wyatt now needs to save is his own.

And he has no idea what saving it is going to cost.

Or if he's willing to pay it.

99.

Wyatt presses forward as quietly as he can, trying to imagine his feet barely touching the ground, pretending he's a ghost.

Every few minutes—minutes that feel more like hours—he stops to look around.

Stops and listens.

Every time he does, he thinks about turning around and walking away.

Wyatt thinks about running, and not just for cover.

He thought he had a solid plan for himself from the time he'd shown up in Ohio. Except plans have a way of changing. He'd learned that fairly early in his life.

Man, have I ever learned that.

A family trait, maybe?

But what did they say in the military? Plans change when the situation on the ground changes. Jack McHenry had told him that one night when the two of them had taken an after-dinner walk in Maine. Or maybe it had been in Kentucky.

Well, now the situation on the ground—*this* ground—was changing with every step he took deeper into the woods.

Where's Zhi?

Am I tracking him or is he tracking me?

This was supposed to be about me becoming a man, Wyatt tells himself.

Just not a dead man.

All Wyatt does know, one hundred percent, is that he's more frightened than when he had been hanging on for dear life to Mount Washington, right before he watched Reg Drummond lose his own grip and fall all the way to what looked like the bottom of the world.

Right after the same thing had nearly happened to him.

Wyatt's heartbeat? Out of control. His mouth feels as dry as dirt. His right hand, the one with the old-fashioned revolver in it, continues to shake so much he wonders what will happen if he does need to take a shot at Zhi Lin. He looks down and hates what he sees.

If I have to shoot, I'll miss.

And then I'll die.

Unless the Chinese gymnast gets his shot off first.

Could Zhi really shoot him dead? Zhi is an athlete, after all. A champion in his sport. One night when Wyatt was quizzing him about that, Zhi had told Wyatt that it wasn't ever a burning desire to compete that drove him.

No.

It had been his hatred of losing.

Only he doesn't have to hate me to kill me.

Still plenty of light left. Or half-light. The rain had stopped, and the clouds had rolled out, making for what would've been a pleasant evening under any other circumstances. Wyatt tries to slow his breathing in the hope of somehow slowing down his heartbeat. Then looks down at the gun and still sees his hand shaking like a leaf in a strong wind.

He hears something behind him now. Something more than

just the wind. Wyatt wheels around, raising his gun as he does. But it is some small forest creature scurrying away.

The next noise Wyatt hears doesn't come from behind him.

It is Zhi landing on the ground up ahead.

He's jumped down out of a tree.

As startled as Wyatt is, frozen in place, he manages one crazy thought:

Guy stuck the landing.

Before Wyatt can decide what to do next, he sees Zhi's gun pointed at him.

Zhi's hand isn't shaking at all.

Wyatt hears Zhi say, "Winner or loser."

In the instant before he pulls the trigger, Wyatt drops into a forward roll. Zhi fires and misses, the bullet smashing into a tree behind him.

They were told they each had one bullet.

The Host had told Zhi to trust him. Wyatt doesn't. *There's more than one bullet in his gun . . . because that man lies. Every time.*

Zhi wasn't sent out here to "compete."

Zhi was sent out here to win.

The Host wants him dead and, like always, the rules bend to his desired outcomes.

Wyatt doesn't wait. He can't.

He aims and fires because he feels he has no choice.

He aims for the shoulder. For the arm. To stop. To survive.

The recoil punches his wrist.

Zhi jerks back with a sharp cry, his gun dropping. Blood darkens his sleeve instantly. Zhi stares at Wyatt like he can't believe it. Like losing is something that only happens to other people.

Wyatt backs away, gun still up, breathing hard.

"Don't," Wyatt says.

He doesn't know what he means by it.

Don't shoot me. Don't die. Don't make me live with this.

Zhi staggers, collapses against a tree, and slides down into the wet leaves. Wyatt stands there shaking, watching him, waiting for the next lie to reveal itself.

Because he can feel it in his bones now:

Nothing about this was ever going to be as simple as one bullet.

100.

Hannah Wagner is gone by the time Wyatt makes it back to her cottage.

It's Alek sitting on the steps instead, arms wrapped around herself like she's trying to hold her world together.

"She left," Alek says.

Wyatt stares at the door like it might open if he stares hard enough. He has survived his duel. He walked out of the woods alive. And now he's lost Hannah, this time for good, he's certain of that. On a day when he's done what he needed to win, somehow he still feels like he lost.

He sits down next to Alek on the front steps—to keep from falling down. It takes some time for either one of them to speak again.

Finally Wyatt says, "Did *you* at least get to say goodbye to her?"

Alek shakes her head.

"No goodbye," she says. "No note. I think she'd had enough."

"She wanted to win so bad," Wyatt says, staring out at the lawn in front of them.

"Maybe in her own way she did," Alek says.

Alek knows what happened between Wyatt and Zhi. All the survivors do. She says she still wants to hear all about it from him, maybe just because it's a way for them to stop talking about Hannah.

Wyatt takes her through it, almost step by step, from the time The Host handed him his gun until he used it to shoot Zhi in the upper arm right after Zhi had missed.

"Remember when I told you I'd taken gymnastics in high school one time?" Wyatt says. "Well, if I make it out of this thing alive, someday I have to tell my old coach it saved my life twice."

"So you're telling me you saved your own life today from a gymnast because of a gymnastics move?"

"Kinda," Wyatt says.

He grins.

"Think of me as the Artful Dodger," Wyatt says.

"Wasn't he a con man in *Oliver Twist*?" she says.

"Kinda," Wyatt says again. After a long pause, he continues, "I hit him in the shoulder . . . I didn't—" He stops. Tries again. "I didn't mean to—"

Alek's voice is gentle, but it doesn't let him off the hook.

"Did he live?"

"I don't know," he says.

And that's the worst part. Not knowing. Not being able to undo it. Not being able to call it anything clean.

"You still want company?" Alek says after another lengthy silence.

"No," Wyatt says quietly.

"Come find me later," Alek says.

"I will."

Wyatt looks at Alek and thinks about how lucky he is to have her as a friend, even not knowing for how much longer.

"I'll always be here for you," she says.

"I know you will."

He walks across the lawn and down toward the woods, where they'd all gathered for that phone conversation with Jimmy last night. It feels more like last month, or last year, after the events of the day.

At least Hannah is alive, he thinks.

It doesn't lessen the hurt he's feeling. He sits down in the grass, facing the trees.

He had thought he'd lost her once before. But then he felt they had found their way back to each other, if not with the same closeness he'd felt in those first days, when he'd been knocked off balance by her beauty and intelligence and sheer goodness.

Now she's gone without so much as a goodbye, and there is a part of him—big part—that really does know he will probably never see her again.

He's experienced so much loss since arriving in Ohio, they all have.

But he was the one carrying so much extra baggage around, and not just from one game to the next. All the secrets about himself he'd wanted to share with Hannah. And Alek. And Jack.

I really am the Artful Dodger.

These were the secrets he wished he could have shared with Reg Drummond, before losing him, too.

And even though he knows Hannah is alive, Wyatt has a partial understanding of what Jack had felt after he lost Elena.

Jack had told him about all the things he regretted leaving unsaid with Elena, and how that would always haunt him.

There is so much Wyatt wished he had told Hannah.

Maybe even the truth.

Wyatt stares at his hands. They won't stop shaking. Fear doesn't explain all of it.

Guilt does.

He sits here for a long time, feeling as alone as he ever has in his life.

Alone with his regrets.

And with his secrets.

101.

There are six competitors left:

Jack McHenry.

Alek Andrich.

Ant Tipton.

Wyatt Jordan.

Marcelo Oliveira.

Somehow, against every expectation, the sixth is Lin Zhi—the one who took the bullet.

"I'm not eliminating someone for taking a bullet," The Host had told them at dinner last night.

"Still making up the rules as you go along?" Wyatt had asked.

The Host smiled. "No. Just choosing which ones to enforce."

Alek is still processing Hannah being gone. But she is gone, and Jack is still here because of the decision she'd made to help him.

The A Team is down to three:

Alek, Jack, Wyatt.

That's what Alek keeps telling herself, anyway.

They will be told at tonight's dinner what their next destination is, when they are leaving.

Before that, Alek decides to check in on Jack, see how he's recovering. She finds him stretched out on his living room sofa, one hand on his ribs.

Jack tells her that the worst of the damage, according to the doctor—and his portable X-ray machine—is a hairline fracture of his kneecap, of all things. His ribs are badly bruised, but not broken. Nor is his nose.

"The doc's English was thin. The diagnosis wasn't," he says. "I'm basically fine, which is doctor talk for: 'You're going to hate your life for a week.'"

It's plain to see how swollen his nose is, even underneath the bandage the doctor had applied.

"Let's face it, the biggest bruise is my ego," he says. "No offense, but I got my ass kicked by a girl."

"No offense taken," Alek says. Now she grins. "Well, maybe a little bit."

"By rights, I'm the one who should be out of here," Jack says.

"She didn't seem to think so," Alek says.

They talk for a few minutes about what they might be facing next. Both Alek and Jack agree that they must be approaching the end of this competition, even though The Host hasn't come right out and said anything like that.

"All I know is that we're still here," Jack says.

"Are we sure that's good news?" Alek asks.

Jack reaches up and pulls the bandage off his nose.

"Don't you still need that?"

"Probably," he says.

He groans as he slowly raises himself up off the sofa. Alek can see he's favoring one side. *He is tough, though*, she thinks, and she loves that about Jack.

Alek leans in. "Easy."

Jack waves her off. "We should go get Wyatt. He needs us."

When they arrive at Wyatt's cottage, Alek gives a couple of quick raps on the door.

No answer.

Alek does it again.

Still nothing.

"Hey kid," Jack shouts through the closed door. "It's Alek and me. Let's go eat."

Still nothing from inside.

"He said he'd be waiting for me to come get him," Alek says. "And my experience with Wyatt is that he generally does what he says he's going to do."

Jack tries the knob. The door is open.

They both step inside.

"Hey, Wyatt," Alek calls out. "Where you at?"

They walk into Wyatt's bedroom. It looks so neat to Alek, the bed made, towels folded on top of the spread. The counters in the bathroom are empty. No products of any kind on the shelf in the shower.

The closet is empty.

Even the empty hangers are neatly hung.

"No sign of that duffel bag he carries," Jack says. "This is bad."

"No, it isn't." She calls out, "Wyatt!"

Silence.

They walk back into the living room. They take a closer look around.

Nothing appears to be out of place here, either.

It's when they open the door to the kitchen that they see it on the table.

The necklace with the red button.

Alek stares at it, not moving. Like if she doesn't move, it won't be real.

Jack's voice is low. "He quit," he says.

Jack doesn't touch it. He just stares, jaw tight, eyes scanning the room again like Wyatt might step out of a closet and laugh and say *got you.*

Alek lifts the chain. It's heavier than it should be.

There's something else on the table, tucked under the red stone—one sheet of paper, folded once, like it was placed there on purpose. Neat. Centered. Like Wyatt couldn't leave without making it look right.

Alek opens it.

It's only a few lines. Handwritten.

She reads silently at first, then out loud because Jack is looking at her like he can't breathe.

> *I'm sorry.*
>
> *I wouldn't do what he asked. Not like that.*
>
> *I also realized there's something important I need to do.*
>
> *I couldn't do it and stay.*
>
> *Tell Alek I'm safe.*
>
> *–W*

Alek's throat tightens on the last line.

Jack takes the paper from her and reads it again, slower, like if he looks hard enough the words will change. Then he crushes it in his fist.

"That kid doesn't leave notes," Jack says, voice low and shaking. "He leaves jokes."

Alek looks back at the empty closet. The folded towels. The cleared shelves. Wyatt didn't storm out. He packed. And he planned.

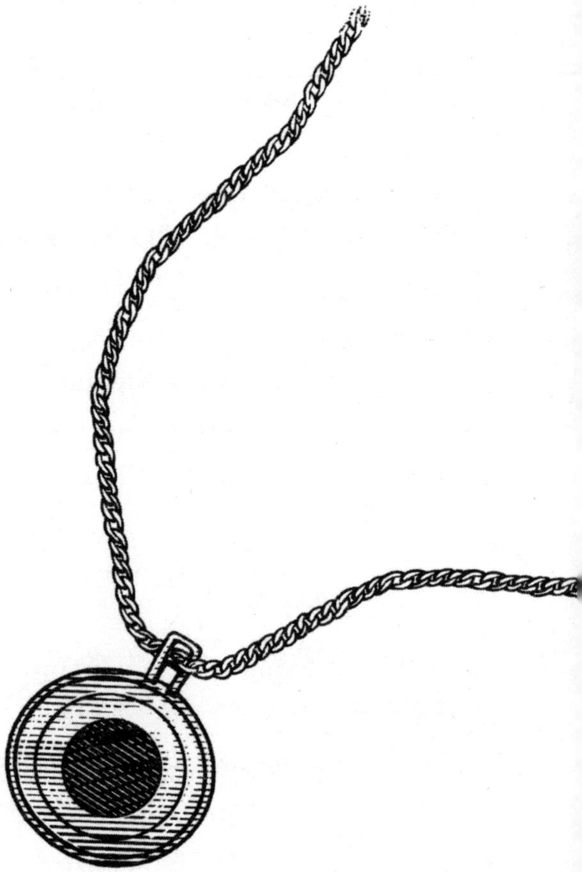

102.

THREE DAYS LATER

Jimmy Donaldson is still running.

Feeling he really is running for his life this time.

If not for his life, for the lives of Jack, Alek, Wyatt, Hannah, and whoever else survived their duels.

He hasn't slept. It's been like this for nearly three days.

He's in London again. He's soaked to the bone, rain slashing sideways through the streets. His mouth throbs where he lost a tooth in a fight that shouldn't have happened in a hotel room that shouldn't have been compromised.

At that moment, he didn't care.

None of this should be happening. None of it. Especially the deaths.

And whatever insane deadly duels had been forced on them.

An hour ago, he was nearly captured in the Royal Horseguards Hotel by three very large men. In his damn room.

None of that matters.

Just keep running.

Finally he stops, has to stop, under the dripping awning of a pub. The Ship & Shovell.

He needs to send a text. To Jack, Alek, Hannah, Wyatt.

And does:

Hope you're all safe. Crazy days. Getting crazier all the time. I've been back to New York. Then Frankfurt for a day. Now back in London. I'm closer than I've ever been to solving this puzzle. Finding the murderer, because that's the way I think of him now. Really close. Continue to trust me if you can. Be safe. Make good choices. I'll try to do the same. Just know this, and know it's important, even though you don't know why yet:

Gavin Hillshire might be alive.

Then Jimmy is running through the teeming rain, again. His shoes keep making loud squishing noises with every step. He's never been this exhausted in his life.

What a terrible night. He finally sees a cab up ahead.

Finally, he catches a break.

But before he can get in—the cab is cut off. Two black Escalades.

Doors fly open. Men fly out.

He immediately recognizes the thugs from his hotel.

Hands grab him. Yank him. Drag him into the back of one of the SUVs before he can even get his feet under him. He fights, but it's three on one and they've done this before.

Once inside, he hears a voice. Smooth. Familiar. It's coming from the very rear of the SUV.

"So nice to see you again, James," The Host says.

"Wish I could say the same," Jimmy says. "But no worries. I'll take a free ride anytime. Just tell the driver to drop me at Heathrow."

A soft chuckle.

"Actually," the man says, "we're going to Farnborough. Private. You deserve the best. None of this could've happened without you. I really do owe you a debt of gratitude."

Jimmy stares into the rear cabin until the man's face becomes visible.

The Host.

Jimmy's voice hardens. "No. I'm not responsible for this. Not for these deaths. Not for your games."

"You helped open the door," The Host says. "Now you get to see what's on the other side."

Jimmy leans forward, jaw clenched. "Where are you taking me?"

"To a place where all your questions will finally be answered. And where a winner will be crowned."

He pauses.

"Do you know who the winner is, James?" he adds.

One more pause, before The Host adds, "I do."

103.

SIX DAYS LATER

The five of them stand at the base of the tallest building they've ever seen, sunlight flashing off glass high enough to make you dizzy. The Burj Khalifa had served in Dubai for the past two decades as international headquarters for Gavin Hillshire, Inc.

Hillshire had moved his primary offices there from New York City just before the global financial crisis of 2008.

There are just five of them standing outside, feeling more pressure than they have since the field in Ohio when they found out they were among those who had made the cut.

They are in a place known as the City of Gold and, once again, they have no idea what's coming next.

Are they about to put their lives on the line one more time, maybe for the last time?

Five of them this close to the ultimate prize, one they all still think is worth it, despite the cost. Five. Not six.

Hannah is gone.

Wyatt is gone.

And no one got to say goodbye.

Jack, Alek, Tipton, Zhi, Marcelo.

They stand shoulder to shoulder, like strangers forced into the same photograph. Above them, the building disappears into haze and glare.

Alek squints up. "What number do you think they press to get to the top—one thousand?"

No one laughs.

No one even pretends.

Their nerves are too raw for humor. Everything in them is tuned to danger now, like animals that have learned the sound of the trapdoor.

They're just waiting to go inside to meet with The Host.

Wyatt is the latest to have left them, without a trace, without an explanation or a goodbye of his own.

More mystery to go with every other mystery they have encountered so far. But all of it has brought them to this place, this building. And as awe-inspiring as Burj Khalifa is, it also inspires unbearable fear and dread. They have absolutely no clue what awaits them inside.

"Are we ready to do this?" Jack asks.

"As we'll ever be," Alek says.

She turns to Jack.

"Just—" Alek says.

He has a feeling he knows what it's going to be. It's the same one they've all been asking since they left Tuscany.

Alek asks it again, anyway, as much for her own benefit as theirs, because there's one question that keeps looping in her head like an alarm that won't shut off:

"Where's Wyatt?"

104.

The view provided by the wraparound windows on the 147th floor is truly spectacular, even more spectacular than they had imagined it might be. The city spreads out below them—roads, towers, sunlight bouncing off everything—almost too neat to be real.

"If I look hard enough," Jack says, "I can see my old rig in West Texas."

Jack and Alek have taken seats on one side of a long conference table. Tipton and Marcelo and Zhi are on the other. Before they'd boarded the plane in Florence, The Host had only told them their next destination, not what the next test would be, even after teasing it.

"Will it be a grand finale? A spectacle?" he'd said coyly. "I guess we'll have to just wait and see."

The Host had not accompanied them on their flight to the Jetex Dubai terminal at Al Maktoum International Airport. He said he had another important stop to make before Dubai. So the five of them have been waiting at a mansion in Emirates Hills for the past few days. No phones. No explanations. Just the feeling of being watched.

The door to the conference room opens now. The Host appears. Impeccably dressed as always. Dark suit, white shirt, freshly shaven, no hair out of place. He faces them from the head of the table, the city spread out endlessly behind him.

"What happened to Wyatt?" Alek says.

"Not your concern, Ms. Andrich. He's out of the contest. That's the only thing of import."

"We have a right to be concerned," Alek says. "He's our friend."

The Host offers her a smile as thin as paper. "He's one less competitor. And not your friend. Trust me on that."

He lets out that disgusting laugh of his.

"He's a big boy," he says. "Though so often too big for his britches."

Jack's voice is low and dangerous. "Cut the games. What's next?"

"All in due time, Mr. McHenry," The Host says. "All in due time. Right now, I have a proposition for all of you."

He leans forward, palms on the table.

"If you can agree among yourselves who should be declared the winner," he continues, "I will immediately present checks of $25 million to the other four."

He lets that sink in.

"What did you just say?" Alek asks, as stunned as the rest of them.

"Hold on," Jack says. "After all of us have fought as hard as we have, you want us to decide the winner now by a vote among ourselves?" He shakes his head. "It will all come down to a damn show of hands?"

"Basically, yes," The Host says. "Think of it as a parting gift. A clean ending."

"And that's it?" Alek says. "That's how it ends?"

"If you agree to my terms, yes," The Host says. "It's time for us all to move on."

Alek hears her own breathing. Too loud.

"And if we don't?"

His eyes brighten, like that's the question he wanted.

"Then we proceed," he says simply. "And I promise you: It will hurt."

"That sounds ominous," Alek says.

"You have no idea," The Host says.

No one speaks as he turns to leave, giving them the room.

"Think it over," he says.

He's about to make another dramatic exit, Alek thinks to herself. *Maybe his last.* For now, his words are still hanging in the air, in this rarefied air, 147 floors up from the street.

"Wait."

Alek's voice stops him as he gets to the door.

"Something you'd like to add, Ms. Andrich?" he says. "You do so often like to have the last word."

"You're being serious?" she says. "You'd call the whole thing off–just like that–and we'd all just walk away?"

"Indeed," he says.

He slowly shifts his gaze from one face to another, then he continues. "All but *The One*. He, or she, gets to stay."

105.

Alek is the first to speak once the door has closed.

"Are we actually going to vote on this?"

The words are barely out of her mouth when Tipton responds.

"I'll go first," he says. "I vote for me. Thanks to the rest of you for playing. Safe trip home."

He looks around the room. "Where's the champagne?"

Zhi, who rarely says much of anything, speaks up.

"You're voting for yourself. Shocking," he says.

Despite the tension in the room, Alek smiles at that.

Even Tipton can't help himself and smiles, too.

Alek looks at the others. "Okay," she says. "Let's do this like adults. First question: Do we even believe him?"

"Absolutely not," Jack says.

"Second that," Zhi says.

"Let's pretend for a second we do and talk it through, and not take all day to do it," Alek says. "I'm not saying we couldn't ever agree on which one of us should be the big winner. But let's say, for the sake of conversation, that we could arrive at a consensus. It would mean no more guns, no more knives. Or mountains or deserts. Or snakes or sharks."

"No more dying," Jack adds quietly.

Alek says, "But the first order of business is deciding if we even want to consider his proposal. Or think that we ever could get a consensus."

"I say we play it out," Jack says. "Winner take all."

"Even though he's the one still making up the rules as he goes along?" Alek asks. "And even though we still don't know how he's going to come up with a winner if we don't accept this offer?"

"I know you've all heard me say this before," Jack says, "but screw him."

Tipton and Marcelo and Zhi slowly nod their heads in agreement.

"I might have put it more colorfully," Tipton says. "But on this one, I'm actually with the rest of you."

"Well, at least we're in agreement on that," Alek says.

In the next moment, The Host reappears, clearly having been listening to their conversation from the next room. It is much the way he's been listening in on them from the start whenever it's suited him, and without them knowing for sure when he was.

"Fifty million," he says.

"Wait," Marcelo says. "You just doubled the offer that quickly."

The Host shrugs. "It's what you do in a negotiation. And to be honest . . ."

"Good one," Alek says.

"Even I fear what comes next," The Host says. "But what's necessary can be terrifying. It's locked into a process for a reason." He lets that sit. "Take the money. Call it mercy. Or stay and pretend you're better than those of us who built this."

Marcelo leans forward, voice careful. "So to be clear. Fifty million each to walk away. And a billion for whoever we agree is *The One*."

"Indeed," The Host says again. "More money than any of you will see in your lifetimes. In ten lifetimes."

"But not a billion," Tipton says.

The room falls into silence until Marcelo blurts out, "I'll take it!"

The rest turn to stare at him. But Marcelo isn't looking at them. He's looking directly at The Host, as if they're the only ones in the room.

"I'll take the money and walk away," he says. "No questions asked."

"But he said that first we have to agree who in the room should be *The One*," Alek says.

"Maybe *I* already have," The Host says.

Chuckles. The sound is even more jarring than usual.

"You have a deal, sir," he says to Marcelo.

Then he adds: "Now get out of here."

Marcelo stands. He gives them a quick nod—apology, or farewell, or both—and heads for the door. But before he can leave the room, The Host reaches out and yanks the red button off the chain around his neck.

"Loser," The Host says.

"Maybe," Marcelo says, "but a rich loser." He gives the rest of them a quick nod, then walks out of the room.

The Host walks back to the head of the table and addresses the four people still left, out of the original one thousand.

Jack. Alek. Tipton. Zhi.

"Anyone else?"

Tipton's gaze flicks to the door—like he's listening for a sound nobody else can hear. *Could this be a way out?* he allows himself to think for a second. *But what if he doesn't hold up his end? He can't risk anything happening to her.*

Tipton looks at Alek, then the others. "Let's get on with it."

The Host says, "Put your red buttons on the table."

Alek doesn't move.

"What for?" she asks.

The Host's voice stays calm.

"No more safety nets."

106.

Alek and Jack and Tipton and Zhi take off their necklaces as ordered, slowly slide them to the middle of the table.

Alek does it as quickly as possible so the others can't see how badly her hand is shaking.

This time The Host is on the money, in every conceivable way. No net. No reset button. No deal you can talk your way into.

The Host says, "You're certain no one else wants to take the deal that Mr. Oliveira just took?"

Alek looks at Jack, then across the table at Tipton and Zhi.

Jack says, "We've talked about this. We've all come too far. We've seen people we care about die in front of our eyes. Or up and leave the way Hannah did. Or disappear the way Wyatt did." He stops himself there, before going on: "But as different as we all are, we have one thing in common: We're still here."

"We're survivors," Tipton says, almost like he hates the word.

Zhi gives a small nod.

The Host studies them, annoyed now, trying not to show it.

"Have it your way," The Host says. "Just understand that there's no going back, for any of you."

Alek can't decide whether he sounds disappointed, or angry—or both. She's not even sure what she herself is feeling at this moment, if she even feels like a survivor, other than this: She needs to get out of this room for a few minutes. She wants to be alone and breathe and think about this deal they were all just offered and whether or not she wants to change her mind and take it.

And just go home.

She looks at her hands, in front of her on the table.

They're still shaking.

She discreetly places them in her lap, then shoots a look over at Jack McHenry, who is seated next to her. If he is feeling as nervous or as anxious as she is, he's not showing it. But then he never does show you much of anything, unless he's talking about Elena. He still does from time to time, often late at night, when he is willing to share his feelings.

One more time, Jack says, "We play the sucker out."

He looks at Alek. "Right?"

She doesn't hesitate. Jack is asking for her permission, deferring to her. Alek has begun to believe she's more and more of a leader the longer the competition has gone on. She's become more and more confident, despite the nerves she's feeling at the moment, and despite sitting right next to a former Army Ranger.

"Right," Alek says.

Tipton and Zhi nod in agreement.

"The four of you will soon regret the decision you just made," The Host says. "Sooner than you think."

He is once again walking back toward the door when they all hear another voice, this one coming from a speaker at the far end of the conference table that has been silent the entire time they've been in here.

It is a voice they all know.

Wyatt Jordan's.

"You still can't read the room, can you, Dad?" Wyatt says.

107.

As shocked as Alek is to hear Wyatt Jordan's voice, The Host looks more shocked, staggering back a few steps, his back to the wall. For the first time in as long as Alek can remember, he doesn't look in control.

"How–"

"Still think I'm too big for my britches, Dad?" Wyatt says.

What did we just hear? Alek thinks.

Is that really Wyatt?

Here?

Calling The Host his father?

Jack is the one who jumps to his feet, furious, running hot that quickly. He looks angrier than when Ant Tipton pulled the knife on him.

He points a finger now at the gray speaker, wanting to grab it and smash it on the floor, or throw it against one of the windows.

Maybe it's Wyatt Jordan he wants to throw across the room.

Whoever he really is.

"No. No way," he snaps at the speaker. "Wyatt, is this really you?"

"It is, Jack," they hear. "Not sure if that's the good news or the bad news."

"And you're calling him–"

"My father," Wyatt says.

Alek tries to put a calming hand on Jack's arm, get him to sit back down. He shakes it off.

Alek says, "What are you saying?"

Wyatt takes a breath on the other end. Like he's been holding it for days.

"My full name is Wyatt Jordan Hillshire," Wyatt says.

Jack says, "Hillshire. As in Gavin Hillshire? The guy Jimmy texted us about?"

"He was my grandfather," Wyatt says.

There is a brief silence before he adds, "And the man with you is Ward Hillshire. Dear old Dad, unfortunately."

Ward Hillshire still looks like he's seen a ghost. Or is hearing one.

"So it's the two of you behind this thing?" Alek says. "And you let us think you were one of us the whole time?"

"That part was real," Wyatt says. "I was being tested, too, right along with the rest of you. I just couldn't tell you."

Alek is shaking her head, slowly, side to side, in disbelief.

"So which one of you is the boss?" Alek asks.

"My father was, right up until a few minutes ago," Wyatt says. "Now I am." They can hear him sigh. "It's complicated. But it's why we're here in Dubai."

"Hey, kid, here's something that's not complicated at all," Jack says. "You've got things you want to say to us? Get in here and say them to our faces."

He turns to look at Ward Hillshire, still frozen in place.

Jack steps toward Ward, voice low and dangerous. "Did you know he was going to do this? Did you know he was listening the whole time?"

"Do I look like I knew?"

The door behind him opens.

Wyatt isn't the one who comes walking into the room.

There are four guards in black jumpsuits instead. They silently come and stand behind each of them at the table.

"Time for the final tests," they hear Wyatt say over the speaker.

"We're still doing this?" Jack says.

"Not my call," Wyatt says. "But yes. The final act was always supposed to be here."

"Where?" Alek demands.

"Downstairs," Wyatt says.

Then he adds: "Good luck to all of you. I mean that, whether you feel like believing me or not."

Wyatt pauses.

Then his tone changes—harder, aimed to cut.

"And now, Dad, as your last official act as the person in charge of these games, take them to the rooms," he says.

He waits one more beat and adds:

"I'm in charge now."

108.

Ward Hillshire reluctantly accompanies them in the elevator, the city spread out below the glass.

He exhales through his nose, like he's already tired of them all.

"Think of what is about to happen as endgames," he says. "Extreme tests designed for you all individually. Predetermined by my father long ago. And ones that he always said were nonnegotiable, unfortunately."

"More extreme than the duels?" Alek asks. "Or the lies you've been feeding us from the beginning?"

"Take it up with my son afterward, if you survive one more time, Ms. Andrich," he says. "It really has been our firm belief all along that what doesn't kill you in these games will make all of you stronger, and help us identify the strongest possible leader among you. Many things have changed—just in the past few minutes. But not that."

Alek says, "More mind games."

Ward gives her a thin look. "Everything has been a mind game. Even when it looked like something else."

Jack says, "What about your father? Is he actually dead? Or is that another layer?"

Ward's jaw tightens. "He's dead."

Tipton says, "And your boy just took your crown."

Ward's eyes flicker. Not denial. Humiliation.

"He did," Ward says. "And if you survive long enough, you can ask him why."

He shakes his head. He's lost a duel with his own son.

"In a few minutes, I fervently hope to be done with you, once and for all," he says.

Tipton says, "So what's next?"

"You will essentially be asked to compete against yourself," Ward says. "All of you will be asked to do the same."

Ward looks at the doors. He'd rather be anywhere else.

"You'll be alone," he says. "Each of you. In a room made for you."

Jack's voice is flat. "Made how?"

Ward meets his eyes.

"By your worst fear," he says. "And whatever you do—don't confuse discomfort with danger. That mistake costs people everything."

109.

Alek Andrich is as frightened as she's ever been in her life as soon as the door to her small room closes behind her.

Not because of the unknown.

Because of what she knows in this moment.

The reality of the inside of this room.

To this point in her life, she has survived wars, real ones, first at home and then in this "game." She survived a knife fight with a man she's still certain would have finished the job if given the opportunity.

But none of that has prepared her for the snakes and spiders crawling toward her now on the floor of this room.

Snakes and spiders of all sizes.

What appears to be an advancing army of them.

Making her skin crawl.

This is fake, Alek is already telling herself.

It has to be an illusion, some trick of technology.

Special effects.

Except that the terror and revulsion she feels couldn't be more real.

This is her nightmare, slowly advancing toward her.

And there is no place for her to run.

Or hide.

No chair or table on which she can stand.

No way for her to somehow climb up the wall to get away from these crawly things.

And isn't that what people say when they describe the feeling of losing their minds?

I was ready to climb the walls.

Alek wishes there was a way for her to do that right now.

Except these creatures would probably follow her.

She looks down, already feeling them on her even though they aren't, at least not yet.

Alek has always had a phobia—a pathological one, really—about any kind of snake or spider. The "creepy crawlies," she'd called them as a child.

It was why, when she'd been given her choice, she had chosen Antarctica over Chile, which she'd been told was crawling with awful creatures.

She'd admitted that all the way back in Ohio.

Only now the creatures are everywhere.

This can't really be happening, she tries to tell herself.

The Host often spoke about mind games.

That's what these had to be.

It. Can't. Be. Real.

Somehow it is.

She is wearing white jeans.

She can clearly see the first spider moving up from her left ankle now, taking its sweet time.

She starts shaking her leg frantically to get it off her.

It doesn't work.

The spider keeps moving.

There isn't a lot of light in this room. But there's enough for her to see other spiders, and now snakes, circling her feet.

She tries to kick them away.

It just makes more of them appear.

Alek can't help herself now.

She screams.

And then feels the first bite.

Looks down and sees the first black spider, which has already made its way up her left leg to her thigh.

She slaps at it frantically with her hand.

Still screaming as she does.

Now there is one on her arm.

She tries to swat it away.

Another appears.

Her skin is crawling now, in every possible and terrible way.

Now she is crying. Not just crying but sobbing in a way she never has in front of the others. Not wanting to look weak in front of them.

She sees the huge rattlesnake at her feet, coiling, looking up at her almost indifferently, its tail beginning to vibrate.

She tries to scream again.

But can't.

No sound comes out of her.

She's back in the freezing water in Antarctica, unable to breathe. Afraid then that she was going to drown before she got any air back into her.

She hears the hiss of the snake as she feels another sting. Looks down and sees an even bigger spider making its way up her right leg.

She swats at this one as she backs away from the snake, nearly falling down into the snakes and spiders between her and the door.

She tells herself she is hallucinating.

Has to be hallucinating.

Alek had told herself she would never quit.

Promised her mother she wouldn't quit.

But this is finally too much, even for her.

Finally she is able to speak.

"Stop it!" she screams. "Please–stop!"

Alek turns and reaches for the door handle.

Locked.

More movement at her feet. Her hands shake so hard she can't control them. She hates that. Hates it more than the fear.

She wasn't a victim in the desert. She wasn't a victim in the war. But this–

This is the thing she has never been able to outthink.

And that's what makes it cruel.

"I give up!" she screams again. "Please–!"

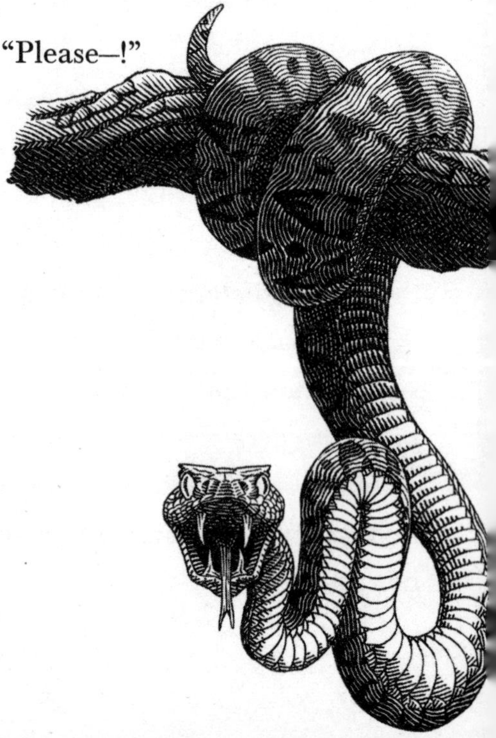

110.

Ward Hillshire stands with Jack outside the next door, a guard on either side like this is a prison transfer instead of a "game."

"Where are the others?" Jack asks.

"All on this floor, in their own chambers," Hillshire says. "Alone with their demons."

"Care to tell me what that means?" Jack says.

"You need only concern yourself with your own demons at the moment," Hillshire says. "You know the unfortunate expression of modern times, Mr. McHenry? 'You do you.' Surely you recall sharing with your interviewer back in Ohio that you detest confined spaces. That's what is waiting for you on the other side of this door. Do you remain convinced you can handle this?"

Jack looks down at his tattoo.

"I don't lose," he says.

"If you come to find you can't handle this, we of course can let you out of here," Hillshire says. "But just know that once you step back outside, you will have lost. No arguments. No second chances. No red button."

"I won't leave the room," Jack says. "And I won't lose."

He gives Hillshire a long look.

Jack's voice drops. "How confined."

Ward looks at the door like he doesn't like the answer either.

"A coffin," he says.

Jack holds still for a moment. Then he nods once, like it's a decision and a promise at the same time.

"I'm on the one-yard line," Jack says.

He takes a deep breath, then lets it out. Then does the same thing again. Jack knows how important it's going to be for him to control his breathing once he's inside. It's a tool he's used before in moments of great stress.

And moments of great fear.

I had no fear jumping out of airplanes, he thinks, *not even the first jump without a trainer.*

Maybe because all he had around him was space.

And air.

This is different.

He turns to Ward: "Open it."

111.

The box into which the guard lowers Jack is smaller than a coffin. At first there's room to breathe.

Then Jack hears a low whirring. The walls shift. Telescoping panels slide inward until his shoulders are pinned and his knees can't rise. His arms are trapped at his sides, not quite crushed, but close enough that panic lights him up.

Even with Jack knowing he could call this off before the guard leaves the room if he wanted to.

He doesn't want to, even if he already feels he's suffocating. Even with no lid to the coffin.

Jack can look up, and out. He can see the ceiling. He can see the rim of the opening above his face.

He just can't get out.

Can't move either his arms or legs enough to climb out, even if he wanted to.

"The boss will be watching, and listening," the guard says. "He told me to give you a safe word you can use. One word."

Jack's heart is already racing. He is starting to sweat, already feeling he's about to be sick.

"What word?" he asks.

It doesn't even sound like his own voice.

"Quit," the guard says. "Easy to remember."

"He'll never hear me say that," Jack says.

"If you say so," the guard replies, like he's heard that before.

When the guard closes the door behind him, it sounds like the door to a jail cell being slammed shut.

Jack starts to feel the tingling sensation he always feels in his hands and feet when he is in any sort of confined space and wants to move around but can't. It's the sensation he sometimes feels on an airplane when it encounters turbulence, his seat belt securely fastened, knowing he can't get up and move around, as much as he'd rather do that than just . . . sit there and wait for it to be over.

He barely fights off the first real wave of nausea.

There is only a tiny lightbulb in an upper corner of the coffin.

Other than that, he is mostly in darkness.

It makes Jack feel even more trapped than ever.

It's not just his heart racing now, it's his mind. It's the memories of other times when his claustrophobia has paralyzed him with fear this way, and there wasn't a thing he could do about it.

This is as bad as it has ever been.

Or could be.

In the next moment, though, it gets worse.

Much worse.

The smell hits.

It pours in convincingly physical and choking. Rot and garbage and sewage—wet, sour, thick. It fills the coffin, fills his lungs, fills his head. It's so strong it feels like he can taste it.

Jack's eyes water instantly.

He knows it's a trick. Some system through vents, a gas line, a canister. A weapon that doesn't leave bruises. What else could it be?

He tells himself these are only special effects. Illusions. Artificial whatever, designed to make him lose his freaking mind.

Or crawl out of his own skin.

Whatever it is, they're succeeding like freaking champions. His body doesn't care that it's fake.

Jack feels he's at the bottom of a sewer, not this coffin, the stench that terrible, and overwhelming.

And disgusting.

Now he's certain he's going to be sick.

They know.

Know that it's not just claustrophobia with him.

It's more than that, and something he dealt with in his normal life on a daily basis.

He hadn't told the interviewer back in the red tent about being a germaphobe. He'd never told anybody with whom he'd played football, even getting down in the dirt the way you had to. He hadn't told anybody with the Rangers. Especially not anybody with the Rangers. He never told anybody in the caves or the jungles in which he'd fought, sometimes crawling around on his belly. Or in the filthy rooms that served as temporary barracks.

He kept it to himself. Jack wore it. Got through it. The only person he'd ever told was the therapist he'd seen after he got out of the Army, when he was about to take the job on the oil rig.

They must have gotten to her somehow.

Because they obviously know.

And then it gets worse, because the smell isn't the only thing.

Something damp splatters against the side of the coffin near his cheek. Something soft brushes his forearm. He can't see what it is, only feel it, and his brain does what it always does in the dark: It fills in the blanks with the worst version.

Jack clenches and unclenches his fists. It's the only movement he has.

His nostrils are filled with a smell he'd only encountered a few times with the Rangers, when they'd discovered a decomposing body.

He has only been in here a few minutes, Jack's certain of that. But it already feels like hours. Or days.

In so many ways, this is his ultimate nightmare:

The complete loss of control.

He can't even control his breathing now. He's afraid to breathe. That would mean taking in more of the stench.

Feeling he can taste it.

He thinks he'd rather suffocate than do that.

This is what hell must be like.

My hell.

This can't be happening, he tells himself again.

But it is.

Jack feels he might black out.

But he's not going to say the word, no matter what.

He's not going to quit.

Somewhere, in the back of his mind, he hears his mother's voice—an old prayer she taught him when he was small.

He reaches for it like it's a rope.

But it's not there.

112.

Ant Tipton has spent most of his life selling one simple story: Fearless. Untouchable. Built different.

It's always been a lie.

One he's told to the rest of the world since childhood. Just not to himself. Never to himself. As much as he wants to believe it.

He knows why, of course, just because he could teach a bloody master class on the reasons for his darkest and worst fears:

When he was twelve, Tipton had walked away from a twin-engine plane crash near Cornwall. His parents and his younger brother had died fiery deaths that day. Somehow Ant Tipton had survived. It was like one of those stories you read about, wild stories about sole survivors involving luck or destiny, about insert-tragedy-here not being your time, at least not yet.

That had been him.

Not his parents, not his little brother. Just him.

He remembers the sound more than anything—metal tearing, the engine screaming, the pitch of human voices when panic turns them into something raw and animal.

Now he's securely strapped into a chair in a room that looks too clean, too modern, too controlled. A huge wall-screen in front of him, one big as life.

Or death.

He's back in that small plane, just looking out from the cockpit this time as the plane dips and rolls and barely pulls out of one dive after another.

Tipton's riding a roller coaster through the sky, gripping the sides of his chair so hard he's afraid they might break apart.

If he doesn't break first.

And in the next second, the room disappears.

He's back in the plane.

Not as a passenger this time—front row, looking out through the windshield as the horizon tilts, rolls, dives. The sound is so loud it vibrates his bones. His hands clamp the chair arms so hard his knuckles ache.

The plane drops.

It yanks up.

It drops again.

The screen in front of him abruptly changes again.

Now he sees other planes, all around him, falling out of the sky, before crashing and burning.

He tries to tell himself that it's all just a movie, that he hasn't left this room, or this chair—he'd been in simulators plenty of times.

Tipton tells himself that it's all just a bad dream.

Only it doesn't feel like a dream.

Or a simulator.

It won't stop.

And he can't turn away.

His nervous system doesn't know pixels. His nervous system knows that day in Cornwall.

Tipton, strapped in, can only sit and watch the plane crashes happen, and keep happening.

In the next moment, he's back in the cockpit, in even more of a death dive, the sound of the plane making his head feel it's about to explode before the plane does the same, and this time he'll be the one engulfed by flames.

Just the way it all happened when he was twelve.

The volume surges until it's not just loud—it's inside his skull. He hears screams, which sound exactly like the screams of his parents and his brother in the last few seconds before their plane crashed that day, before they perished, even if he miraculously did not.

Ant Tipton bites down so hard on his lower lip that he can taste blood, to keep from screaming himself.

He's not going to give them the satisfaction of that.

Or hearing him beg them to make it stop.

He squeezes his eyes shut.

The sound doesn't stop.

It gets worse.

Smoke. Heat.

The man who acts like he's afraid of nothing is afraid to open his eyes back up.

The volume in the room is pumped up even more.

He tells himself to keep his eyes closed.

He does want to tell them to make it stop now.

But he won't.

Or can't.

Tipton tries to convince himself one more time that none of this is real.

Only nothing has ever felt more real to him.

Not since he was twelve and it was really happening to him.

Now Ant Tipton is screaming, because he opens his eyes, looks down, and sees he's on fire.

113.

Lin Zhi is petrified of needles.

Not pain. Not heights. Not the moment in midair when the world spins and you have to find the floor again.

Needles.

The fear has humiliated him his whole life, because he can't reason his way out of it. He can be brave in a thousand ways and still go cold at the sight of a syringe.

He had nearly blacked out at the little hospital in Tuscany where he'd been taken after being shot by Wyatt. But it wasn't because of the pain from the gunshot wound.

It was because of the needles. First the injection he'd been given for the pain, and then being conscious when the Italian doctor had gone in to remove the bullet from his upper arm.

When Zhi had been competing in gymnastics for his country, he'd never been afraid when he'd become disoriented in midair, a condition known as the "twisties" in his sport. No, the loss of control, the chance that he could land on his back, had never panicked him the way needles did. Trypanophobia. The fear of needles.

The one time he'd had knee surgery, early in his gymnastics career, he'd had a panic attack as he was being wheeled into the operating room, before finally being sedated.

As he had walked into this room on the 146th floor, the guard had quickly reached over and pressed a cloth over his mouth before Zhi could resist.

It carried a sweet, chemical smell.

"Just let it happen," the guard murmured.

Now Zhi wakes strapped to an operating table.

A doctor and nurse, both wearing surgical masks, are standing over him. Bright lights glare down. The room is so white it feels unreal.

The doctor speaks calmly, like this is a routine appointment.

"Tissue damage," he says. "Infection risk. We need to do a repair."

The nurse steps closer. In her gloved hand is a syringe.

"Nerve and vascular repair," the doctor says, making it sound so pedestrian.

"We need to put you back under," the nurse says.

The needle in her hand looks as big to Zhi as a carving knife. He struggles in vain to get loose. But both his hands and feet are secured.

The nurse leans forward and swabs alcohol on his bare upper arm.

"Stop," Zhi says, too sharply, voice cracking.

He knows this is a form of madness he's dealt with his whole life, but he can't do anything to combat it in the moment. Or stop it himself.

Zhi is convinced these people aren't here to help him. They're here to inject him with something and kill him.

Do what the bullet hadn't done.

The nurse has the needle touching Zhi's arm now.

"We know this is torture for you, Mr. Zhi," she says in a

soothing voice. "But all of us in this room know there's a way to end it, don't we?"

He doesn't answer right away. Zhi's eyes dart to the syringe. Then the scalpel on the tray. Then back to the syringe.

"Don't we?" she repeats.

Zhi forces air into his lungs. "Yes," he whispers.

"Would you like for us to help you off this table, so you can walk out of this chamber?" the doctor says. "And walk out of your nightmare?"

Zhi focuses on the nurse's needle again, then on the scalpel in the doctor's hand. But then he tells himself—hears his own voice screaming at him inside his head—how close he is to winning.

Despite the full-blown terror he is feeling.

"No," he says, louder now—like he can scare the fear away with volume. "No!"

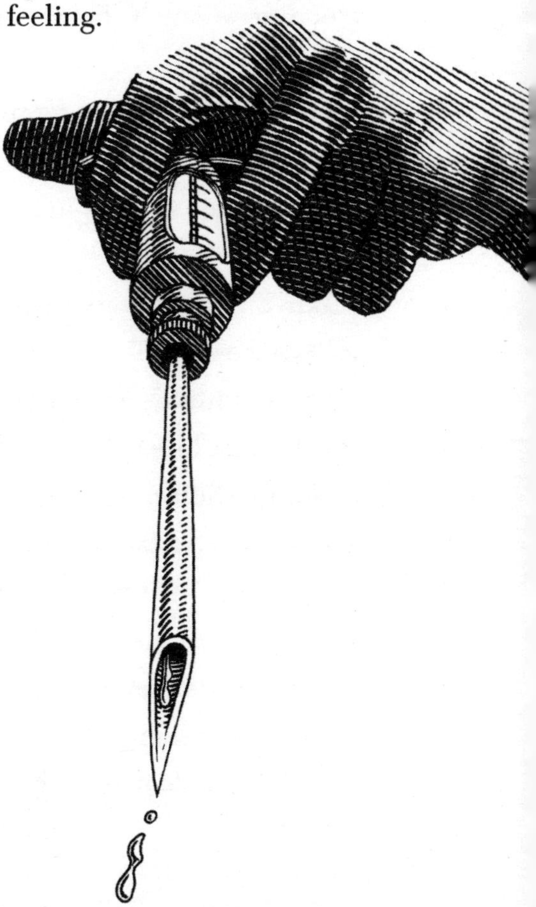

He squeezes his eyes shut just as he feels the tip of the needle puncture his arm.

Zhi keeps screaming—through the panic, through the humiliation, through the flooding terror—until the room tilts and the lights smear and his mind finally lets go.

114.

Ant was going to outlast them all.

He just was.

He was supposed to win in the end, that was his deal with The Host, back at the beginning, before he knew Ward Hillshire's true identity. He would spy on the other contestants. Not that he ever learned very much. From the start they'd all kept their distance from him.

And ultimately, Ant would act as The Host's henchman that day up on Mount Washington.

"My money's on you," The Host had told him when they'd struck their deal. "Quite a lot of money."

"Why?" Tipton had asked.

"Because we're very much alike," The Host had said.

"In what way?" Ant had asked.

"Kill or be killed," The Host had said that day.

"Not by choice."

"I know. Also like me you need a reason. Mine is the salvation of the world. Yours is her. The one person that you know I can still reach."

His hand wanders to the chain around his neck, the last gift she gave him before she left.

Ant had made it entirely clear he was willing to kill whoever got in his way to save her. He had shown how far he was willing to go on the mountain, where he'd been ordered to kill Reg Drummond and make it look like an accident.

Knowing now that the man had wanted to kill his own son. That way Ward Hillshire would have been the last man standing in the family. He'd never come right out and told Ant to kill the boy. He'd never used those exact words. But it had been understood. The closest Hillshire had come was saying, "Once Reg is gone . . . it would be a shame if the boy didn't make it down either."

But Ant Tipton had failed in his mission that day. Wyatt had survived.

Looking back now, having never discussed this with Ward Hillshire when he still thought of him as The Host, Ant wonders if the grenade at the hospital was supposed to kill Wyatt.

But Tipton learned something that day: If you win by breaking someone, you lose. Maybe even if it meant losing her. Maybe even if it meant losing the world.

He's in one of these rooms along with the others. *Maybe*, he can't help but think, *it's because Hillshire has reneged on our deal. Maybe everything changed when I didn't succeed in killing Wyatt. Maybe she's already gone.*

Or it's as simple as this: Ant really does have to pass one final test before being declared the winner. Hillshire can't hand him the trophy simply for showing up today.

Ant has never doubted, not for a minute, that he's better than McHenry. Not just stronger. But more strong-minded than this oil rigger from Texas who fancied himself as such a tough guy because he'd been an Army Ranger once.

And as much as Alek Andrich has surprised him with her own

toughness and resolve, she believed in the group more than she believed in herself. To Tipton, that seemed a fatal weakness. Even if he now saw there was a line that shouldn't be crossed.

Zhi? Formidable for sure. But small and quiet. He couldn't command a group, let alone humanity.

I'm supposed to be the last one in the room.

Just not this room.

He's on fire.

He's the one being burned alive.

Hillshire had spoken of mind games.

Ant is certain he's in the process of losing his.

Tipton has always believed he can outlast anything.

That's been the point.

Not the medals. Not the money. Not the talk.

Outlasting. For himself. For her.

But the room won't let him outlast it.

Because it's not testing his body.

It's testing the part of him that was twelve years old and trapped in a world that suddenly decided to burn.

The heat in here feels real. The smoke looks real. It crawls across the ceiling and down the walls.

Tipton's breath comes in ragged slices. His eyes sting. His throat burns.

His screams are once again drowned out by the primal screams he heard that day in the small plane, the last sounds he ever heard from his parents and brother.

Ant Tipton, survivor of that crash and survivor of war, is succumbing to a different kind of warfare.

Psychological warfare.

It is why, now that he's reached his breaking point, Ant is ready to do the unthinkable:

Surrender.

Tipton violently pulls his arms away from the arms of his chair, ripping away the leather restraints. Not because he's a superhero—because panic makes you strong in stupid ways.

Doesn't just unhook his seat belt.

Rips it off, tearing it into two pieces.

"Enough!" he shouts, voice raw, trying to make himself heard over the cries still being pumped into the room, even louder now than before. "ENOUGH! You win! Okay? YOU WIN!"

He looks down as he sees the flames licking at his black jeans.

"Let me out of here!"

Smoke is filling the chamber. Tipton feels the burn of that on his throat, gagging as he blindly stumbles toward the door, eyes full of smoke and tears. He's now the one inside that burning apartment, inside the fire from which Wyatt had saved that little girl.

Only Ant Tipton is trying to save himself.

When he finally gets his hand on the handle, he's the one crying out again, the same pain of having touched a hot stove.

He jerks back, swearing silently in his head, because even now he refuses to give them the satisfaction of hearing him break.

But the handle won't turn.

He pulls his hand away, takes off his black T-shirt, covers the handle with it, tries to open the door again.

Nothing.

Locked from the outside.

Tipton takes a step back into the smoke and charges the door now, lowering his shoulder like he's the one who played American football the way McHenry did back in Texas, trying to turn himself into a human battering ram.

This time the searing pain is in his shoulder, the sharp ache of having broken it.

Ant Tipton feels broken, gutted, humiliated, after all the times he'd told himself he'd die before he quit.

He slides down the wall next to the door, until he is seated next to it.

Smoke and flames everywhere. The room is a furnace. The air is poison.

Tipton tries to tell himself he can't possibly be burning up this way.

This can't be real.

But it all couldn't be more real.

He tastes the word they gave him—*quit*—right on the edge of his tongue, and it terrifies him more than the fire, so he bites down and swallows it like poison.

Tipton thinks: *This is what it must have been like for my brother that day.*

And for the first time in his life—maybe the first time since he was twelve—Ant Tipton thinks something he's never allowed himself to think.

Maybe surviving wasn't proof of strength.

Maybe it was just delay.

Maybe this is the way he was meant to die all along.

He sighs out one last whispered word. He whispers it like a confession. Not surrender. A trade.

Because somewhere out there . . . he hoped she was still alive. He wishes he could just see her one last time.

115.

When Zhi forces himself to open his eyes again, the doctor and the nurse are still frozen in place over him.

At least he's still alive.

But is it over?

"He shouldn't be awake this soon," the nurse says, as if he's not a person but a machine that turned on too soon.

"Best give him another dose of the anesthesia," the doctor says.

Zhi doesn't cry out this time. His fear spikes—but underneath it is something else now.

Anger.

"Screw this!" he whispers to himself. "I quit."

He uses the immense strength he's always had in his forearms and jerks himself free from the safety straps holding him down.

He breaks loose with even stronger legs.

Then the gymnast, one of the greatest China has ever produced, is bringing his knees to his chest and springing up and off the table like doing one more ring leap from a balance bar.

Neither the doctor nor the nurse makes any move to stop him as he runs for the door. There is no longer a guard in the room with them.

Zhi is afraid the door might be locked.

But to his surprise, the handle turns easily in his hand.

Zhi doesn't hesitate, even realizing the cost of what he's about to do if he leaves this room.

But he can't stay in here any longer.

He can't risk them opening him up.

When he steps into the hall, the rush of cooler air hits him like mercy. Finally able to breathe again. To think.

He sucks in a breath, eyes wide, scanning. And then he sees Jack McHenry standing a few feet away, his face pale, his nose still bruised, but his eyes sharp.

Jack doesn't look surprised to see him.

He looks like he's been waiting.

"They . . . opened yours too?" Zhi manages, still shaking.

Jack nods once. "After a while. After I . . . After I quit."

Zhi swallows. "I couldn't–"

"I know," Jack says, voice quiet but steady. "I know."

Zhi looks both ways down the long corridor. Doors. Cameras. Silence.

"You're all right?" Zhi asks.

"Well as can be expected under the circumstances," Jack says.

"What about Alek and Tipton?" Zhi asks him.

"Still in their chambers as far as I know," Jack says.

Zhi nods.

"So now it's down to two," Zhi says.

Just not for long.

116.

There is no time for Jack and Zhi to share the personal horrors they've just experienced in their chambers. As soon as they're outside they hear Alek's muffled cries for help from down the hall.

Jack and Zhi are sprinting in that direction when they see Alek's door fling open, see her stumbling and falling into the hallway, wildly slapping at her own body with both hands.

She's sitting on the floor when they reach her, arms hugging her knees, crying hysterically, rocking back and forth.

Despite everything that has happened to her—everything that has happened to all of them since leaving Ohio—Jack has never once seen Alek Andrich cry.

Had never seen her lose control like this.

Until now.

She looks up at them, bleary-eyed, trying to catch her breath and stop herself from crying at the same time.

Finally, she uses the same words Lin Zhi just used with Jack after making his own escape:

"I . . . couldn't . . ." she manages.

Then, smaller, as if saying it might make it true: "I'm sorry."

"For what?" Jack says.

He sits next to her. Zhi leans down and respectfully places a comforting hand on Alek's shoulder.

"They finally found a way to break us," Jack says. "Maybe that was the goal all along. Maybe they didn't really want anybody to win."

"It was . . . awful," Alek whispers. Her voice cracks. "I can still feel them."

We're all a wreck today, Jack tells himself.

They wanted us to lose our minds before we lost the money.

She tells them about the snakes and the spiders—how they kept coming, how they climbed, how the bites felt real. How she screamed for it to stop until her throat went raw.

"It was like death in there," Alek says. "I can't believe Wyatt let this happen."

"Maybe he's no better than his father," Jack says. "Bad apple not falling far from the tree and all like that."

Jack gets back to his feet and opens the door just a crack, looking back into her room to see for himself if somehow Alek's demons had been real.

"They'll get out!" Alek shouts, scuttling farther away from the door.

When Jack looks inside, Alek's chamber is completely empty.

No snakes. No spiders. No movement at all. Just a clean floor and cold, indifferent air. Jack closes the door and turns back to her.

"Nothing," he says.

Alek squeezes her eyes shut, shaking her head, hating herself for believing her own senses.

"It was real," she insists. "It was real to me."

"We know," Zhi says quietly, because they do.

117.

They stand in the corridor for a long moment, the three of them not sure what to do with the fact that their bodies are safe but their minds are still trapped inside those rooms.

Up here—high above the city—the world feels very far away.

All they know is that they had made it this far only to end up defeated this way—crushed—their worlds shrunk to the size of these small rooms.

"I'm starting to wonder how much of the whole thing was real," Jack says.

Zhi's face is pale, his eyes fixed on the floor like he's still watching a needle descend.

"I have never felt more like a failure," he says. "I thought I was stronger."

It's clear that they all feel the same sense of loss. It is because of everything they had overcome along the way—the whales and sharks and deserts and mountains and caves and the death of friends. All of it. They had experienced the reality of war, only to end up beaten by the hideous augmented reality of these rooms.

Alek looks at Jack, then at Zhi. She wipes her cheeks with the heels of her hands, furious that she has tears at all.

"Why drag us all the way here," she says, "to end it like that? Not with courage. Not with skill. With . . . humiliation."

"Maybe that really was the sick plan all along," Jack says. "Cruelty is easy. That's the whole playbook."

"They made us believe we were pursuing a higher calling," Zhi says. "But it was all a lie."

"Like that was their endgame," Alek says. "To see if we lost every form of hope." Alek takes a shaky breath. "So what now? We just . . . wait?"

Jack looks both ways down the empty corridor.

"What are you looking for?" Alek asks.

Jack stops walking. "If we're all out here . . . and Tipton's still inside—" He doesn't finish. Doesn't have to. "He outlasted us. He's *The One*."

Alek's stomach turns.

"He said all along he was going to be the last man standing," Alek says. "As much as I hate to admit it, he was right."

Jack shakes his head and whistles softly.

"People always talk about the last man out," he says. "He's the last man in."

Ward Hillshire appears from around the corner, moving slower than he used to, like the building itself is heavier on him now.

"Just so you know, Tipton didn't win," Ward says to them.

"You're still here?" Alek says.

"Not by choice," Hillshire says. "And on that you can believe me."

Jack's eyes narrow. "Why isn't Tipton out here?"

He ignores Jack and points at Alek.

"You won," he says to her.

118.

Alek opens her mouth and closes it, staring at the silver-haired man, dapper and put together as ever, but somehow diminished at the same time.

She feels her world is spinning—out of control—one final time.

I won?

How can that possibly be?

She can't find the right words because she has no idea what they might be.

She closes her eyes instead. When she does, she finds one moment of peace: Imagining her mother's face once Alek gives her the news.

"I . . . what?" she says.

"It has been decided that you are officially *The One*," he says flatly, like he's reading a weather report.

"We all failed," Alek says. "Why me and not them?"

"And why not Tipton?" Jack asks. "He's the only one of us not out here."

"You didn't quit," he says. "You broke. You begged."

Alek swallows. "But I didn't surrender."

Jack stares at him. "The safe word."

Ward nods once. "The system only recognizes that one thing."

He motions for them to follow him back around the corner, to a different elevator than the one that had brought them down to the 146th floor from the conference room.

As they approach it, they hear someone crying out for help from behind one last closed door down the hall.

This voice clearly belongs to Ant Tipton.

Clearly still locked inside his chamber.

Ward Hillshire doesn't even break stride.

"Why is he still locked inside?" Alek demands. "If he said it—if he surrendered—why isn't he out here?"

She is still dizzy after having been declared the winner, almost like one more jolt of augmented reality.

Ward doesn't even slow down as he gestures for them to follow him toward the elevator.

"Because this isn't mercy," he says. "It's procedure. And punishment."

"I still don't understand," Alek says.

Another rasp of sound leaks from the door, small now, almost private—like the room is forcing it out of him again and again.

Alek takes a step toward the door, but Jack catches her gently by the elbow.

"Don't," he says. "That's what they want. One more fight. One more panic. One more mistake."

Ward presses the elevator button.

"All is about to be explained," he says, sounding very tired all of a sudden. "By your new hosts."

The elevator doors open. They all step inside.

The next voice they hear is Wyatt's, coming from a small box high up in the corner of the elevator.

"I'd like to congratulate you on your great victory, Alek," Wyatt says. "Well done."

Alek looks up at the speaker. "Go to hell," she says. "But heads-up—you're not going to like it much. We were all just there."

Jack looks up at the small box. "Where are you, Wyatt?" he asks. "I'd still like a word."

"Waiting for you a couple floors up," Wyatt says. "And before you say it—yes, I know. I know what it looked like. I know what it felt like."

Alek's hands curl into fists. "You let it happen."

Then Wyatt says, "I didn't design those chambers. And I didn't have the legal authority to stop them once they started."

"Legal," Jack spits.

Wyatt exhales. "It's frustrating because my father used the rules as weapons. He knew what the contract demands and where the wiggle room is. But when it comes to the final outcome: Rules are rules. The only way any of you could win the money was to finish the final stage. You can hate that. We do too. But it's true."

Alek's eyes narrow. "You said 'we.' Who else is involved?"

Wyatt doesn't answer.

The doors begin to close. A hand shoots in and stops them.

Jimmy steps into the elevator. There is a bruise on his left cheek. There is a bandage over his puffy right eye.

But it's him.

"Don't worry," he says, "I won the fight."

Without saying a word, he reaches past Ward and presses "PH."

He looks at Alek and Jack and Zhi.

Jimmy touches the bruise on his cheek.

"We don't get to quit," he says. "So we get smart."

They ride the elevator in silence.

119.

Alek keeps replaying Ward's words.

You never said the word.

She can still hear Tipton's muffled voice behind that door, like the building itself is swallowing him.

Then the doors open into another conference room—bright, expensive, unreal.

Wyatt is there waiting for them.

So is Hannah Wagner.

Alek freezes. It's like seeing a ghost walk into sunlight.

"How?" Alek finally blurts. "What are you doing here?"

Hannah looks tired. Alive. Real. She takes one step forward.

She doesn't run. She doesn't do melodrama. She just says, "I'm sorry."

Alek's throat locks. "For what?"

"For leaving you with him," Hannah says.

Alek is already moving. She grabs Hannah—hard. Not gentle. The type of hug that's half relief, half anger.

Hannah's voice is in her ear. "We're alive. That's the first miracle."

Alek pulls back, eyes wet. "Why didn't you say goodbye?"

Hannah swallows. "Because if I said it out loud, it would've been real."

"After this . . . you and me. No more disappearing. Deal?"

Hannah nods once. "Deal."

Wyatt lifts both hands, palms out, like he's trying not to get hit.

"I know it's a lot, Alek," Wyatt says. "We're gonna need a minute."

"More than a minute," Jimmy says, jumping back in. "Everybody just hang in, because the story you're about to hear is worth it. And you know I love a good story."

He pauses and says, "There have been times over the past few days when I wasn't sure. But now here we are, we're still together, and it's finally going to end the way it should've ended a long time ago."

The air in this spacious, sunny room is crackling with excitement and Jimmy's energy. Alek thinks it might be enough in the moment to power this skyscraper.

But she continues to feel dumbstruck by the presence of Hannah. In Dubai. In this room. Back with Wyatt, back with all these people who mean so much to her.

Alek doesn't know whether to cry or scream. For the first time in a long time, she feels something close to hope.

And it scares the hell out of her.

120.

Jimmy points at Wyatt like he's calling the first speaker at a meeting.

"You start," Jimmy says to Wyatt. "How you got here is just as wild as how I got here."

"Never a doubt, right?" Wyatt says, bumping fists with him. "I heard a guy say people think you're crazy until you're a genius."

Jimmy smiles. "Some nerd must have said that."

Wyatt looks at Alek, then Jack, then Zhi—meeting their eyes like he owes them something he can't dodge anymore.

"It started in Hamburg," Wyatt tells them. "I left the villa in Tuscany, spur of the moment, running hot on impulse, because I couldn't live with what I'd helped set in motion. And because there was one person I needed to see before the end."

He nods toward Hannah.

Wyatt tells them he went to find her—not for strategy, not for optics, not for the game—just to talk. To say what he didn't say when she walked away.

Hannah's mouth tightens with emotion, but she doesn't look away. "I didn't say goodbye," she says quietly. "Neither of us did."

"While I was there," he says, "Jimmy called me. He told me that he was in Dubai and had managed to sneak his way to a phone. He'd been transported there after he was caught by The Host's men in London, even got beaten up along the way."

Jimmy jumps in. “And on that call, Wyatt dropped two nukes on me. One: Who he really is. Two: He wasn’t alone.”

Wyatt continues. “Jimmy said that my father was moving the endgame here. And that if we didn’t act, the last stage would chew up whoever was left and spit them out.”

Jack’s voice is flat. “So you came to stop it.”

Wyatt hesitates. “I came to take control of it. There’s a difference.”

At that moment, the conference room doors swing open. Another unexpected surprise. Two guards escort Ward Hillshire into the room. Not looking anything like a Host.

Alek takes a step forward. “And Tipton?”

Wyatt’s expression hardens.

“My father built those chambers to break people,” Wyatt says. “Tipton broke.”

Alek feels it in her ribs. “He said the word.”

Jack’s jaw clenches. “Then why was he still locked inside?”

Wyatt’s eyes flick toward Ward—like the answer makes him sick. Ward says it instead.

“Because I don’t believe in letting go,” Ward mutters. “I believe in making an example.”

Jimmy’s voice drops, dangerous now. “That part ends today.”

Hannah, quietly, chimes in, “It ends without us becoming them.”

“So here we are,” Wyatt says to his father, “where your winner gets crowned. And where we decide what kind of people we are going forward.”

Wyatt looks around at the view from up here.

“High time for it, don’t you think?” Wyatt says.

121.

Alek had one question:

How did I win?

Ward Hillshire looks like a man who just watched his own life get repossessed.

"There was one area where I told the truth, as it turns out," he says. "That part about everything being explained. I just assumed I'd be the one doing the explaining."

Alek stares at him. He does look diminished, reduced to being a bit player in the final scene playing out all around him.

"Sadly," Ward Hillshire adds, "I appear to have lost that privilege."

"You lost it a long time ago," Wyatt says. He doesn't raise his voice. He doesn't need to. "And by the way, I was never a part of this to prove anything to you. I was proving something to myself. And to my grandfather's memory."

Ward's mouth twitches, like he wants to laugh it off. He can't.

Wyatt stares scornfully at his father.

"I always suspected I would have to take you down," he says. "I just didn't know when. Or how."

Jimmy steps in, calmer now.

"Sometimes you choose," Jimmy says, "and sometimes you get chosen. Either way, when the moment hits—you meet it."

Alek speaks up. "Wyatt. Jimmy. I still have questions."

"Of course you do," Wyatt says. "You're thorough. You want the whole chain of cause and effect."

"I'm sure we all do."

"My grandfather always believed in me," Wyatt says. "So I had allies, helpers. I still do. Most of the guards here were loyal to my grandfather. Now they're loyal to me. One last game changer."

Alek finally manages to smile. "Thank God for that. But you haven't really answered my questions."

"I will," Wyatt says. "First I'd like to ask everybody to please follow me."

"Where are we going now?" Alek asks.

He nods toward the door.

"Boardroom," Wyatt says.

"I thought this *was* the boardroom," Alek says.

Wyatt's expression hardens.

"There's another one," he says. "And the people in it are the reason this competition stopped being a game."

"This mysterious board?" Jack asks.

Wyatt looks at them—Alek, Jack, Hannah, Zhi—like he's about to turn a key in a lock.

He nods. "Yes. They're the ones who benefited every time you suffered," he says. "The real enemy."

122.

Wyatt leads them through a small anteroom, then down a long, bright corridor. Finally, he walks them into the real boardroom, giving his father a slight shove in ahead of him.

Alek is trailing behind, ready to watch another strange scene play out.

"Hey," she hears Ward Hillshire say as he stumbles forward after another shove from Wyatt.

"You're lucky he doesn't kick your ass," Jack says to Ward.

There are four men and two women at the boardroom table. Expensive clothes. Controlled faces. But their eyes flash the same way predators' eyes do when the door opens on something unexpected. They look angry.

"Ward?" one of the women says. "Would you care to fill us in on what exactly is happening?"

Ward spreads his hands. "There was nothing I could do to stop them."

"True," Wyatt says. "And now there's nothing you can do to stop *me*."

Ward looks over at his son.

"As it happens, my son did prove something to me, whether that was his motivation or not," he says. "But as full of himself as he's feeling, I still think he's making one more monumental mistake."

"Trust me," Wyatt says. "I've made bigger. The biggest was trusting you to do the right thing at the start of all this." He shakes his head. "So much of this didn't need to happen."

Wyatt walks to the far end of the room. He motions for Alek, Jack, Hannah, and Zhi to come stand behind him, and for Jimmy to take the seat at the head of the table. Whoever had been in charge before, Alek sees that Wyatt Hillshire is in charge, at least for now.

Wyatt remains standing at the front of the room.

"This doesn't need to take long," he says. "You thought this was one man's sickness. It wasn't."

He points at the table.

"This was a board decision."

The room goes cold.

Wyatt starts naming names—controlled, clinical, lethal.

Alek watches the faces as he does. Not guilt. Not horror. Annoyance. Like he's interrupting a meeting.

Thomas Waldrip, tech titan.

Jeanne Starr, international finance.

Li Chang, arms.

Juan Escarra, manufacturing and influence.

Helen Trengove, supply chain.

Gianni Volpe, pharma.

Wyatt slides a folder across the table. Six signatures stare back.

"Congratulations," he says. "You're all on the murder paperwork."

Jeanne Starr speaks first. "Ward, you told us the games would be contained. A controlled stress test. You promised no . . . headlines."

Ward looks at the ground. She rolls her eyes.

"The people we see here at this table are among the richest and most powerful on earth," Wyatt says. "Unfortunately, it's why over time they've proven themselves to be the most dangerous, while they line their own pockets."

Wyatt smiles without warmth.

"My grandfather foolishly thought these people would be loyal to him even after he was gone, and remain loyal to his ideals," Wyatt says, spitting out the words. "He wasn't wrong about a lot, my grandfather. But he was wrong about that."

"You have no idea what you're talking about," Thomas Waldrip booms. "Gavin was my friend and everyone at this table knows it."

"Sure, he was," Wyatt says. "Whenever you needed another favor from him. Or to cut you another sweetheart deal on your latest merger or acquisition."

Waldrip starts to respond, but Wyatt holds up a hand to stop him. He is very much in charge here, Alek sees. More confident than she has ever seen him.

"And how exactly do you know all this?" Helen Trengove asks. "Nobody saw Gavin for the last year of his life. Perhaps longer than that."

Jimmy leans forward.

"I can answer that," he says. "He didn't want any of you to see him. But I found him in London, just over a week ago. As weak as he was, we spoke for hours that night. He was one of the most amazing people I've ever met face-to-face. And still full of fight. And he had one message for all of you."

Jimmy looks around the table, one face at a time.

"He said you were going to pick his bones the second you thought he couldn't stop you. And the only thing he regretted was that he wasn't young enough to fight right along with us when the time came!"

"Sounds like him," Wyatt says.

Ward scoffs. "Pity."

Wyatt snaps his head toward him. "Shut up."

Ward smiles. "Or what?"

Wyatt doesn't blink.

"Or I put you in a room," Wyatt says, "and let you learn what it feels like to have no exit from your own nightmares."

Jimmy starts addressing the people watching him stone-faced from the table.

"He asked if I would be his advocate after he was gone," he continues.

"Why not Wyatt?" Alek asks.

"Because at the time, he was worried that Ward might still try to have Wyatt killed," Jimmy says, getting revved all over again.

"Oh please, even I wouldn't go so far as to harm my own son," Ward says.

"Of course you would," Wyatt says. "With me out of the way, you would become the only heir."

"Something else your father wanted me to know?" Jimmy says to Ward. "He was about to fire everybody on this board–including you. He said he should have cleaned house a long time ago and the other board members were never going to come around to his way of thinking. The next day, he was dead."

"How?" Alek asks.

"A great heart finally stopped beating," Wyatt says.

"I was gutted," Jimmy says. "But I knew it was time for me to step up, like he asked."

123.

Jimmy and Wyatt remain standing next to each other at the front of the boardroom. Huge floor-to-ceiling windows tower behind them. They look like partners, or maybe conspirators, but definitely friends.

Alek finds herself thinking back to Ohio, when Wyatt turned into a starstruck kid upon first meeting his hero.

Wyatt: Not his father's son. Gavin Hillshire's grandson, in all the best ways.

Jimmy exhales like he's been holding in anger for days.

"I want to say something else," he tells Wyatt. "A bunch of things."

"The floor is all yours," Wyatt says.

"I didn't ask for any of this," Jimmy says. "But I'm not walking out the way I walked in."

Jimmy takes a deep breath and goes on, almost like he's caught a second wind. He faces the board and looks around the table, stopping at one face after another.

"Here's what Gavin would've said if he were standing where I'm standing: You wanted to fix the ending. You wanted a winner you could control. You wanted Tipton because he was obedient. Because he'd do what you told him to do. Because he'd keep the machine running."

Alek cuts in. "So he was supposed to win instead of me?"

"Tipton," Wyatt says. "Yes. That was the plan."

Ward opens his mouth.

Wyatt points at him. "Don't."

Thomas Waldrip, red-faced, stands before anyone else can speak. "You all keep calling it cruelty. I call it selection. The world doesn't need kinder leaders. It needs effective ones."

Jimmy doesn't raise his voice. He sharpens it.

"Sit down," Jimmy says.

"Security!" Wyatt calls.

Five uniformed guards enter the room.

Wyatt looks at Waldrip. "Sit."

Waldrip bristles. "You can't talk to me that way."

Wyatt's smile returns—small, dangerous.

"Just did."

"Are you people really going to sit out a fight like this?" Jimmy asks. "Are you so deep into your own pockets that you're not going to do anything to keep us all from going right over a cliff?"

"We *were* trying to save the world," says Li Chang.

"It takes people like us to do that. People who are willing to do what needs to be done, despite the costs," Jeanne Starr adds.

"You're children. You're being naïve. Idealistic. You want the world to be a place that we can fix with rainbows and unicorns," Helen Trengove mocks.

"We were trying to get you to see that," Ward finally speaks up again. "We were trying to show you how dark the world is."

Wyatt points a finger at his father.

"You know, *Dad*," he says. "You really should have had me killed when you had the chance."

"You all ignored something important, really important. We got this far without compromising our values," says Alek.

Thomas Waldrip, still standing, barks out a harsh, mirthless laugh.

"You people actually think you're going to save the world?" Waldrip says. "That's adorable."

"*Enough*," Alek raises her voice, which is unusual for her. "More than enough! There's still things I don't understand. Why would Gavin Hillshire let Wyatt anywhere near this competition in the first place?"

"Mr. Hillshire told me that he had to find out once and for all who should be his real heir," Jimmy says. "To carry on his work, his vision of the future. He wanted to see who Wyatt really was—by the games."

Wyatt turns back to his father.

"You couldn't have that, could you?" Wyatt says.

Wyatt gives his father the same disdainful look Jimmy had just trained on Thomas Waldrip.

Alek takes a step forward. "I still need one answer. Why am I *The One*?"

Wyatt doesn't hesitate.

"Because my grandfather's rules were written in steel," he says. "Not feelings. Not fairness. Not 'almost.'"

He looks at Alek.

"You never said the word."

Alek can't believe it's that simple.

Wyatt continues, "Zhi said it and left his chamber, that's why his door was unlocked. Jack said it. Tipton said it. Quietly. But the system recorded it."

Jack nods once. "So she actually won."

"She did," Wyatt says. "By the only rule the system recognizes."

"Makes sense to me," Jack says.

Lin Zhi nods his head in agreement. "Congratulations," he says.

"Thank you. But I don't feel like *The One*," Alek says.

Wyatt's expression softens for the first time.

"My grandfather believed in *The One*. I don't," Wyatt says.

"Me either," Jimmy says. "Not anymore."

Wyatt continues, "One person can start something, but they can't do everything alone. That's the lesson of these games."

Waldrip starts laughing. "Idealistic idiots. You'll see. When the pressure is real, when the stakes are real, when the decisions are right in front of you, you'll come to the same conclusions we did."

Alek clears her throat, "Honestly, Waldrip, shut the hell up."

The room goes still.

"One last question, and then I promise to stop," Alek continues. "Where's Tipton?"

"Still in his room downstairs," Wyatt says. "I made a brief stop there. When I said I'd let him out if he told me the truth, he couldn't wait to confess that he was supposed to let me die on Mount Washington."

"Did you let him out then?" Alek asks.

"No," Wyatt says.

He puts his hands out helplessly.

"What can I tell you. I told one more lie."

Wyatt takes a long look around the boardroom.

"Do any of you have anything you'd like to add before I declare this meeting adjourned?" Wyatt says. "Because we all have a lot of work to do."

"I have one more thing to say, for the record," Thomas Waldrip snaps. "You're not half the man your grandfather was."

Wyatt smiles at the man.

"You know something?" he says. "I'll take that as a compliment."

Alek speaks again. She takes charge. "Guards! Take them away. The former board members. The rest of us have work to do."

124.

When they're all back inside the lightning-fast, gold-plated elevator, Alek tells them where they're going. And who they're going to see.

"Seriously?" Wyatt asks. "You're sure about this?"

"I'm sure," Alek says. "This needs to get done."

The elevator doors open. Then they're walking back down a long and familiar corridor.

Alek is the one to open the door after Wyatt has pointed the right one out to her.

Ant Tipton is where Wyatt had left him, lying in the corner of the room, half-conscious but breathing, shallowly. The only light in the room comes from the corridor with the door cracked open. It's enough for them to see that Tipton's black shirt is loosely wrapped around his right hand, his body is dripping with sweat, his eyes distant, only half present.

Alek kneels down next to him, takes one of his hands, and softly says, "Tipton."

He doesn't stir at first.

She squeezes his hand harder, says his name even louder.

His eyes flutter and then open wide—wild, haunted, still trapped in whatever fire the room fed him.

As soon as he does, they can see the terror in them. He's waking from a nightmare but somehow still in the middle of it. They understand. They were in the same place today, with their own nightmares.

"Tipton!" Alek snaps, as a way of focusing him. Bringing him back.

Tipton cries out, anyway, jerks his hand away from hers.

"It's all right," she says. "It's us."

Tipton's voice is sandpaper. "How . . . ?"

He points at Wyatt like it costs him strength. "You . . . left me."

Wyatt doesn't flinch. "You said it."

Tipton's eyes flicker. Shame flashes there–fast.

Alek watches him. Really watches him.

Then Tipton, his eyes wild, is the one shouting:

"I have to get out of here!"

He tries to stand, but doesn't have the strength, collapsing into a sad heap.

His head snaps against the wall.

"We're not here to punish you," she says.

"Why are you here?" he rasps.

Alek doesn't hesitate.

"Get up. You're not done," she says.

Tipton is fully awake now, if not fully alert. He still appears disoriented. Or delirious.

"After everything? After . . . Wyatt?" His voice trails off.

"Wyatt is here," Alek says. "And the fact is, we're going to need warriors like you." She shrugs. "Whether we're totally comfortable with that or not. Or with you. I believe you won't cross the line if you don't have a knife at your throat making you do it."

Hannah looks at Wyatt, her eyes apologizing, "I read your file. She's safe."

Tipton looks at her. Recognizes the gesture. All that rage, all that posture—gone for a second. He swallows hard. His hand goes to the chain at his neck like he needs air.

"What are you talking about?" Wyatt asks her.

"Later," Hannah replies.

"He did try to kill me," Wyatt says.

"But he didn't," Jimmy says to Wyatt. "Despite what was at stake."

"Okay, someone, catch me up," Wyatt says.

Jack and Zhi reach down and help Tipton to his feet, still having to prop him up once they do.

Tipton swallows hard. His eyes are wet and furious at the same time.

"I thought I was going to die in here," he says.

Alek nods. "So did we."

She is tall enough to look Tipton in the eyes. "You want a way to make this mean something?" she asks. "You want a way to pay it back?"

Tipton's jaw clenches. He nods once.

Alek leans in slightly.

"Then fight with us," she says. "Show us who I believe you are when you're free from their leash."

Tipton's breath shudders.

"Understood," he says.

In that moment, after everything, they see the last scraps of the old Tipton:

"Just give me the mission."

125.

The others are waiting for Alek in the lobby of Burj Khalifa an hour later. The plan is for them all to go to one of Dubai's finest restaurants for dinner and then to feel like normal humans again.

Even Tipton is slowly turning back into himself, for better or worse.

Alone in the boardroom, Alek uses her phone—the one that had kept her connected to Jimmy—to call her mother.

Once she answers, Alek tries to sum up the crazy events of this day—of the past few days. She tells her the truth, but not all of it, choosing to leave out the parts about the horrors inside her chamber.

When she finishes, her mother says, "Are you still certain this is what you want?"

"Yes," Alek says without hesitation. "And not just for me. For you, too, *maty*."

Then Alek adds:

"This is for everyone under attack the way we have been."

"So you're ready for whatever comes next?" her mother asks.

Alek looks out over Dubai like she can already see the future moving.

"Yes," Alek says again. "I'm ready. We all are."

Then, surprising even herself, Alek Andrich puts her phone

down on the table, leans back in her chair, and screams her head off in the empty conference room.

On the other end, her mother's voice cracks through. "Alek? Is everything okay?"

Alek laughs, breathless and disbelieving.

"Okay?" she says. "Okay?"

She wipes her face.

"I won, *maty*," she says. "Me. Your daughter. I won."

She says it again, softer this time, careful, almost afraid.

"I won."

Then she can't help herself, she really is laughing at the sheer improbability of it all.

She tells her mother she loves her and ends the call.

Alek sits for a minute and thinks about the journey here from Ohio, the one that really began for her in the freezing water of Antarctica. That was the first time she nearly died.

She closes her eyes and remembers those who did lose their lives.

She thinks about the child they'd saved from fire, picturing Wyatt and the girl falling out of the sky one more time.

Now the whole world seems on fire.

Now we're the ones who have to take a leap of faith.

The entire time, she'd had one question she couldn't shake: *Can one person really save the world?*

That was the story The Host sold them. What the board treated as religion. Find *The One*. Crown *The One*. Let *The One* do whatever needs to be done.

The end justifies the means.

Alek understands now why people want to believe that story.

How it could even come from the right place. When the world is burning, you want somebody to put it out. But she's seen what that story becomes when you push it far enough.

That story buys you one thing: permission. And once you have permission, you'll call anything "necessary."

You can call cruelty "necessary" and feel proud of it.

Alek thinks about the duels. The rooms. The dead. The way they tried to turn fear into a weapon.

That wasn't leadership.

That was control.

And the "one" wasn't a person.

It was an excuse.

Alek closes her eyes and sees Reg again. Sees Hannah's face. Sees Jack crawling out of his own hell. Sees Zhi forcing himself to breathe through his terror. Sees Jimmy showing up bruised and smiling like the whole world can still be fixed.

And she thinks of Tipton, too—shaking in that room, finally learning what it feels like to be powerless. A man who'd told himself he'd do anything, right up until "anything" meant losing the last piece of himself.

There are lines you don't cross. Not for money. Not for power. Not even to save the world.

Because if you win by becoming the thing you're fighting . . . you didn't win.

Alek opens her eyes and looks out at the city again. Maybe the truth is simpler than all of them wanted it to be.

Nobody saves the world alone.

You save it the only way it's ever been saved.

Together.

With loyalty. With courage. With care.

With people who refuse to surrender their souls, even when they're terrified, even when they're hurting, even when it would be easier to go numb and call it "strength."

And then you make that group bigger.

At last she stands. Time to go to dinner and celebrate with her friends. Her team.

Jimmy had a phrase for moments like this. Not heroic. Practical. *Okay. Now we work.*

Quietly she says, "Let's do this."

EPILOGUE

Alek is taking one last look at the City of Gold from this awesome height when the door opens.

Ward Hillshire walks back in.

"We need to talk," he says to Alek.

Alek doesn't turn right away. When she does, her face is calm. "I've said everything to you I needed to say. Enough to last a lifetime."

He smiles at her, as smug as ever.

Finally: "Make it fast. I've got somewhere to be."

Ward sits–far end of the table. Not the head.

"You think you're walking into a clean world?" he asks. Then, in the same dismissive tone he'd used with them before today: "While you've been in Dubai, winning, the map has started bleeding, the world has continued burning. That's the part you don't get to pause."

She doesn't respond right away, making him wait.

"Thanks for the apocalypse briefing," she says.

"Do you not understand where I'm going with this, Alek?" Ward says.

"I don't," she says. "But I'm sure you're going to enlighten."

He sighs.

"Do you really think you can be '*The One*'"—he puts air brackets around that—"to solve the kinds of problems that are literally cropping up every day, and all over the map?" he asks.

"The only thing we can do is try," she says.

"Good luck with that," he says. "Though you're going to need a lot more than luck."

"On that we agree," Alek says.

She stands.

"Are we done here?" she asks.

"Almost," Ward Hillshire says.

"To the end, you remain in love with the sound of your own voice," Alek says.

"I actually came back here to do you a favor," he says.

"Did you?" she says drily.

Ward's smile sharpens.

"I came back here to tell you about the other games," he says. "Just concluded on the other side of the world, but just as dangerous as your own."

Alek finally stills.

"What other games?" she asks.

He chuckles one last time, as if he has once again become The Host.

"Let me put it to you another way," he says. "You may be *The One*."

There is one last dramatic pause from him.

"Just not the only one," he says.

THE END

(OR IS IT?)

ABOUT THE AUTHORS

JIMMY DONALDSON, also known as "MrBeast," is the creator behind the most subscribed YouTube channel in the world and founder of global entertainment, CPG, consumer products, and philanthropy empire, Beast Industries. He entertains and inspires a global audience through viral spectacles, engaging challenges, and massive giveaways, including millions of dollars in food and supplies for those in need. @MrBeast @BeastPhilanthropy

JAMES PATTERSON is the most popular storyteller of our time. He is the recipient of an Edgar Award, ten Emmy Awards, the Literarian Award from the National Book Foundation, and the National Humanities Medal.